VICIOUS

He watched her unload the jack, wrench, and spare tire from the trunk of her old Toyota. All the while, Susan Blanchette kept looking over her shoulder. He'd given her the flat tire, his way of welcoming her to Cullen—and an ominous start to the weekend he'd planned for her. Susan had no idea he was calling all the shots. He knew Susan would be coming to Cullen before she did.

And he knew she would die.

He'd been watching her for weeks now, and she continued to fascinate him. He'd seen her coming and going at Dr. Chang's office. He often parked across the street when she picked up Matthew at Yellowbrick Road Day Care. And sometimes he watched from outside her bedroom window as she climbed into bed alone.

He knew the whole layout of her first-floor duplex. He'd even broken in once. He smelled her hair on her pillow—and thought about how he could touch her and smell her as she was tied up.

He could do whatever he wanted to her.

And maybe after he killed her, he would even taste her blood. . . .

Books by Kevin O'Brien

ONLY SON

THE NEXT TO DIE

MAKE THEM CRY

WATCH THEM DIE

LEFT FOR DEAD

THE LAST
VICTIM

KILLING SPREE

ONE LAST
SCREAM

FINAL BREATH

VICIOUS

DISTURBED

TERRIFIED

UNSPEAKABLE

TELL ME YOU'RE
SORRY

NO ONE NEEDS
TO KNOW

YOU'LL MISS ME
WHEN I'M GONE

HIDE YOUR FEAR

THEY WON'T BE
HURT

THE BETRAYED WIFE

Published by Kensington Publishing Corporation

KEVIN O'BRIEN
VICIOUS

PINNACLE BOOKS
Kensington Publishing Corp.
www.kensingtonbooks.com

PINNACLE BOOKS are published by

Kensington Publishing Corp.
119 West 40th Street
New York, NY 10018

All Kensington titles, imprints, and distributed lines are available at special quantity discounts for bulk purchases for sales promotions, premiums, fund-raising, educational, or institutional use. Special book excerpts or customized printings can also be created to fit specific needs. For details, write or phone the office of the Kensington sales manager: Kensington Publishing Corp., 119 West 40th Street, New York, NY 10018, attn: Sales Department; phone 1-800-221-2647.

PINNACLE BOOKS and the Pinnacle logo are Reg. U.S. Pat. & TM Off.

ISBN-13: 978-0-7860-4521-1
ISBN-10: 0-7860-4521-3

First printing: June 2010
First premium mass market edition: December 2019

10 9 8 7 6 5 4 3 2

Printed in the United States of America

Electronic edition:

ISBN-13: 978-0-7860-2520-6 (e-book)
ISBN-10: 0-7860-2520-4 (e-book)

This book is for my friend and fellow author,
David Massengill.

ACKNOWLEDGMENTS

John Scognamiglio has been my editor and friend for fourteen years, and he's the best. Thank you, John! Thanks to everyone else at Kensington for all their hard work and support, especially my pal, the marvelous Doug Mendini.

I'm grateful to my hardworking agents: the lovely and talented Meg Ruley and the talented and lovely Christina Hogrebe. Thanks to all the cool people at Jane Rotrosen Agency, and that includes Peggy Gordijn, for helping make me an International Man of Mystery with all those foreign sales.

Thanks also to Thomas Dreiling, for believing in me. Tommy, you rule.

My writers' group is terrific, and I'm very, very lucky to share works in progress with generous, supportive friends like Cate Goethals, Soyon Im, David Massengill, and Garth Stein.

For sharing his expertise in psychology, I want to thank my neighbor John Simmons. And for information on boats and boating equipment, my thanks go to Peter Sherman of Orcas Boats.

Many thanks to the following friends for their encouragement or for pushing my books to their friends: Dan Annear and Chuck Rank, Marlys Bourm, Terry and Judine Brooks, Kyle Bryan and Dan Monda, George Camper and Shane White, Jim and Barbara Church, Anna Cottle and Mary Alice Kier, Paul Dwoskin and the gang at Broadway Video, Tom Goodwin, Debbie and Dennis Gotlieb, Cathy Johnson, Ed and Sue Kelly, Elizabeth Kinsella, David Korabik, the cool people at Levy Home Entertainment, Cara Lockwood, Stafford Lombard, Jim Munchel, Jake, Sue, and Conor O'Brien, Meghan O'Neill, David Renner, Eva Marie Saint, John Saul & Michael Sack, the gang at Seattle Mystery Bookshop, Jeannie Shortridge, Dan, Doug, and Ann Stutesman, George and Sheila Stydahar, Marc Von Borstel (photographer extraordinaire!), Michael Wells and the gang at Bailey/Coy Books, and my nice neighbors at the Bellemoral.

Finally, thanks to my family. Adele, Mary Lou, Cathy, Bill, and Joan, you're the greatest.

CHAPTER ONE

"It's probably been going on a lot longer than he says, the son of a bitch. I have to be the world's biggest sap—"

Pamela Milford realized she'd been talking to herself.

Approaching her on the park's pathway, a fifty-something ash blonde in lavender sweats gave her a puzzled look.

Pamela was pushing Andy in his stroller; so maybe the woman thought she was babbling to her baby. Dressed in a hooded blue jacket, Pamela's ten-month-old was enjoying the stroll through Volunteer Park on that chilly April night. He'd point to joggers or people walking their dogs, and then squeal with delight. Now he waved to the blond woman.

It was just after seven o'clock, and the park's lights were on. The walkway snaked around bushes, gardens, and huge, hundred-year-old trees. Up ahead in the distance, just beyond the greenhouse, was a dark, slightly creepy forest area that Pamela had no intention of exploring.

She usually didn't take the baby out for a stroll this late, but she was furious at her husband right now. Throwing on her pea jacket and grabbing her scarf, she'd told Steve to cook his own damn dinner. Then she'd loaded Andy into his stroller and taken off for the park.

"He's adorable!" declared the lady in the lavender sweats. She squatted down in front of Andy, gaped at him in mock surprise, and laughed. "Oh, you're just so cute, you take my breath away!" She caressed Andy's cheek. "And where did you get that gorgeous curly red hair?"

"Not from me," Pamela said, with a strained smile. Andy had inherited his father's red hair.

Pamela's chestnut brown hair used to cascade down past her shoulder blades. But she'd gotten it cut short after Andy's birth. Along with the excess pounds from her pregnancy, the haircut made her look frumpy, more like she was forty than thirty-one. Though she'd lost most of her postnatal pounds, she was still waiting for her hair to grow back.

Perhaps Steve had also been waiting for her hair to grow back—before he started to pay attention to her again. The baby had put a crimp in their love life; all the spontaneity and the passion had dissipated. She'd half expected that.

But Pamela hadn't been prepared for what she'd discovered this afternoon.

She was an editor for the *Seattle Weekly*, and usually spent her lunch hours at Andy's day care. But today, she'd decided to surprise Steve at work and treat him to lunch at Palomino. Lombard-Stafford Graphics was only four blocks from the *Weekly* offices. Steve wasn't in his cubicle, and the office was nearly empty. A thin young Asian woman with a pink streak in her hair and a nostril stud, two cubicles away, tersely explained that Steve and everyone else were in a meeting. It was supposed to let out any minute now.

Pamela sat in his cubicle, twisting back and forth in his swivel chair as she waited for him. A "fish-tank" screen saver illuminated his computer monitor. Pinned to the grey cubicle wall were a *Far Side* calendar; Steve's football team portrait from New Trier High School in Winnetka, Illinois; a cartoon picture of Homer Simpson; three photos of Andy; and one photo of her—back when her hair was still long.

Pamela got tired of waiting and decided to leave him a note and then take off. But first, she wanted to change his screen saver.

Back when they were first married, Steve gave her—as a joke—a 5 x 7 photo of exercise guru Richard Simmons and faked an autograph: *You make me sweat! I feel the heat! XXX—Richard.* Two days later, Pamela surprised him by taping it to the steering wheel of his car. A few days after that, she found he'd left the photo for her in the refrigerator's crisper drawer. The joke had gone on for weeks and weeks. The Richard Simmons Wars, they called them. They'd had time for such silly stuff back then—back when their relationship had been passionate and fun.

Pamela reached for the computer's mouse. She'd go on the Internet and find a photo of Richard Simmons and turn it into his new screen saver. Chuckling, she imagined Steve as he tried to explain to his coworkers why he had Richard Simmons for his screen saver. She clicked the mouse.

That was when Pamela noticed an e-mail from Jill@ Evanstonproperties.com, and the smile ran away from her face.

Jill Pondello had been Steve's girlfriend at New Trier High. Evanston Properties was probably a real estate firm or something. And Evanston was close to Winnetka; she knew that much. Pamela glanced up at Steve's high school football team portrait. He still clung to the memories of that time. Steve would be going back to Winnetka in three weeks for the Class of '83 Reunion. He'd asked if she wanted to come, but Pamela had figured she would be bored to tears at the festivities and stuck with her oppressive in-laws the rest of the time. She'd told Steve he could go alone.

It had never occurred to her until that moment in Steve's cubicle: He couldn't really be trusted. Pamela stared at the computer screen and clicked on the OPEN MAIL icon:

Hey, Mister,

Ha! I can't believe U still remember making out in Debi Donahue's basement rec room & the pink panties! U naughty boy! Do U remember what we were listening to??? Air Supply . . . Even the Nights Are Better. J Maybe I should ask the DJ to play it at the reunion & see if it puts U in the mood again! I'm so glad we'll be doing dinner together after—just the 2 of us. Maybe I can persuade U to stay a few more days. J Like U say, we have a lot of catching up to do. I'm counting the days until I see U (19). I can't wait! Give me another call, OK? E-mails are fine, but I really like hearing your voice ☺.

XXXXXXXXX—Jill

"What the hell?" Pamela muttered, hunched in front of his computer monitor.

From what she could discern, Steve and this slut, Jill, had been talking on the phone and e-mailing—at work—for a while now. Did this woman even know he was married—with a ten-month-old baby?

Well, if she didn't know, she certainly would now.

Pamela hit the reply key. Her fingers worked furiously on the keyboard:

> Dear Jill,
>
> Steve won't be coming to the reunion after all. He needs to spend more time with his wife and 10-month-old son. Perhaps you can hook up with some other former classmate, someone who is actually single. If you don't receive any more e-mails or phone calls from my husband, I'm sure you'll understand why. ☹ By the way, Air Supply was a suck band.
>
> Sincerely,
> Pamela Milford (Steve's wife)

She barely glanced at what she'd written before clicking on the SEND icon. Then she stood up so fast, she almost tipped over Steve's chair. Bolting toward the exit, she heard the young woman with the pierced nose call to her: "Hey, I hear the meeting just got out! Steve should be back any minute now!"

But Pamela ignored her and hurried toward the elevator. Tears welled in her eyes, and she felt sick to her stomach. She jabbed the elevator button. When it didn't arrive right away, she took the stairs—five flights. She just had to keep moving.

There was still time to go to Andy's day care.

More than anything, she longed to be with her sweet

baby boy. His adorable face always lit up whenever he saw her walk into the day care's nursery.

"I mean it, he's just adorable," said the fifty-something jogger in the lavender sweats. "Just look at that smile!"

Pamela wished the lady would stop touching Andy's cheek. It always secretly bothered her when strangers came up to Andy and started touching him. Fawning was fine, but not touching. God only knew where that lady's hand had been.

"Tickle, tickle, tickle!" the woman chimed, brushing Andy's chin with her finger. The baby squealed.

Pamela inched the stroller forward. "Wave goodbye to the nice lady, Andy!" She managed to smile at the jogger. "Have a great night."

"Bye-bye!" the woman cooed to Andy as she backed away.

Glancing over her shoulder, Pamela nodded at the blond woman. She turned around again and then stopped dead. Just up the trail, she spotted a tall, lean man emerging from some bushes by a curve in the pathway. She just glimpsed his silhouette. Then as quickly as he'd appeared, the lean figure ducked behind an evergreen tree.

Pamela froze. For a few moments, she just stood there, staring at the towering evergreen. Her hands tightened on the stroller's handles. She thought about heading in the opposite direction, maybe catching up with the blond woman. At least there was safety in numbers.

Andy let out a bored little cry.

"We're heading on home now, honey," she said nervously. Pamela's eyes were still riveted to the evergreen's trunk. She couldn't see the man, but she knew he was behind there, waiting.

She glanced around for other people in the area. Pamela noticed an attractive young brunette strolling up another path that intersected with the one she was on, right by the giant evergreen. Dressed in a trench coat, the young woman was tall and willowy with long, wavy hair. She had a cell phone in her hand and was too busy flipping open the mouthpiece and pulling out the short antenna to watch where she was going. She passed under an old-fashioned streetlight that illuminated only that section of the trail. Soon the young woman would be in the shadows of the big evergreen.

"Miss?" Pamela tried to call to her, but her throat closed up. Her warning was barely a whisper. Her hand came up to her throat as she watched helplessly. The young woman got closer and closer to the towering tree.

"Miss?" Pamela said, louder this time. Her voice cracked. "Excuse me . . ."

All of a sudden, the dark figure leapt out from behind the evergreen.

Pamela screamed.

So did the young woman. And then she burst out laughing. "You idiot! You almost made me drop my phone." The man put his arm around her, and they kissed. "I was just about to call and ask what was keeping you. . . ."

Pamela caught her breath and then pushed Andy onward. Her heart was still racing. She'd almost made a fool out of herself.

Arm in arm, the young couple strolled up the path toward Andy and her. As she passed them, Pamela noticed the girl glancing down at Andy in his stroller—and then at her. "That's me in a year and a half," the girl whispered to her companion. "I'll be pushing around little Justin Junior. I'm going to be her. . . ."

For your sake, I hope not, Pamela thought. Did that young woman—eighteen months from now—really want to discover that Justin Senior, the father of her child, was a cheating slime bucket?

Okay, so maybe Steve hadn't actually cheated yet, but he'd been working up to it.

Pamela had taken Andy out of Rainbow Junction Day Care early and gone for a long drive. The phone was ringing when she came through the front door with Andy in her arms at 4:30. It was Steve. He'd left several messages for her at the office—and then at home. "Jill phoned me, and said you e-mailed her," he admitted. "Listen, you're freaking out over nothing. This e-mail thing with her is all very innocent—and—and *harmless*. It's so dumb. It started when they sent the notice about the reunion. I was going to tell you about it, only I . . . well, listen, just do me a favor and stay put. I'm leaving work right now. I should be there in a half hour. . . ."

Pamela waited. She put Andy in his crib for a late nap, poured herself a glass of merlot, and plopped down at the kitchen table. She kept busy painting her nails—a honey-brown color called Cinnamon Sin. Ninety minutes later, she was still sitting there, impatiently clicking her newly painted nails on the kitchen table. She sat there and glared at Steve as he paced in front of her, apologizing, explaining, and groveling.

Apparently, *poor Jill* had just been through a messy divorce and was very fragile. He didn't want to hurt her feelings by telling her that her e-mails were inappropriate. Yeah, sure, maybe he kind of liked the attention, but it was all very innocent.

"I was going to tell you about it," he claimed. "Only I knew you'd go ballistic. This is just the sort of reaction I've been afraid of. Can you really blame me for not saying anything?

Yes, indeed, I blame you, you son of a bitch.

She took Andy and left. She just needed to cool off for a while.

That had been nearly an hour ago. Steve was probably going out of his mind with worry. Maybe she thought he'd never see her and their baby again. Well, good, let him think that a little while longer.

Up ahead, past the dahlia garden, Pamela thought she saw him, walking along another intersecting trail. Then she realized—although he had Steve's loping gait and wore a navy blue windbreaker very much like Steve's—the man wasn't her husband. For a few moments, a streetlight behind him cast a shadow over his face. But as he came closer, Pamela saw he was extremely good looking and he was smiling at Andy in his stroller. "Well, well, well, what a handsome little rascal you are!" he said.

Pamela stopped for him. The stranger crouched down to grin at Andy. He wasn't a toucher. He kept his hands in his pockets. "What's your name, fella?" he asked.

"Andy," Pamela answered for her son.

The handsome stranger looked up and locked eyes with her. He had such a sexy smile. Pamela felt herself blush. She could always tell when guys were interested in her, and this one was interested. Not that anything would happen, but it sure was nice. In fact, this impromptu flirtation in the park was just what the doctor ordered to make her feel desirable again.

The man glanced down at Andy once more. "Is this beautiful lady your mommy?"

Pamela let out a coy laugh. "Well, I don't know about 'beautiful,' but I'm the mommy."

He locked eyes with her again. "Listen, *Mommy*," he said quietly. "I have a gun aimed at Andy right now. Unless you want to see his little head blown off, you're going to do exactly what I tell you to do."

Pamela wasn't sure she'd heard him right. Dumbfounded, she gazed at the man. The smile disappeared from her face. She glanced down at his hands—still in the pockets of his windbreaker. She could tell he was holding something in his right hand.

Andy let out a screech and squirmed in his stroller. He clapped his little hands and giggled.

The man furtively pulled the automatic out of his pocket for a moment—the barrel pointed at Andy's face.

"Oh, God, please, no," Pamela murmured, paralyzed with fear. White-knuckled, she clutched the stroller handles. She glanced around to see if there was anyone else in the vicinity—anyone who might help her. A man in track shorts and a sweatshirt ran along another paved trail about thirty feet away—but he was moving too fast to even notice them. Within moments, he was gone.

Tears stinging her eyes, Pamela gazed at the stranger. "What—what do you want?"

With an odd, little smile, he nodded toward the greenhouse—and the dark, wooded area beyond it. "Let's take a walk down there, and I'll tell you what I want."

Pamela hesitated.

He reached up and gently tugged at the pale green scarf around her neck. "C'mon."

Pamela swallowed hard and then started walking toward the darkened woods. Her legs felt wobbly. Wincing, she felt something grind against her spine, and realized it was the barrel of his revolver. Pamela realized something else. She was going to die.

As she pushed Andy in his stroller, she could only see the little hood covering the back of his head. He let out a squeal, then giggled and kicked.

"Please . . . please, don't hurt my baby," she whispered to the man.

"I won't hurt him," he promised. "Just you, *Mommy*, just you . . ."

Pausing under a park light, Hannah McHugh pressed two fingers along the side of her neck and ran in place. Warily, she glanced back at the winding pathway. The strange man had been on her tail for about ten minutes now, and he was still there—about twenty feet behind her. He was dressed in tan corduroys, a flannel shirt, and a light jacket—and he was *jogging*. He wasn't even wearing running shoes. From this distance, they looked like loafers, for God's sake.

A paralegal in a law office downtown, Hannah had been varying her after-work running course from day to day, and it had paid off. She'd gone from a size 10 to size 6. Divorced and thirty-eight years old, Hannah had convinced herself forty wouldn't be fatal. She'd recently made the transition from medium-brown brunette to Sassy Ginger (at least, that was the name on the Clairol box) and joined an online dating service, www.lifeconnexxions.com. So far, the guys she'd met had been drips, but Hannah wasn't giving up. Though she hadn't been in the mood to run tonight, she'd still donned her sweats and taken the Volunteer Park route. Just her luck, her persistence was paying off in the guise of some weirdo following her around the park's paved trail.

Hannah continued to jog in place and watched the bizarre man coming closer and closer. She studied his brown crew cut and the determined expression on his pockmarked face. He passed by her without even a glance her way. He was muttering to himself in an odd, singsong monologue. Hannah couldn't make out the words. She watched him retreat down the darkened pathway past the greenhouse—until he disappeared in the shadows.

"Talk about strange," someone said.

Startled, Hannah swiveled around and gaped at the man.

With his hands tucked in the pockets of his blue windbreaker, the handsome stranger gave her a crooked grin. "Looks like he just stepped off the crazy bus," he said.

Hannah shyly smiled, wiped the sweat from her forehead and flicked back her Sassy Ginger hair. She nodded toward the darkened trail in front of them. "Yeah, I think I'll wait a minute before I head down there. He's probably harmless, but I'm giving him a wide berth just the same."

"Smart," the handsome man replied. "A pretty woman like you shouldn't take any chances at this hour." He gave her a little wave. "Well, take care." Then he started to walk away.

"You too!" Hannah called. "Take care!" Biting her lip, she watched the good-looking man wander toward the shadowy trail. *Don't just stand there, stupid,* she thought. *He's cute. Go after him, talk to him!*

"Hey, wait a second, okay?" Hannah called. She hurried to meet up with the man.

Stopping, he turned and half smiled at her.

Suddenly, she was a little breathless. "Listen, would you mind if I walked with you—just to be on the safe side?"

"No problem, c'mon," he said, taking a step toward her. For a moment, Hannah thought he'd touch her arm. But his hands remained in the pockets of his blue windbreaker. He nodded toward the paved pathway that snaked through the gloomy woods ahead. "I'll make sure no one bothers you. Do you live close by?"

"Yes, near the Cornish School," Hannah answered, strolling beside him. "Lucky for me you came along."

He didn't respond. They'd just passed under the last streetlight for a while, and now headed into the wooded section. A few empty cars were parked on the side of the winding road. Hannah kept a lookout for the weird jogger, but she didn't see him in the darkness ahead. She didn't see anyone at all.

She felt the stranger's shoulder brush against hers. Was he flirting? She stole a furtive sidelong glance at him. No, he wasn't even looking at her. He seemed to be scoping out the area. Maybe he was on the lookout for the crazy jogger, too.

A cool wind kicked up. Tree branches and bushes

seemed to come alive for a moment. She could hear the man's breathing grow heavier. Hannah glanced at him again. He looked so serious—and tense. His gaze shifted from side to side as if he were making sure no one else was around. Then he peered over his shoulder.

Hannah glanced back in the same direction. There was no one behind them. "So—did you lose something?" she asked.

"What?" he said.

"I was wondering if you'd lost your dog or your cat, the way you keep looking around as if you . . ." She trailed off.

He wasn't listening. As they walked side by side, Hannah became more and more uncomfortable. Finally, the stranger paused and whispered, almost to himself. "We're all alone here, aren't we?"

Hannah swallowed hard and tried to veer away from him ever so subtly. "You know, I think I'm okay now," she said, finally. "I—I'm going to finish my run. It was—it was nice of you to—"

"Did you hear that?" he interrupted, stopping suddenly.

Hannah stopped, too. "Hear what?"

He took hold of her arm and led her off the trail—toward some bushes. Twigs snapped under their feet. "Listen to it," he said. "Sounds like whimpering. . . ."

Hannah's whole body stiffened up. She gently pulled her arm away. Any minute now, she expected him to slap a hand over her mouth and drag her into the bushes. She thought about making a break for it—while he was staring into the thicket. But then she heard it, too: a strange, muffled whining. It sounded like a wounded animal.

He weaved around some bushes. "You're gonna think I'm crazy," he said, his back to her. "But I recognize that crying. . . ."

Hannah didn't move. She gazed into the woods, but couldn't see anything beyond the first group of shrubs and trees. There was just darkness. Still, she heard the whimpering.

"Sounds like my kid," the man said. He squinted over his shoulder at her. "Earlier, you didn't see a pretty brunette with a baby in a stroller, did you?"

Confused, Hannah just shook her head.

He heaved a sigh. "My wife and I had an argument tonight. She left with the baby. Last time she blew up at me, she came to this park. That's why I'm here. . . ." The man ran a hand through his red hair, then turned and gazed into the forest. "I can't hear him anymore," he said, a panic in his voice. "Pam?" he called out. "Sweetie? Is that Andy I hear? Sweetheart?"

Hannah dared to venture a few steps farther into the woods. At the same time, she widened the gap between her and the man. Just beyond a cluster of shrubs, she detected movement. Moonlight reflected off something shiny and metal; it looked like a fallen bicycle's handlebars. With apprehension, Hannah moved in closer. The muffled whimpering became louder. The man was right. It sounded like a baby's stifled cries.

"Andy, is that you?" the man called, heading in the other direction. "Pam?"

Hannah crept around the bushes and gasped. It wasn't a bicycle's handlebars shining in the moonlight. She could see the baby stroller now—and the gleaming metal struts. "Over here!" she screamed.

She hurried toward the baby. Writhing and kicking

in his stroller, he wore a hooded blue jacket and held a little stuffed yellow giraffe that looked a bit tattered. Someone had wrapped a green cloth around the lower part of his face. Hannah wondered how the baby could breathe with that thing over his nose and mouth. The cloth—it looked like a scarf—muted his cries but didn't stop him from trying to shriek in protest. His face was red, and tears slid down his cheeks. He vainly swatted at the scarf with one little hand. The other hand clung to the dilapidated stuffed animal.

Instinctively, Hannah lifted the wriggling baby out of his stroller seat. *How could his stupid mother just abandon him like this?* She held him tightly with one arm and started to unravel the scarf from his face. "You poor thing," she murmured. It was hard holding on to him; he kept squirming and twitching. His little face was so red, it almost matched his hair.

The man staggered through the bushes. "Oh, Jesus, Andy!" he cried, reaching out for him. "It's Daddy. . . ."

Hannah gave the child to his father, but kept unraveling the scarf—careful not to scratch the baby's cheek with her fingernails. His screams became louder, and he wiggled fiercely. "What in the world?" she muttered. To her horror, Hannah found part of the silky material crammed into the baby's little mouth. She pulled out the makeshift gag, partially stained with his saliva and tears.

The little boy gasped, then let go an ear-piercing scream. He trembled in his father's arms. The man kept hugging him and kissing his forehead.

"Do you know whose this is?" Hannah asked, showing him the green silk scarf. She had to shout over the baby's cries.

"That's his mother's," the man replied, dazed. He rocked the baby in an effort to calm him down. "She— she had it on when she left the house earlier. But she— she wouldn't have done that to him, not Pam. She's a good mother, she—"

Hannah gazed at him and shook her head.

The man seemed to choke on those words, *She's a good mother*. Tears came to his eyes as he stared at the frayed stuffed giraffe in his son's grasp. "Oh, my God, that's not his. . . . It's not his toy. . . . Oh, Jesus, this isn't happening. . . ."

In horror and disgust, he knocked the stuffed animal out of the boy's hand. The child shrieked even louder, and his father held him against his chest. He anxiously glanced at the dark woods around them. "Pam?" he screamed. "Sweetheart? Pam?"

The green scarf slipped out of Hannah's grasp. Numbly, she stepped back and bumped into a tree. But she barely felt it. She couldn't feel anything beyond the terrible sensation in her gut.

Most everyone in the Seattle area knew about the string of recent murders. Three women had disappeared in the last few months. Their ages varied, but they had one thing in common. They were all mothers, each one abducted in front of her son. In what was becoming an eerie calling card, their abductor always left behind a used toy for the child.

And each of the mothers was later found dead.

The local TV and newspapers had given this killer a name: *Mama's Boy*.

People in the Seattle area were scared—especially women with young sons. But maybe Andy's mother hadn't been thinking when she'd taken her baby for a walk after dark. Didn't her husband say they'd been quarreling? In the heat of anger, she must have grabbed her son and left the house in a hurry.

"Pam?" the man screamed over his son's wailing. He kept rocking the baby in his arms. "Honey, can you hear me? Pam? Sweetheart . . ."

Hannah stood with her back against the tree. She listened to the man crying out and the baby's screaming. She felt sick to her stomach. A cool wind whipped through her. Leaves scattered. Shuddering, Hannah stared down at the frayed, stuffed yellow giraffe, leaning against one of the wheels of the child's empty stroller.

Hannah had an awful feeling that no matter how many times this man called out for her, Andy's mother would never answer him.

Two days later, someone found Andy's mother. The story made the front page of *The Seattle Times* on April 5, 1998:

FOURTH VICTIM DISCOVERED IN 'MOTHER' KILLINGS

'Mama's Boy' Continues to Elude Police

LATEST CASUALTY LEFT BEHIND AN INFANT SON

SEATTLE—An intense, 36-hour search for a missing Seattle woman, Pamela Baiter Milford, 31, ended early Friday morning, when workers found her body partially buried under a tarp at a Greenwood area construction site. According to sources at the King County Medical Examiner's Office, the victim had been beaten and strangled to death at least 24 hours before her body was discovered.

Seattle Police Detective Keith Stuckly, on a special task force for homicide investigation, said: "Ms. Milford's death has all the earmarks of another Mama's Boy killing. The circumstances of her disappearance and death all but confirm it."

The elusive serial killer dubbed "Mama's Boy" is believed to be responsible for at least three other Seattle-area murders in the last eight months. Each victim was abducted in front of her son and later found beaten and strangled to death.

Milford was last seen with her only child, a 10-month-old boy, around 6 p.m. Wednesday in Capitol Hill's Volunteer Park, four blocks from her home. . . .

The article went on to explain about the three others before Andy's mother.

On November 8, 1997, an intruder attacked the first victim, Sarah Edgecombe, twenty-four, in her home in Auburn while she was giving her three-year-old son a bath. Her husband, Kyle, had stepped out for cigarettes. Returning home twenty minutes later, he discovered the traumatized young boy, shivering in the cold tub. In the boy's bedroom, on his pillow, Kyle found a dilapidated teddy bear. Hikers spotted Sarah's remains three days later in the woods at Seattle's Discovery Park. Unfortunately, woodland scavengers had found her first. Police had to scour nearly a mile of the forest before they found all of her, and even then, it was mostly bones, picked near-clean. Sarah was the only one who had been dismembered.

After that, it seemed Mama's Boy wanted his victims to be discovered—eventually.

Anita Breckinridge, forty-three, disappeared on December 29, 1997, in a Safeway supermarket two miles from her Lynnwood home, leaving her four-year-old son in the shopping cart's child seat. The abandoned boy's screams resonated through the store for ten minutes. In the cart, a store employee found an old Raggedy Andy doll. The boy's father confirmed that it didn't belong to his son. The following morning, a jogger noticed Anita's nude corpse in a ditch near the Burke-Gilman Trail by Lake Union in Seattle. The jogger called 911 from her cell phone. "For a moment, when I saw that pale thing lying there in the gully, I thought it was a dead deer," she said.

With his learner's permit in his back pocket, fifteen-year-old Greg Sherwood drove his mother, Lila, forty-nine, to China Gardens in Ballard on March 22, 1998. It was raining that night. Greg parked in an alley behind the restaurant. He left the motor running and his mother in the front seat while he dashed into the restaurant to pick up their carryout order. Greg returned five minutes later with two bags of Chinese food. He found the car's passenger door open, and the windshield wipers still moving and squeaking. One of his mother's shoes was in a puddle by that door. In the passenger seat was an old G.I. Joe doll. Lila Sherwood's body was discovered in a Dumpster behind a Texaco station in Issaquah the following morning.

The toys Mama's Boy left behind were all used, slightly damaged, and untraceable.

Psychologists on the case speculated that the killer's mother must have deserted him, and there was probably abuse, too. It would explain why this killer was acting out. Typically, they would have expected all of the victims' children to have been the same specific age—the age the killer might have been when abandoned by his mother, or when he might have experienced a severe trauma.

But that just didn't apply to Mama's Boy—and his killing pattern. The oldest surviving child was fifteen, and the youngest, Andy Milford, was ten months old.

No one saw the man who had abducted Andy's mother in the park that night.

A twenty-seven-year-old construction worker, Chad Schlund, was the one who had found her. The building site was for a proposed forty-unit luxury condominium, Greenlake Manor. A two-story-deep, giant hole had been excavated for the basement and underground garage. A black tarp covered most of the vast crater, and that was where Chad Schlund wandered off from his coworkers to have a cigarette break. The ground beneath the tarp was hard and flat. So when Chad stepped on something soft and mushy beneath the black plastic sheeting, he balked. He noticed a bulky lump in the tarp and figured a large raccoon or dog must have made its way under that plastic sheet and suffocated.

Chad almost moved on. He had only a few minutes left of his break. Already one of the tall cranes began to sweep across the grey horizon again, and his coworkers were lumbering back to their workstations. Chad figured he had time for only half a cigarette now. Yet he stopped, and with his foot, pushed back the loose piece of tarp. He stopped when he saw the woman's hand sticking out from under the tarp's folds. The skin was so pale, it was almost blue. And her fingernails were the color of cinnamon.

The Seattle Times article on April 5, 1998, included a photo of Mama's Boy's fourth victim. The picture of Pamela Milford showed a pretty, fresh-faced woman with a big smile. Andy's mother looked so full of hope. The picture had been taken around the time Pamela found out she was pregnant—back when her hair was still long.

CHAPTER
TWO

Mount Vernon, Washington—ten years later

No *Signal,* it said in the window on her cell phone. This was the second time she'd tried calling him.

Susan Blanchette shoved the phone back in her purse, then sipped her Diet Coke. She smiled at her toddler son in the booster seat across from her. "You've had enough French fries, Mattie," she said gently. "I want you to work on your Arby's Junior. Just a few bites and you'll make your dear old mother very happy."

Mattie dared to eat one last fry; then he adjusted the napkin tucked in the collar of his Huskies sweatshirt. He was a bit short and underweight for his age, but healthy—with pink cheeks, straight, light brown hair, and long-lashed blue eyes. Cautiously touching the top bun of his junior roast beef sandwich as if it were the shell of a snapping turtle, he frowned at her. It was a perturbed expression Susan used to see on his father from time to time. Now she only saw that look on Mattie.

It was 1:45. The drive up from Seattle had taken an hour, and Susan guessed they had another hour to go before reaching Cullen, a sleepy little resort town, where her fiancé had rented them a house on Skagit Bay. Allen was there right now—or at least he was supposed to be. Susan just wished she could get ahold of him.

She hoped Mattie might sleep the rest of the way in the car, after their late lunch. The Arby's—by a casino off Interstate 5 near the Mount Vernon exit—wasn't too crowded. She and Mattie took a table in the middle of the restaurant, one of those two-seaters attached to another two-seater. The Formica table and plastic chairs were the color of mustard.

Mattie still hadn't taken a bite out of his Arby's Junior. He held it in his hand, but paid more attention to the Woody doll in his other hand. He was skipping Woody across the adjoining tabletop. The slim cowboy doll from *Toy Story* had belonged to Mattie's older brother and was becoming something like a security blanket for Mattie lately. For months now, the cartoon cowboy doll had never left his side, and it was starting to smell.

In a nearby booth, three guys in their early twenties had been leering at her—to the point at which it had almost become more irritating than flattering. But they looked as if they were about to leave, thank God.

Susan was tall and pretty and often passed for twenty-five. But she'd just checked herself in her compact mirror—between attempts to phone Allen—and under the restaurant's glaring fluorescent lights, Susan thought she appeared tired, haggard, and every one of her thirty-four years. That table full of twentysomething guys must have been really hard up. She didn't exactly look glamorous in her knock-around black V-neck pullover and jeans—even if the ensemble accentuated her trim figure. She had hazel eyes, a pale complexion, and wavy, shoulder-length, tawny brown hair. Lately, Susan had noticed the occasional wild grey strand, and she always yanked them out with trepidation (*pluck one, and five more will come to its funeral*). At this rate, Susan figured she'd be bald by her fortieth birthday.

With a shifty glance her way, Mattie put down his junior roast beef and reached for another fry.

"Don't even think about it, kiddo," she warned him. "You need to put a dent in that sandwich, and only then can you have some more fries. Now, c'mon, put Woody down and eat. . . ."

With a sigh, Matt set Woody aside and lifted the top of the bun and peeked at the roast beef.

"They're pretty great at that age, aren't they?"

Susan glanced up at a handsome man in his mid thirties. He had black hair, parted to one side, and a heavy five-o'clock shadow. He gave her a cocky smile and then sat next to Mattie on the other tandem table. He set down his soda and started to unload his Arby's bag.

Baffled, Susan gaped at him. Was this a pickup or something—in an *Arby's,* for Pete's sake? The restaurant was practically empty, and this character had decided to sit right next to her and her son.

"How old are you, little fella?" the man asked Mattie.

"I'm four and a half years old," Mattie replied, putting down his sandwich to show four fingers on his right hand. He also wiggled his left index finger—to emphasize the extra half year.

"And what's your name?" the man asked him.

"Matthew Blanchette," he answered proudly. "And I live at eight-fifteen East Prospect Drive in Seattle, Washington, USA."

Taking out his sandwich, the man grinned at Susan. "Well, you certainly have him well-trained in case you're ever separated. You folks are a long way from home."

Susan tried to work up a smile. So far, the man hadn't done anything inappropriate. And he was quite attractive. Yet he was just a little too friendly, a little too pushy.

He sipped his soda, winked at her, and then leaned close to Mattie. "I heard your mom trying to get you to eat your sandwich there," he said in a stage whisper. "You should listen to her. That sandwich is packed with protein, and it'll help you grow up big and strong—like me. Here, take a look at how big my hand is. . . ." He put his hand up—palm out—almost inviting Mattie to press his little hand against it and compare.

Fascinated, Mattie did just that.

Susan nervously glanced around the restaurant and saw the twentysomething guys lumbering out of their booth. She'd figured if this man got any more familiar—and he had, he was already touching her son—she might have counted on these twenty-year-olds to run interference. One distressed look their way might have prompted one or all of them to get chivalrous and come over to her table. But instead, they were now filing out of the restaurant.

The man growled like a tiger and clamped Mattie's tiny hand inside his own. Mattie squealed with delight.

The stranger leaned in close to him and growled even more fiercely. Mattie shrieked with laughter.

Susan cleared her throat and winced a little. "I'm sorry. I don't encourage him to make a lot of noise in restaurants and public places." She turned to Mattie. "Remember what I've told you, honey? There are other people here, trying to enjoy a nice, quiet meal. You have to be considerate of them." She reached across the table and gently pried his hand away from the man's grasp.

"We were just having fun," the man said—with a crooked smile and a slightly wounded look. He sat back in his chair. "C'mon, *Mommy*, don't be a spoil-sport."

"Yeah, Mom. Don't be a boil's port," her son chimed in.

Susan took Mattie's sandwich and fries, quickly wrapped them up, and loaded them in the Arby's bag. "It's getting late, and we need to skedaddle," she said, not looking at the man. "You can eat your sandwich in the car, honey. Don't forget Woody. Say good-bye now."

The man let out a stunned laugh. "Hey, listen, I didn't mean anything, I was just—"

"Of course you didn't," Susan said, getting to her feet. She managed to smile at him, then grabbed her purse and the Arby's bag. "We just need to hit the road. It was awfully nice talking with you." She took Mattie by the arm and helped him off his booster seat. "Say good-bye, Mattie," she repeated.

"G'bye!" he called, waving at the stranger with his free hand.

The man stood up, but didn't leave the table. "Hey, listen, I'm sorry. I was just . . ."

Susan kept walking, pulling Mattie along. But she realized they couldn't make a clean getaway. They had a long drive ahead, and Mattie would need to use the restroom. She bypassed the glass door exit and headed toward the alcove where there was a wooden highchair along with several orange plastic booster seats in a stack. In the alcove, she bypassed the men's room and started into the women's lavatory.

"NOOOOOO!" Mattie screamed. In his latest mode of resistance, he stopped and tried to sit down on the dirty tiled floor. He was at that age when little boys start to realize places like this were only for *girls*. So getting him into a women's room to pee or poop was a major ordeal lately. "No, I don't want to go in there!" he protested loudly.

"What did I just tell you about making a lot of noise in restaurants?" Susan growled. She took him by the arm and pulled him up. She tried not to drop her purse, the bag of food, and her Diet Coke. With her hip she pushed open the women's bathroom door, and then she peeked inside. "No one's in there, honey," she said with a sigh. "C'mon, the coast is clear. Let's go. . . ."

"NOOOOOOOO!" he screeched, resisting.

A shadow swept over the alcove, and Susan glanced up to see the stranger coming at them. "So—Mattie, you don't want to go in the ladies' bathroom?" he was saying. "Well, I don't blame you, sport." He grinned at Susan and started to reach out his hand for Mattie—his big, grown-up hand. "I'll take him into the men's room for you—"

"Would you please just . . . no, thank you!" Susan snapped at him. "We're fine here!" She yanked Mattie into the lavatory, and felt cold Diet Coke spilling down the front of her sweater. It seeped through her T-shirt to her stomach. Mattie let out another wail of protest, but in he went. With her shoulder, Susan quickly pushed the door shut behind her—right in the man's face.

She still had a firm grip on Mattie's hand. Whining, he twisted around and tried to sit down on the restroom floor. He kept Woody firmly tucked under his other arm.

"That's enough out of you, young man," Susan barked, pulling him up. "Now, get in here. . . ." Guiding him toward the open door to a toilet stall, she made sure the toilet was flushed. Why in the world some people didn't flush after using a public toilet was beyond her. This one was clean. "Do you think you might have to go number two?" she asked.

Pouting, he shook his head.

Susan took his Woody doll and then lifted the toilet seat for him. "All right, you know what to do," she said briskly. She left him standing in front of the toilet. "And I don't want any more screaming or crying. I've just about had it, mister."

"You're mean!" Mattie retorted.

"Yes, you have the meanest mother in the world," Susan shot back. She retreated toward the sink and unloaded Woody, her wet purse, and the wet bag of food on the orange Formica countertop. The half-crushed drink container was only a quarter-full now, and the plastic lid had come undone. "Shit," she muttered.

"You said a swear!" Mattie called from the stall.

Someone knocked on the women's room door. "Hey, you know," the man said loudly. "I was just trying to help!"

Leaning over the sink, Susan took a deep breath. "Yes, thank you!" she called back. "We're fine in here! You can go now, thank you!"

She waited for a response. But there was none. She tossed the soggy bag of food and what was left of her drink into the trash. With a paper towel, she dabbed the front of her pullover. Then she shoved Woody inside her purse. Maybe she'd overreacted with that man. But the guy had unnerved her. And she wasn't about to entrust her son to this stranger. Her older sister, Judy, claimed she was way overprotective with Matt. Maybe that was true, but she had good reason to be—considering what had happened eighteen months ago. Susan still hadn't completely recovered from it. She doubted that she ever would.

She paused to listen for a tinkling noise in the stall. Nothing.

"Sweetheart?" she said, eying the dirty mirror over the sink. Behind her, Susan could only see Mattie's red Converse All Stars and the cuffs of his jeans beneath the stall's partition. It looked like he was still standing in front of the toilet. But obviously, nothing was happening.

"Honey, can't you tinkle?" she said. "C'mon, I know you can't rush these things, but give it a try. We still have a long drive ahead." She turned the water on full blast in the sink. It was a trick she'd picked up in nursing school. She always used to turn on the faucet in the bathroom when a bladder-shy patient had a problem providing a urine sample. There was something about the sound of running water that helped prod them along. In her early twenties, Susan had been on the staff at Harborview Medical Center, a very stressful job. After she'd married and had Mattie's older brother, Michael, she'd kept up her nursing credentials part-time, consulting for an insurance company. She'd been able to work out of her home—and look after her babies. Of course, Susan hadn't realized it then, but that was the best time of her life. She should have savored every minute.

Now Susan was a single mother with one child, and working full time again—for a dermatologist in Ballard. Fridays at Dr. Chang's office were half days. She usually spent those free afternoons at home, grabbing a nap or just doing absolutely nothing (and loving it) for those two hours alone before picking up Mattie at Yellowbrick Road Day Care. She cherished her Friday afternoon routine and had been a bit reluctant to give it up today. But Allen had been so insistent they take this weekend getaway to Cullen.

So—instead of napping on the sofa right now with the soft Pottery Barn throw blanket over her and Joni Mitchell on the CD player, she was in an Arby's bathroom, seventy miles from home, doused with Diet Coke and despised by her toddler son. No doubt, she'd also offended that slightly creepy wannabe Good Samaritan, too. Well, tough.

Susan stepped over to the stall and found Mattie standing in front of the toilet with his pants up and fastened. He was idly playing with the toilet paper dispenser. All this time, Susan had thought he'd had a shy bladder. "Oh, for Pete's sake," she muttered, leaning over him. "You aren't even trying!" Susan unfastened his jeans and yanked them down; then she pulled down his underpants. "Now, tinkle, okay?"

Nothing.

Susan hovered behind him with the stall door open. "C'mon, sweetie, give it a try," she said, more gently. "Listen to the water in the sink. I know you hate being in the ladies' room. As soon as you go, we'll get out of here." But nothing was happening. At times like this, the kid really needed his dad.

Susan was about to throw in the towel and pull up his pants. That was when she heard the restroom door yawn open. A woman with her little girl had just stepped into the lavatory. Mattie saw them, too. He let out a shriek, and then so did the frightened little girl. Their screams reverberated within the tiled walls of the small bathroom. Mattie kept crying—screeching angrily—while Susan fastened his pants back up and led him toward the restroom door. All the while, she apologized to the woman and her startled daughter. Mattie continued to scream and squirm as she hustled him toward the restaurant exit. Susan figured everyone in the Arby's probably thought she was kidnapping him.

She half expected to see her wannabe Good Samaritan among the patrons, sitting at another table—perhaps trying to hit on another woman, some young mother.

But Susan didn't see him at all. There was no sign of him in the parking lot either.

She strapped Mattie in his booster seat on the back passenger side of her old-as-the-hills but reliable red Toyota. It had a bent antenna, and the indicator handle easily screwed off the steering column—a discovery she'd made while nervously twisting it during a traffic jam. But the old car got her around just fine. Besides, she couldn't afford a new one.

She gave Mattie his Woody doll, and he started to calm down. He let her wipe away his tears with a Kleenex from her purse.

"Is he coming with us?" Mattie asked.

"Is *who* coming with us?" Susan was crouched down by the open back door of her car.

"The man we ate lunch with," Mattie said. "Is he coming, too?"

She shook her head. "No, he's not coming with us, sweetheart," she said. "I don't even know him. We won't be seeing him again. . . . God willing." The last part, she muttered under her breath. "Fingers and toes!" she announced, straightening up. Then she closed the car door.

As she walked around to the driver's side, Susan took one last look around the parking lot. There was still no sign of the man anywhere. She ducked inside the car, started up the engine, and pulled out of the lot.

She didn't look back.

"I have to go potty."

Hands on the steering wheel, Susan glanced in the rearview mirror at Mattie. He'd set aside his book and now squirmed in his booster seat. The breeze through the partially open window made a mess of his hair. He impatiently tapped his feet against the back of the passenger seat.

"Do you have to go number one or number two?" Susan asked.

"Both," he whined urgently. "I have to go bad!"

"Oh, Lord," she muttered under her breath. Susan gazed beyond the dirty, bug-splattered windshield at the road ahead. The narrow highway weaved through a dark forest and beside a creek. At times, the road took her along the edge of a cliff with only a short guardrail to prevent her from careening into the gulch. Every once in a while, the late-afternoon sun would peek through the tall trees and momentarily blind her.

After his hissy fit in Arby's, Mattie had turned quiet. By the time they'd reached Cullen—with its picturesque harbor, quaint shops, and galleries—he'd been mesmerized by the scenery. Checking a MapQuest printout on the passenger seat, Susan had followed the directions here to Carroll Creek Road, north of the town center. That had been a mere fifteen minutes ago, and she'd asked Mattie if he needed to go to the bathroom.

"Naw," he'd muttered, distracted by the boats in Skagit Bay.

Now he acted as if he were about to explode.

Along the road, there were several signs with symbols that warned of FALLING ROCKS, CROSSING DEER, STEEP INCLINES, and HAIRPIN TURNS. Watching for all these hazards, Susan kept glancing back at Mattie. She wondered what the symbol might look like warning drivers of a toddler passenger about to poop in his pants. "Honey, try to hold on," she urged him, tightening her grip on the wheel. "Allen said there's a mini-mart on the way to the house. I'm sure it's coming up soon. I'll bet they have a bathroom. Have you—have you been looking for deer, sweetheart? The signs say a lot of Bambi's relatives and friends live here in these woods."

And here's hoping your frazzled mother doesn't plow into one of them, Susan thought.

She'd never gotten ahold of Allen. Her fiancé had driven up earlier that morning to open the lakeside rental house and make arrangements for a special "surprise." So far, the only real surprise was the lack of cell phone reception, probably because of all the mountains and trees. Susan hoped he was waiting for her at the house right now, because she didn't have the key.

Biting her lip, she glanced at the MapQuest directions again. They claimed it was 5.1 miles on Carroll Creek Road before the turnoff for the rental house on Birch Way. Susan was beginning to wonder if she'd missed it. She'd passed several turnoffs—mostly dirt roads or one-lane paved arteries. Maybe one of them had been Birch Way. For all she knew, she could be headed deeper into these godforsaken woods.

Susan had had some initial misgivings about this trip, but kept them to herself. Allen had seemed so bent on going—and quite suddenly, too. He'd only started talking about the trip a few days ago, saying they needed a break from the city and Cullen was the perfect spot. The strange part was he didn't seem very eager about it, just determined.

Susan went on the Internet to learn more about where they were spending their weekend. The first few search results were from the City of Cullen, the Washington State Tourist Bureau, and *The Seattle Times*'s "Best Places to Visit in the Pacific Northwest." According to the articles, Cullen was a terrific destination for sailing, fishing, camping, and hiking. Charming shops, art galleries, and restaurants made the town center a

must for visitors, who could also view the eighteen-
foot bronze sea lion statue in historic Harbor Park. And
Cullen was a haven for antique collectors. The town's
lovely inns and B&B's were the perfect romantic getaway for travelers visiting the nearby casino and vine-
yard.

Susan found another link on the Google listing for
Cullen, Washington. The article was a year old:

Missing Bellingham Woman Assumed Dead – Bellingham Herald
October 7, 2008 . . . Local police discovered Matusik's
abandoned car on Timberlake Drive in **Cullen** . . .
www.bellinghamherald/news/100408 – 22k

It wasn't what Susan had hoped to find in her search
for information about Cullen; nevertheless, she clicked
on the link to the article.

Beneath the headline, there was a photo of the missing woman, a twenty-seven-year-old bank clerk named
Wendy Matusik. The snapshot must have been taken at
a party, because someone—cropped out of the picture—had their arm around the chubby, pretty-faced,
curly-haired blonde. From her bright smile, she looked
like she was having a great time.

MISSING EIGHT WEEKS, the caption said. *Wendy
Matusik of Bellingham, shown here at an engagement
party for a friend. Matusik disappeared on Friday, August 8, while driving to Arlington for a bridal shower.*

Susan read the long, detailed article with interviews
that profiled the missing woman and examined her last
known hours. The author of the piece obviously wanted
to bolster the public interest in Wendy—and keep the
search for her going. The first reference to Cullen
caught Susan's eye in the second paragraph: *Local po-*

lice discovered Matusik's abandoned car on Timber-
lake Drive in Cullen. One of the rear tires was flat.
Wendy Matusik was last seen that Friday afternoon
around 2:30 at Rosie's Roadside Sundries in Cullen.
She was alone. . . .

The journalist had interviewed the store clerk, who
said that Wendy had bought a Diet Coke, an eight-
ounce bag of Lay's barbecue-flavored potato chips,
and a pack of Juicy Fruit gum.

Wendy's best friend, a Seattle resident, Margarita
Donavan, had also been interviewed for the article.
She mentioned that Wendy had a tabby named Chow-
der. She was a crossword puzzle fiend and had recently
joined Weight Watchers. She wanted to lose fifteen
pounds in time for her friend's wedding. Margarita was
getting married in October, and Wendy was to have
been her maid of honor.

That Friday afternoon she'd planned to meet Margarita at Angel of the Winds Casino in Arlington. Wendy
was throwing an early, unofficial bachelorette party for
her pal. The other two bridesmaids had agreed to join
them at the casino hotel the following day.

She'd left a voice mail for Margarita that afternoon,
and her friend had saved it: *Hey, Margarita, it's moi,*
and I-5 is insane. So I'm taking the scenic backwoods
route down. I'm going around Cullen, and I'll be at
least an hour late. Have a wine spritzer, and start the
nickel slots without me. I'll give you another update as
I get closer to Arlington. I don't think you'll be able to
call me because the cell phone reception here is awful.
Talk to you soon!

That was the last Margarita Donavan ever heard
from her friend.

At ten o'clock that night, during a routine patrol, Cullen's sheriff, Stuart Fischer, noticed the abandoned car on the shoulder by Timberlake Drive. The sheriff said his headlights caught sight of a raccoon lazily stepping out of the vehicle's driver's side. The door had been left open—and the interior light was still on, but dimming, due to the drain on the car's battery.

Sheriff Fischer found a Diet Coke in the dashboard's cup holder—along with a map and an open bag of potato chips on the front passenger seat. The raccoon had eaten all but a few chips, still scattered on the seat and the car floor.

The sheriff said he didn't find a purse or any car keys. But in the trunk, authorities later found a small suitcase. The article pointed out that among the clothes in the overnight bag was a black cardigan with a colorful spade, heart, club, and diamond design. According to Margarita Donavan, Wendy always wore the cardigan when she gambled. It was her lucky sweater.

Susan had gotten a memory jolt reading the last three paragraphs of the story. And those memories were from a very scary time:

> According to Cullen's Sheriff Fischer, "It's been ten years since we've had a missing persons case like this one."
>
> On September 3, 1998, a Bellevue resident, Stella Syms, 38, was abducted from her summer home in Cullen, while vacationing there with her 8-year-old son. Syms' body was discovered 36 hours later in some woods near her home. She had been strangled. Syms is believed to be the seventh known victim in the Mama's Boy murders that plagued the Seattle area from November 1997 through

October 2000. The vicious serial killer is believed to have strangled at least 13 women, all mothers who left behind sons. Mama's Boy was never captured, and his identity remains a mystery.

"They keep searching the area over and over for clues to Wendy's disappearance," said longtime Cullen resident, the Rev. George Camper of First Episcopal Church. "These are the same woods, streams, and ravines the police were combing ten years ago for Stella Syms. It's hard not to remember the Mama's Boy slaying. But no one wants to say it out loud. No one even wants to think something similar has happened. . . ."

Hands tight on the steering wheel, Susan watched the winding road ahead. She remembered Mama's Boy, too, and shuddered. He'd killed most of his victims that first year, 1998, when Susan had been a new mom. In fact, her son, Michael, was the same age as the baby boy left behind when the fourth victim was abducted in Volunteer Park. That literally hit too close to home for Susan, Walt, and Michael. They lived five blocks away from the park.

Susan had read *The Seattle Times*'s accounts of each new murder, the endless speculation from police and forensic psychologists, and the warnings. She remembered the widely released police-artist's sketch of the suspect—based on vague descriptions from the surviving sons and other witnesses. The result was a creepy half-photo, half-cartoon of a man with dark hair, thin lips, and a dead-eyed stare. It gave Susan chills to look at it. The image burned in her head. Some nights, she imagined a stranger with that stark, caricature-like face quietly sneaking into their home while she was looking in on the baby. She could almost see him, with those cold, lifeless eyes, glaring at her from the doorway of Michael's nursery.

By the end of 1998, he'd killed eight women. He'd broken into the homes of two of them. Walt installed a home security system and fit dead-bolt locks on both the front and back doors of their duplex. He insisted she buy a cell phone and got her a small canister of in-dustrial-strength pepper spray. Susan wasn't the only one taking precautions. Seattle mothers armed them-selves with handguns, switchblades, or knitting nee-dles. Police encouraged women to have whistles or alarms on their key chains whenever they stepped out with their sons. Playground dates became group excur-sions. Police beefed up security at playgrounds through-out the area—ironically, more for the safety of the mothers than their children. Whenever Susan needed to go somewhere with little Michael, she called her neighbor, who was also a new mom, and they went out as a team.

It should have been an idyllic time for Susan, with her first baby. In so many ways, it was. She felt lucky to work at home with the part-time consulting-nurse job. Walt was a great dad, very doting. He was an engi-neer for Boeing, and every afternoon, when he re-turned home from work, he'd look after Michael so she could have a run, go to the store, or just steal some alone time. Susan remembered many an afternoon, handing the screaming baby to Walt before he even made it through the front door.

Walt. If someone had ever told her she'd end up marrying a man who was *follicularly challenged*, she would have told them they were crazy. She usually liked a guy with a nice, full head of hair. But Walt was practically bald on top. He had a handsome, chiseled face—with intense blue eyes and thick, dark brows. Both of his sons had inherited his long eyelashes. Walt was a fitness nut, and he had the lean, wiry body to prove it. As soon as Michael could sit up, Walt regularly took him out in the special jogger's stroller—or he set him in the little canopied attachment that trailed after his bike. Susan couldn't do that. She couldn't risk going out alone with her son.

She remembered one case in particular in November 1999, because she'd planned to take Michael to his first movie, a matinee of *The Borrowers*. But then she read about Dianne Rickards, thirty-nine-year-old Bellevue stay-at-home mom, who took her seven-year-old son to see the same movie at Factoria Cinema. During the film, she left her coat on the seat and went to use the restroom. Dianne's son never saw her again. In the pocket of his mother's coat, police found two slightly banged-up Matchbox trucks. Dianne's son remembered a man sitting behind them, but he'd never gotten a look at his face in the darkened theater. An engineer with the Burlington Northern Railroad spotted Dianne's bruised and battered body in a marsh beside the railroad tracks in Kent two days later.

At Walt's urging, Susan postponed taking Michael to the movie. Mama's Boy often waited just long enough between victims so that mothers let down their guards— and then he'd strike again. And everyone would be on edge once more. Sometimes, Susan got fed up always looking over her shoulder, and she'd resolve not to let this creep scare her. But then little things would happen—like someone calling and hanging up, or a piece of trash that mysteriously made its way into their back-yard—and suddenly she'd feel hunted.

One solace: at least none of the victims' sons had been harmed, not physically anyway. But Susan often worried that if anything were to happen to her, Michael wouldn't have any memory of her.

It was strange, after all the precautions they'd taken, they still couldn't escape tragedy. But it was Mattie who couldn't remember his father or older brother. Susan kept plenty of framed photos of them at home to help her son feel connected to them. She didn't want to lose that connection either.

She still needed it—even now, with Allen in her life.

"You know, maybe Allen will rent us a boat tomorrow," Susan said, with a glance at Mattie's reflection in the rearview mirror. "We could go sailing. Your daddy used to take us sailing all the time. Do you remember going out on a boat with Mikey and Daddy?"

Her son let out a long sigh. "Mom, I gotta go *now*!"

"Okay, honey, okay." Biting her lip, Susan slowed down for another curve in the tree-lined road. She considered taking him out to the woods and letting him go there. But she thought about Wendy Matusik, and the notion of venturing into those woods with Mattie right now gave her the willies.

Wendy's wasn't the only recent missing-person case in Cullen. In her Web search, Susan had found a link to a brief story about a thirty-six-year-old woman from Vancouver, British Columbia, who had been camping with friends in Cullen earlier in the summer. Monica Fitch had gone hiking in the woods by Skagit Bay one morning and never come back. A weary rescue worker on the unsolved case said he believed Monica might have attempted to go swimming in the bay and drowned.

None of those "Best Places to Visit" articles that Susan read had mentioned any casualties among Cullen's hikers and campers.

After another curve in the road, she noticed an intersection up ahead. At the corner stood a slightly rundown, one-story cedar shaker with an illuminated sign over the front porch. ROSIE'S ROADSIDE SUNDRIES, it said between twin Coca-Cola logos.

"Hallelujah," she sighed. "Hold on just a little longer, sweetie. We'll stop in here. I'm sure they have a bathroom. That's my good boy. . . ."

As Susan pulled into the gravel lot, she noticed a neon sign for Rainier Beer in the front window. A sandwich board by the screen door advertised:

Gourmet Deli & Snacks! – ATM
Beer & Wine – Fresh Coffee – Ice Cold Drinks
Camping Supplies & Live Bait
RESTROOMS

"Thank God," Susan whispered as she read the last line.

Also on the porch, on the other side of the door, was an old-fashioned, coin-operated bucking bronco for the kiddies to ride. Someone had tacked a faded, weather-beaten handwritten placard on the front porch post: THIS IS A KID-FRIENDLY ZONE—WATCH WHEN YOU BACK OUT!

Susan parked beside a dark green Honda Civic, the only other vehicle in the small lot. Switching off the ignition, she glanced up at the illuminated sign again and remembered the *Bellingham Herald* news article:

Wendy Matusik was last seen that Friday afternoon around 2:30 at Rosie's Roadside Sundries in Cullen. She was alone. . . .

As she helped Mattie out of his booster seat in back, Susan glanced at her wristwatch: 2:30. *And Friday, too,* she thought, hesitating for a moment.

She told herself she was being silly. "C'mon, sweetie," she announced. "Let's leave Woody in the car. He can sit out this little excursion. I'll crack a window for him. . . ."

Once Mattie climbed out of the car, he made a beeline for the bucking bronco on the store's front porch. Clutching the front of his pants with one hand, he bounced on his heels and pointed to the coin-operated pony ride. "Can I, Mom? Can I, please?"

"First, the bathroom," she said, shutting the car door. "Then you can take on the mechanical bull." Stepping up to the front porch, she took Mattie by the hand and pushed open the screen door. Inside Rosie's Roadside Sundries, it smelled like stale coffee and popcorn.

Two teenagers—a pretty brunette and her gangly, goofy-cute boyfriend—wandered up the aisle with shopping baskets. Susan guessed they were both about eighteen. "We're getting this," the young man declared, waving a box of Cap'n Crunch at his girlfriend. "I have breakfast with the captain every morning."

The girl rolled her eyes. "Do you sleep with him too?" She tossed a box of Pop-Tarts into her basket. "God, you're so retarded—" The slim, pixie-haired girl stopped and grimaced with embarrassment when she locked eyes with Susan and Mattie.

The boy let out a laugh and nudged her. "Hey, nice talk, Moira, real sensitive. . . ."

Susan ignored them and headed up another aisle with Mattie in tow. The shelves were full of slightly dusty canned goods, from pork n' beans to corned beef hash to Chef Boyardee—all stuff that could be heated over a campfire. There was Cheez Whiz and Saltines and Progresso and Campbell's Soup cans. The store had old hardwood floors and somewhat poor overhead lighting—all the better not to see the dust or the expiration dates on the merchandise. On one side of the store, there was a movie-theater-type popcorn maker, a microwave oven, two kinds of coffee brewing, a Coca-Cola fountain, and a heated display case with rotating spits that kept hot dogs and corn dogs warm.

Pulling Mattie by the hand, Susan headed up to the counter. Beside the register and a lottery ticket display stood a plump, kind-faced woman with bright orange hair that had to be a wig. Susan guessed she was around seventy years old. "Excuse me," Susan whispered to the woman. "Where's the restroom, please?"

"Oh, this looks like an emergency. Am I right?" The woman didn't even wait for Susan to respond. She motioned for her to step behind the counter. "C'mon, let's take the shortcut, honey. It's right here out back."

"Thanks very much," Susan said, following her. Between the counter and the back door, they passed by a little play area with a mat, some Fisher-Price toys, and a multicolored, plastic mini jungle gym for toddlers. Mattie stopped dead in his tracks to gaze at it. He was still clutching himself in front.

"C'mon, sweetie," Susan urged him.

The woman waddled to the back door, opened it, and looked back at them. "Oh, that's for my grandson when he visits," she explained. She smiled at Mattie.

"He's just about your age. You can play here, too, honey—after your bathroom break." She pushed open the screen door. "You can come back in this way, too, if you'd like. I'll leave the door open for you."

"Thanks again, you're a lifesaver," Susan said, prodding Mattie out the doorway.

They hurried up a short dirt path, past a Dumpster and some recycling bins, to a chalet-style, white stucco hut. Susan noticed a paved pathway that wound around from the front of the store, intersecting with this trail. There was a bicycle rack and a phone station at the junction point. The hut housed the men's restroom on one side and the women's on the other. Pulling Mattie by the hand, she headed toward the women's side.

"NOOOOOOOOOO!" he shrieked. He must have noticed the international women's symbol by the door. He stopped and tried to sit down on the ground. "Don't take me in there!"

"We're not going through this again," Susan hissed, hoisting him up to his feet. "Now, c'mon, please—"

"No! I don't want to go in there!" he protested. He tried to wriggle free from her grasp. He started crying. "Please, Mom! Please! I want to go in the *boys'* room!"

"Oh, Lord," she muttered. She took a deep breath. "Okay, fine, fine. The boys' room it is. I haven't got time for the pain." She led Mattie to the other side of the little chalet hut. He went back to holding himself in front. Susan paused at the men's room doorway and cracked it open a few inches. "Excuse me!" she called. "Is anyone in here?"

"Yeah! I am!" someone answered.

Susan could hear water running—and then, a hand-dryer roaring. She stepped back from the door and glanced down at Mattie, who was doing an *I-have-to-pee* dance. "Hold on, sweetie. I can't take you in there just yet."

The door swung open, and a handsome young man almost bumped into her. He drew back for a moment. "Um, excuse me. . . ."

He was about eighteen. Susan guessed those two kids in the store were his friends. His short, dark brown hair was messy and wind-blown—and somehow looked perfect. It gave his boy-next-door good-looks a sexy edge. About six feet tall, he had a lean, solid build. He wore a leather jacket over a black T-shirt and olive cargo pants. For a moment, he blocked the doorway and gaped at her.

"I'm sorry, but is there anyone else in there?" Susan asked. "I want to take my son in."

"Oh, go for it," he said, nodding. He stepped aside. "If you'd like, I'll stand guard out here, make sure no one goes in."

"Thanks a lot." Susan started to lead Mattie past him.

He touched her arm. "Um, someone wrote a nasty message on the stall divider," he whispered. "You might want to—avert his gaze."

"Thanks," Susan said. Then she took Mattie inside the men's room. The young man hadn't told her that the place stank or that someone had thrown a roll of toilet paper—now yellow—in one of the urinals. But thanks to the young man's warning, she managed to distract Mattie so he didn't see *"SUCK MY BIG DICK"* carved on the wooden stall divider. Mattie was just learning to read, too, so she was grateful for the warning. While Mattie did his business, Susan thought about Holden Caulfield in *The Catcher in the Rye*, saying how he wanted to go around erasing all the *Fuck yous* so little children wouldn't see them. It was sweet of that young man to warn her about the graffiti, sweet of him to stand guard, too.

After all that panic and drama, Mattie didn't go number two. He didn't even tinkle much. Susan kept his attention diverted from the stall divider while he washed his hands at the sink. When they stepped out of the men's room, she found the young man standing by the door.

"Thanks, you're very nice," Susan told him. She nudged Mattie. "Can you say thank you?"

"Thank you!" Mattie said, squinting up at the young man. "Do you play football?"

He smiled at Mattie. "I'm on my high school's lacrosse team. It's almost like football, but much cooler. Are you a Huskies fan?" He nodded at Mattie's sweatshirt.

"The Huskies rule!" Mattie announced, though he'd never seen a Huskies game. It was just something he'd picked up from the other boys at Yellowbrick Road Day Care.

The young man smiled at Susan. "You from Seattle?"

She nodded. "Yes. We rented this house for the weekend, and I'm not exactly sure where it is. Are you from around here?"

"No, I'm from Seattle, too. But my family has a cabin not far from here. I'm staying there with some friends. Anyway, I know the area. Where are you headed? Maybe I can help."

"Birch Way," Susan replied. "It's a house on the water, number twenty-two Birch Way."

The young man just stared at her. His smile faded.

"Do you—do you know where that is?" she asked, a bit puzzled by his sudden, somber reaction.

He nodded glumly and cleared his throat. "Sure. Just keep going north on Carroll Creek Road for about fifteen minutes. Birch Way will be on your left. Look for a red mailbox. Number twenty-two is the only house on that road. It's pretty isolated." He seemed to work up a smile. "I'm one of your closest neighbors. My family's cabin is a little over a mile away."

"So this house, is it nice?" Susan asked. "Is it okay? I mean, the way you looked at me when I mentioned the address—"

"No, it's fine," he said coolly, cutting her off. "There are a lot of rental houses around here, and that's one of the loveliest."

Susan gave him a puzzled smile. It struck her as odd that this high school lacrosse player would use the word *loveliest.* It seemed rehearsed, as if he had been told to describe the house that way to people. Susan automatically tightened her grip on Mattie's little hand.

"Well, I should take off," he said after a moment. He glanced toward the gravel lot at the front of Rosie's Roadside Sundries. "My friends are probably waiting for me. Nice talking to you. Enjoy your weekend." He smiled at Mattie, made a fist and shook it. "Go, Huskies, right, dude?"

"Go, Huskies!" Mattie enthusiastically agreed, shaking his little fist, too.

Susan watched the young man retreat up the pathway, toward the parking lot in front of the store. She could hear his friends talking, and the girl laughed about something. As Susan retreated toward the store's back entrance, she heard car doors shutting and the motor starting up, and then the sound of gravel under tires.

Inside Rosie's Roadside Sundries, the nice woman with the Lucille Ball hair—who turned out to be Rosie herself—let Mattie run wild in the small play area. Susan picked up a few things for the weekend. Allen had probably already stocked the house with groceries and supplies. But Susan figured she ought to give Rosie her business, after they'd used her bathroom and play area.

"I'm staying the weekend at this house on the water," Susan told Rosie at the counter. The plump older woman was ringing up her items. "It's—um, Twenty-two Birch Way," Susan said. "Do you know it?"

"Oh, yes, that's a very nice house," Rosie answered, momentarily distracted. She donned a pair of cat's-eye glasses dangling from a chain around her neck to read the price sticker on a box of Ritz crackers. She kept them on while totaling up the sale. "You'll like it there, hon. That'll be twenty-one-oh-five."

Mattie didn't want to leave the play area, but Rosie assured him he was welcome to come back and play there any time. She opened her till drawer, fished out a quarter, and handed it to Susan. "That's for a ride on Seabiscuit outside—for my new little buddy there."

With a bit of prompting, Mattie thanked Rosie, and then they headed out of the store. The coin-operated pony was pretty tame, rocking Mattie very gently. Still, Susan put down her grocery bag to keep ahold of his arm while he rode the pony. Mattie squealed with delight. He'd only been on the pony for half a minute when Susan noticed a red MINI Cooper turning into the store lot. The car pulled up a few spaces away from hers and parked.

"Gimme up, gimme up!" Mattie squealed. He must have meant *giddyup*.

Susan turned to him and smiled. "Pretty fun, huh, sweetie? Yippee-eye-oh . . ." She glanced over toward the car once again. The driver hadn't gotten out of the front seat yet. Susan couldn't see him because the late afternoon sun reflected on the windshield. But then some clouds moved in front of the sun, and Susan noticed the driver, sitting alone in the car. She saw his handsome face, the dark hair parted to one side, and the rugged five o'clock shadow. He stared back at her, unsmiling.

It was just a few fleeting seconds, and then the glare on the windshield wiped his image away. Susan could no longer see him, but she still felt his eyes on her. She remembered his cocky grin as he'd sat down next to them forty-five minutes ago. *Well, you certainly have him well-trained in case you're ever separated,* he'd said. *You folks are a long way from home.*

"Yippee!" Mattie sang out, kicking the toy pony's flanks. "Gimme up! Gimme up!"

Susan tightened her grip on his arm. "Um, honey, that's enough for now," she said, pulling him off the pony in mid-ride. "We need to get a move on. Allen's probably waiting—"

"NOOOOOOO!" he screamed, his legs kicking in the air.

"Enough of that," she said firmly. Susan managed to grab her grocery bag while wrestling with him. "The pony needs to rest up. He'll give you *two rides* tomorrow." She carried Mattie to the car.

Susan hated turning her back to the stranger in the MINI Cooper, but she had to put down her bag and strap Mattie in his booster seat. Her hands shook as she fumbled with his seat belt. All the while, she listened for a telltale click of the door handle of the car behind her. Any minute now, she expected to see a shadow creeping up on her and Mattie.

"Okay, sweetie, fingers and toes," Susan said, a bit out of breath. She shut his door, then glanced back at the red sports car. She could see the man, still at the wheel, his head slightly tilted in her direction. Part of her just wanted to scream at him to leave her and her son alone. But instead, Susan hurried around to the driver's side of her car. Tossing the bag on the passenger seat, she scooted behind the wheel, then shut her door and locked it. Her hands were still trembling as she turned the key in the ignition and shifted into reverse. Then she backed out of the space, turned the car around, and headed out of the lot.

Speeding down Carroll Creek Road, Susan checked her rearview mirror several times. The MINI Cooper hadn't moved. Finally she took a curve in the tree-lined road, and she couldn't see the store anymore.

Susan started to wonder if she'd overreacted back there. The man really hadn't *done* anything—except come on as overly friendly and solicitous at the Arby's earlier. Yes, he'd shown up at the store, but fifteen minutes after her. Was he really following her? Maybe he was a local.

Something buckled under the car. Susan glanced in her rearview mirror to see if she'd hit a piece of metal on the road—or had lost some part of the car. But the road was clear behind her.

The car suddenly rocked and wobbled as if it were going over a series of potholes. Biting her lip, Susan clutched the steering wheel. It vibrated from the rough ride. She nervously glanced at the driver's side mirror—shaking so much the reflection was just a blur.

Mattie was jostled in his booster seat. "Gimme up! Gimme up!"

Easing up on the gas, Susan steered over to the side of the road. The car seemed to be limping. It felt like she had a flat tire. "Oh, I really don't need this now," she muttered to herself, a pang of dread in her stomach.

She switched on the emergency blinkers, cut the ignition, and then glanced back at Mattie. "Well, that was pretty exciting, wasn't it?" she asked.

Wide-eyed, he nodded and put his thumb in his mouth.

"I'm just going to take a look at the damage, okay, sweetheart?" she said. "I'll be right outside where you can see me." Climbing out of the car, Susan checked around the back. The rear tire on the driver's side was flat; the hubcap pressed against the gravel roadside.

"Oh, swell," she murmured. She remembered that article again: *Local police discovered Matusik's abandoned car on Timberlake Drive in Cullen. One of the rear tires was flat. . . .*

Even though she knew it wouldn't work, Susan took out her cell phone and tried dialing Allen. Her hands were shaking. *No signal available* came up on the tiny screen.

With a nervous sigh, she popped open the trunk and

started to unload their suitcases so she could get the spare tire, jack, and other equipment. She glanced over her shoulder at the empty road behind her.

The narrow highway curved around a wall of tall evergreens, but there was a gap between some of the trees, and she saw another little stretch of road—and a car. Susan was too far away to see the color or the make of the car.

But it was coming her way.

He watched her unload the jack, wrench, and spare tire from the trunk of her old Toyota. All the while, Susan Blanchette kept looking over her shoulder.

He stood behind a tree in the woods, about thirty feet away, snacking on a Three Musketeers bar.

He'd given her the flat tire, his way of welcoming her to Cullen—and an ominous start to this weekend he'd planned for her. Susan had no idea he was calling all the shots. He knew Susan would be coming to Cullen before she did.

And he knew she would die.

He'd been waiting for Susan and had kept a lookout for her red Toyota—license plate: MLF901. While she'd been in Rosie's Roadside Sundries, he'd set a small device under her rear left tire. It was a foot-long spiked metal strip—a section cut from a long grid that rental car companies used at their lot exits and entrances to prevent theft. Those spiked strips instantly punctured tires and disabled cars. His smaller, portable version perforated only one tire, but it got the same job done. It just took a bit longer for the tire to deflate.

In fact, last year, Wendy Matusik had driven at least two miles from the grocery store before all the air left her back tire. He hadn't gone to any great lengths to hide the perforating device afterward. He'd merely tossed it on the ground by the cellar storage doors on the shady side of Rosie's. And there it remained for days—much to his amusement—while state police combed the area for clues to Wendy's disappearance.

The Wendy episode had been unplanned, a mere impulse. He kept her alive for a few days until he got bored with her. It was the same with that hiker, Monica, who was a bit too mannish for his tastes. After the initial capture, the thrill had worn off pretty quickly. As a kid, when he'd grown tired of a toy, he would smash it with a hammer, and there was always a bit of regret afterward. Except with Wendy and Monica, there were no regrets after he'd slit their throats. Those were departures from the Mama's Boy killings. All of them had been strangled. And neither Wendy nor Monica had been mothers—not to his knowledge anyway.

He finished up his candy bar and watched Susan struggle to loosen the tire's lug nuts. He shoved the Three Musketeers wrapper in his jacket pocket.

He couldn't imagine growing tired of Susan. He'd been watching her for weeks now, and she continued to fascinate him. He'd seen her coming and going—sometimes wearing her white nurse's lab coat—at Dr. Chang's office. He often parked across the street when she picked up Matthew at Yellowbrick Road Day Care. And sometimes he watched from outside her bedroom window as she climbed into bed alone. She wore a man's T-shirt to bed. She only wore a nightgown when her fiancé spent the night.

Of course, he knew her fiancé's whereabouts most of the time, too.

But he had become far more interested in studying Susan. He knew the whole layout of her first-floor duplex on Prospect Avenue in Capitol Hill. He'd even broken in once. He'd gotten so close to her, but in her home, he could actually touch her clothes, her shoes, and her panties. He smelled her hair on her pillow— and thought about how he could touch her and smell her as she was tied up. He could do whatever he wanted to her. And maybe after he killed her, he would even taste her blood.

He'd been looking forward to this weekend for quite some time. He had to be patient. He couldn't rush it.

When he'd spotted that teenage girl outside Rosie's a few minutes ago, he'd thought about going after her, too—just something to tide him over until he had Susan. He'd heard of some guys who masturbated before a big date—to take the edge off. Killing that cute teenage girl before starting in on Susan might serve the same purpose. It was something to think about.

On the shoulder of Carroll Creek Road, Susan took her young son out of his car seat in the back. "All right, sweetie," she told him, handing him a wrench. "I need your help with these thingamajigs! I can't get them unstuck!" Hovering over him, she showed him how to unscrew the lug nuts she'd already loosened. The kid seemed to get a real kick out of helping.

Watching them, he had to admit, it was pretty damn cute.

Thirty feet away, Susan stood bent over her son by the rear bumper of the old Toyota. Her brown hair was blowing in the wind. Soon he would be close enough to touch it.

And soon, before the end of this weekend, her little boy would be an orphan.

CHAPTER THREE

"**W**ell, what did this joker look like?" Allen asked. He stood at the gas barbecue on the rental house's back porch. Moths fluttered around the porch light. Over his navy blue fisherman's sweater and khakis Allen wore a *Hail to the Chef* apron they found hanging on a hook in the pantry. He was a tall, ruggedly handsome thirty-eight-year-old. Susan had fallen in love with his thick, wavy salt-and-pepper hair and pale green eyes. He had a scar on his left cheek that looked like a dimple, so it appeared as if Allen were smiling even when he wasn't. With a pair of tongs, he set four marinated chicken breasts on the grill. That barbecue smell mixed with the crisp, cool night air.

Susan had Tater Tots and French bread in the oven and a salad in the refrigerator. The kitchen had modern, stainless-steel appliances. She'd been expecting to "rough it" in a squat, rustic, bayside shack. But their rental house was a lovely, comfortable, two-story white wood-veneer house with green shutters. The property was surrounded by trees on three sides—and in the back was this quaint porch. In addition to the barbecue, it had a porch swing and a view of the backyard dock on Skagit Bay. That was where Allen had moored her "surprise," a beautiful sailboat with an indoor cabin—complete with a small galley, dinette, and V-berth sleeping quarters. He'd rented it from a charter place in town, and tomorrow afternoon, they'd go sailing.

Mattie was thrilled about it, of course. At the moment, he was in the sunroom, on the other side of the sliding screen door, watching *WALL-E* on DVD. *So much for roughing it*, thought Susan, but she wasn't complaining one bit.

Susan was wrapped in a russet cardigan sweater. She poured some more pinot noir into Allen's wine-glass, hoping it might take some of the edge off. He seemed far more upset about her Arby's encounter than she'd been.

"Actually, this guy seemed perfectly normal," Susan told him. She spoke in a hushed tone so Mattie wouldn't hear. "In fact, he was good looking—tall, with dark brown hair. I'd say late thirties, and nicely dressed, too. I would have been flattered if he hadn't been so overly familiar and pushy."

"He didn't tell you his name or where he was from? Any clue—in case I want to report this to the police?"

"No, he didn't say a thing about himself." She sipped her wine. "But listen, I don't know about involving the police, Allen. I mean, this man really didn't do anything *wrong*. He—"

"What are you talking about?" Allen interrupted hotly. "The guy followed you all the way to Cullen, and then you got a flat—with practically new tires. We just got them—what—three months ago? I don't like it, I don't like it one bit." With the tongs, he flipped over the chicken breasts on the grill. All the while, he was frowning and shaking his head. "I really wish you'd gotten the license plate number off that red MINI Cooper."

"Sorry, it didn't occur to me," Susan murmured. "At the time, I just wanted to get the hell out of there."

"Well, if you remember anything else about this creep that would help us track him down, let me know."

"All right already, I will," she sighed. "Y'know, I didn't encourage the guy—if that's what you're thinking."

"I wasn't thinking that at all," Allen replied.

"Well, you act like you're mad at *me*." She took her wineglass and retreated to the edge of the porch.

"I'm not mad at you," he answered quietly. "I'm just upset thinking about what could have happened."

Susan didn't say anything. She gazed out at the moon and the stars—so bright this far away from the lights of the city. Slivers of white and silver reflected on the bay, and the boat gently rocked in the water. Susan leaned against the railing and heard it creak.

Grabbing the top rail, Susan gave it a shake. It groaned again, and she could see a gap in the corner between the top-rail beams. "Better not let Mattie play out here alone," she said. "It's not safe. This thing looks like it might give way."

"Oh, he'll be fine, babe," Allen said, focused on his barbecuing. "I'm sure the railing will hold. Besides, the drop's only two feet. He'd do worse rolling off the sofa."

"Well, I still don't want him playing out here unsupervised," she insisted.

"Yes, cupcake, anything you say, cupcake," he replied in a whiny, milquetoast voice that sounded a bit like Truman Capote.

She rolled her eyes at him and then started into the house. "God, I hate it when you do your henpecked husband act."

"Yes, pudding," he said—with that whiny voice again. "Dinner will be ready in about five minutes, pudding."

Susan could hear him chuckling as she slid the screen door shut behind her. She didn't think it was very funny, not when they were discussing the safety of her child.

Lately, she found herself cutting Allen very little slack. She wasn't quite as enamored of him as she'd been when they'd first met. Then again, maybe that was just what she needed right now. If she wasn't completely in love with him, she wouldn't get her heart broken.

Susan set the dining room table—with plaid cloth mats that had seen better days, plain white plates, and mismatched stainless pieces. This was about as close to "roughing it" as they got here. That nice young man she'd met by the restrooms at Rosie's had been right about this place. It was lovely.

She could smell the Tater Tots cooking; they had about five more minutes. She remembered the Tater Tot casserole she'd made that one time—eighteen months ago. She would probably never make it again.

Walt and she had been invited to a party.

Tater Tot casserole was the "kitsch-dish" Susan had

decided to make for Connie and Jim O'Mara's Fourth of July potluck. The hosts, old friends of Walt's from college, were barbecuing hot dogs and hamburgers. Connie encouraged their guests to bring a side dish or dessert that was some guilty-pleasure comfort food, parish picnic delicacy, or trailer-trash cuisine. Connie had explained to Susan over the phone that one guest was baking a mock apple pie from Ritz crackers. Another guest was bringing a Jell-O ambrosia salad.

"And Melissa Beale is bringing a Seven-Up cake—whatever the hell that is," Susan said, folding a load of still-warm laundry on the bed while Walt dried off from an after-work shower. Steam wafted out the open bathroom door. Dinner was on the stove, and the kids were in front of the TV in the living room. Susan could hear it blaring. "Anyway, I told Connie we'd be there."

"I really don't want to go," Walt grunted from the bathroom. "Can you call and cancel?"

"But why?" Susan asked while folding a pillow-case. "I figured you'd be all for it. They're all your old college friends. . . ."

The O'Maras had recently moved into a new luxury condominium on the edge of Capitol Hill. They were supposed to have a spectacular view of the Puget Sound and the fireworks. Kids were invited, too. Connie had hired a nanny to look after the little ones and read them to sleep in the guest room while the adults and older kids enjoyed the fireworks. Susan thought it sounded terrific—what with a sitter for two-year-old Mattie, and Michael, age eight, begging to stay up and watch the fireworks this year. It was an ideal arrangement—and she didn't even have to cook, except for the Tater Tot casserole.

"I'd just as soon skip it," Walt sighed, emerging from the bathroom with a towel around his waist. He was working a Q-tip around his ear.

Susan caught him furtively looking at her in the mirror over her dresser, and she could tell something was wrong. She stopped folding one of his T-shirts and tossed it on the bed. "Okay, what's going on?"

"Nothing," he said. "I just don't feel like going to a party on July fourth. Traffic is always a pain in the ass. And the parking . . ." He snatched a pair of boxer shorts from her pile of laundry, then shed the towel and stepped into his boxers. The whole time his eyes avoided hers. "It's too much of a hassle. I'd rather not go. . . ."

Folding her arms, Susan stared at him. "Something's wrong, I can tell. You're not even looking at me. I've never known you to turn down a party. At the risk of repeating myself, what's going on?"

With a long sigh, he strode across the room and closed the bedroom door. He stood there in his undershorts for a moment, one hand on the doorknob. He looked down at the floor. "Melissa Beale," he muttered, frowning. "I'd rather not see her."

"Why?" she asked, half smiling. "Don't you like Seven-Up cake?"

He kept staring at the floor, and Susan kept waiting for him to say something.

She knew Melissa from the occasional get-togethers with Walt's college friends. Melissa was a petite, pretty redhead with a killer body. She taught yoga and had a back tattoo (Walt's old college gang had had a pool party last summer). She also had a younger live-in boyfriend, Jason Something, with a pierced nipple.

Susan had asked Walt ages ago if he and Melissa had ever had a thing in college, and he'd told her no.

"I'm trying to avoid her, because she's been calling me and e-mailing me at the office," Walt said, finally.

Susan sat down on the edge of the bed. "And exactly why is she doing that?"

"She and Jason broke up," Walt explained. "She came by the office about two weeks ago—just before lunch. It was a sneak attack. She said she needed a sympathetic ear. At lunch, she got a little buzz on and asked me to drive her home. I—I wasn't comfortable about it, because clearly she was flirting with me at the restaurant. But we'd taken her car, and I didn't want her to get in an accident. . . ."

"Always the Good Samaritan," Susan murmured numbly. She didn't like where this was going at all. This wasn't like Walt. She kept waiting for him to burst out laughing and say it was all a joke—a very, very stupid joke. But he was still standing over by the door in his underwear, gazing down at the floor.

"I parked in front of her place over in Wallingford, and she invited me in to wait for a cab." Walt finally looked at her. "But I said no thanks. I gave her the car keys and I was just about to climb out of the car, and that's when she kissed me."

"On the lips?"

He nodded glumly.

"Did you kiss her back?"

"For only about five seconds," he whispered. "Then I pulled away and got out of the car."

Dazed, Susan stared at him. "But you kissed her back," she murmured.

"I'm sorry, honey." He shook his head. "I told her I

was happily married and very much in love with you, and that this wasn't ever going to happen again. Then I tried to make some kind of joke, because it was just so damn awkward, and I got the hell out of there. . . ."

He kept saying he wasn't interested in Melissa. He didn't mean to kiss her back, it "just sort of happened." He was sorry he didn't tell her about it, but he didn't want to upset her over something that meant nothing to him. But the trouble was Melissa had called him at the office the next day to apologize. Then she'd wanted to buy him lunch just to show how sorry she was. He'd given her a polite "No thanks, not a good idea." But Melissa wasn't giving up that easily. She was on a campaign. And that was why he didn't want to go to the damn Fourth of July party.

Susan sat there in a stupor, growing angrier and angrier. She still couldn't believe he'd kissed that woman back—and for five seconds. It probably went on longer than that, but he didn't want to admit it. If they hadn't been invited to this party, would he have ever bothered telling her any of this?

She finally got to her feet. "I need to get out of here, I need to be alone," she said in a low voice. "You can serve up the kids their dinner. Make up any excuse you want for where I've gone. I promised Michael I'd help with his math homework. So you'll need to do it now. I'm not sure when I'm coming back—"

"Wait, Sue, please," he said, moving toward her.

She shook her head. "Get the hell out of my way," she growled, brushing past him as she headed for the door. "I need to be alone. I need to get out of here before I hit you or something. . . ."

Then Susan hurried out of the bedroom. She ducked

out the kitchen door, so the boys didn't see her leave. She drove to a lookout point on Fifteenth, near Lakeview Cemetery. The little park had benches and a panoramic view of Husky Stadium, Lake Washington, and Bellevue. Directly below the park was a wooded ravine with trails. It was just the kind of remote spot she wouldn't have taken Michael during the heyday of Mama's Boy. But that night, Susan sat there for three hours. She managed to cool off. It wouldn't be easy forgiving Walt, but she would. And going to that Fourth of July party would be terribly uncomfortable for him.

But go they would—Walt, the boys, and her. Susan saw to it.

Driving to the O'Maras' on July Fourth, Susan balanced the Tater Tot casserole in her lap and tried not to kick the two six-packs of Redhook India Pale Ale at her feet in the front passenger seat. Though she and Walt had pretty much made up, he'd been tense and taciturn all day. Clearly, he saw going to this party— with his college friends and Melissa in attendance—as some kind of punishment. And it was. Except for when he yelled at Michael for teasing Mattie in his car seat, Walt said nothing for the duration of the ride. Susan didn't utter a word either.

She looked for Melissa when they got to the O'Maras' home, but the pretty redhead yoga instructor wasn't yet among the thirty or so guests. The O'Maras had a large wooden deck off their living room, and that was where Jim was barbecuing. Though only on the second floor, the condominium stood on a hillside, so the deck was at least four stories above the ground. They looked over the treetops at the Space Needle on the horizon.

An occasional skyrocket or firework from some other private party burst against the darkening sky.

Walt opened up a Pale Ale, while she had a Coke and watched for new arrivals. After three doorbell rings and three more couples made their entrance, Melissa finally appeared—in a clingy blue and white striped halter-top dress that she'd accented—no doubt, for Independence Day—with a red belt. She had her stupid 7-Up cake with her—in a Tupperware cake container. Making her way to the kitchen to unload the cake, she smiled and waved at Susan—one of those, *Hi-haven't-got-time-to-talk-now* deals. But minutes later, Susan watched her hug Walt out on the deck, kiss his cheek, and then whisper something in his ear.

"She said, 'Why haven't you called me?' and 'We really need to talk, handsome,'" Walt told Susan under his breath during dinner.

"She called you *handsome*?" Susan whispered. "She was flirting with you while the kids and I were right there across the room?"

She waited until after the horrid 7-Up cake was served for dessert (even the kids didn't like it) before she approached Melissa, who, in a rare moment, stood by herself near the guest-room door. She was sipping a glass of red wine. "Melissa, can I show you something?"

"Why, sure, Susan," she said with a big phony smile. "I haven't had a chance to talk to you all night long. I just had a smidge, but your Tater Tot casserole was to die for!"

"Well, thank you." Susan opened the guest-room door, then nodded toward the bed. A pretty, brunette teenager was sitting there with an open book in her lap.

Two toddlers sat on one side of her, and Mattie was curled up on the other side, just starting to doze off. "I don't think you've had a chance to really see my boys," Susan whispered. "That sleepyhead is our two-year-old, Matthew. . . ."

"Oh, he's a darling," Melissa said.

"Isn't he though?" Susan replied, quietly closing the door. She pointed to Michael, out on the deck. Holding a sparkler, Michael turned and smiled at her. "And that's our eight-year-old, Michael. He looks a lot like his dad, doesn't he?"

"He sure does," Melissa agreed. "And just look at those eyelashes. He's going to be a real heartbreaker."

"Speaking of breaking hearts," she said, pulling Melissa to the corner of the living room. "Now that you've seen my children and talked a little bit with me, I hope you understand what I'm about to say, Melissa. If you come near my husband or try to call him again, I'm going to come after you. And you'll have a very difficult time teaching your yoga class with two broken arms."

Melissa let out a bewildered laugh. But then she must have seen the seriousness in Susan's eyes, because the smile vanished from her face.

"Do you understand?" Susan whispered. "I know what's been going on. Walt told me everything. I'm only going to say this to you once. Lay off."

Melissa stared at her and nodded. "All right," she murmured. Her hand was shaking a bit as she gulped down the rest of her wine. Her eyes avoided Susan's. "I—I'm really sorry. . . ."

"I'm sorry, too," Susan said quietly. "And I'm sorry

you're going through a difficult time right now. I hope you figure out some other way to cope with it."

Susan patted her arm and headed toward the deck to join Walt, Michael, and several others who were waving around sparklers. Walt eyed her nervously. To take the edge off, he'd consumed at least three India Pale Ales. She wasn't sure of the exact count, but he was feeling no pain. "Is everything all right, my love?" he asked. He'd just started to slip into his fake British accent, which he took on whenever he got tipsy. That was how Susan knew he was too drunk to drive. He didn't stagger, or slur his words, or get loud; he just got *British*. And it was the worst imitation of Brit she'd ever heard. His old college friends were used to it, and like Susan they knew, when Walt started referring to other guys as *blokes*, it was time to cut him off. He hadn't gotten that far along just yet.

"Everything's peachy," she said, sliding an arm around him. "Don't look now, but I believe Melissa is making her excuses."

The redhead was indeed talking to their hostess and moving toward the door with an empty Tupperware cake container under her arm. She glanced over her shoulder at the two of them. Susan just smiled and nodded.

"So all is forgiven?" he whispered.

Susan just nodded.

"Any chance for a bit of makeup sex tonight?" he asked in his awful British accent.

"Don't push your luck, *Nigel*," she whispered. "And by the way, I'm driving us home tonight. I don't want any arguments."

"Anything you say, old girl." He kissed her on the cheek.

Susan glanced over at Michael, with a sparkler in his hand and the darkening cityscape behind him. From across the balcony, he smiled at her and Walt. Her sweet son looked so beautiful.

That was when she heard the loud crack. Susan thought it was a firework's pop, but it was too close. The noise seemed to come directly underneath them. Everyone was looking around for something in the sky.

Then it happened again. Susan realized the sound was wood splintering. The deck floor shook and creaked.

"Oh, my God," she murmured, a panic sweeping through her.

People started screaming, and they tried to scramble off the faltering deck, but it was too late. Another thunderous crack rang out.

Susan saw Michael on the other side of the deck. "Mom! Dad!" he cried, reaching for them.

She broke away from Walt and tried to get to her son. He was just outside her grasp. Then all at once, the deck's wood floor opened up beneath her feet.

Suddenly, she was falling. As she plunged toward the ground, Susan heard all these horrible screams around her. Her arms and legs flailing, she felt so helpless—and doomed.

Someone from a neighboring condominium later said that the bodies, wood beams, and broken concrete all toppled down in unison. Some of the people— along with chunks of debris—bounced off the balcony below the O'Maras' condo. Others careened straight down to the ground.

Susan had no idea of this. She remembered slamming against something hard. Then she must have blacked out from the pain and shock. It couldn't have been more than a minute or two.

She was still disoriented as she regained consciousness. Her vision was blurred, but she realized she was lying in a pile of debris. She tried to sit up. But a heavy wood beam pressed against her arm and pinned her to the ground.

All of the casualties had landed in an unfinished garden area on the side of the hill—amid piles of dirt and newly planted trees and bushes. The O'Maras had turned off the outside lights to better view the fireworks, and it was dark at the bottom of the building. A cloud of dust and dirt loomed over the scene. It got in Susan's eyes, and she tasted grit every time she took a breath. She could hear the agonizing screams and moans all around her. A child cried out for his mother. But it wasn't Michael.

Susan tried to sit up again, but her whole body ached—and as much as she tried, she couldn't free her left arm. Her hand was ensnared on something. She was pretty certain the arm was broken. Helplessly, she called out for Walt and Michael.

As the dust cleared, she saw the others, mangled in a mess of broken concrete, wooden planks, and dirt. Some of them were moving; others were perfectly still. She couldn't see Walt or Michael among them. Part of her kept hoping they were okay. She continued to call out for them. But hers was just one of many voices crying out for help.

Finally, she spotted the silhouette of someone climbing over some rubble toward her. She never got a good look at the kind man's face, but he lifted a few splintered, heavy wood beams—and at last, Susan could move her arm. Blood oozed from a six-inch gash along her forearm. The pain was excruciating. Still, she kept thanking the man. "Have you—have you seen Walt or Michael Blanchette?" she asked anxiously as he helped her to her feet. "Are they okay?"

He shook his head. "I don't know. I wasn't at the party. I'm a neighbor. . . ."

Susan staggered through the wreckage, desperately searching for her husband and son. She could hardly walk. Every time she found someone, she tried to help them—as much as she could with her left arm out of commission. Everything she'd learned from her days as a nurse back in Harborview's ER was coming back to her. She tried to identify people's injuries or, at least, figure out whether or not they could be moved. She asked someone to get some sheets to make bandages and ice for the fractures and breaks. She remembered there had been two coolers full of ice at the party. So many people from the party and from neighboring buildings had rallied together to help. Susan kept looking for Michael—and Walt, hoping against hope he was among those good Samaritans.

The ambulances, cop cars, and two fire trucks finally showed up. But they had to park half a block away from the site. A stone path was the only access to the back of the condominium. Still, the nearby strobe lights from all the emergency vehicles bathed the area in an eerie red glow. The paramedics and firemen were just starting down the slope toward the casualties when Susan heard someone call her name.

She saw a man waving at her from farther down the

hill. He stood over a heap of split boards and rubbish. Susan couldn't see any bodies, but she knew they were there. She hobbled through the twisted ruins on the hillside. Tears streamed down her dirt-smudged face. As she got closer, she recognized Jim O'Mara, standing over Michael's battered, broken body. Jim was shaking his head. There were tears in his eyes.

Susan plopped down on the ground, and she pulled Michael into her lap with her one good arm. She didn't want to believe he was dead. She held on to his wrist and kept rocking him. But there was no pulse.

A rocket shot across the sky above them and then burst with a dazzling display of color. Susan glanced up for a moment.

"Walt's just over here," she heard Jim O'Mara say. "He's unconscious. He—he's still breathing. . . ."

Walt never regained consciousness.

He had an epidural hematoma due to massive head trauma. They took him to Harborview Medical Center, where he died twenty hours later. Susan was at his bedside.

Later, when the lawsuits were filed against the condominium's designers and builders, Susan remembered one of the arbitration hearings. She sat at a varnished walnut table in the conference room on the twenty-sixth floor of a downtown-Seattle office building. She listened to some hotshot attorney in a three-piece dark blue suit go on and on about how the materials used to build the decks on those condos had been up to code specifications. He kept talking about the odds of such a catastrophic accident ever happening. He said the odds were something like a million and a half to one.

And yet against all the odds, it had happened.

Michael was one of three people who had been killed on the scene. Walt was the fourth casualty. Nine more partygoers were seriously hurt and hospitalized, including Susan. She hadn't realized the extent of her injuries from the fall until later. She'd been walking around the wreckage with two cracked ribs, a sprained ankle, and several cuts and bruises. Her left arm had been fractured in three places—and bled so profusely that she'd passed out in the ambulance with Walt.

When she came to in the hospital's ER, it was like waking up from a dream. For a moment, she was reaching out for Michael again.

She'd known back in the ambulance that Walt would never recover—and that Michael was dead. She'd asked about Matthew. They'd told her that her younger son was fine. When the deck had collapsed, he'd been safely in bed with three other toddlers in the O'Maras' guest room.

Yet when she'd regained consciousness in the emergency room, Susan had convinced herself that Mattie was dead, too. She thought they were lying to her when they said her friends, Jim and Barbara Church, had taken Mattie for the night. She didn't calm down again until they called the Churches, and Barbara put a tired, confused Mattie on the phone with her.

If it wasn't for Mattie, she would have completely fallen apart. She had to be brave and carry on for him. But that didn't stop her from having moments when she'd think about Walt and Michael and start sobbing uncontrollably. Thank God most of these crying jags hit her when she was alone—driving in her car, or in bed at night. But occasionally they snuck up on her— in the checkout line at the supermarket or during her lunch break at the sandwich place near Dr. Chang's office. All it took sometimes was a song on the radio or the sight of a young dad and his son, and then the damn waterworks would start.

It was silly of her to think these awful, empty, heartbreaking episodes would suddenly stop now that Allen was in her life. He didn't know that she still had those moments. He didn't ask about Walt much—and for that, she was grateful.

The accident had been almost two years ago, and yet she still couldn't help worrying that she'd lose Mattie, too. So if she was a bit overprotective of him at times, that was why.

At the kitchen sink, Susan blew her nose and wiped her tears away with a paper towel. Then she splashed some cold water on her face.

With a sigh, she took the Tater Tots and French bread out of the oven and set them out on the warm stove. Then she went back to the sunroom, sat down beside Mattie, and mussed his hair. "We'll have to put *WALL-E* on hold for dinner, honey," she said. "Let's get your hands washed, okay?"

Gazing wide-eyed at the TV with the Woody doll at his side, Matthew didn't respond.

"C'mon, Mattie," Susan said, reaching for the remote. "You can . . ."

A hammering noise outside silenced her. Susan got to her feet and wandered toward the sliding screen door. She looked out at the porch. On the table by the gas grill was the platter of barbecued chicken breasts with a sheet of tinfoil over it—fluttering slightly in the night breeze.

She saw Allen by the corner of the porch, bent over

the faulty balustrade with a hammer in his hand. In his mouth, he had an extra nail. He was repairing the loose railing.

Obviously, he had no idea she was watching him. Every once in a while, Allen stopped his hammering and looked out at the woods surrounding their rental house. Susan figured he was on the lookout for that man who had followed her here from the Arby's in Mount Vernon. Maybe he was being a bit overprotective himself. But Susan didn't mind, not at all.

She told herself that Allen was only doing his best to keep them safe—against all the odds.

CHAPTER
FOUR

"**Y**ou guys just want to see me naked," Moira Dancey said.

Jordan Prewitt and Leo Forester stood by the kitchen door, each with a rolled-up bath towel under his arm. Jordan had a flashlight. It was already dark outside, starting to get chilly; they both wore fall jackets over their street clothes. Yet they were ready to hike through the woods so they could sit naked in some secluded hot spring.

Leo rolled his eyes at her and shook his head. "Jeez, full of yourself much?" he said. "I don't want to see you naked. I want to see Jordan naked. We just need you for a chaperone—so things don't get too *Brokeback Mountain*."

"You wish," Jordan said, bumping his shoulder against Leo's.

The buffed, handsome lacrosse player and his lean, gangly best buddy made an odd-looking duo. But they'd been best friends for six years. "It's weird to think," Leo had mentioned in the car on the way up from Seattle. "Jordan and I have known each other B.P.H. That's before pubic hair."

"And we're all still waiting for Leo to grow some," Jordan had chimed in from the driver's seat, never taking his eyes off the road.

"Stop, stop, please," Leo had rejoined in a deadpan tone. "My sides are aching. You're so hysterical. I think I just ruptured my spleen from laughing."

Riding alone in the backseat of the Honda Civic, Moira had felt a bit like an outsider with the two of them. She was Leo's friend. He and Jordan went to Garfield High School, and she attended Holy Names Academy, an all-girls Catholic school. A year ago, her mother and Leo's mother had fixed them up at a Sadie Hawkins dance—or the *Sadie Hawkins Disaster*, as they now referred to it. Mrs. Dancey had been really pushing for the date, because most of the guys Moira hung out with were a bit dangerous. Mrs. Dancey described them as "hoody." Her mother needn't have worried too much. Moira was still a virgin—technically. She never let it get too far with any of those guys, but sometimes, she felt like she was pushing the envelope—and her luck. One of her friends said she was a "virgin on the verge." Moira wasn't exactly sure how she felt about that label, but it didn't make her happy.

Unlike the guys who usually turned her head, Leo was safe—and nice. His dad had been killed in Iraq, and Leo worked nights, busing tables at Broadmoor Estates Country Club to help his mom with the finances. He also had a kid sister he helped care for. How much nicer could a guy get?

Moira and Leo had a horrible time at the dance, probably because she was—admittedly—a jerk to him for the first two hours. She'd made up her mind not to like this guy her mother was forcing her to go out with. But afterward he'd taken her to the Deluxe Restaurant, and during their one-on-one time together over burgers, she realized he was funny and sweet and genuine. He even had an offbeat kind of cuteness. But she just wasn't that attracted to him.

Leo later said he'd caught on to her lack of passion when he'd tried to kiss her good night on that first date. Moira had let him kiss her on the lips, but she'd kept her mouth closed and punctuated the kiss with a *mwah* afterward. "You gave me the *mwah*. That's the way my aunt Sonja kisses," Leo had later told her.

Moira liked him—just not *that* way. So they were good friends—with a little something extra, that *something extra* being his slight crush on her. He was always there for her. As long as Leo was around, Moira had a date for every dance or social occasion that came up. She still had an occasional date with some other guy, but never anything serious.

She'd met Jordan four times—always with Leo, of course. She thought he was very handsome and sexy, but the less Leo knew about that, the better. So she did her damnedest to conceal her attraction to this brooding, sensitive jock.

She wasn't sure how Jordan felt about her. Earlier, when they'd stopped at that ma-and-pa grocery store down the road, he'd shown a lot more interest in that pretty brunette woman with the little boy than he had in her throughout the entire drive up from Seattle.

The Prewitts' Cullen retreat was a brown-shingle, two-story cabin—quaint and rustic looking on the outside. But inside she found a gracious living room with a big stone fireplace. The kitchen was wallpapered with a tacky design that must have been called *Spice Rack,* because it had olive and brown-tone renderings of spices and jars—sage, oregano, rosemary, pepper, and thyme. The matching avocado oven and refrigerator were kind of ugly, but she liked the lime-colored dinette set from the fifties.

There was a basement. Moira had peeked at it from the top of the cellar steps of the kitchen when Jordan had given her a tour. It was cluttered with junk—and creepy. Throughout the tour, Jordan had occasionally touched her arm, and Moira had liked that.

Right now he was standing by the back door, giving her a guileless smile. "If you want, while you get undressed, we'll close our eyes until you're in the hot spring. Plus—it's pretty dark out there anyway, Moira. You shouldn't miss this experience. Some people drive half a day to get to a hot springs, and this is a ten-minute walk for us."

"C'mon, where's your sense of adventure?" Leo asked.

One hand on the kitchen counter, the other on her hip, Moira frowned at her friend. "I'm sorry, but this reminds me too much of that Friday night last month when we were alone and you kept challenging me to a game of strip poker." She turned to Jordan. "Did he tell you about that?"

Nodding, Jordan laughed. "You can't blame the guy for trying."

"Hey, I just wanted to hone my card-playing skills for a possible appearance on *Celebrity Poker*," Leo said. "Don't flatter yourself."

Moira sighed. "Yeah, well, you guys go have fun. I

can't get too excited over the prospect of traipsing through those creepy woods so I can sit bare-assed in some muddy water. I don't care how warm the water is."

"Okay," Jordan said. "Make yourself at home. We should be back in about an hour, and then I'll fire up the barbecue."

"Yeah, let's get *traipsing*," Leo said, opening the screen door. "I didn't want to see her naked anyway. Did you want to see her naked?"

"Hmmm, maybe," Jordan allowed, and then he winked at her.

Moira felt herself blushing. "Oh, I know who you wouldn't mind taking to the hot spring and seeing naked, Jordan," she said, teasingly. "That pretty lady at the grocery store you were talking to earlier. I think you were flirting with her. You must have a thing for older women. Maybe it's some kind of mother complex or some—" Moira stopped herself when she realized what she'd just said.

The smile seemed to freeze on Jordan's face. He let out an uncomfortable chuckle.

"C'mon, let's get cracking," Leo announced, pushing his friend out the door. "You can analyze Jordan later, Moira."

"See ya!" Moira called. "Have fun!" She jumped a bit when Leo let the screen door slam shut behind them. She felt like an utter moron, bringing up the subject of mothers to Jordan—and in such an idiotic way, too. Leo had told her ages ago that Jordan's mother died in a car accident when he was eight.

"Nice going, Moira," she muttered to herself. "That was real charming." Rubbing her forehead, she turned toward the refrigerator.

She heard the screen door yawn open behind her, and she turned around.

Leo stepped into the kitchen. "Why did you bring up *his mother*?" he whispered. "Jordan's crying. You made him cry."

"Oh, no," Moira murmured, a hand on her heart. "I'm so sorry—"

Leo broke into a grin. "Relax, I'm screwing around with you. He's fine."

She slapped him on the shoulder. "You shit."

"I told him I wanted to come back for some water." Leo opened the refrigerator and pulled out a bottle of Smartwater. He stopped and looked her in the eye. "You like him, don't you?"

"What do you mean?" she asked.

"You always get tongue-tied or say something stupid in front of guys you're interested in," Leo explained. "And what you said to him just now was pretty stupid. Don't worry, he's cool. He didn't notice. But I did. That's why I came back. I knew you were in here, kicking yourself." He hesitated at the kitchen door. "So—do you like Jordan? I mean, I want you to *like* him, but are you *interested* in him?"

She shrugged uneasily. "I think he's nice, that's all." Moira knew it would kill Leo if she said yes.

He gave her a wary sidelong glance. "Are you sorry you came?"

"Of course not, this is fun." She worked up a smile and patted Leo's arm. "You guys do your hot-spring thing. I'm going to finish unpacking and maybe have a *civilized* bath."

Leo threw her a crooked smile. "See ya in a bit, Moira." Then he let the screen door slam shut behind him as he headed back outside.

Moira wandered over to the door and gazed out past the screen. Off to the side in the small backyard was a flagstone patio with a barbecue pit, a picnic table, and two deck chairs. The woods lay beyond that. She watched Leo and Jordan head for a break in the trees—obviously the trail to the hot spring.

They disappeared in the darkness past that first row of trees.

From behind some bushes alongside the cabin, he watched the two young men forge into the woods with bath towels tucked under their arms. Then he peered through the kitchen window at the girl. She was a tall, willowy thing with a short pixie-style haircut. She looked very fetching in those tight jeans and the long-sleeved white T-shirt. She seemed like the type who came from money, read books, and got straight A's at school.

He imagined the public outcry when a girl of her pedigree suddenly vanished. With her slim figure, she would be a radical change from the pleasantly plump Wendy and the mannish Monica. She was younger and prettier than them, too. Maybe he'd even keep her alive for a while—something to amuse him after he finished off Susan.

Watching her in profile at the kitchen door, he wondered if she knew what she was doing. The girl seemed unconscious of it. As if in a trance, she ran a hand down her neck, then her T-shirt, and over her breasts. *Budding teenage sexuality*, he thought, licking his lips.

He only had to wait a little longer—until the boys were farther along in the woods. Then he'd make his move. They just had to be a bit farther away.

He didn't want them to hear her screams.

With a sigh, Moira stepped away from the screen door. She grabbed a Smartwater out of the refrigerator and retreated upstairs. The guys had her staying in the master bedroom—very cozy with a slanted ceiling, a four-poster queen bed, and a potbellied stove. The large window looked out at the forest and a long, private driveway to the cabin. Jordan and Leo would share a cramped loft space with a futon down the hall. They had a window, too—a little porthole, like something in the steerage section of a ship. Moira felt a bit guilty scoring the better accommodations, but Jordan and Leo had insisted.

She bypassed her bedroom and checked out their sleeping quarters off the hallway. Jordan had changed out of the black T-shirt he'd been wearing earlier. Now it was draped over the loft-space railing—just off the hallway. Moira couldn't resist pulling it down from the banister. His scent was on it—a musky smell mixed with a subtle, spicy cologne fragrance. She put the shirt to her face and breathed it in.

"Oh, what the hell," she murmured. Moira pulled her long-sleeved top over her head, took off her bra, and then donned Jordan's shirt. His bare skin had been against this same, thin, soft material. Her whole body tingled. She started to unzip her jeans. She wanted to be naked—except for his T-shirt.

That was when she heard a noise outside. It sounded like something had bumped against the side of the cabin.

Alarmed, Moira quickly fastened up the front of her jeans, then headed up the hallway to her bedroom. She gazed out the big window, but it was so dark outside, she couldn't see anything except her own reflection.

Moving close to the window, her breath fogged the glass. She cupped her hands around her eyes and peered outside. Directly below, she noticed a patch of light and her own shadow on the dirt ground in front of the house. It was so dark out there she couldn't see much else beyond the first row of trees on the other side of the driveway. "Probably just a raccoon or something," she muttered to herself.

Backing away from the window, she caught her reflection again. She looked like an idiot in Jordan's oversized T-shirt. What the hell was wrong with her?

Moira shuffled back down the hall toward the loft area. Pulling off Jordan's T-shirt, she carefully draped it on the railing—exactly where it had been. Then she put her bra and top back on. Returning to the master bedroom, she started to unpack her overnight bag.

She wished she hadn't come here. This weekend getaway had been Leo's brainchild. His eighteenth birthday was tomorrow. She and Jordan had asked him—separately—what he wanted to do to celebrate the occasion. He'd proposed a mini vacation with his two best friends at Jordan's family cabin. Apparently, the Prewitts sometimes rented out the place, and Jor-

dan had to get the okay from some local leasing company so they could use the cabin this weekend. Leo
had been here only twice before.

Moira didn't know if either of those previous visits
had included a skinny-dip in the hot spring, but maybe
that was one reason Leo had wanted her along on this
trip. In addition to his lame-o strip poker proposition a
few weeks ago, earlier this summer on a particularly
sultry evening, he'd suggested they go skinny-dipping
in Lake Washington—at a spot near Madison Park
Beach. "Do you know the meaning of *fat chance*?"
she'd replied.

Yet a part of her had wanted to go along with them
to the hot spring tonight. She imagined being naked in
that warm spring with Jordan right now—after a scary,
exciting trek through those dark woods. She imagined
his muscular leg accidentally brushing against hers
under the water.

Of course, Leo would be there, too—so that would
have put a damper on things. Still, as much as Leo's
clumsy overtures annoyed her, she was flattered, too.
She cherished Leo and didn't want to lose that friendship.

Moira unpacked a pharmacy container of sleeping
pills her doctor had prescribed. It seemed like all her
friends were on some kind of medication or another—
for their weight, ADHD, or depression. Moira's problem was that she'd go to bed and think about school
and her grades and college, and then she'd stare at the
ceiling all night. The pills helped, but she was trying
not to get too dependent on them.

Moira stashed the prescription bottle in the bureau

drawer along with her socks. She didn't want Jordan seeing it and figuring out just how neurotic she was.

She suddenly realized no one except Leo and Jordan knew where she was right now. What if something were to happen to them—or her?

Her parents had gone to Scottsdale to visit her sister. Moira's older brother and sister had already moved away and gotten married by the time she started high school. One advantage to being the youngest was that her parents had mellowed with age and allowed her a lot of independence. So leaving her alone in the house for a week was no huge deal.

On her own, Moira had engaged in the usual *Risky Business* behavior—dancing around the house in her underwear, doing her homework while sipping Chivas Regal from her dad's liquor cabinet, and masturbating a lot. Still, she'd been nervous about sleeping alone in the house, and, twice, she'd gotten Leo to stay overnight in the guest room.

He'd come up with plans for this sojourn two weeks ago. Moira had told her parents she'd spend this weekend at a girlfriend's house. She'd said they could get ahold of her on her cell. She hadn't known then that cell phones didn't work around here. She'd call them from the pay phone at that grocery store tomorrow. She didn't want them to worry.

Moira was just putting away the last of her things when she heard another noise outside. She went to the bedroom window again, cupped her hands against the pane, and peered out. She didn't see anyone. It was pitch black after that first cluster of trees on the edge of the woods.

She was a city girl. She wasn't used to all this darkness and quiet. She'd never felt so alone in all her life.

Downstairs, the screen door slammed in the kitchen.

It gave her a start. "Leo? Jordan?" she called, stepping out to the narrow hallway. "Is that you, guys?"

No answer.

Maybe she wasn't so alone after all.

It was too soon for them to be back from the hot spring already. They'd left only a half hour ago.

She crept to the top of the stairs and glanced down. She could see only part of the living room and a bit of the kitchen. Moira wasn't sure, but she thought she noticed a shadow sweep across that *Spice Rack*–patterned wall in the kitchen. A chill raced through her.

"Guys?" she called again, her voice quivering. She listened for a moment, but heard nothing. "Dave? Dave, I think I hear someone downstairs. . . ." She felt a bit stupid, but if someone had broken in, she didn't want them thinking she was alone. "Dave, maybe you should check it out. . . ."

Moira paused, but still didn't hear any movement down there.

Retreating to the bedroom, she grabbed her cell phone off the bureau, but then she realized it was useless. Who would she have called anyway? The police? She wasn't *positive* she had an intruder, not yet.

Glancing around the bedroom, Moira spotted a fireplace set attached to the potbellied stove. She grabbed the poker and tiptoed back to the top of the stairs again. She saw the shadow flutter across the kitchen wall once more. It wasn't just her imagination.

Slowly, Moira crept down the stairs, the poker clutched in her fist. She winced every time a step creaked. If this was Leo and Jordan playing some kind of joke on her, she'd kill them. This wasn't funny, not one bit.

Her heart racing, she hesitated at the bottom of the stairs. At last, she peeked around the corner into the kitchen. She noticed a couple of moths fluttering near the ceiling light. Moira turned and studied their shadows on the *Spice Rack* wall. She let out a tiny laugh.

But she couldn't quite relax, not just yet. She glanced over her shoulder at the empty living room. With the poker still ready, she ventured back into the kitchen and gazed out the screen door. She didn't see anyone. But a candy wrapper drifted across the back stoop. Moira squinted at it: a Three Musketeers wrapper.

Stepping back, she closed the kitchen door and locked it. That was when she noticed the dirt footprints on the kitchen floor. Were they there before? Or had someone just made them a few minutes ago—when he'd come in from those woods?

She tried to determine where the footprints were headed, but the dirt marks faded in the middle of the kitchen—about halfway to the basement door, which was open.

That door had been closed earlier; Moira was almost certain of it.

"Shit," she whispered. Paralyzed, she stared at the darkness beyond the open doorway and those first few steps down. The poker shook in her sweaty, trembling hand.

Moira's breathing grew heavier as she started toward the cellar stairs. She didn't see a light switch near the basement door, so she reached past the doorway and felt around for a switch on the wall. She found it and turned on the light. "Who's down there?" she demanded.

Slowly she descended the stairs, but only a few steps. The place was unfinished and dirty—with cobwebs between exposed pipes running along the ceiling. There was a dust- and lint-covered washer and dryer, and a laundry sink. Garden equipment, collapsed folding patio chairs, a big, blue plastic kiddy pool, and two bicycles that looked broken leaned against one wall. There was a workbench, cluttered with tools, and a couple of old paint cans. In the corner, where a ceiling light was out, stood the furnace and a hot-water tank. She couldn't tell if anyone was hiding back there or not. She noticed another door, which was closed. It looked like it might be a closet or a storage room. She didn't want to go down any farther and check.

Suddenly, she heard a noise above her. The floorboards were creaking. Moira glanced up and saw a shadow move across the cellar doorway. She told herself it was probably those damn moths again—but she couldn't be sure. If it was an intruder, he could switch off the light down here. Any moment now, she could be helpless, swallowed up in darkness.

Upstairs, a door shut, and Moira jumped. It was too far away to be the kitchen door. "Who's up there?" she yelled.

No response. But there was more noise. It sounded like they were closer.

Biting her lip, she remained frozen on the stairs. "Goddamn it, who's up there?"

Someone started pounding on the back door. Moira

recoiled at the sound. "Oh, Jesus," she whispered, tightly clutching the fireplace poker.

She heard the doorknob rattling, and then a muted voice: *"Moira! Moira, are you in there?"*

It sounded like Jordan. Catching her breath, she raced back up the stairs and saw him on the other side of the window in the kitchen door. He and Leo were wet and shirtless. Leo slouched against his friend as if he were half dead. Jordan pounded on the door again. "Moira, c'mon, let us in!"

She hurried to the door, unlocked it, and swung it open. "My God, what happened?"

"He needs some juice," Jordan said. Helping Leo into the kitchen, he left their shirts and the bath towels in a heap on the back stoop. "C'mon, buddy." He sat Leo down at the kitchen table.

Leo appeared dazed. He struggled to talk, but no words came out.

Moira set the poker on the counter and then ran to the refrigerator. Pulling out a carton of orange juice, she opened it and took it to Leo. But he was in too much of a stupor to reach for it. Jordan grabbed the carton instead. "Thanks," he said. Sitting down next to his friend, he put the open end of the juice container to Leo's mouth. "C'mon, drink this. . . ."

Moira hovered over them, uncertain what to do. She knew about Leo's diabetes, but had never been with him when he'd had an episode. She watched the orange juice spill past Leo's lips and run down his neck to his bare chest. He was shaking.

"Swallow it, buddy, c'mon." Jordan tipped his friend's head back and tried to pour the juice down his throat. "Damn, we should have eaten first," he grumbled. "I wasn't thinking about his sugar levels. We just got into the spring, and he started to feel woozy. . . ."

Leo started choking and coughing. Jordan got sprayed in the face with some orange juice. He pulled back the carton for a moment. "Okay, ready to take some?" he asked. As soon as Leo stopped coughing, Jordan put the orange juice carton to his lips again.

Leo drank, and his hands eventually came up over Jordan's. "Atta boy," Jordan whispered.

Moira fetched a dish towel and wetted one end. She held it to Leo's forehead for a moment, then dabbed at the spilt orange juice on his chin, neck, chest, and torso. He stopped drinking for a moment. "Thanks," he gasped. He tried to smile. "Jesus, this is embarrassing."

"Hey, compared to your attempt at the Macarena at the homecoming dance, this is nothing," Moira replied, trying to smile.

Leo started to laugh.

"Keep drinking," Jordan told him. He patted Leo's shoulder and then stood up.

Moira turned to him. "You got some orange juice on you, too," she said, dabbing at his face with the dish towel.

"Thanks," Jordan said, smiling at her. "I got it." He took the dish towel from her and kissed her hand. Then he wiped off his face.

Unconsciously, Moira touched her hand where he'd kissed it. She noticed Jordan's lean, muscular physique—and realized his pants were still unfastened in front. He must have put them on in a hurry. She could see a trail of black hair moving down from his navel. He still had a tan line.

Leo cleared his throat.

Moira turned to find him glaring up at her. It was obvious he knew what she was feeling for his friend. He'd stopped drinking and took several long, labored breaths. All the while, he kept staring at her—wounded and disappointed.

Jordan was oblivious. He mussed Leo's hair. "Well, you know the diabetic drill, stay put for a while and have a little more juice. I'm going to get cleaned up."

Moira didn't dare look at him as he started to walk away. She couldn't look at Leo either. She glanced down at the floor—and the different patterns of dirty footprints on the kitchen tiles. The ones she'd noticed earlier were lost amid the others now.

On his way out of the kitchen, Jordan hesitated and turned to Moira. "What were you doing with the poker?"

Moira shrugged. "Nothing," she said. "It was nothing."

As he raced through the woods in front of the Prewitts' cabin, he couldn't help chuckling. He'd come so close. He'd had her trapped in the basement when he'd heard Jordan's voice in the backyard: *"C'mon, Leo, hang in there. . . ."*

Five minutes later, and those boys would have come home to an empty house.

Maybe he should have been angry that his plans were thwarted. But it was kind of exciting almost getting caught. He'd made his escape—out the front door—with mere seconds to spare.

He slowed down and got his breath back. No one was chasing him. No one had seen him.

The girl must have not said anything to her friends. Perhaps right now, she was chalking up her terrible fright to being a stranger in a strange house. Maybe she was telling herself that the sounds she'd heard were the cabin settling or a raccoon outside one of the windows. People thought up all kinds of explanations to avoid thinking the unthinkable.

Tonight had whetted his appetite for Moira. He had to have her now. She'd be alone again soon enough, and he'd get another chance at her.

Deep in the forest now, he listened to his own breathing—and twigs snapping under his feet. The car was parked on a nearby trail.

He hadn't forgotten about Susan Blanchette. In fact, he was already thinking of a clever way to incorporate this girl into his grand plan for the weekend. He chuckled again when he considered it.

Killing two birds.

CHAPTER
FIVE

She didn't realize where she was at first. Susan rolled over on her right side, expecting to see the alarm clock with the glow-in-the-dark numbers on her nightstand. But there was nothing, just unfamiliar shapes in the murky blackness. And she was alone.

It took a few moments, but then she knew. They were in that house by the bay in Cullen, their weekend getaway. Allen must have gotten up to read. He did that sometimes. He had problems sleeping.

She had problems, too. Tonight, for example, when they'd made love, she had to fake it again. She'd become quite the actress lately. It wasn't Allen's fault. He wasn't doing anything wrong. She just had a hard time letting herself go with him. Susan chalked it up to the fact that she was too cautious, afraid of loving someone again—and possibly losing them, too.

After Walt's death, she'd gone to this grief counselor for a while, a skinny, fifty-something East Indian woman who dressed like a conservative lawyer and wore her hair in a tight bun. Six months after the accident, Dr. Kumar had told her that she needed to move on. She suggested Susan start by taking down some of Walt's and Michael's pictures at home. The woman acted as if Susan had a regular shrine to her dead husband and son in the duplex. Yes, she had a few pictures out. She wanted Mattie to feel a connection to those images. And okay, maybe she still needed that connection, too. It was tough enough giving all of Walt's clothes to Goodwill. So Susan didn't get rid of the photos. She got rid of the counselor.

That first year without Walt was like sleepwalking. She felt numb. It was all about taking care of Mattie and finding work, going through the motions to survive each day without her husband and firstborn. Thank God her lawyer brother-in-law, Bill, jumped in and got a local attorney to represent her in the class-action lawsuit. Everyone who had been injured or lost a loved one when that deck had collapsed was suing the construction company—which, in turn, was trying to blame the city inspectors and the architectural firm. It was a mess, and the blame game promised to drag on for at least another year. Susan's lawyer was asking for 1.5 million dollars.

She couldn't get excited over the money, though, God knows, they needed it. Walt's insurance had only covered seventy percent of the hospital bills. A year after the accident, Susan was still in debt.

She still missed Walt horribly, but started noticing other men. In fact, some days—and most nights—she just wanted to be *near* a man, any man. Dr. Chang had a few attractive, athletic male patients—men who spent too much time in the sun with their shirts off. Susan would sit in the small examining room with them, the

clipboard in her lap, taking notes and doing her best
not to get caught looking as Dr. Chang examined those
tanned, toned bodies for moles and melanomas. At
some point in the session, the gown often got tossed
aside, and the patient would be naked or in his underpants. Susan managed to keep a clinical, business-as-
usual expression on her face, and then she'd go home
that night alone and frustrated.

Her friends tried to set her up, but not too many men
were looking to date a woman in her mid-thirties—
with a three-year-old, no less. So one of her girlfriends
bought her a month's subscription with an Internet dating service: MatchMate.com. Susan met several interesting men through the service, but most of those
interesting men were just interested in getting laid.

When she agreed to a coffee date with Jack—*38, 6
feet, 175 lbs, brown hair, blue eyes, ad executive, non-
smoker, occasional drinker, spiritual, no tattoos, Tau-
rus*—Susan was skeptical. They got together one
February afternoon at the Top Pot on Capitol Hill. Jack
was actually better-looking than his photo. Coffee
turned into a romantic dinner at That's Amore restaurant, and then a long kissing session by Susan's car. By
the time they said their final good night, her head was
swimming, and she felt almost giddy.

They made a date for dinner at Daniel's Broiler at
Leschi on Lake Washington that Friday. The same afternoon, she had to appear at a deposition—four grueling hours in a conference room. One of the defense
attorneys made wild claims about people jumping up
and down on the deck—and filling it beyond capacity.
Susan was furious. The SOB made Jim and Connie's
Fourth of July gathering sound like a frat toga party.

She didn't even get to testify. At the end of it, her lawyer gave her a pile of documents to review and said they might have to wait another six months before they saw any money.

Susan got home late that afternoon to a voice mail from her babysitter, canceling on her.

"It's okay," Jack said, when she phoned to tell him what had happened. "We can still have dinner at Daniel's. Bring Matt along with you. I'd love to meet him. Maybe afterward, I could follow you home, and we can put Matt to bed. I'm pretty good at reading bedtime stories. We can stay in and have a nightcap or something. How does that sound?"

It sounded wonderful. And *nightcap* sounded like code for something else.

She didn't know Jack very well and wondered if he'd really show up to this date with her—*and her child*. Maybe he'd just been jerking her around. When she pulled into the parking lot by Daniel's Broiler, Susan kept looking for Jack's car. She remembered he drove a white Mazda Miata.

The restaurant was in a little marina-type complex off Lake Washington, across the street from several secluded lakefront homes. The gravel parking area could have used a few more lights. Carrying Mattie toward the restaurant, she spotted Jack's white Miata under the shadow of a tall oak tree. *So he'd come, a man of his word. Nice.*

And he was great with Mattie. Sitting at the lakeview table, Susan had her beautiful, blessedly quiet son in a booster seat on one side, and her gorgeous, charming potential boyfriend on the other side. Mattie

got a special kiddy meal while she and Jack each enjoyed a glass of merlot. Then their salads arrived.

And then Mattie kicked the table.

Jack went to grab his wineglass and knocked it over.
Merlot spilled into his pear and butter lettuce salad,
across the white tablecloth, and onto Jack's lap. "Shit!"
he hissed.

"Oh, my God," Susan murmured, steadying the
table—and then, Mattie's leg. "I'm so sorry—"

"Shit, my good khakis," he muttered, dabbing his
trousers with the cloth napkin. "Goddamn it. . . ." He
stood up.

Susan started to stand, too. "Maybe some club soda
from the bar will get out the stain—"

"Just—just—never mind, okay?" he growled, throwing his napkin down on the wine-soaked tabletop. "Be
right back."

Biting her lip, Susan sat back down and watched
him hurry toward the restaurant's bar. People were
staring at her. Mattie started to whine, and she patted
his shoulder. "It's okay, sweetie," she murmured.

Susan managed to flag down a busboy. "Could you
please take that away?" she whispered, nodding at
Jack's salad—swimming in merlot. "And could you
have our waiter bring my friend another salad and another glass of the merlot?"

But the waiter didn't do that. Instead, he brought their
dinners. By then, Mattie was crying—quite loudly.
Susan politely asked the waiter to check on her dinner
companion in the men's room. She knew what had
happened before the waiter even returned to the table.
Her charming, handsome potential boyfriend wasn't in

the restroom—or the bar, or anywhere else in the restaurant. He was gone.

Five minutes and $135 later, Susan made the walk of shame toward the restaurant door, clutching a carry-out bag in one hand, and her cranky, screaming toddler in the other. "Good God, about time," she heard one man at a nearby table mutter to his date. "That stupid woman's finally taking her brat out of here. . . ."

She hadn't quite made it to the door when Mattie spun around and knocked the carryout bag from her grasp. The bag ripped, and two cartons—Lobster Newburg and the garlic prawns and pasta—spilled over the tiled floor. Some of it got on Susan's legs.

The hostess called a busboy over. Susan kept apologizing. "It's all right," the hostess said edgily. Frowning, she opened the door for her. "You can go. We'll clean it up. Really, just go. . . ."

After slinking out the door with Mattie, she noticed the empty spot where Jack's car had been parked. What had made her think she'd ever find another nice guy like Walt?

Susan couldn't help it. She started crying before she even got her car keys out. She strapped Mattie in his child seat. Before climbing in the driver's side, she tried to wipe off her hands with a Kleenex, but they still felt sticky. As she scooted behind the wheel, Susan noticed all the lawyer's documents on the front passenger side, where she'd left them. She blew her nose, wiped her eyes, and then turned the key in the ignition.

Click, click, click. That was all, then nothing.

"Oh, no, please, God, enough already," she murmured. She turned the key again and stepped on the gas. *Click, click, click.*

She tried two more times, but nothing.

"Damn it," she whispered, tears welling in her eyes again. She rested her forehead on the top of the steering wheel for a moment.

A knock on the passenger window startled her.

Susan gaped at the handsome man with the wavy salt-and-pepper hair. He gave her a shy, friendly little wave on the other side of the glass. "Need some help?" he called.

Wiping the tears from her eyes, Susan stared at him.

He walked around to her side of the car and then twirled his finger to indicate she should roll down her window. Susan lowered it about two or three inches. She realized her door was still unlocked.

"I don't know much about cars," the man said. The cute scar on his cheek looked like a dimple. "But I have a cell phone and Triple A. Do you want me to call them for you?"

"It won't do any good. I don't have Triple A," Susan said through the window gap.

"But I do," he replied. He pulled out his wallet, then checked a card he had in there. "If I tell them I'm a passenger in your car, you're covered." He took out his cell phone and made a call. He stepped back from the window. "Hi, my name is Allen Meeker, and I'm with a friend who's having car problems. . . ." Susan couldn't hear any more because he wandered away from the car for a few moments. She wasn't sure about this guy. He seemed too good to be true. And his timing was almost too perfect, showing up exactly when he did.

In the backseat, Mattie yawned.

"What's wrong with the car, they want to know," he asked through the gap in the window.

"It just won't start," Susan answered. "When I turn the key in the ignition, it makes this weird, clicking noise—and nothing."

He turned away and talked into the phone again. She watched him finally slip the phone back in his pocket, and then he lumbered back to her window. "It's going to take them forty-five minutes to an hour to come out here."

She smiled politely. "Well, I couldn't ask you to wait here all that time. I'll call a tow. . . ."

He nodded at the mini-marina complex. "I was about to have dinner. Ruby Asian Dining is where I always go for Thai. Hi there, sport!" He smiled at Mattie in the backseat. Then he pointed to the stack of papers on her passenger seat. "Better move those so when Triple A gets here it'll look like I was riding shotgun. What is that, legal stuff? Are you a lawyer?"

"No, my lawyer gave me these documents today," Susan explained. She rolled down the window a bit farther. "I'm involved in a lawsuit right now."

"Is somebody suing you?" he asked with concern.

"No, just the opposite," she admitted. Susan didn't know why she was telling him this, and she didn't know why she was starting to tear up again. She'd told others about what had happened to Walt and Michael without getting all weepy about it. Maybe she was just feeling terribly vulnerable tonight. "My—my husband and older son were killed when they were on this balcony that collapsed . . . and . . . and two others died, and several people were injured. Anyway, there's this lawsuit, and I don't give a shit about the money. I just miss my husband and little boy. . . ." She was sobbing now.

Turning away, she opened her purse and tried to find another Kleenex.

"Mommy's crying," Mattie announced.

"That's right, sweetie," she said. She turned toward the man again. "I'm sorry, I don't know why I—why I'm unloading all this on you, a perfect stranger. . . ."

He offered her a handkerchief through the car window opening. "My name's Allen Meeker," he said. "So I hope I'm no longer a stranger. I was just about to have some Thai food by myself. You and your son have probably already eaten. But as long as we're all waiting for your car to get fixed, I'd really enjoy your company. Maybe you could have some coffee or dessert."

Susan wiped away her tears with his handkerchief. She managed to smile up at him. "As a matter of fact, I—I haven't had my dinner yet."

In the Thai restaurant, Allen paid for dinner and Mattie's ice cream. He also tipped the man from Triple A, who had to tow Susan's car. Allen gave them a ride home.

Ever since that night, he had been there for her. Even when he went out of town for his job—selling hospital equipment—Allen still called her practically every day. He was good with Mattie, too. So what if Susan didn't see skyrockets every time they made love? That was okay. She cared for Allen and was beholden to him. Since meeting him, every few weeks she'd put away another photo of Walt. It wasn't premeditated. It just seemed the right thing to do as Allen became more and more a part of her life.

He hadn't come with much baggage. His mother

died in a car accident when he was eleven and his father passed away a decade later. He had a stepmother and a younger stepbrother he wasn't close to at all. There was also an ex-wife from six years before, whom Susan had no interest in ever meeting.

They'd been seeing each other for seven months when Allen paid for their trip and accompanied her and Mattie to Vero Beach, Florida, to visit her parents—a gesture that, in Susan's opinion, made him a candidate for canonization. He kept Mattie entertained during the duration of the seven-hour flight, and then won over her parents, who were getting crazier and crazier in their old age. Without complaint, he even slept on the lumpy sofa in her dad's small study—in their stuffy, sultry, mothball-scented retirement village condo. Susan and Mattie shared the guest room. During that trip Allen asked her parents if he could marry their daughter.

That had been five weeks ago. Susan didn't want him spending money on an engagement ring, and they still hadn't set a date. She wasn't in any real hurry. Maybe it had something to do with the fact that she still had two framed photos of Walt on display in her living room.

Allen didn't ask her to put them away, nor did he pressure her about setting a wedding date. So when he'd started pushing for this trip to Cullen a few days ago, she couldn't very well refuse. Allen didn't ask for a lot.

Half sitting up in bed, Susan groped around in the darkness until she found the lamp on her nightstand. She switched on the light, then picked up her wristwatch and squinted at it: 2:50 AM. She gazed at the vacant spot beside her on the bed. There was a noise downstairs; it sounded like the sunroom's glass door sliding open.

Susan crawled out of bed and threw on her bathrobe. Pushing her hair back from her face, she padded down the corridor and checked in on Mattie in his bedroom. He was sleeping. From the top of the stairs, she could see a light was on—probably in the kitchen or the sunroom. Susan crept down a few steps. "Allen? Honey?" she called softly.

No answer.

From the bottom of the stairs, she didn't see anyone in the first-floor hallway. "Honey?" she called again—a little louder. "Allen, are you down here?"

She poked her head in the kitchen. Only the stove light was on. She heard water steadily dripping from the faucet—and then, outside, a rustling noise. In the window above the sink, she spotted someone—or something—darting past the house outside. Susan gasped. "Allen? Allen, where are you?"

She retreated toward the sunroom, where she saw the sliding glass door halfway open. A chilly night breeze drifted into the house. Susan felt it kissing her bare feet. She clutched her robe at the neck. There was a light on by the sofa—and a small glass, half filled with bourbon on the end table. The Robert Dugoni book she'd given Allen was open, pages facing down, on the sofa cushion.

Susan heard floorboards creak on the porch outside. She swiveled around toward the glass door and gaped at the shadowy figure standing there.

A hand went to her heart. "Oh, Lord, Allen, you scared the hell—"

She fell silent as he stepped inside. He wore sneakers, sweatpants, and a Rainier Beer T-shirt. Allen looked frayed, and he had a gun in his hand.

"Where did you get that?" Susan murmured, staring at the gun. "I didn't know you had that. What—"

"I thought I saw someone out there," he said. He glanced outside again before sliding the glass door shut behind him. "But it's okay now. . . ."

Dumbfounded, Susan stared at him. "Was that you I saw running past the kitchen window?"

Nodding, he adjusted the safety on the gun. "If someone was out there, he's not coming back."

"Where did you get the gun?"

"I've had it for years," he answered. "I just didn't mention it because I knew you'd freak out if I told you I owned a gun."

"Well, you were right," she replied. "I *am* freaking out. I hope you haven't been bringing it inside my house—"

"Relax, I've never smuggled any firearms inside the Blanchette duplex," he said wryly. He set the gun on the end table and then picked up his glass of bourbon. "Just be glad I brought it along for this trip—what with that creepy son of a bitch following you here and probably giving you that flat tire." He took a gulp of bourbon.

Booze and guns, good combination, Susan thought. Frowning, she shook her head. "Well, I don't want that thing in this house, not with Mattie around. I'll be a nervous wreck."

"I had it in the glove compartment of my car," Allen assured her. "I only took it out about an hour ago when I heard a noise outside. I'll put the gun back tomorrow morning. Until then, I'm holding on to it, okay? I'll make sure it stays out of Mattie's reach."

With a sigh, she leaned against the sunroom doorway. She still didn't feel very reassured. "I don't understand why you felt you needed to bring a gun along this weekend. I mean, were you expecting trouble?"

He wandered over and rested his arms on her shoulders. Then he leaned in to kiss her.

Susan kept her arms folded in front of her. She could taste the bourbon on his lips.

Allen touched his forehead against hers. "Please, don't freak out about the gun, okay? I've had it for years, and I know how to handle it. I'm just looking out for you and Mattie. Why don't you go back upstairs and try to sleep, babe? I'll be up in a little while—as soon as I'm sure we're all safe and sound here."

Susan still felt uncomfortable. Her eyes wrestled with his. "Listen, do me a big favor and don't have any more to drink, not while you're toting that gun."

He smiled and kissed her again. "No problem, point taken. Besides, believe me, I don't want to be hungover while we're sailing tomorrow—" he glanced at his wristwatch, "or today, rather." He chuckled. "Yikes, he'll be up in about four hours. You better go to bed, Mommy. Get some shut-eye."

He kissed her again, and this time, Susan kissed him back.

Heading up the stairs, she nervously rubbed her arms. She thought she knew everything about Allen, but until a few minutes ago, she had no idea he owned a gun. And it still seemed odd that he'd brought it along on this carefree weekend retreat, which he'd planned. He'd never really answered her question. Had he come here expecting trouble?

She stopped by Mattie's room again and peeked in on him. He was still asleep, undisturbed. Susan moved on to the master bedroom.

Shedding her robe, she draped it over a chair. Then she crawled under the covers, reached over, and switched off the light. Allen had told her to get some sleep. But she knew it wouldn't come easily, not while he was downstairs keeping watch—*with a gun*, for God's sake. Clearly, he was expecting something bad to happen, and she couldn't ignore that.

Her head on the pillow, Susan took a few deep breaths and tried to relax. But she knew—as much as she tried—she wouldn't fall asleep.

It would be hours until morning.

CHAPTER SIX

At first, Jordan didn't pay any attention to the other customer who walked into Rosie's. From where he stood by the refrigerated foods and drinks section, Jordan briefly glanced at the guy—a good-looking man in his late thirties with wavy, silver-black hair and a cocky manner. Except for Rosie, behind the counter, they were the only ones in there.

Jordan was on a mission. He'd already driven into town and picked up the birthday cake he'd ordered for Leo. Just for kicks, he'd told the bakery it was for a young boy, so the cake had Speed Racer's likeness in the multicolored frosting and a miniature plastic race car by the *Happy Birthday, Leo!* Jordan figured his buddy would get a good laugh out of it.

Leo would definitely like his birthday present. He'd flipped over a leather aviator jacket they'd first seen at Nordstrom about six weeks ago. Leo had gone back on two separate occasions to try it on again—even though he couldn't afford the damn thing. Now it was wrapped and hidden in the back of Jordan's Honda Civic. It cost three hundred and ninety-nine bucks. But that didn't break the bank for Jordan, not at all. His dad was rich, and he'd also inherited a ton of money from his mom.

While in town, he'd also picked up birthday candles, streamers, and balloons. The plan was Moira would go for a walk with Leo in the woods. By the time they returned at one o'clock, Jordan would have the cabin decorated and the cake on display.

It wasn't even noon yet, plenty of time. So, Jordan had stopped by Rosie's for some Tim's barbecue-flavored potato chips and Cheetos, and—after Leo's diabetic episode last night—they also needed to re-stock on OJ.

Jordan opened the refrigerator door and reached for a big glass jug of orange juice. He heard the other customer talking to Rosie: "Say, listen, do you sell sunscreen here?"

The sound of that voice made Jordan's stomach lurch. For a moment, he couldn't breathe—or move.

"You bet we carry sunscreen," Rosie was saying. "Let me show you. . . ."

"We're going sailing this afternoon," the man continued. "Sometimes you can really get burned on these cool, overcast days—"

Jordan listened to the voice and to the man's footsteps as he followed Rosie down the next aisle. Bent over by the refrigerator, Jordan started to shake violently. The jug of orange juice slipped out of his hand. It crashed on the wood floor. Glass shattered, and a puddle of orange juice bloomed across the aisle. Shards of glass were everywhere.

"Are you okay, hon?" Rosie called to him.

Jordan couldn't answer her. He stood paralyzed in

the middle of the puddle. Splattered orange juice soaked the legs of his jeans and his black Converse All Stars. He gaped at the man one aisle away, and they locked eyes. Jordan thought he was going to vomit.

"Hey, Mr. Destruct-o," Rosie called, "what are you doing over there? Jordy, are you tearing the place down or what?" She waddled around the corner and balked at the mess on the floor. Then she gazed at Jordan. "Hon, you're as white as a sheet. . . ."

Numbly, he turned to her. He was still shaking. "I— I'm sorry, Rosie. I—don't feel well." For a moment, he thought he'd pissed in his pants, but then he realized it was orange juice. As he bent down to pick up some of the glass, everything around him started spinning.

"Leave that," he heard Rosie insist. Rushing to his side, she took the bags of chips and Cheetos from him and set them on the counter. She quickly led Jordan down the aisle toward the door. "Careful of the juice on the floor, don't slip now. Let's get you some fresh air. . . ."

As they passed the older man, Jordan couldn't look at him. He couldn't get out of that store fast enough. He broke away from Rosie and ran out the door. He raced around the corner—to the shaded side of the store so he could throw up without anyone seeing him. Over by the doors to the cellar storage space, he braced one hand on the wall.

"Sweetie, should I call somebody?" Rosie asked, coming around the corner. She stopped a few feet away from him.

"No, it's okay," Jordan managed to say. He took a deep breath. "I'm sorry, Rosie. Could you—could you please just leave me alone for a few minutes?"

She backed away. "Give me a yell if you need anything. You hear me?"

He nodded. Rosie patted her orange hair and then headed back around the corner.

Jordan took a few deep breaths. He told himself he wasn't going to puke. And he wasn't going to start crying either. No, he had to keep his cool—and figure out what to do. Yet he was still shaking. His throat began closing up—and the tears streamed down his face. He slumped back against the cedar shingle wall and let go. He couldn't stop sobbing.

Then after a few moments, he became enraged.

He couldn't believe how he was acting—like a frightened little boy.

Wiping his face and nose with his shirtsleeve, Jordan paced back and forth by those cellar doors. He needed to *do something*, for God's sake—before that guy jumped into his car and drove off.

A metal object on the ground by a woodpile caught Jordan's eye. It resembled the head of a spiked rake. Part of it was rusted, but the prongs were still sharp and shiny—as if someone had recently sharpened them. Jordan picked it up and wandered toward the gravel lot in front of Rosie's. He paused behind the thick trunk of a tall evergreen.

The only other car in the lot—besides his own Civic—was a black BMW. Jordan took a long look at the car's tires. Then he examined the strange spiked object again.

He knew what he had to do.

That son of a bitch wasn't getting away, not this time.

* * *

In the distance ahead, he watched the BMW listing to one side as it hobbled onto the gravel shoulder of Carroll Creek Road.

Jordan pulled over as well, leaving about a block-long gap between them. There weren't any other cars in sight. He imagined the guy looking in his rearview mirror and barely making out the Honda Civic down the road behind him. He hadn't stepped out of his BMW yet.

"Your cell phone doesn't work around here, asshole," Jordan whispered, his voice shaky. "Never mind trying to call anyone. Just get out of the car. See what the problem is. . . ."

After setting the pronged device under the BMW's rear passenger-side tire, Jordan had hidden behind a tree on the shady side of the store. He'd watched the man emerge from Rosie's with a small plastic grocery bag and then climb inside his car. The spiked device remained on the ground while the BMW pulled out of the lot. Jordan couldn't be certain if it had punctured the tire.

Once the BMW disappeared around a bend, Jordan retrieved the device and hurled it into the woodpile at the side of the store. He hurried up to the front porch. "Sorry, I'm leaving you with a real mess, Rosie!" he called through the screen door. "I still don't feel so hot. I'll be back to pay for the orange juice later. . . ."

"Oh, don't worry about it, Jordy," she called back. "I hope you feel better!"

He barely heard her as he rushed toward his Civic. Jumping inside, he gunned the engine and peeled out of the lot—not slowing down until he'd finally spotted the BMW up ahead in the distance.

It couldn't have been more than a quarter of a mile before the car had started listing to the right.

Now Jordan watched and waited inside his idling Civic. He nervously drummed his fingers on the steering wheel. He'd parked in the sun at Rosie's lot earlier, so the car was hot, and it smelled of orange juice, sweat, and birthday cake. Jordan cracked a window. "C'mon, c'mon," he muttered, eying the crippled vehicle ahead. "Get out and look at the goddamn tire. . . ."

He didn't want anyone else coming along to help the guy. Jordan wasn't sure yet exactly what he was going to do, but whatever it was, he didn't want any witnesses.

At last, the driver's door opened.

Biting his lip, Jordan watched the man step out of the BMW, then slam the door shut. He was wearing sunglasses. He stomped toward the back fender and checked the flat tire on the rear passenger side. He kicked at the gravel and then treaded back to the driver's door. Opening it, he reached into the front for something on the dashboard. The trunk popped halfway up. The man moved around toward the trunk, but suddenly stopped and stared down the road.

Jordan shrank back in his seat. He couldn't discern the man's expression—and his eyes were hidden by his sunglasses—but Jordan was almost certain the guy was glaring at him.

Finally, the man turned and opened the trunk lid all the way. Taking off his jacket, he draped it over the edge of the trunk, and then he began to unload the spare tire and the tools.

Jordan waited a few more minutes. He found it tough to breathe right, and his heart was racing. He felt a little sick again. Glancing around to make certain no other cars were coming, he slowly pulled onto the road. He didn't have to drive far before veering back onto the shoulder and crawling to a stop behind the disabled BMW.

The man had just set the spare tire and the last of the tools on the ground. He stopped and took off his sunglasses to stare at the Honda Civic. He reached for his jacket again.

Jordan swallowed hard and then climbed out of the car. He worked up a friendly smile and tossed him a little wave. "Need any help?" he asked.

The man didn't return the smile. He squinted at Jordan. "Say, weren't you in the store earlier? Are you following me or something?"

Jordan stopped in his tracks. He chuckled nervously. "Yeah, I was at the store, but I—I'm not following you, no."

Holding on to his jacket, the man patted it down for something in the pockets. "Well, this is a pretty weird coincidence. Something just like this happened yesterday. Do I know you?"

"I don't think so," Jordan replied, moving a step closer. "I'm Brad—Brad Reece." It was the name of his English Lit teacher.

The man found whatever he'd been searching for in the jacket's pockets, but he didn't take it out yet. "If you weren't following me, what were you doing parked back there?"

Jordan shrugged. "Oh, well, huh, I thought you might be in trouble or something. There isn't a lot of traffic on this stretch of the road. I didn't want to leave you stranded." He laughed and then shrugged again. "Then again, you could have been sitting in there lighting up a joint for all I knew. I just—I just wanted to make sure you were okay before I passed you by."

"That's extremely nice of you," the man said, with a skeptical sidelong glance.

Jordan took a deep breath and then stepped over to the car. "So—do you live here in Cullen, or are you visiting?"

"Visiting," the man answered, still guarded.

Jordan nodded a few more times than necessary. "Well, my family—we live in Everett, but we spend a lot of weekends here. We own a cabin down the road a bit." He feigned interest in the flat tire. "Wow, that's shot to shit, isn't it?" Rolling up his sleeves, he picked up the tire wrench. Jordan hoped the man didn't notice his hand trembling. "I bet the two of us can get this tire changed in less than five minutes."

The man didn't respond. He seemed to be watching Jordan's every move.

With one end of the wrench, Jordan pried the hubcap off the flat tire. His palms were sweating, but he kept a firm grip of the wrench as he started to loosen the lug nuts. "Damn," he grunted. "These suckers are on here tight—tighter than a bull's ass in a snowstorm, as my dad likes to say." He forced a laugh. "Hey, um, you know, you never told me your name—or where you're visiting from."

Bent over the flat tire, Jordan wasn't looking at the man. He just had to go by the tone of his voice. The guy waited a few beats before answering. "My name's Allen Meeker. I'm here for the weekend with my fiancée and her little boy. We drove up from Seattle yesterday."

"Oh, really? So—how old is the boy?" Jordan asked.

"He's four. Why do you ask?"

"Just curious," Jordan replied. He knew the man was lying. He'd taken a long look at this BMW, and if the guy had driven up here with a child under five, there would have been some kind of child safety seat in the back.

"Are you camping, or did you guys rent a cabin?" Jordan asked, keeping his eyes on his work.

"We've rented a very nice house on the bay."

Jordan hesitated. He remembered the woman and the little boy he'd met yesterday afternoon outside Rosie's. "Is—um—the house about two miles farther down this road?"

Standing over him, the man nodded. "How did you—"

"Twenty-two Birch?"

"Yeah. How did you know?"

Jordan felt a bit sick again. He tried to keep his voice steady as he answered: "It's the only rental house on the water on this side of the bay." He glanced up at the man again.

Allen Meeker put on his jacket—and his sunglasses. It struck Jordan as odd, because he didn't need the jacket. Despite a slight autumn chill in the air, the sun was strong and warm. There were even beads of sweat on his forehead. He'd been feeling around for something inside that jacket earlier. Jordan figured he had a gun, a switchblade, or *something* in there. Right now, he kept his hands in his jacket pockets—and he kept sweating.

Jordan loosened the last of the lug nuts. "Is this your first visit to Cullen?" he asked—as casually as he could.

"I—um, yeah, this is my first visit," the man answered with hesitation.

He was lying again. Jordan knew.

"So—Allen," he said. "If you don't mind getting your hands a little dirty, could you roll that spare over here and hand me the jack?"

He laughed. "Shit, I'm sorry. I didn't mean to make you do all the work. Listen—um, *Brad*, thank you very much. You really deserve a Good Samaritan award." He took his hands out of his pockets and retrieved the jack. He set it by Jordan, and then went to fetch the spare tire.

Jordan wedged the jack beneath the car and started cranking it up.

The man rolled the spare tire over to him. "I think you were right," he said. "You'll have this done in five minutes." While Jordan worked the jack, Allen unscrewed the loose lug nuts by hand. They made a hollow clanking noise every time he dropped one of them inside the upturned hubcap. They were both squatting down by the car's rear passenger side. Allen stopped to glance at him. He took off his sunglasses and put them in his shirt pocket. "Say, your color looks better now—at least, better than it did in the store earlier. I thought you were going to be sick back there."

"So did I," Jordan calmly admitted. "But it's all under control now."

The man's eyes narrowed at him. "The clerk in the store seemed pretty concerned. She knew you. . . ."

Jordan just nodded. He slowly reached for the lug wrench.

"She called you something back there, it wasn't *Brad*. It was—*Jordy*. . . ."

"That's right." He had the lug wrench in his grasp now. "My name is Jordan—Jordan Prewitt, and you killed my mother, you slimy fuck."

Wide-eyed, the man stared at him and started to reach into his jacket pocket again. "No, wait—wait!" he cried.

Jordan hauled back the wrench and brought it crashing down on his scalp. Allen Meeker flopped forward, his face hitting the gravel.

A gun fell out of his jacket pocket.

CHAPTER
SEVEN

"**B**ang, bang!" Mattie said.

Susan stared at him, a hand over her heart.

Her little boy wore an orange life vest over his grey sweatshirt from Disney World—with Mickey, Donald, Pluto, and Goofy on it. He stood near the storage locker in the cabin of the boat Allen had rented for them. He had a flare gun in his hands—and Susan had no idea whether or not it was loaded. She didn't even know where he'd found the thing. Mattie pointed the gun directly at her. "Bang, bang! You're dead, Mommy!"

"Mattie—honey, that's not a toy," she said, as calmly as she could. Susan wasn't even thinking of herself; it just panicked her to see her four-and-a-half-year-old handling a gun—no matter what direction it was pointed. Nevertheless, the bulky yellow life vest she had on couldn't deflect or diminish the deadly impact of a flare—especially one shot at such close range. She was in the cabin's small galley, by the stepladder-stairs to the deck.

The boat was tied to the dock in back of the house. She'd just put some food and cans of soda pop in the mini refrigerator, and then she'd turned to see Mattie with the flare gun in his little hand.

Susan remained perfectly still. "Put the gun down on the table," she said. "Right now, sweetie, I mean it. That's not a toy, Mattie. It's very dangerous."

"Bang, bang!" he repeated. Now he gripped the gun with both hands. His finger wiggled near the trigger.

Slowly, she took a step toward him. "Did you hear me, Mattie? Put that down this instant. It's not yours." She pointed to the heavily varnished, narrow table in front of the settee. "Put it down on the table—right now. . . ."

He stared at her for a moment, the gun still pointed at her. His tongue poked out past the corner of his mouth. The boat swayed a bit from side to side. Susan could hear water lapping along the sides of the vessel and against the dock pilings.

Susan reached out to him. "Okay, then, just hand it to me, sweetie. That's a good boy."

Smiling, he plopped it in her outstretched palm.

Susan let out a long sigh. The gun felt heavy. It was probably loaded. "Thank you," she muttered, working up a smile. "That's my guy. Where did you—um, find this, sweetheart?"

"There," he pointed to a half-open drawer by the storage closet. Susan noticed two big flashlights and about ten flare cartridges in there. She gingerly set the flare gun in the drawer. Closing it, she noticed the lock.

Allen had given her the keys to the boat earlier. Susan dug into the pocket of her jeans and pulled them out. There were three keys on the ring. Her hands were still shaking as she tried each key in the drawer's lock. The third one worked—thank God.

She'd brought along a whole bin of Mattie's favorite toys for this boat trip; so naturally, he had to go looking for something else to play with—like a loaded flare gun. She didn't remember Michael being this much of a handful, but then again, she'd had a lot of help with Michael.

It was ironic; she'd been up half the night worried that Mattie would somehow get his hands on Allen's gun, and here he'd found another lethal weapon on the boat. So far, except for one nice, mild surprise, it had been a pretty sketchy morning.

Allen had finally come to bed around 4:30 AM. He'd stashed the gun on the top shelf in the bedroom closet. Susan kept tossing and turning, but managed to nod off about an hour later. She stirred a bit when Allen got up again at seven, but he told her to sleep in. He even volunteered to make breakfast for Mattie.

Susan dozed off again. She had a dream about Walt and Michael. Her firstborn was about Mattie's age in the dream. They were in a crowded train station, but she could see Walt over by the newsstand, looking at a magazine. She tried to hold on to Michael's hand, but he kept slipping away. Her husband wasn't paying any attention to them at all. She was terrified that Michael would get lost. She kept calling to her husband, "Walt, I need you to help me!"

She woke up, feeling as if she were still reaching out for her lost little boy.

It used to be she'd awaken from such dreams and

tell herself everything was all right. But now after dreams like this one, she almost always sat up in bed and cried. This morning was no different.

Susan used up three Kleenexes before she smelled the coffee—and there was bacon cooking, too.

It was 9:35. She threw on her robe and paused by the open closet door. She checked the top shelf, but the gun wasn't there.

Downstairs, she found Mattie in front of the TV again, watching the DVD of *Finding Nemo* for about the zillionth time. Allen was in the kitchen, at the stove. "I looked, but couldn't find the *you-know-what* in our closet," she whispered to him. "Please tell me this doesn't mean you're packing heat right now."

"It means I locked the *you-know-what* in the glove compartment of my car two hours ago," Allen replied, removing bacon from the grill with a set of tongs. He set it on a paper towel on the counter. "And I know bacon sandwiches are your favorite breakfast guilty pleasures, so here we are, babe."

Susan put her arm around him and kissed him. "Will you marry me?"

"Yeah, come to think of it," he replied, kissing her back.

While she poured the coffee and made toast, Susan couldn't quite look her handsome, considerate fiancé in the eye. He had no idea she still had dreams about Walt.

Later, she cut up last night's leftover chicken, tossed in some bacon, and made a chicken pasta salad to serve up cold with Tuscan bread while they were on their nautical excursion around Skagit Bay. Susan put on sneakers, jeans, a heather-green pullover, and a wind-breaker; then she got Mattie into a pair of jeans and his Disney World sweatshirt.

They'd been on their way down to the boat when she'd realized they had no sunscreen. So Allen had said he'd drive to Rosie's Roadside Sundries and buy some. He'd told her to put the food in the boat's refrigerator and don their life vests so they'd be ready to sail by the time he returned.

That had been over a half hour ago. Susan sweltered in the life vest and windbreaker. Then again, maybe she was perspiring because she'd just had one of the major frights of her life seeing Mattie with that flare gun.

She led him to the built-in sofa and sat him down. "Now, what did I tell you when we first came aboard this boat?" she asked.

He pouted slightly. "Not to touch anything without axing you."

"That's right," she said. "And did I tell you it was okay to touch that flare gun and play with it?"

"No."

She nodded. "That was very, very dangerous. One of us could have been seriously hurt. Now, if you can't obey the rules of being a good sailor, you can't go sailing. You sit here and think about that while we wait for Allen to come back from the store." Reaching into the toy bin, Susan laid out some things on the table to keep him occupied. "I want you to stay put and play quietly—like a good sailor, okay?"

"'Kay," Mattie murmured.

Mussing his hair, Susan walked back toward the galley area. She climbed two of the three steps up to the deck. The wind whipping at her hair, she peered out at the back of the house for a few moments. She kept hoping to see Allen's BMW come around the driveway. But there was no sign of him.

"Well, Allen must have had to go all the way into town for the sunscreen," she announced, stepping down into the cabin again. She'd said it more for herself than for Mattie, who was bringing a little Fisher-Price airplane in for a landing on the narrow table.

Susan got busy putting away the plastic plates and glasses—and checking out all the drawers and cupboards of the compact galley.

There was a *click* from the operating panel on the other side of the steps. One of the two built-in monitors had a flashing icon that said *You've Got Mail!*

It struck her as odd that they couldn't get decent cell phone service in the area, but they were able to get e-mail on this boat. She sat down at the navigating station and found the pullout drawer for the keyboard and the mouse.

"Will we see any pirates?" Mattie asked, focusing on his toy plane.

"Not on this trip, honey," she said. She was thinking at this point, they might not even see the rest of the bay. Allen was awfully late. Maybe this e-mail was from him. She clicked on the icon, and the e-mail listing popped up on the screen. The sender was chris@orcasleasing.com, and the subject was: Welcome & Happy Sailing!

Susan opened the e-mail.

Dear Mr. Meeker,

Thanks for renting your Catalina C28 Cruiser Sailboat from Bayside Rentals Partners, and welcome aboard! We're glad we were able to secure the Seaworthy for you. We apologize again for the confusion with the other boat, and we're happy we could meet your specific request. As you can see, your Internet access is up and working. If you have any problems or questions, don't hesitate to e-mail me or phone: 306/555-0416. For more information on the operating features of your Catalina C28, simply click on the link below or refer to the instruction manual. We appreciate your business, and happy sailing!

Sincerely,
Chris
Bayside Rentals Partners

http:///www.jCatalinaC28/features.html.

Susan clicked KEEP AS NEW, to save the e-mail for Allen. It looked like he'd gone to a lot of trouble to reserve this particular boat. He'd been adamant about getting out on the water before noon today.

Susan glanced at her wristwatch: 12:40. This was getting ridiculous. He'd been gone nearly an hour.

"Mommy, can we go up on top?" Mattie asked.

Susan got to her feet. "Sure, sweetheart." She found his Mariners baseball hat in the toy bin and put it on his head. Mattie grabbed his Woody doll from the bin of toys. Susan helped him off the settee and led him up the steps to the deck. "You'll have to hold on to me while we're up here—the whole time, okay?"

"'Kay," he said. "Where's Allen? When's he coming back?"

"That's what your dear old mother would like to know," she muttered. Susan glanced over at the house again as she came up on deck. There was still no sign of him.

She sat down with Mattie in the cockpit. Susan

started to adjust the visor of Mattie's baseball hat so he wouldn't get sunburned.

"Is that Allen?" Mattie asked, pointing toward the house.

Susan turned and gaped at their rental house. At first, she didn't see anything. She'd been focusing on the driveway that wound around near the back porch. It took a few moments for Susan to realize what Mattie had seen.

She gasped. Her son was pointing to a man at the edge of the woods—only a few feet away from the far side of the house. He wore sunglasses, an oversized army camouflage jacket, and a matching hat. She couldn't quite see his face. He was creeping toward the sunroom window.

"Is Allen wearing a disguise?" Mattie asked.

For a moment, Susan couldn't move. She sat there, paralyzed.

"HELLO!" Mattie yelled cheerfully. He waved his Woody doll at the man. "HELLO, ALLEN!"

The stranger in the camouflage fatigues spun around and faced them.

Susan jumped up and grabbed Mattie. Her sudden movement made the boat rock. "That's not Allen," she said, panic-stricken. Susan could barely keep her balance as the boat teetered from side to side. Bracing herself, she grabbed on to the edge of the boat with one hand and held on to Mattie with the other. "C'mon, sweetie, let's get down below. Hurry!"

As she guided Mattie to the steps down to the cabin, Susan glanced back at the man by their rental house. Threading through the trees at the edge of the forest, he made his way toward them.

Mattie hesitated at the top of the cabin steps. So Susan scooped him up under her arm and scurried down the steps to the cabin. Setting him down on the settee, she turned and pulled shut the cabin door. She locked it with the dead bolt. The boat was still swaying from side to side.

Any minute now, Susan expected to hear the thunder of footsteps on the old, dilapidated dock. Unsteadily, she hurried toward the storage closet—and the drawer where she'd locked up the flare gun.

"What's wrong, Mommy?" Mattie was asking.

"It's okay, honey—everything's okay!" she tried to assure him, though her voice was shrill. All the while, Susan tried to get the correct key to unlock the drawer. Her hands wouldn't stop shaking. At last, she got the drawer open. She took out the flare gun and several cartridges. Shoving the cartridges in her pocket, she tried to figure out how the gun worked. She tugged at the handle, and the barrel, and then yanked at both ends simultaneously. To her utter astonishment, the gun bent in two. She could see the chamber—and the cartridge snug inside it. Snapping it shut, she went to the long, narrow, horizontal window by the operating panel, and she glanced out at the dock. She didn't see the man out there. But her view was limited, and for all she knew, he could be hovering near the boat—just out of her line of vision.

"Mommy?"

Susan turned toward her son. "Sweetie, I need you to wait in here." She led him into the berth at the front of the boat. "I want you to hide in here until I tell you to come out. Do you understand? I—I want to see how good you are at hide-and- seek. Now, I'm going to shut the door. Okay?"

Wide-eyed, Mattie clutched Woody to his chest and gazed up at her. He nodded.

She closed the door and then hurried to the window again. She saw the man retreating. He ducked behind the bushes near the house's back porch.

Susan wished she could see his face, but he moved so fast, he was just a blur. It might have been the man who had followed her from Mount Vernon yesterday, but she couldn't be sure.

The boat still swayed a bit. Susan turned to the operating panel, set the flare gun on the desk, then pulled out the keyboard drawer, and clicked on the e-mail icon again. "How are you doing in there, Mattie?" she called, focusing on the monitor.

"Can I come out yet?" he replied—in a slightly frightened tone.

"Not just yet, honey," she said, typing furiously.

Dear Chris,

THIS IS AN EMERGENCY! My little boy and I are trapped on boat docked off backyard. Some man is lurking around our house—22 Birch. No phone. Please call Cullen Police for me. Don't know if man is armed. Tell police to hurry. Thank you.

Susan Blanchette (Allen Meeker's fiancée)

She hit the *Send* button. Then she glanced up at the cabin door—still expecting any minute now for someone to start tugging at it from outside. Susan looked at the flare gun—within her reach.

She pulled up Google.com and typed: Cullen, Washington, police emergency. But the closest she got to that was a CONTACT US option for the police department on a *Welcome to Cullen!* Web site. Susan e-mailed them anyway, telling them pretty much what she'd told Chris at Bayside Rentals.

Standing, she grabbed the flare gun and peered out the narrow window again. She didn't see anyone, but she was convinced he was still out there. She kept hoping to hear that *click* sound from the computer, signifying a new e-mail—and perhaps an answer to her distress call. But the guy at Bayside Rentals was probably at lunch. Susan glanced at her wristwatch: 1:05. For all she knew, Cullen might have a police force of two—and with her luck, they were both at lunch, too.

She wondered if there was any connection between Allen's disappearance and this strange man now lurking around their rental house. It was strange that they were both happening at the same time.

Suddenly, the boat tipped toward one side, and she heard a scraping against the hull. Had the man just climbed aboard? Susan clutched the gun tighter. She glanced out the window once more, and then up at the cabin door. The boat rocked—and the vessel grazed against something a second time. She realized it must have been a wave. The craft was bumping against one of the dock pilings.

The gun poised, Susan stood at the bottom of the cabin steps until the boat steadied itself again.

"Mommy?" Mattie whined from the other side of the bedroom door. "I want to come out now!"

"In a minute, honey!" she called back. "You're doing really well so far. I—I'm so proud of you!"

She spotted a pair of binoculars with a strap, dangling from a hook by the operating panel. Grabbing them, she hung the binoculars around her neck and moved up the steps. The flare gun ready in one hand, she unlocked the cabin door's dead bolt. Taking a deep breath, she pushed the door open and stuck her head out the opening. They seemed to be alone on the boat. Yet she couldn't stop shaking as she climbed up on deck. She nervously glanced around and then put the binoculars up to her eyes. She gazed out toward the house and the forest around it. She kept waiting to catch that creepy man in her sights, but there was no sign of him.

Her heart was still racing as she returned below. She couldn't stay aboard this claustrophobic vessel any longer—with her poor, scared son locked in the V-berth. Their best bet was making a run for the car, then driving into town—or at least to the grocery store so she could call the police from the pay phone. She only hoped once they got to the car, the tires would be okay.

Turning off the boat's main power switch, she called to Mattie, "You can come out now, sweetie."

"'Kay," he replied.

She moved to the door and heard the lock jiggling. On the other side, he seemed to be tugging and tugging at the door, but to no avail. She realized he must have locked himself in.

"Sweetheart, can you—"

The lock clicked, and the door finally opened.

Susan swept Mattie into her arms. "C'mon, we're going for a ride," she announced. She carried him up the steps to the deck.

Eyeing the house and grounds, Susan set down Mattie and the flare gun so she could lock up the cabin. "You're my lookout, honey," she said nervously. She tried to find the right key for the lock. "You need to tell me if you see that—that *soldier* again, okay?"

With his Woody doll tucked under his arm, Mattie nodded and gazed over toward the woods.

Susan finally got the cabin door locked. She grabbed the flare gun and then picked up Mattie. The vessel started to rock again as she carried him onto the dock. Even off the boat, her legs still felt unsteady and wobbly. She set Mattie down again.

She wouldn't be able to fit him into the car's child safety seat while he was wearing the bulky vest, so she took it off. Then she shed hers as well. "Okay, piggyback," she said, turning her back to him and squatting down.

"Yippee!" Mattie cried. His arms went around her neck, and he jumped on her back. "Gimme up!"

Leaving the life vests on the dock, Susan hurried up toward the house, Mattie bouncing against her back the whole time. She had the flare gun ready. As she came closer to the driveway, she could see only the front of her car. But the tires looked all right. She was already digging into her pocket for the keys.

By the time she reached the car, Susan was out of breath. Her throat had dried up, too, and sweat glistened on her forehead. She kept glancing around to make sure they were alone. She set the gun down on the hood so that she could secure Mattie in his safety seat in back. She worked quickly, but still took the time to kiss Mattie's forehead once he was strapped in. "You've been so good," she said.

"There he is!" Mattie declared excitedly. He pointed his Woody doll at something beyond the windshield. "There's the soldier!"

Susan snatched the flare gun off the car's hood, and she swiveled around in time to glimpse the man as he darted behind a tree at the edge of the forest—not far from the driveway.

"I see you!" Susan yelled, the anger rising up in her voice. "Who are you? Answer me!"

"Mommy?" Mattie cried.

"Stay there, honey." She shut his door, but didn't move away from it.

She could hear twigs snapping and the rustling of bushes. A figure scurried through the trees, but he wasn't running away. She could tell; the sound wasn't fading. He was just as close—only in a different spot. It was as if he were playing a game with her.

"Damn it, I'm going to fire this thing if you don't speak up right now!" She had both hands on the gun now.

The bushes moved behind an old wooden rain barrel about twenty feet away—just past the driveway. "I see you there!" Susan screamed. She pulled the trigger and felt an electric-like jolt course through her hands and arms.

With a hiss, the flare left a tail of smoke in its path as it hit the rain barrel. The wooden barrel burst into flames, sending fiery splinters and cinders into the air. Susan heard a howl—as if the intruder might have been hurt or, at least, startled.

She quickly dug into her pocket and pulled out another flare cartridge. Her hands still tingled with rever-
berations from the blast. But she managed to pull out
the spent cartridge and load another into the gun. All
the while, she heard bushes rustling. The sound grew
fainter, and she could tell he was running away.

Catching her breath, Susan stood guard by Mattie's
door, ready to fire again. Considering the blast and the
inferno, she was pretty sure the guy was well on his
way to the Canadian border by now.

She opened Mattie's door, expecting her poor son to
be traumatized. "Sweetie, it's okay now—" she started
to say.

"Do it again! Do it again, Mommy!" he cheered.
His legs kicked at the back of the passenger seat, and
he clapped his hands. Wide-eyed, he watched as flames
engulfed the empty barrel and spread to the bush behind it.

"There will be no encore," Susan muttered, shaking
her head, "God willing."

Shutting his door, she retreated from the car for a
moment to retrieve the garden hose, on the same side
of the house. Susan managed to douse the fire. All the
while, she kept a lookout for the return of their unin-
vited visitor.

She was watching out for him on the way to Rosie's
Roadside Sundries, too. Checking her rearview mirror
every few moments, she didn't see any cars behind her.
But as Susan got closer to the store, she saw an empty
car pulled over to the side of Carroll Creek Road.

It was a dark green Honda Civic, the same car those
teenagers had been driving yesterday. She remembered

how that nice, handsome young man had acted a bit strange when she'd asked how to get to Twenty-two Birch.

He seemed to know the house very well.

Frowning, Susan took another long look at the empty car in her rearview mirror, until she took a curve in the road. Then she couldn't see it anymore.

CHAPTER
EIGHT

Jordan stopped running to glance over his shoulder. Between all the trees, he could see slivers of the road in the distance—and a car approaching. His lungs were burning as he gasped for air. Sweat rolled off him, and his clothes were soaked. The splattered orange juice had made the legs of his jeans sticky and itchy. Burrs clung to his socks.

He was accustomed to running several miles a day—but not in his street clothes, and not along a crude forest path. He'd had to navigate around fallen branches, rocks, divots, and tree roots. He already had a few scratches on his hands and forehead from brushes with low-hanging branches.

Jordan had just chalked up seven miles through the woods in less than forty minutes. Though he'd figured it would be okay to leave his car for a while along that lonely stretch of Carroll Creek Road, he didn't want to push his luck. And forty minutes was pushing it.

Less than an hour ago, Jordan had hastily dumped Allen Meeker into the trunk of his BMW. The unconscious man's cheek had been bloody from falling face-first onto the gravel. And under his wavy black and silver hair, he'd had a cut on his scalp where Jordan had hit him with the tire wrench, but it hadn't bled much.

With Meeker in the trunk, Jordan had quickly finished changing the tire. He'd figured the old, abandoned Chemerica plant would be the best temporary spot to hide the BMW—and his captive.

Back in the sixties, the facility had been a government-subsidized lab. They'd even had some army personnel on staff. Jordan wasn't sure exactly what they'd researched or manufactured there. Rumor was they'd been working on something top secret, related to chemical warfare or rockets—hence, the isolated location. At least, that was the story Jordan heard. Apparently, for a while, that part of Carroll Creek Road had seen a lot more traffic, and the deli stop, which was now Rosie's, had done a brisk business. But by 1977, the army no longer needed whatever Chemerica Corporation provided for them, and the facility was shut down.

The government still owned the now-dilapidated two-story facility and the square mile of neglected land it sat on. A high rusty chain-link fence surrounded the property, and concrete barriers blocked the access drive off Carroll Creek Road. But Jordan—along with some resourceful locals—had found a remote dirt road that merged onto the Chemerica facility's driveway. There was a lot to explore in the deserted forty-room building—if one could find a window that wasn't completely boarded up. There were also five old bunkers to attract curious or horny teenagers in the mood for exploring. Yet despite evidence to the contrary—fast-food

wrappers, beer cans, and pop bottles littered the
Chemerica grounds—these instances of trespassing
were few and far between. They were even rarer in
daytime.

So Allen Meeker and his BMW would probably be
safe—for the time being—at the Chemerica facility.
Jordan parked Meeker's car off an old driveway between the back of the building and a swamp.

There, he had more time to search the car. For
someone who claimed to have driven up to Cullen with
a four-year-old, Meeker had a pretty immaculate car,
devoid of any toys or kids' books. No child safety seat,
no food wrappers, no empty juice boxes. Jordan
checked the glove compartment. He discovered maps
of Washington and Oregon, a BMW owner's manual, a
flier for Domino's Pizza with coupons that had expired
a year ago, and the vehicle registration. The guy's
name was Allen Meeker, all right.

Jordan verified this again when he checked on
Meeker in the trunk. He found him still unconscious
and still breathing. The driver's license in his wallet re-
confirmed the name: *Meeker, Allen Lloyd,* along with
the birth date, which made him thirty-nine. The rest of
the stats were already pretty apparent: *Height: 6-00,
Weight: 175; Eyes: GRN.* He had a Seattle address.
Jordan also found $140 in cash; a gym pass; credit
cards and insurance cards—all for *Allen L. Meeker*;
and a punch card for Tully's Coffee. There were no
photos of his alleged fiancée—or of anyone else for
that matter.

Jordan couldn't tell much about him from the wallet. Nor could he find anything in his pockets. He took
Allen Meeker's jacket and tied up his ankles with it.

Then he used some twine already in the trunk to bind his hands behind him. Taking a handkerchief from Meeker's pocket, Jordan stuffed it in his captive's mouth. Meeker barely stirred through any of this.

But just before Jordan shut the trunk, Allen's eyes had fluttered open. Past the gag, he'd let out a muffled moan—a pathetic, panicked sound.

Jordan had slammed the BMW's trunk shut.

And then he'd started running.

He was six miles away now—very close to where he'd left his own car along the shoulder of Carroll Creek Road. But Jordan could still hear that helpless, muted cry in his head. And he couldn't help wondering if he'd made a terrible mistake.

He ducked deeper into the woods as the car sped up the road. He hadn't been paying attention to that woman's car yesterday at Rosie's, and he wondered if this was her in the old Toyota headed toward Rosie's. Was she really Meeker's fiancée?

Wiping the sweat from his forehead, Jordan watched the Toyota slow down as it approached his empty Honda Civic. But then it picked up speed again and finally disappeared around a bend in the road.

Jordan didn't see any more traffic on the lonely highway. He didn't think anyone saw him climb into his car and drive away. He didn't spot any vehicles in his rearview mirror as he turned off the road onto the narrow, uneven dirt trail. It wound through the forest and had an array of dips, puddles, and rocks. At least it was easier to negotiate all the obstacles on this second trip.

But his hands were still sweating against the steering wheel, and he hadn't quite gotten his breath back yet. Jordan wondered if he'd return to the old driveway behind the deserted Chemerica plant and find nothing—no BMW, no Allen Meeker. It was a stupid, impossible notion. He had the keys to the BMW in his pocket. He'd locked Meeker in the trunk. How could the guy get out or get away?

Jordan went over one last big bump before the dirt trail merged with the old access road to Chemerica Corporation. As far as he knew, it was the only break in the chain-link fence that protected the worthless property.

Though paved, the two-lane access road was full of potholes and divots. Everything from blades of crabgrass to small trees had sprouted through the pavement cracks. Hunched close to the steering wheel, Jordan picked up speed and did his best to avoid these obstacles.

The Chemerica Corporation building finally came into view—just beyond an open gate and the shell of a guard station. It was an old, ugly beige brick structure, decorated with graffiti. The front entrance and all the first floor windows had been boarded up. Nearly all of the second-floor windows were broken—some completely hollowed out so their ragged, brownish-yellow blinds flapped in the breeze.

As Jordan approached the lonely, decrepit building, it was hard for him to imagine there had once been an army guard in that little sentry post—and at least fifty cars parked in the now deserted lot. He followed the driveway as it wound around to the back of the facility. To his utter relief, he saw the BMW just where he'd left it. And the trunk was still closed.

He pulled up behind the BMW, shifted to park, and turned off the ignition. Then he heard the pounding. It was coming from the BMW's trunk.

Reaching under his seat, Jordan pulled out Allen Meeker's gun. He grabbed the tire wrench from the floor of the passenger side and climbed out of his car. Gravel crunched beneath his feet, and he knew Meeker heard him approaching. The pounding got more intense and frantic. The muted moaning sounded so pitiful, like a wounded animal.

Jordan tucked the gun inside the waist of his jeans—in the back. He dug Meeker's car keys out of his pocket and pressed the trunk-lid button on the remote control. The trunk's lid popped—and then Meeker gave it a fierce kick. He tried to sit up, but Jordan was right there with the tire wrench ready.

Wide-eyed, Meeker recoiled. His feet were still tied up, and his hands still bound behind him. He tried to speak past the gag, but it was just more muffled, indistinguishable pleading. He shook his head over and over again.

Jordan swallowed hard. He hit him with the wrench, the other side of his head this time.

Allen Meeker let out one last moan and then slumped back into the trunk.

Jordan stared at him. The guy was still breathing. But this blow broke the skin, and blood trickled along Meeker's greying temple and down the side of his neck.

Jordan began to tremble, and tears filled his eyes. He still had some doubt. What if this man was totally innocent?

He gazed at the cluster of scuff marks on the left inside of the hood, where Allen Meeker had been kicking at it.

Wiping the tears from his eyes, Jordan noticed similar markings on the right side, too—just above Allen's head. It didn't make sense. Meeker couldn't have shifted positions in that confined space.

That was when Jordan no longer had any doubt about what he was doing.

Now he knew. Allen Meeker wasn't the first person to be locked inside that trunk.

Jordan had meant to drive the BMW to the edge of the swamp, but he overshot it. The area was so overgrown and muddy, it was hard to tell where land stopped and the marsh began. The front of the vehicle started tilting forward and sinking while he was still in the driver's seat. Quickly climbing out of the car, Jordan found himself ankle-deep in mud that felt like quicksand. A panic raced through him as he struggled toward hard ground. All the while, Meeker's BMW sunk deeper into the muddy water. Once Jordan reached the edge of the swamp, he leaned against the car's trunk and pushed with all his might. The water made a strange gurgling sound as it started to swallow up the car. The front hood completely disappeared below the dark, murky surface. Backing away, Jordan watched as the mire enveloped the windows. It pulled the vehicle deeper into its depths. He couldn't tell if it was the mud or some mechanism in the car, but he heard a strange, hollow moan as the vehicle finally sank out of sight.

Jordan hurried back to his own car, still parked behind the old Chemerica plant. He did his best to shake the excess mud off his shoes before climbing behind the wheel and starting up the engine. He drove around to the front of the facility. As he passed the decrepit little shack that had once been a guard gate, he heard a loud, startling wail.

Jordan gaped in his rearview mirror and saw a police car bearing down on him with its strobe lights flashing. It seemed to have come out of nowhere.

"Oh, Christ," he murmured, a sudden dread overwhelming him. He automatically hit the brake pedal. Frozen, he sat there with a tight grip on the steering wheel, staring in the rearview mirror.

The patrol car pulled up behind him. Its eardrum-splitting siren ceased, but the strobe lights kept swirling. The cop sat in the front seat for a few moments. That seemed to be their routine: sitting in the cop car and letting the busted driver sweat it out for a spell. Jordan could see it wasn't Cullen's sheriff, Stuart Fischer. That was one solace, because Fischer was an asshole—and useless, too.

The Cullen Police Department consisted of Fischer, his deputy, and a clerk. So this had to be the deputy, who had been around for about two years. Jordan didn't know him. And he didn't know how long the deputy had been parked there in front of the Chemerica building. Had he seen anything?

Earlier, Jordan had stashed Meeker's gun under his front seat. The tire wrench lay on the floor of the passenger side. If the deputy asked him to get out of the car, how would he explain the mud all over his shoes?

His stomach in knots, Jordan rolled down his window all the way. He watched in the side mirror as the

deputy finally climbed out of his patrol car and mo-
seyed up toward him. He was about thirty, with short,
thick dark blond hair. He had the slightly worn good
looks of an ex-jock just starting to let himself go soft.
He still possessed a fairly muscular build—and the
swagger that came with it. He had one hand poised on
his gun holster as he approached Jordan's window.
"Hey there, dude," the deputy said. "Turn off your
motor, okay?"

Squirming in the driver's seat, Jordan switched off
the ignition.

"How about coughing up your license and registration for me?"

Jordan took his driver's license out of his wallet and
handed it to him. "Um, the registration is in my glove
compartment, okay?"

"That's where most people keep it, ace. Go for it."

Jordan glimpsed down at the tire wrench—and
hoped the deputy didn't notice. It was too late to try
hiding it. He quickly retrieved his registration from the
glove compartment and gave it to the cop. He stole a
glance at the deputy's nametag: *Dep. Corey Shaffer*.
"Is there—is there a problem, officer?" he asked.

"So you're Jordan Prewitt," the deputy said, grinning at him. "Well, I've heard your name bandied
about. Your family has that place on Cedar Crest Way.
Are you staying there this weekend with your mom
and dad?"

Jordan cleared his throat. "Um, I'm here with—"

"Oh, excuse me," the deputy interrupted. He shook
his head. "I mean your dad and your *step*-mom. Sorry."

"It's okay," Jordan replied. He managed to smile up

at him through the open window. "I'm staying at the cabin with two friends of mine. Is there a problem here, officer?"

Deputy Shaffer glanced at the large, wrapped present and the bakery box in Jordan's backseat. He leaned against the roof and sighed. "Well, yes, Jordan, as a matter of fact, we do indeed have a problem. See, this is private property. It belongs to Uncle Sam. You're trespassing here."

So are you, Jordan wanted to say. *You're not with the feds*. But he decided not to be a smart-ass. His best bet was to suck up to Deputy Shaffer and try to get the hell out of there as quickly as possible.

"Sorry," he said finally. "I've always been kind of curious about this place, and today I decided to go exploring."

Deputy Shaffer handed him back his license and registration. "Could you step out of the vehicle, please?"

Jordan stared up at him. "Why?"

"I'd like to show you something." Shaffer backed away from the car. His hand went on the gun holster again.

Jordan swallowed hard; then he opened his door and climbed out of the car.

Eyes narrowed, the deputy stared down at his muddy shoes. "What happened there?"

Jordan gave an uneasy shrug, and he stomped his feet. "Yeah, kind of a mess, isn't it? Taking that back road on the way here, I got stuck in the mud. I had to get out and push."

The deputy frowned. "Well, Jordan, I guess you should have taken that as a sign and turned back, because you're in a lot of trouble. Trespassing is a serious offense. I'm afraid I'll have to haul you in and book you."

"What?" Jordan murmured, dazed.

Deputy Shaffer burst out laughing. "Ha, you should see the look on your face! I'm fucking with you, man!"

Jordan could barely work up a smile. For a moment, it had felt as if his heart had stopped. He was having a hard time figuring out this guy.

Nudging him, the deputy swaggered toward the back of Jordan's Honda Civic. "Take a gander at this left tire back here. It's getting pretty low. That's what you get for driving down these rough back roads. Better have it checked soon."

"I will, thank you," Jordan nodded. "So—you aren't giving me a ticket or anything?"

"Not this time," Deputy Shaffer said with a friendly smile. "But don't come back here, okay? Sheriff Fischer has got a bug up his butt about this place because some of the high school kids come here to do drugs."

He stopped to gaze at the deserted building. Most of the first floor was boarded up. The ragged blinds in the second floor's broken windows flapped in the autumn breeze. "I hate patrolling this old dump," Shaffer said. "Gives me the royal creeps, y'know?"

Jordan didn't answer. He thought he heard a knock—coming from his trunk. He wondered if Deputy Shaffer had heard it, too.

With his elbow, the deputy nudged him again. "Anyway, be glad it's me and not Fischer catching you here, because that old hard-ass would have thrown the book at you."

"Thanks for cutting me a break," Jordan said. "So— is it okay if I go now? I should probably get back to my friends—"

Jordan heard it again—a knock and then some rumbling from inside his trunk. He wandered away from the back of the car, hoping to draw Shaffer from the source of the noise.

The deputy moved with Jordan toward the driver's door. "So—where did you leave these guests of yours while you went on this sorry expedition?"

"Well, um, they went for a walk in the woods," Jordan explained. Any minute now, he expected Meeker to start pounding and banging against the trunk's lid. "But they should be back soon. I really ought to get going. . . ."

"Wait a sec," Deputy Schaffer said. "Did you hear something?"

Jordan started to shake his head. But then he did hear a noise, and it wasn't coming from the trunk of his Honda Civic. It was a static-laced announcement on the radio of Shaffer's police car. The words were all fuzzy and muddled together.

"Oh, shit, just a second," Shaffer said. He turned and hurried back to his patrol car. He climbed in the front seat.

Watching him, Jordan stood by his own car, his fingers poised on the door handle. He heard the knocking and rustling again. Allen Meeker had regained consciousness inside the Honda Civic's small trunk. No doubt, he could hear the police radio, too. He had to know help was very near. The pounding started.

Jordan's whole body tensed up as he walked back

toward the police car. Passing his Honda's trunk, he could hear Meeker's muffled screams, and then more pounding and kicking. He stood by the cop's door.

"Okay, gotcha, see you there, over and out," Corey Shaffer was saying into the dashboard mike. Then he hung it up. He started jotting something on a clipboard.

"Is it cool if I take off?" Jordan asked. He could still hear the pounding and kicking, but Meeker had some competition from the flapping blinds in the second-floor windows of the plant. Jordan stole a glance at his Civic. The car was rocking up and down in the back.

"Yeah, go ahead, scram, Jordan." The deputy tossed aside his pen and clipboard. "But I'm beating you out of here. I have an emergency. Some babe on Birch Way has her panties in a twist over a Peeping Tom."

"Is she okay?" Jordan asked, thinking of the pretty brunette with the little boy.

Shaffer nodded tiredly. "Stuart's with her at Rosie's right now. I tell ya, it's always something. See ya, dude." He shut his door.

Jordan stepped back as the cop peeled around the wobbling Honda Civic. He watched the patrol car speed down the Chemerica Corporation access road.

The knocking and pounding continued from inside the trunk of his car. Jordan lumbered toward it, then rested his hand on the lid. He felt the vibrations. "You can kick and kick all you want, asshole," he growled. "It's just you and me here. There's no one to save you."

The pounding stopped. Then there was just whimpering.

Jordan leaned closer to the lid. "Did you hear what that cop said back there in his car?" Jordan asked, his voice cracking. "Did you hear where he's going? A woman's in trouble on Birch Way. Does that sound familiar?"

The pounding and muffled pleading started up again—more intense than ever. But Jordan ignored it.

Wiping the tears from his eyes, he climbed inside his car, started up the engine, and prepared himself for the rough road ahead.

CHAPTER NINE

"**I** wasn't even in the house when you took a shower this morning," Leo said. He swatted at a bush along the path through the woods.

Moira studied Leo's face as she walked beside him. She could usually tell if he was lying, because he always blinked a lot and tilted his head to one side. She got the head tilt, but no blinking, so she couldn't be sure if he'd given her an honest answer or not.

Leo had obviously made an effort to clean up nicely today. His unruly brown hair was combed, and he wore a sage-color V-neck sweater she'd once mentioned looked good on him. Moira figured he was hoping for something to happen during this woodland hike— maybe a surprise birthday make-out session or something.

She'd planned to keep him on this outing until at least one o'clock, so Jordan could pick up the cake and get the house decorated. But the way Leo was acting, it might as well have been his idea that Jordan get lost so he and she could sneak off by themselves. An hour before, when they'd first ventured down the forest path, he'd tried to put his arm around her. She'd carefully wiggled away. She didn't want to encourage him or give him the wrong idea. Yet several times along the way, he'd taken hold of her hand. And she always found some excuse to pull away after a moment. She'd smooth back her hair or point to something in the woods and make a comment.

Moira was pretty certain he'd peeked at her while she was showering this morning. He and Jordan had gotten up earlier, had their Cap'n Crunch and coffee, and then gone out for a walk. While still in bed, Moira had heard them leave. She'd figured she ought to pull herself together before they returned. Her fantasies about sleeping with Jordan Prewitt did not include him seeing her after she'd just woken up.

So Moira crawled out of bed, brushed her teeth, and jumped in the shower. There was no lock on the bathroom door, which made her a little uneasy. Ever since seeing *Psycho*, she was wary about showering in an otherwise empty house and always locked the door. After last night's scare, she was even more skittish. The plastic shower curtain was transparent—with blue and green cartoon fish on it. So Moira kept an eye on the bathroom door while she showered. But after getting soap in her eyes twice, she decided she was being silly. She finally started to relax and enjoy her shower. Her back was to the curtain when she saw a strange shadow on the tile wall in front of her. Automatically covering herself, she swiveled around. "Who's there?" she asked in a panic. Through the transparent shower curtain, she caught a glimpse of the bathroom door just as it was closing.

Unnerved, Moira shut off the water and quickly wrapped a towel around her. She was wet—with conditioner still in her hair. But she stepped out of the tub and went to the bathroom door, leaving a trail of water footprints. She opened the door a crack. "Who's there?" she demanded. Tightly clutching the towel, she stepped out to the corridor. "You guys? Jordan? Leo? Are you home?"

She waited a few moments. No answer. She heard floorboards creaking—then footsteps on the stairs. There was someone else in the house—again. She realized that last night was no fluke. It was real. Gooseflesh covered her bare, wet skin.

"Jordan? Leo?" she called, backing toward the bathroom.

"Did you just yell for us?" she heard Jordan ask.

"Oh, God," Moira gasped, slumping against the wall.

Jordan stepped around the corner at the end of the hallway. An iPod was clipped to his belt, and he had the earphones on. "Oops, sorry. . . ." He shielded his eyes.

"Were you or Leo just in here?" she asked.

"You mean in the bathroom?" he asked, lowering his hand away from his eyes. "I was in the one downstairs, but not up here. I think Leo's still outside. We just got back—like a minute ago. What's going on?"

Moira let out a long sigh. "Nothing, I—I thought someone came into the bathroom while I was in the shower."

Jordan shook his head. "Not me, not without an invitation."

She managed a smile and then ducked back into the bathroom. She went to lock the door behind her and realized once again that it had no lock.

Moira hadn't said anything to either one of them about her little scare last night. She figured either they were playing an extended prank on her—or she was just nervous about being in a strange house in the middle of nowhere. She wasn't completely giving up on the first explanation. Teenage boys were always punking each other. They could have decided to frighten her for a good laugh.

Or maybe Leo had thought scaring her was one way to make her more clingy and submissive this weekend. Was that his tactic? *Oh, Leo, I'm so scared, I can't sleep in that big bed alone tonight. Will you come to bed with me?*

Walking alongside him in the woods, she was still trying to read his expression. "Are you sure you didn't just happen to open the bathroom door and stick your head in for a free peek?" she asked.

"Jeez, I told you, *no*," Leo said. "You think I'm so hard up that I'm sneaking peeks at you in the shower and then lying when you ask me about it? God, get over yourself, Moira."

"Well, somebody opened the door while I was in there. I didn't imagine it." She shrugged. "Maybe it was Jordan."

Shoving his hands in his pocket, Leo grunted. "Huh, you wish."

"What's that supposed to mean?" she asked, indignant.

"It means you've got the hots for my best friend,

and you're probably hoping the feeling is mutual. And I think that really sucks."

She squinted at him. "I don't have *the hots* for Jordan. What are you talking about?"

"Oh, now who's the liar?" he grumbled. "I saw the way you were looking at him last night, the way you were acting around him. How do you think that makes me feel? I've been—*campaigning* to win you over for a year now, hoping you'll eventually come around. You treat me like your stupid little puppy dog or something. You've got me following you around. You call me up when you're lonely or can't get some guy you *really like* to take you out—"

"That's not fair," she argued.

Leo started to walk faster, and Moira grabbed his arm to stop him. "I've been honest with you from the start, Leo," she said, her eyes wrestling with his. "I like you. I like you a lot. I don't want to ruin a good friendship. My feelings for you are strictly—"

"Strictly platonic," he finished for her. He yanked his arm away from her. "Yeah, I know. You've told me that before, and it's emasculating."

Moira said nothing. She didn't even know he used words like *emasculating*.

Leo gave the ground a kick. "Just once, I wish you knew how it felt. In fact, huh, you want to hear something?"

"I'm not sure I do," she admitted.

"Jordan's not interested in you—not at all, not even *platonically*, Moira."

She stared at him, wondering if it was true. After all,

Jordan had kissed her hand last night. If that wasn't flirting with her, then what was?

"I asked him this morning," Leo said. "I told him to be honest, because he knows how I feel about you. And get this—he knows you're hot for him—"

"Did you tell him that?" she asked, raising her voice.

"No, he figured it out. It's obvious, Moira. I could see it last night—when I was getting over my diabetic episode, and hell, I was half out of it! You couldn't stop looking at him. Jordan said you made him uncomfortable. He said it was embarrassing. He told me, 'She's not my type.'"

Moira frowned at him. "Okay, now you're just being hurtful."

He shook his head at her. "You want to talk about hurting? How do you think I feel, Moira? Shit, it's my birthday, and you won't even let me hold your goddamn hand."

She started to walk away, but then stopped and turned toward him. "Well, if I'm such an *emasculating* bitch and your friend thinks I'm an *embarrassment*, why the hell did you invite me here for the weekend? Why are you even walking with me right now?"

"I'm wondering the same damn thing," Leo shot back.

"Fine, then just leave me alone," Moira retorted, tears in her eyes. She turned and stomped away, deeper into the forest.

"Okay, listen, listen," she heard him groan. "I'm sorry, Moira. I didn't mean to make you cry—"

"I mean it, leave me the fuck alone!" she screamed. Her voice seemed to echo through the trees. She started running up the forest trail, swatting at stray branches in her path. She almost stumbled over the roots of a tall cedar and grabbed on to the trunk to keep from falling.

Moira caught her breath and wiped the tears away. Gazing back at the trail snaking through the thick forest, she saw no sign of Leo. She heard leaves rustling in the distance, but the sound seemed to be fading.

Then, closer, some twigs snapped.

"Leo?" she called. "I'm serious. I need you to leave me alone!"

Glancing at all the trees and bushes looming around her, Moira tried to spot where her friend might be hiding.

"Leo?" she called out once more.

No response.

She stood by the towering cedar for another few moments. Part of her wanted to find Leo and smooth things over. But how could she explain it to him? *I didn't want to hold your hand, because that would have been leading you on, and then you'd think I was a tease. I can't help it if I'm not attracted to you that way. And yes, I like your best friend. I can't help that either. . . .*

What did it matter? Leo was furious at her, and Jordan found her interest in him embarrassing.

She had a weird thought about how sorry they'd be if she got lost in these woods and was missing for hours and hours. It was such a juvenile notion—like when she was a kid running away from home, mostly to worry her parents.

Yet a part of her truly wanted to disappear for a while—to shut out everything and everyone else.

Moira gazed at the path she'd been taking—the one that led back to the cabin.

Then she started walking in the opposite direction.

"All right, Ms. Blanchette," the sheriff said on the other end of the line. "You stay put there at Rosie's, and I'll be by in about five minutes. Over and out."

Susan heard a click. "Okay, thanks," she said to no one. Then she hung up the receiver and slid the desk phone closer to the clerk's side of the counter at Rosie's Roadside Sundries.

One elbow resting on top of the lottery ticket machine, Rosie was watching Mattie in the small play area near the back door. She glanced over her shoulder at Susan. "The sheriff on his way?" she asked.

Susan nodded. "Thanks for letting me use the phone—and watching Mattie. I owe you big-time."

"Oh, it's my pleasure looking after this one," she replied, with a nod toward Mattie. "Y'know, I bet you had a wayward hunter poking around your backyard earlier, that's all. Some of these guys are absolutely nuts. They start chasing after a deer, and totally forget where the heck they are. You want anything?"

Susan shook her head. "No, thanks." She moved down to the end of the counter, closer to Rosie. She could see Mattie on the multicolored plastic jungle gym in the little play area. "Sheriff Fischer said he'd be here in five minutes."

"If Stuart Fischer tells you five minutes, you can expect him in ten," Rosie said out of one side of her mouth. "Unless it's a major emergency, which I haven't seen in my seven years working here—with one notable exception—the sheriff always takes his sweet time. So . . . get comfortable, honey."

Susan nervously drummed her fingers on the counter. "The one notable exception," she said. "Was that the missing person case last year?"

"Oh, then you heard about that," Rosie said soberly. She nodded. "They never did find her, the poor thing. I was the last one to see her before she disappeared, a very sweet girl, too. She stopped into the store on a Friday afternoon, and the sheriff came across her abandoned car that same night. You wouldn't believe how many detectives and policemen and special investigators were through here asking me questions. And all I could tell them was the same thing, over and over again. She drove up, came in alone, bought some stuff, left alone, and then she drove away." She gave Susan a sidelong glance. "You sure I can't get you anything, honey?"

"Well, as a matter of fact, you might be able to help me," Susan replied, lowering her voice so Mattie couldn't hear. "Did a good-looking man with silver-black hair come in here a little over an hour ago?"

Rosie squinted at her. "Nice dresser, about thirty-five?"

Susan nodded. "Yes, that's him, that's Allen. He's my fiancé."

"Well, well, congratulations, honey. He's a looker."

"So—he was here?"

Rosie nodded again. "Yes, ma'am, he stopped in at around—eleven forty-five. He bought some sunblock lotion. . . ."

"And that's it?" Susan asked. "Did he ask for anything else? I mean, something you might not have had, something he'd need to go into town for?"

"Nope," Rosie replied, shaking her head.

Susan sighed. "I'm sorry to be asking all these dumb questions, but the thing of it is, he never came home."

"Oh, dear," Rosie murmured. "And then this business with the hunter. No wonder you're on edge, you poor thing."

"Did he say anything to you about where he was headed—anything at all?"

Rosie fingered the glasses on a chain around her neck. "Hmm, just that he needed the sunblock because he was going sailing this afternoon."

"Was there anyone else in the store who might have talked to him?"

"Yes, there was another customer, Jordy Prewitt, a nice young man from Seattle. His folks have a cabin on Cedar Crest Way, not too far from where you are—"

"Was he in the store yesterday—with some friends?" Susan asked. "I spoke with a tall, handsome, dark-haired boy. . . ."

"Yes, that's Jordy. He was here again today, when your fiancé dropped by. But I don't think they talked at all. Jordy was feeling sick, and he left rather quickly."

"So there was no one else in the store when Allen left? No one who might have talked to him or seen which way he was headed?"

Rosie shrugged. "I'm sorry, honey. I wish I could be more help. He just drove up, came in alone, bought some sunblock—"

"He left alone, and then he drove away," Susan finished for her. She winced at the thought of him vanishing like that.

Rosie reached over the counter and patted her hand. "Oh, honey, I'm sure he's fine." She glanced back at Mattie, oblivious, playing with one of the toys. Then her voice dropped to a whisper. "Your fiancé looked like a man who can take care of himself. He probably decided to go into town for something at the last minute and got sidetracked. . . ."

Susan tried to smile at her. "Thanks," she said. "Maybe that's what happened."

She wished she could believe it. She wished right now that Allen's black BMW would pull in front of the store. And she'd see him step out of the car.

But right now, she didn't see any other cars in the lot but her own. And all she heard was the distant wail of a police siren.

As he hit the first rough patch on the dirt road, Jordan heard more knocking and kicking from inside the cramped trunk of his car. No doubt, the son of a bitch was getting quite a pounding back there over the rear tires.

Meeker had been out cold during their last trek on this bumpy trail. In a way, Jordan had done the guy a favor knocking him unconscious earlier, because he hadn't been awake to feel every jolt of the bouncy, nausea-inducing ride.

Jordan watched the road ahead, resisting the temptation to torture his indisposed passenger and steer toward the rough patches.

Jordan remembered: "A rough patch" was how his mother had described the divorce. Jordan had been eight years old at the time.

"This is going to be a rough patch for you," she'd told him when she was getting ready to move away from their house in Bellingham to her own apartment ninety minutes away in Bellevue. "I really wish you could stay with me, but the people who decide these things think you're better off with your dad—for now, at least. But don't you sweat it, kiddo, because we'll get to spend weekends and holidays together. It'll be a lot of fun, you'll see. . . ."

A beautiful, curvaceous blonde, his mother looked like a movie star. All of his friends thought he had the coolest mom. She came to every one of his Little League games and threw parties for the team afterward—the worse the defeat, the grander the party. After one particularly humiliating trouncing, she even rented two ponies to give the kids rides in the backyard. As one of the most affluent families in one of the most affluent sections of Bellingham, they had a huge house, which had become headquarters for Jordan and all his pals—much to his mother's delight. She was always cooking up something for them to do—putting on skits, water-coloring, shaping clay, and a ton of sports activities. One bitter-cold winter afternoon, she suggested they flood the driveway so he and his friends could play hockey. She didn't tell his dad about it, and that night, the old man pulled his Mercedes-Benz into the driveway and slid right into a tree. That impromptu hockey game cost $5,300. At least, that was the repair bill for his dad's precious Mercedes.

"What the hell were you thinking?" Jordan overheard him yelling at her. "Jesus Christ, Stella, this house is a sty half the time because of you and your projects. And I'm still finding pony crap in our backyard. Haven't we talked about this? Did you go off your medication again?"

When their parents had first separated, Jordan had been kind of glad, really. It would mean an end to all the fighting. He'd imagined he would stay with his mom and that his dad would move out. But it was his mom who left, and "the people who decide these things" forced him to stay with his dad—and a series of nannies and housekeepers.

His first weekend with his mother after the divorce was at the family's bayside house in Cullen. It had been three weeks since he'd last seen her, his longest time between visits. He remembered seeing the name *Syms* on the mailbox at the end of the long driveway on Birch Way and realizing she'd changed her name back. She wasn't Mrs. Prewitt anymore. The summer home in Cullen had originally belonged to her parents, so her maiden name was on the mailbox now.

Jordan remembered how she came running out the front door as his dad pulled down the driveway. Jordan got so caught up in seeing her again that he almost jumped out of the car while it was still moving. His dad had to hold him back for a moment. Once the car stopped, he bolted out and raced into his mother's arms. She hugged him so fiercely, Jordan could barely breathe.

One of the first activities she'd lined up for them was a hike through the hilly woods beside the house. She'd donned a big backpack for their excursion, and after a while trudging uphill on the forest trail, Jordan could tell she was having a hard time lugging it. Her breathing became more and more labored, and sweat glistened on her forehead. He kept asking if he could carry the backpack for her, but she said she was fine. They found a bald spot in the woods she'd been talking about for most of the hike. There was a break in the trees that offered a gorgeous, sweeping view of Skagit Bay. Jordan gathered sticks to build a fire. They roasted hot dogs his mother had packed in a cooler. She'd also brought Cokes and potato salad. For dessert, they made s'mores with marshmallows, Hershey bars, and graham crackers.

It was during this feast that she asked him if he'd noticed anyone following them. She insisted a man was always a few feet behind them, hiding behind the trees and shrubs just off the trail.

"I didn't really see him, Jordy, but I know he's there," his mother said. She moved her marshmallow-roasting stick away from the fire so she could wave it in the general direction of the woods. "He's hiding out there somewhere. I'll bet your father hired someone to spy on us. He doesn't trust me with you. I'm sure that's why he bought that dumpy little place over on Cedar Crest Way last month, just to keep an eye on us when we're here together. He says it's because he loves it here on the bay, but no . . . no . . ." Shaking her head, she moved her marshmallow away from the flame and started making another s'more.

After they put out the fire, his mother left behind the backpack and the cooler. "Some lucky hiker will be happy to find this stuff," she reasoned out loud.

For the whole rest of the hike back, Jordan was scared. He kept looking around for the man his mother said was following them. At one point, he thought he saw someone duck behind a berry bush. "Who's there?" he shouted.

His mother shushed him. "We mustn't let him know that we're on to him," she whispered. "We have to pretend he's not there."

But later, as darkness fell over the house on the bay, his mother could no longer pretend the elusive man wasn't there. She claimed she saw him in the backyard, creeping up to their windows. Jordan didn't even want to pass by a window—for fear of seeing some kind of apparition hovering outside. He was terrified and clung to a baseball bat while watching a video with his mom in the sunroom after dinner that night.

The movie was *The Russians Are Coming! The Russians Are Coming!* Just when he'd forget to be scared and laugh at something in the movie, his mother would jump up from the sofa, saying she heard a noise or saw something move outside the window. She'd pause the movie each time she went to investigate a potential threat. For at least ten minutes, Jordan sat alone in the sunroom and watched Alan Arkin frozen in mid-sentence on the TV. All the while, his mother was on the kitchen phone with the Cullen police, reporting a prowler.

When Sheriff Stuart Fischer's patrol car pulled into the driveway, he had the red swirling strobe going, but the siren was off. Jordan watched from the living room window. He was relieved to see the police lights out there, where it once had been so dark and foreboding. He quickly put the bat away because he didn't want the police to think he was scared. Seconds after he returned to the window, a bright searchlight on the side of the police vehicle went on. Aimed at the house, it blinded Jordan for a moment. He stepped back from the window and rubbed his eyes. When Jordan peered outside again, Fischer had turned the cop car around and was shining that intense light toward the forest at the edge of the driveway. As the bright beam moved across the trees, it created a ripple of shadows. Jordan kept waiting to see a man hiding amid those trees, but there was nothing.

Sheriff Fischer got out of the car, then lumbered around the house with a flashlight. He even went down to the dock and checked around where they'd moored the junior kayak his mother had recently bought.

"Well, if someone was truly out there, Ms. Syms, I'm pretty sure I've scared him away," Fischer said. He stood in the dining room with a can of Sprite in his hand. Jordan's mother had offered him something to drink—and she'd told Jordan to go watch the movie. But he was distracted by the other drama unfolding in the dining room next door.

Fischer was a tall, wiry but potbellied man with a mustache and dark, receding hair. When he called Jordan's mom *Ms. Syms*, he seemed to make a point of extending the *Ms.* so it sounded like *Mizzzz*. And while he talked to her, his eyes kept wandering over to the TV in the sunroom.

"You don't have a description of the guy?" he asked—for the second time.

"No, like I told you, I only caught glimpses of him," Jordan's mother explained, shaking her head. "I never really saw his face—not this afternoon in the daylight. And tonight, it was just shadows and—and movement. But I could see someone was out there." She shuddered, then tugged together the front of her white cable-knit cardigan. She was always cold at night; even during the summer she usually put on a sweater after dinner.

"Well, you probably just ran into some hikers or

hunters in the woods earlier," the sheriff surmised. He glanced toward the TV in the sunroom. "Who's that blonde? She looks familiar."

"Eva Marie Saint," Jordan's mom answered, rubbing her forehead. "Listen, Sheriff, hikers or hunters wouldn't be lurking around this house at eight-thirty at night."

"Well, I'm guessing you had some teenagers checking the place out, Ms. Syms," Sheriff Fischer said. He sipped his Sprite. "They go around looking for empty rental houses they can mess around in. On top of that, you have a dock, and it's a pretty night. That's an invitation to all sorts of shenanigans." His eyes strayed toward the sunroom again. "Isn't Jonathan Winters in this movie?"

The sheriff didn't stay long. He assured them that he'd make another drive-around search on his way out, and he'd have his deputy conduct an extra patrol of the vicinity tonight. "You folks will be all right—right as rain," he told them.

Jordan's mom was still scared and asked Jordan to sleep in bed with her. Several times that night, she threw back the sheets and got up to look out the bedroom window. Jordan would watch his mother as she stood by the window, a sweater over her nightgown. Then she'd climb back into bed.

"Didn't the sheriff promise we'd be okay?" he asked her—after she'd gotten up and come back to bed for the fourth time.

"I suppose," she muttered, patting him on the hip. "I'm sure he knows what he's talking about. I'm just kind of wound up. Pay no attention to me. You try to get some shut-eye, kiddo. . . ."

"The police will protect us, Mom," Jordan remembered saying—just as he'd started to drift off that night.

But of course, he'd been wrong. . . .

There hadn't been any noise from the trunk since he'd pulled off the bumpy dirt trail and turned onto Carroll Creek Road. Either Meeker had passed out, or he'd just gotten tired of pounding, kicking, and whining.

It was out of his way, but Jordan drove to Birch—as far as the end of the driveway, where there had once stood a mailbox with *Syms* stenciled on it. He stared at the police car parked in front of the house.

He wondered if Sheriff Fischer was now explaining to that nice woman about the hunters and hikers who sometimes strayed too close to private property, and the teenagers who liked to party in deserted rental cabins.

Jordan turned the car around and glanced at the house in his rearview mirror.

He could almost hear the good sheriff telling the frightened woman that she and her little boy would be all right—right as rain.

CHAPTER TEN

Outside the sliding glass door, the handsome, husky blond deputy held his hands up in the air. Wearing the deputy's cap—which came down almost over his eyes—Mattie stood in front of him on the porch. He pointed his finger at the deputy and kept his thumb extended. "You're under a dress!" he proclaimed.

The deputy got a big kick out of this, but kept his hands above his head and played the part of the crook to the hilt.

Barely cracking a smile, the sheriff ignored the skit going on outside. He was a tall, paunchy man in his early fifties, with a thin grey mustache that had turned brownish-yellow at one corner—maybe from smoking a cigar or something. Hairy arms akimbo, he stood near the sliding glass door in the sunroom, beside a chair that had a basket of dirty laundry in it. At the top of the heap were Susan's bra and a pair of panties. She might have been a bit embarrassed if she weren't so worried right now about Allen's disappearance—and that creepy man in the army fatigues who had paid them a visit earlier.

Sheriff Fischer seemed to think she was overreacting about Allen. After all, her fiancé had been gone less than two hours. "Ordinarily, he would have phoned you by now, right?" Fischer said. "You know, it's too bad they yanked the landline phones out of this house when they converted it into a rental. And I'm sorry about the cell phone reception around these parts. But in some ways, it's a blessing. Just imagine how many accidents we'd have around here with kids trying to maneuver these winding roads while yakking away on their cell phones and texting and Twittering and what have you."

Sitting in one of the dining room chairs, Susan nodded. At Rosie's earlier, she'd already given the sheriff a description of Allen, what he was wearing, and his car. He'd jotted it down and told her not to worry. They'd keep a lookout for him. "I'm sure he's fine," the sheriff had said back at the store.

He was saying it again now: "I bet, any minute, your fiancé will be pulling into the driveway in that fancy black BMW of his. In the meantime, I wouldn't let this Peeping Tom business upset you, Ms. Blanchette." He put a strange emphasis on the *Ms.*—as if after forty years he still hadn't gotten accustomed to saying it. "I doubt it's this fella you say followed you down from that McDonald's in Mount Vernon—"

"Ah, it was an Arby's," Susan gently corrected him. "Why do you think—"

"Arby's, right," he nodded, interrupting her. "Nevertheless, we will keep our eyes peeled for this—" he consulted the notes he'd scribbled down at the store earlier, "Ah, red MINI Cooper you told me about."

"Thank you," Susan said. "But why do you think it couldn't be this man who followed me from Mount Vernon? As I told you, he was awfully familiar and pushy. . . ."

Sheriff Fischer tucked his little notebook in his back pocket, then cleared his throat. "Well, Deputy Shaffer and I had a good look around here, and there's no sign of an attempted break-in. It's obvious someone has recently been in the woods surrounding this house. But I don't think he's after you or your little boy. And I don't think it's this fella you're worried about. Let me show you what I mean." The sheriff turned and called over his shoulder. "Corey, would you like to come in here and join the adults? Bring in what you found."

The blond deputy took the police cap off Mattie and put it on his own head. He reached for something on the porch step and lugged it into the sunroom. It was a big rock, at least ten pounds. The bottom of it was covered with dirt.

"What is that?" Susan asked, getting up from the dining room chair.

"It's a mineral rock, a salt lick," the deputy explained, setting it down on the sunroom floor—dirt side up. "Some hunters use them as bait to lure deer or antelope. I found this in the woods over there. . . ." He pointed in the general direction of the forest bordering the driveway. "There was another one just like it about a hundred feet away." Stepping toward the sliding door, he nodded at the forest on the other side of the house. "And if you check those woods south of here, you'll find one just beyond that first set of trees near the water there. . . ."

But Susan wasn't looking toward the trees. She noticed the sheriff, staring at the basket of dirty laundry. His stubby fingers casually brushed against the top of the load, touching her bra and panties. He didn't seem too conscious or sneaky about what he was doing—just curious.

Her mouth open, Susan numbly gazed at him. She thought about saying something, but just then he took his hand away and hooked his thumb in his pants pocket. He turned to gaze out at the section of forest bordering the bay.

"You see, ma'am," the deputy was saying. "This guy's obviously been using these woods as his own little hunting ground, and he—"

"What we have here, Ms. Blanchette," Sheriff Fischer interrupted, "isn't a stalker or a Peeping Tom. We have some amateur hunter who's using this land unlawfully. And that's a serious offense around these parts. But I don't think you or your son are in any real danger." He frowned at the mineral rock on the floor, then turned to his deputy. "Get rid of that thing. And then you can go, Corey."

The younger cop seemed a bit perplexed. "Well, I can get around Ms. Blanchette's car, but your prowler is blocking me in."

With an impatient sigh, Sheriff Fischer dug into his pocket and tossed the keys at him. "Then move it, and park it back where it was after you've backed out."

"Yessir," the deputy muttered. He shoved the keys in his pocket and then hauled the rock out to the back porch. "Hey, want to help me carry this back into the woods, partner?" he asked Mattie. "Then you can ride in a police car. . . ."

"Cool!" Mattie exclaimed, chasing after him.

Outside, Mattie let out a labored grunt as he put his hands under the rock, though it was clear the deputy was toting all the weight. "We'll need to wash our hands after this," the handsome cop was telling him as they moved down the porch steps together.

"Anyway, I doubt this hunter character will be back," the sheriff said. "I saw what was left of that barrel you shot with the flare. If this joker was anywhere near there, he's not about to make a return appearance. It's kind of ironic, but most hunters I know don't like being shot at." He laughed at his own remark.

Susan tried to work up a smile.

"Anyway, you probably scared him more than he scared you." Sheriff Fischer chuckled. "I'll tell you who got the biggest fright. It was Chris over at Bayside Rentals. You really had him going with that e-mail you sent. He thought for sure you were a goner."

"So did I for a while there," Susan said. "I'm very grateful he called you."

The sheriff nodded. "Well, you got to us first. In the meantime, Ms. Blanchette, I wouldn't worry about your fiancé too much. I'm sure he's close by. If he's not in town, maybe he swung by the winery to surprise you with a bottle of wine. I know I wouldn't stray too far if I had such an attractive lady waiting for me at home."

"Well, thank you," she said coolly. She might have

been flattered if he hadn't been touching her under-things two minutes ago.

"So—do me a favor," Sheriff Fischer said. "Once your fiancé turns up, I'd appreciate it if you'd pop on over to Rosie's and give us a call. Let us know he's okay. If I don't hear from you in a couple of hours, I'll be sure to check in."

Susan nodded. "I'll do that, thank you again."

"Can I ask for another favor?" He smiled and licked his lips. "You wouldn't happen to have something cool to drink for a thirsty policeman, would you?"

"Oh, I'm sorry. Where are my manners?" Susan started backing toward the kitchen. "Would you like bottled water? I also have some Coke—*Coca-Cola*, I mean, and root beer."

"A Coke would hit the spot nicely, thank you."

She ducked into the kitchen and retrieved two cans of Coke from the refrigerator.

By the time she brought them into the sunroom, Mattie and Deputy Shaffer were back, shaking off their wet hands. "I rode in a police car!" Mattie announced excitedly. He wrapped himself around Susan's leg.

"We rinsed off our hands with the garden hose, but you better give him the soap and hot water treat-ment," the deputy recommended, grinning at her. "You don't know what kind of cooties get on those salt licks." The smile faded as he turned to his boss and gave him a set of keys. "The prowler's back just where you parked it."

Sheriff Fischer wordlessly took the keys and put them in his pocket.

"Um, here's a cold drink for the road," Susan said, handing them each a can of soda.

The deputy thanked her. Sheriff Fischer opened his Coke can, took a sip, and smiled at her. "Y'know, I can stick around—if you're still a bit uneasy and lonely."

Susan held Mattie against her. "Oh, I think we'll be all right. I'd feel better if I knew you were out there looking for Allen. Besides, I've already taken up enough of your time. Thanks."

They left by the back porch. Susan was glad to be rid of that sleazy sheriff, who made her skin crawl. She'd been so afraid he would insist on staying.

She led Mattie into the kitchen, propped him on a stepstool by the sink, and washed his hands thoroughly. "I think we'll go ahead and have our lunch," she said, with a glance out the window.

The deputy's car pulled out of the driveway. But the sheriff's car remained.

"Is Allen under a dress?" Mattie asked.

"What?" she asked, distracted for a moment. "Um, it's *under arrest*, honey. And no, the police are just going to look for Allen, and tell him to hurry home, because we're worried about him." She dried off Mattie's hands with a dish towel. "Will you be a good boy and wait for me on the back porch while I go down to the boat? I left our lunch in the little fridge there."

Mattie nodded.

Susan looked out the window again.

The sheriff's patrol car was still in the driveway. She couldn't see if anyone was actually inside the vehicle. *Why didn't he go already?* she thought.

Taking Mattie by the hand, she walked him out the sliding glass door to the back porch. He sat down on the bottom step, grabbed a long stick, and poked at the ground with it.

As she started down toward the dock, Susan turned back to wave at him. She saw the sheriff's car was still parked beside the house. She noticed something else— the red Coke can sitting on the corner of the porch railing. It was odd that the sheriff would just leave it there.

Hesitating, Susan headed back toward the house— and the driveway.

The cop car finally backed out of the drive, just as she was about twenty feet away. Susan watched him use the turnaround and then continue out the driveway. She retreated toward the house.

"Bizarre," she murmured. She glanced over at the Coke can on the railing again. "What a pig." She reached up for the empty can, and felt it was near full. Baffled, she poured it out and then pitched the can in the recycling bin by the side of the house.

Susan shrugged it off and hurried down toward the boat. Stepping around the life vests they'd abandoned on the dock earlier, she climbed aboard, unlocked the cabin door, and went below. She'd shut off the power before, so the lights didn't work. But the mini refrigerator was still slightly cold, so their lunch hadn't spoiled. Susan stashed the Tupperware container of food and the Tuscan bread into the bin with Mattie's toys. She managed to lug the bin up the stepladder to the deck and then locked the cabin door behind her. She glanced over toward the house.

For a second, her heart seemed to stop.

Mattie was gone. She didn't see him on the back porch.

"MATTIE!" she screamed, dropping the bin. She almost tripped scurrying off the boat. It rocked back and forth, and the side banged against the dock. But Susan barely noticed. She raced up toward the house. "MAT-TIE, WHERE ARE YOU?" she cried. "MATTIE!"

"I'm here, Mommy!" he called, coming around from the side yard. He still had the stick in his hand, and he waved it at her.

Susan stopped and caught her breath. "Honey, I told you to stay on the porch!" she called wearily. "Now, wait right there. . . ." Slump-shouldered, she returned to the boat to pick up the bin. She wished right now Allen would pull into that driveway "in that fancy black BMW of his." And then, after the hugs, and screaming at him, and listening to his explanations, and more hugs, she could tell him, *My God, what an afternoon I've had. . . .*

Susan carried the bin up to the house. Mattie was telling her how he'd seen a "reindeer" in the woods, and he'd gotten up to "look at it better." But the animal had apparently run away when it had seen him coming. Susan figured with all the deer, elk, and antelope bait in those woods, there would be plenty more "reindeer" around, which was just fine by her—as long as she didn't encounter that creepy hunter again.

She set the bin on the dining room table. "You can eat your lunch in front of the TV for a change, sweetie," she announced. "So go pick out a DVD, okay?"

While Mattie ran into the sunroom to pick through the collection of Disney and Pixar DVDs she'd packed, Susan shut the sliding door. She locked it—just to be on the safe side.

Passing by the laundry basket, she noticed something. Her bra and panties had been at the top of that pile of dirty laundry. The bra was still there, but the panties were gone. Susan examined the heap of clothes, just to make sure the panties hadn't somehow, miraculously, shifted among the rest of the things.

She thought about Sheriff Fischer touching them earlier, and how he'd asked for something to drink. But it turned out, he hadn't really been thirsty.

He'd just needed for her to turn her back on him for a few moments—so he could take what he wanted.

"I'm opening the trunk now," Jordan announced.

He stood in back of his Honda Civic, parked in the driveway by the cabin on Cedar Crest Way. Fortunately, Leo and Moira hadn't come back yet. Jordan had already ducked inside the house and quickly found what he'd needed—a sharp knife, some rope, and a roll of duct tape, all of which he'd taken down to the basement. He'd been in and out of the cabin in less than five minutes.

Meeker banged on the inside of the trunk's lid again. No one was likely to come by and hear him. The nearest neighbor was the woman Meeker claimed was his fiancée, staying at Jordan's old family summer home a mile and a half away.

Jordan didn't want Moira and Leo involved in this. Once he had Meeker in a secure location, he planned to pack their bags and set them out by the car. When Leo and Moira returned from their woodland walk, he'd insist they take his car and drive home. He'd claim he needed to be alone or pretend he was pissed off at them. Whatever it took, he'd get rid of them.

The skies had turned slightly overcast again. Jordan felt a chilly wind against his back as he stood by the car. In one hand, he had the car keys with the automatic opening device for the door and trunk. In the other hand he held Allen Meeker's gun.

"I'm the only one around for about a mile," Jordan announced over the incessant banging. Meeker wouldn't stop hammering and kicking the inside of the trunk's lid. "No one else can hear you, so you might as well stop all that noise and shit. Here, in case you don't believe me . . ." Jordan yelled out: *"I'VE GOT A MAN BOUND AND GAGGED IN THE TRUNK OF MY CAR! WON'T SOMEONE PLEASE COME HELP HIM?"*

The banging and pounding stopped.

"See what I mean?" Jordan asked, staring down at the small trunk. "So like I told you, I'm going to pop the trunk now, and I don't want you making any sudden movements."

He paused a moment to let that sink in.

"I have your gun," he continued. "And I won't hesitate to shoot you or hit you over the head with it if you try anything. Got that? You want to get hit over the head again? I'm figuring you don't. Tap once if you understand me."

Jordan waited. A solitary thump came from the trunk.

"Okay, I'm going to open her up now," he said. He pressed the button on the key-ring device. The trunk popped open a few inches—and stayed there.

Jordan shoved the keys in his pocket. His palm was

sweating against the gun handle in his other hand. With a cautious step toward the back of the car, he pushed open the trunk's lid all the way.

Curled up in the cramped space, Allen Meeker lay on his side. His face was crimson, and wet with perspiration and tears. The gag still filled his mouth, and his eyes seemed to plead with Jordan. Shifting a bit, he let out a sad, sickly moan. The jacket Jordan had used to tie his ankles together had come unraveled. Jordan couldn't see if Meeker's hands were still tied in back of him.

"Roll over on your other side," he said, pointing the gun at him. "I see you freed your legs. I need to check if you managed to untie your hands, too."

Nonplussed, Allen Meeker just stared back at him and blinked.

"Roll over!" Jordan barked.

Meeker nodded obediently, then turned to one side, contorting his body within the confines of the small trunk. He was trembling and looked so vulnerable in that awkward position. Jordan could see the twine, still taut around his wrists. His hands were red and slightly swollen.

Jordan put the gun to his head. "The last time I saw you was ten years ago," he said quietly. "Remember, you said you had car trouble? Funny, isn't it? That's how I got to you today. I gave you car trouble. Do you remember, Allen? Do you recall waving at my mother and me?"

Jordan remembered all of it. His mother hadn't slept well the night before, and her attempt to make pancakes in the shape of bunny heads was an utter disaster.

She had never been much of a cook, and now kept burning the pancakes or screwing up the rabbit's profile. She was trying so hard to make this mother-son weekend something special. Jordan ate her fourth attempt at a pancake and pretended it was scrumptious, even though it was a bit runny inside and one of the bunny ears had fallen off going from the spatula to his plate.

After breakfast, it was kayaking time—finally. Jordan had been looking forward to this since talking to his mother last week, when she'd said she'd bought a junior-size kayak for him. Jordan had been on sailboats and canoes before, but he'd never taken to the water on a kayak all by himself. This had promised to be a real adventure. The previous day, before their hike in the woods, she'd let him climb inside the small, yellow craft with the bucket seat—just to get the feel of it. He'd been disappointed he couldn't take the kayak out on the bay, but—at least in his mother's opinion—the water was too choppy.

The bay didn't look much better that morning. The grey sky gave the water a dull slate color—except for the ripples of small, whitecapped waves. Roped to the dock, the yellow kayak teetered on the water. His mother made him put on the orange helmet and life vest, which was okay. But he was disappointed when she insisted he practice paddling while still roped to the dock. He couldn't wait to take the kayak out on his own—on the open water. But she told him, "Just a little practice, kiddo, a few more minutes so you get the feel of it."

He remembered her standing on that dock, in a pale

blue pullover and khakis. Her blond hair was all wind-blown. When she took off her sunglasses, Jordan could see from her eyes that indeed she hadn't gotten much sleep the night before. Yet she still looked beautiful—especially when she smiled at him.

"Okay, kiddo, I'm letting you go," she said, at last. She moved toward the rope securing the kayak and started to untie it from the dock cleats. "Stay close to the dock. And the minute I wave you in, you paddle back. Understand?"

"Yeah, Mom, I will," he said. He would have agreed to anything at that moment. He just wanted to be out on the water.

Once he was on his own, it was a bit scary. The current quickly carried him away from the dock, and the small boat rocked back and forth. Biting his lip, he worked the paddle from side to side until he got a rhythm going and the craft moved more steadily.

"That's it, kiddo! You're doing great!" his mother cheered him on.

He risked taking one hand off the paddle to wave at her. The kayak teetered for just a few seconds, but he got it balanced again. Gliding farther away from the dock, Jordan watched his mom become smaller and smaller in the distance. Again, he took one hand off the paddle, just so he could look at his mother and pretend to hold her between his finger and his thumb. He had done that before, looking at people in the distance; and he often pretended to squish them. But he didn't squish his mom. He just laughed, then starting working the paddle with both hands once more.

The cool wind whipped at him, and Jordan loved it. He glanced over his shoulder at the open bay. Out on his own like this, he felt so grown-up and powerful.

"You're getting too far out now, kiddo!" his mother called. "Come on back a little. . . ."

Jordan turned to look at her. That was when he saw the dark-haired man coming around from the driveway side of the house. He wore sunglasses, a black V-neck sweater, and jeans. He walked very quickly—as if at any minute, he might break into a sprint.

Jordan immediately thought of the elusive stranger who had been spying on them the previous afternoon and all through the night. Jordan had never really seen him, but his mother had. At first, she'd been so sure their stalker was a spy for his dad, and she'd been angry about it. But later, she'd just seemed scared.

"Mom!" he screamed, "Behind you!" He took one hand off the paddle again—so he could point to the stranger. He kept stabbing his finger in the air, but she didn't seem to understand. She didn't turn around.

"Come on in, Jordan! That's too far!" She waved him in.

All the while, her back was to the man. Jordan could see him, heading down the sloped yard with that strange, determined, brisk gate. He moved so fast, his face was just a blur.

Waves jostled the kayak, and Jordan started paddling again—toward his mother. "Mom, look out behind you!" he yelled.

She must have heard him that time, because she suddenly swiveled around.

The man waved at her—and then at Jordan, out on

the water. "Sorry to bother you folks!" he called in a friendly tone, advancing toward the dock. "Maybe you could help me. I have some car trouble. . . ."

Even from a distance, Jordan could see his mother's body become rigid and tense. She took a step back as the stranger approached her. He was saying something to her, but Jordan couldn't hear it. But he saw the man's charming smile, and the way his mother seemed to relax a little. Jordan kept paddling toward them. "Mom?" he called. "Mom, what's going on?"

She turned to look at him, a smile on her face.

Jordan noticed something in the man's hand, but he was too far away to see what it was. The man hauled back—almost like a pitcher about to throw a fastball.

"Mom!" Jordan screamed.

She spun around in time to ward off the blow. But he hit her arm with that thing he had. It might have been a blackjack, Jordan wasn't sure. His mom let out a stunned cry.

For a moment, Jordan couldn't move. Trembling, he gripped the paddle, but held it against his lap. The brisk, cool wind kicked up around him, and the kayak started to teeter. But he was paralyzed—until he felt the front of his pants grow warm and wet. Then he was like a little kid, suddenly waking up once he'd wet the bed. Jordan started screaming, and he paddled furiously toward the dock. "Mom, hold on!"

But she was so far away. "Please, no, wait—wait," she cried, recoiling from the man. She was holding on to her arm. Jordan could tell she was hurt. "If you want money," she said. "My purse is in the house—please—"

Tears in his eyes, Jordan kept paddling. The kayak

rocked violently as it surged toward the dock. Cold water from the bay splashed him and sluiced inside the craft's bucket seat. But he was still too far away.

Helplessly, he watched his mother struggle with her attacker. The man knocked her down with one blow. Her sunglasses flew off her face. Jordan heard a thud as she collapsed on the dock. But she got up again and began to pummel the man with her fists.

"Goddamn it, bitch, that's enough!" the man yelled. He grabbed her by the injured arm and yanked her toward him. She shrieked in pain.

Jordan continued to paddle frantically—though his shoulders and back ached from all the effort. The dock seemed just out of reach. He was still too far away to save his mother. All he could do was scream as loudly as possible—anything to distract or delay this stranger who now had his mother in a choke hold. He raised the blackjack above his head again.

"Jordan, help—"

Those were the last words he heard his mother say. The man brought the bludgeon down on Jordan's mother's skull, and she suddenly went limp. He caught her before she crashed down on the dock's wooden planks.

"No, no, no, no!" Jordan shouted. But the man didn't even glance his way. He pulled something out from the back of his sweater and casually tossed it on the dock. Then he lifted Jordan's mother in his arms, turned, and carried her up the back lawn toward the driveway at the side of the house. He looked like a groom, carrying his limp bride toward a threshold. They disappeared behind the hedges bordering the driveway.

Jordan was crying. He was so close to the dock, but not quite there yet.

By the time the kayak rammed into the dock pilings, he heard a car revving up and tires screeching. There was no time to secure the small craft. The kayak almost tipped over as Jordan jumped out of it. Staggering onto the dock, he shed the helmet and life vest. He spotted his mother's sunglasses on the wooden planks and, beside them, something the man had left: a rubbery old Kewpie doll of a smiling sailor boy.

Jordan snatched up his mother's sunglasses. There was something inside him that thought he might be able to give them back to her.

He ran up the sloped backyard as fast as he could, toward the driveway at the side of the house. But the only car he saw there was his mother's.

Racing inside the house, he went for the phone in the kitchen, the same one his mother had used the night before to call the police. But when he took the receiver off its cradle, there was no dial tone. He cried out in frustration, then bolted upstairs to her bedroom and tried the phone on her nightstand. It was dead, too.

Panic-stricken, Jordan scurried back down the stairs and flung the front door open. Rushing outside, he saw the phone line at the side of the house was cut.

The cabin on Cedar Crest Way had no phone. Their neighbor on the bay was actually closer, but not by any paved road or path. It was a mile through a muddy, overgrown forest on the water's edge. Jordan didn't even know if they had a phone. But he had to try.

He plunged into the thicket, hoping to find a path, but it was as if no one had ever ventured through those dense woods before. Jordan kept looking through the trees at the bay to get his sense of direction. He tried to run along the water's edge, but it was just sludge that swallowed up his feet—up to his ankles. Racing through those impenetrable, muddy woods, he thought he might never find the neighbor's house. All the while, he couldn't stop crying. He couldn't stop thinking about what that horrible man might be doing to his mother.

It seemed like forever, but eventually, the ground beneath his feet became harder, and the forest thinned out. Jordan stumbled upon a gravel road and followed it to a frame-style house with big picture windows and a deck across the second floor. Sitting on a hill, surrounded by trees, it looked out at the bay. Jordan didn't see a car in the carport by the house. Staggering up to the front door, he banged on it. His face and hands were riddled with scratches. Bay water, mud, and his own urine soiled his pants.

No one came to the door. He started screaming and pounding harder and harder.

The rest was a blur. Jordan didn't remember cutting his hand when he broke a window in the back of the house and climbed inside. He had no recollection of phoning the police. And he could only take their word for it when they said they found him on the front stoop of the empty house. They said he was sobbing, half-covered in mud, and in his bleeding hand he held a pair of sunglasses.

They found his mother thirty-six hours later.

The casket remained closed at her wake. So Jordan's last glimpse of his mother had been from a distance, when he'd watched her executioner carrying her away.

And despite some false alarms, he never saw that man again—until today.

"Do you remember my mother, Allen?" Jordan asked, pressing the gun against his silver-grey temple. "Or have you forgotten her, after all the others you've killed?"

Contorted in that awkward position inside the small trunk, Allen Meeker could only respond with a confused, pathetic whimper. He seemed to be choking on the rolled-up handkerchief in his mouth.

Jordan reached for the gag. "Go ahead and scream all you want," he said. "There's no one around to hear you."

He carefully pried the handkerchief from his captive's mouth.

Allen Meeker let out a raspy sigh. "I won't scream," he whispered. "I—" But he couldn't finish. He started coughing. His face became even redder. Every time he tried to take a breath or talk, he choked and began hacking all over again.

Jordan gave the rope around his wrists a tug, just to make sure it was still tight. Then he went around to the driver's door and found a half-full bottle of Evian on the floor of the backseat. Returning to his captive, Jordan tossed the bottle into the trunk and helped him turn around to a sitting position. He kept the gun on him the whole time, but the man didn't seem to notice. He was still coughing uncontrollably.

Jordan stepped back to unscrew the water bottle cap. That took two hands, and he didn't want to be anywhere near his prisoner—not even for a few seconds—unless he had the gun ready. Once he opened the bottle, he came in closer again with the gun trained on Meeker. He put the bottle to the choking man's lips.

Meeker gagged on the first gulp, but then drank greedily. Jordan had recently seen someone lift their dog up to a drinking fountain in the park, and that was how Allen Meeker guzzled this water. It dripped from his mouth and cascaded along his neck, but he kept swigging it down.

Meeker finally turned his head slightly, and Jordan pulled the bottle away. "Please," he gasped. "Could you— could you splash some on my face? I'm burning up."

"I can't, you drank it all," Jordan replied, frowning.

"Listen, if you want money, you can—you can take my wallet," the man said, still trying to catch his breath without coughing. His voice was hoarse and gravelly. "There's only—only about a hundred bucks—"

"I already have your wallet," Jordan interrupted. He was thinking about his mother, begging the man to take her purse.

"You can have my car," Meeker said, closing his eyes in a pained way. "It's a BMW; it's nice. The keys are in my pocket."

"No, they're not. I took them and drove your car into a swamp."

Meeker gaped at him. "Are you fucking crazy? Good God, what's wrong with you? Why are you doing this?"

"Why did you kill my mother?" Jordan quickly retorted. He stuck the end of the gun barrel under the man's chin, then grabbed him by the arm and hoisted him toward the edge of the trunk.

"I don't know what you're talking about," Meeker protested. "If you—if you really think I've killed someone, why don't you call the police? I mean it, please, take me to the police station! I have people worried about me, my fiancée and her little boy." Even with Jordan pulling him, he had difficultly climbing out of the trunk. "What you're doing here is insane," he continued. "You're just getting yourself into a lot of trouble. Believe me—you're making a horrible mistake."

"Is that a threat?"

"God, no," he replied. "Listen, I'm sorry about your mother, but—but I don't even know who she is. . . ." He faltered once his feet hit the driveway. "Jesus, my legs are cramped up," he sniveled, leaning against Jordan. "I'm sorry. . . ."

Meeker staggered back like he was about to fall, but then all at once, he slammed his body into Jordan's, full force.

The gun flew out of Jordan's hand. He reeled back and landed on the paved driveway. He fell on his ass, and it hurt. But he'd encountered much worse during a normal lacrosse practice. Jordan sprung back to his feet and leapt for the gun.

Allen Meeker obviously had no use for it right now. He scurried up the driveway—in the other direction. "HELP ME!" he screamed. "SOMEBODY HELP ME! GET THE POLICE. . . ."

He must not have been completely lying about his legs, because he hobbled as he ran. Then his feet suddenly seemed to give out from under him. He slid to one side. With his hands tied behind him, there was no way to break his fall. He went crashing down into some bushes along the driveway. He cried out in pain and tried to roll over.

Jordan slowly walked over to him, the gun drawn.

Defeated, Allen Meeker gazed up at him from amid the crushed bushes. Scratch marks and the bloody gash on his cheek from the earlier fall marred his handsome face. Tears mingled with the sweat running down from his brow. "Please . . ." he whispered.

"You say you don't know who my mother was?" Jordan asked, standing over him. "Haven't you figured it out by now, *Mama's Boy*? My mother was Stella Syms, your seventh victim. And you killed her less than a mile from here."

CHAPTER
ELEVEN

"Leo, please, quit following me!" she announced. "I mean it, give it a rest. I just need to be alone for a while."

Moira had paused along the narrow path she'd been taking through the woods. It had become more and more difficult to navigate the crude trail snaking though all the trees, rocks, and foliage. Moira was afraid if she went any farther she'd get lost on her way back.

For the last ten minutes, she was almost certain Leo had been following her—at least, she hoped it was Leo. She could hear bushes rustling behind her. Yet whenever she glanced back, she didn't see anyone. A few times, she saw a shrub or a tree's low-hanging branches moving. She would call out his name, but never get an answer.

She'd hurt his feelings earlier. But Leo wouldn't get even by scaring her now. He didn't operate that way. He was a wiseass at times, but he was also one of the nicest, most dependable guys she knew. She often thought if he weren't so available, so anxious to please her, she'd be more attracted to him. When Moira had thoughts like that, she wondered if she'd ever have a normal relationship.

It would be just like Leo to trail after her and give her a bit of space—to make certain she was okay. Despite his frequent clumsy attempts to make a pass at her, he was still a gentleman. That was one reason her mother was so gaga about him. He never dropped her off; he always walked her to the door. And he always let her have the last available seat if they got on a crowded bus. So he wouldn't leave her alone in the woods, no matter how mad he was at her. But this was the fourth time she'd stopped to call out to him, and he still hadn't replied.

"Leo, I mean it," she said. "Please, go back to the cabin. It's been a while since you've had anything to eat. You don't want to have another episode like last night. . . ."

She studied the rustling bushes. It appeared as if someone or something was ducking just beneath the tops of those leaves, slowly moving toward her. She heard twigs snapping.

Maybe it wasn't him after all. Maybe it was some forest creature.

"Leo, is that you?" she asked loudly.

Whatever it was, it stopped moving.

A chill raced through her. Moira remembered last night, when she'd thought an intruder had snuck into the house—and this morning, when she'd caught someone spying on her in the shower. Maybe she wasn't so paranoid after all.

"Who's there?" she asked. There was no response,

but she saw some branches shift ever so slightly in that same spot.

"LEO?" she screamed. "LEO, CAN YOU HEAR ME? LEO!"

Moira hoped to hear him call back to her in the distance. But there was nothing. She started to back away. Glancing down around her feet, she found a rock about the size of a baseball. It was covered with dirt and worms. But she snatched it up and quickly brushed it off. She kept walking backward, feeling her way along the path with her free hand. She didn't dare turn around at this point. She clutched the rock and watched as something just below the tops of the shrubs made its way toward her.

"Get out of here!" she yelled. Moira held onto the rock to defend herself. But she grabbed some smaller rocks along the path and hurled them in the general direction of the disturbance. If an animal was in the brush, she didn't want to hurt it; she just wanted to scare it away.

Then again, maybe she was provoking the damn thing. She wasn't sure. She'd heard that these Pacific Northwest woodlands had everything from bears to cougars to wolves. Any minute now, that creature could emerge from those bushes and come charging at her.

Worse, it could be a two-legged creature preying upon her.

"Shit," she murmured. She finally turned and started running, but the path seemed to disappear—until she was randomly zigzagging around trees and shrubs, going wherever she could find even the narrowest pathway. Moira had no idea where she was headed, but she kept moving. And she kept the rock clutched in her hand.

She finally came to a clearing and realized she was at the summit of a slope. She looked down at the tops of trees. In the distance below, she noticed a gap, a long, narrow channel that wove through the woods. At first, Moira thought it was a stream. But then, through the foliage, she glimpsed a blessed sight: a blue SUV sped along that trail. She was looking down on its roof. That wasn't just a clearing down there. It was a road— *civilization, at last.*

"Thank you, God," she murmured. She was fed up with these woods, sick of feeling so lost and scared. On top of that, she was hungry.

Moira guessed that wonderful, paved road was about two or three blocks away, which through this thicket would seem like a mile. But at least she knew where she was headed now—and it was all downhill. There would be other cars after that SUV. She might even be able to catch a ride back to the cabin.

Moira held on to the rock as she started running again. She thought about how she might square things with Leo. Maybe they'd actually have a nice time tonight celebrating his birthday. Jordan had made reservations at some ritzy waterfront restaurant in downtown Cullen—probably the *only* ritzy place in Cullen. She'd brought along a knockout, sleeveless black dress for the occasion, beaded around the neckline, very sophisticated and adult.

She discovered a wider trail easier to navigate and realized she must be close to the road by now. She let the rock slip out of her hands. Moira started giggling as she thought about how freaked out she'd been by that thing in the woods back there. It was probably just a fawn or a squirrel, for God's sake.

Following a curve in the path, she stepped through a pile of leaves, and suddenly, the ground seemed to drop out from under her. Moira heard this loud crackling and splintering sound. All at once, she was falling. She let out a scream and tried to grab at something. But there was nothing to stop her from tumbling into the chasm below. Moira hit the bottom of the trench, feet-first. A searing pain shot through her left foot. She heard something snap, then she collapsed. Leaves, dirt, twigs, and broken branches crashed down on top of her.

Moira got the wind knocked out of her. Struggling for a breath, she tried to wipe the dirt out of her eyes. It was in her mouth, too. Coughing, she sat at the bottom of the pit. It took her another few moments to realize what had happened. The cloud of dust and grit finally cleared above her, and she looked up at the patch of sky. She felt like she was in an empty grave in a cemetery plot, only much deeper, maybe eight or ten feet down.

The top part of the pit was lined with wood supports that had turned black from years of underground moisture. Moss grew between the beams. Below that, the walls to the rest of the hole were just dirt and rock. Moira was cold, and with every breath she took, she could taste dirt. The place smelled like moist, decaying leaves and mud. She guessed someone had meant to dig a well here decades ago, but they'd given up after a while.

At first, Moira thought a bush had taken root and grown at the very top of the hole. That was why she'd mistaken it for a pile of leaves. But as she squinted at the splintered limbs hovering above her, she saw all their leaves were dead. Someone had stuck branches between the cracks of those wood supports along the top—to cover the hole.

Moira was still stunned and catching her breath at the bottom of the deep trench. She hadn't tried to move yet. She lay there and wondered why in God's name someone would camouflage a pit that way. Didn't they realize a person could easily fall into this concealed hole—and be trapped here? Didn't they know something like this might happen?

Then it dawned on her.

Of course they knew.

Leo thought about turning back to make sure Moira was okay.

With a long, thin branch he'd found, he tapped the trees along the trail. Just up ahead was the hot spring where he and Jordan had gone skinny-dipping last night. They'd had a blast—until his stupid diabetic episode. It was probably just as well Moira hadn't come along with them. Truth be told, she'd been right. The main reason he'd wanted her to join them had been so he could catch a glimpse of her naked. But when he thought about it now, it would have been a drag with her there—even if he hadn't had his diabetic meltdown. She probably would have kept her bra and panties on—and made a big deal out of that.

He still couldn't believe she'd accused him of peeking at her while she was showering this morning. Did she really think he was that desperate and creepy?

He wasn't going back there. She'd told him, "Leave me the fuck alone." How much clearer could she have been?

Frowning, Leo lumbered along the forest trail, occasionally kicking at a rock in his path. *Some birthday so far*, he thought. He was eighteen and still felt like a skinny, inexperienced kid. He was graduating this year, too. What was it going to say under his picture in the yearbook? Not much. Because of his diabetes and his work schedule busing tables at the country club, he couldn't go out for any sports. So he wasn't a jock. He couldn't drink and be a party boy—even if he wanted that. And he wasn't part of the theater crowd either. If not for his friendship with Jordan, he'd be a total nobody. So what the hell would it say under his name in the yearbook anyway?

CHARLES LEO FORESTER
"Leo"
Social Club Vice President,
Garfield Big Brothers, Spanish Club
Pathetic Virgin

Sometimes, he got really sick of being the "nice guy" all the hot girls' *mothers* adored. He had to go to another school to find a girl who actually liked him and made him feel important. Moira Dancey was smart, pretty, and funny—and not like anyone else he knew. But every time he tried to get romantic with her—even just a coy, suggestive remark or a hand on her knee or shoulder—Moira's response was something along the lines of "Oh, God, gross, cut it out, Leo!" or "I don't think of you that way!" And he'd feel like an asexual reject-loser. More than anyone, she knew how to humiliate him. It was awful getting that kind of treatment from someone he really liked and felt so comfortable with.

Before crossing over some rocks in the narrowest part of the spring, Leo turned back and glanced at the trail behind him. He thought he had heard Moira yell out his name. He started to backtrack—to get away from the babbling stream and listen for her voice again.

"MOIRA!" he hollered. "MOIRA, ARE YOU OKAY? I JUST WANT TO MAKE SURE YOU'RE ALL RIGHT!"

He retraced his steps along the trail, hoping to hear her answer him. He had a gut instinct that something was wrong. Plus he felt pretty lousy for making her cry earlier. But what had upset her most was the revelation that Jordan wasn't interested in her and that he was embarrassed by her flirting.

Yeah, he was being hurtful when he'd told her what Jordan had said. Jordan had actually said those things, too—but coming from him, it hadn't seemed so critical and cruel.

Jordan had also said that he was wasting his time with Moira: "I think she's pretty and nice and all. But you ought to find yourself a girlfriend who doesn't act like she's about to hurl every time you try to kiss her."

He had a point.

Still, Leo couldn't help worrying about her right now. She was unfamiliar with these woods. Of course, he wasn't exactly Daniel Boone. He didn't know the area very well himself. He'd stayed at the Prewitts' Cullen cabin only twice before.

The first time had been when he was twelve, shortly after Jordan's family moved down from Bellingham. He was Jordan's first friend in Seattle. They went everywhere together on their Schwinns. Leo was in awe of the Prewitts' big-screen TV and the *Penthouse* collection Mr. Prewitt had hidden in a drawer in his walk-in closet. But they spent most of their time at Leo's house, where his dad helped them organize weekend softball games in the park with some of the other neighborhood kids and their dads. Mr. Prewitt never came. That first trip to Cullen was an overnight with Jordan and Mr. Prewitt. It was just about the only time Jordan's dad ever did anything with them, and he was nice enough, but not exactly Mr. Personality.

The second trip had been almost two years ago, a weekend with just Jordan and him. Leo had recently been diagnosed with diabetes, and later that same month his dad had been killed in Iraq. "We're taking the Cullen Cure-All," Jordan had promised him. And he was right, that weekend was the first bit of fun Leo had experienced since finding out his dad had died in the jeep accident. They had some good laughs—and they'd cried, too. It was the only time Leo had seen Jordan cry. "Your dad was really cool, man," Jordan explained. "I liked him a lot."

On that trip, he also talked briefly about his dead mother, and how much he missed her. Leo figured they had something else in common now, both having lost a parent in an automobile smash-up. But when he pressed Jordan for details about the accident—how it had happened exactly—he hit a wall. "I really don't remember the specifics," Jordan told him. "I was eight at the time.

I've asked my dad for more information, but he doesn't like to talk about it. Guess I don't like talking about it either. . . ."

They'd spent a lot of time hiking that weekend, too.

Leo had been able to refresh his memory hoofing to the hot spring last night. So while no expert on the terrain, at least he knew his way around better than Moira.

He was near where they'd parted company earlier. This spot with the three tall evergreens in a row looked familiar. He saw some movement in a clump of bushes off the pathway ahead. Leaves rustled.

"Moira?" he called. "Is that you?"

A deer suddenly scurried across the trail in front of him. It gave him a scare, but he caught his breath and scoped the area again. "MOIRA!" he yelled. "ARE YOU THERE? MOIRA, ANSWER ME!"

There was no response.

Leo started to feel a bit light-headed. He'd brought along a small, Halloween-size Nestlé Crunch bar in case of an emergency. But he needed something more substantial to keep his levels right.

Leo called to Moira several more times before turning back. He didn't want to leave her alone there, but figured he wouldn't do her much good passed out in these woods. He'd go back to the cabin, wolf down some food, and then return with Jordan. The two of them would find her—if she was indeed lost.

By the time he made it back to the hot spring, he'd eaten the Nestlé Crunch and felt steadier. He called out for Moira a few more times. Maybe she'd discovered another trail and hiked back to the cabin on her own.

Leo continued along the pathway until he finally saw the cabin through the trees ahead. Emerging from the woods, he noticed Jordan's car parked in the drive-way, near the back of the house. On his way to the back door, Leo looped around to the car. Peeking inside, he checked out the gift-wrapped package and what was unmistakably a bakery cake box.

With a tired grin on his face, he turned and started down the flagstone walkway for the kitchen door. He hoped Moira would be there with Jordan, waiting for him. And if she wasn't, she'd be back soon enough. Then they'd smooth things over, and everything would be okay.

Leo stepped inside the kitchen and let the screen door slam behind him. "Hey, is anyone home?" he called, making a beeline to the refrigerator. He grabbed the container of orange juice that had saved him last night and guzzled the rest of it down. "Anyone?" he called again.

No one answered.

But he heard a muffled whimpering sound from an-other room. Then someone grumbled, *"Shut up, god-damn it!"* Leo didn't recognize the voice right away. It sounded a little like Jordan, but he couldn't be sure. It was too distant and muted.

Baffled, Leo closed the refrigerator door and put the empty container on the counter. Heading toward the living room, he stopped at the bottom of the stairs. It didn't sound like anyone was on the second floor. But he could still hear a person muttering and realized it was coming from the basement.

"Jordan?" he called, returning to the kitchen. He opened the basement door.

"Stay there!" Jordan yelled—with panic in his voice. "I'll be right up, man!"

Leo laughed. Obviously, his buddy was hiding some birthday surprise down in the cellar. But then he heard a weird, muffled sobbing.

A puzzled smile frozen on his face, he took a few steps down. "What's going on?"

"I mean it, get out!" Jordan shouted.

But it was too late.

"My God," Leo whispered. Stunned, he gaped at his friend in the dank, cluttered cellar. He'd never seen Jordan look so haggard and crazy. His handsome face was red and dripping with perspiration. He had a knife in one hand; the other was clenched in a fist. He held a weird kind of attack stance as he stood there, trying in vain to block Leo's view of a third person in the basement.

But Leo saw the man quite clearly. He was in his late thirties—with tears in his eyes and a wadded-up handkerchief crammed in his mouth. There were scratch marks on his face—along with a bloody gash on one cheek. His arms stretched out in front of him, he was leaning facedown over a wooden worktable. Layers of duct tape bound his hands together. A rope tied to his wrists wound around the tabletop several times. More duct tape had been used to secure his ankles to two of the worktable's thick legs.

The man stared at Leo, his eyes pleading. He tried to cry out past the gag in his mouth.

Jordan swiveled around. "Shut up!" he growled, raising his fist at the helpless man.

Leo stood on the basement stairs and shook his head in disbelief. "Jesus, Jordan, what—what the hell are you doing?"

"I didn't want you to see this," Jordan muttered, his back to him.

"But—what—" Leo couldn't even get the words out. He clutched the banister. "Why are you—"

"Go back upstairs," Jordan whispered.

"No!" Leo said. "What are you doing? Who is that?"

Jordan turned to glare at him. His breathing didn't sound normal, and he still had that strange attack stance.

"Who is he?" Leo repeated.

With the knife, he pointed at the bound and gagged man behind him. "He's *Mama's Boy*," Jordan said steadily. "Remember Mama's Boy? He killed at least sixteen women. And one of them was my mother."

CHAPTER
TWELVE

"**Y**ou definitely need some Tic Tacs or something, because your breath stinks!" the donkey with the voice of Eddie Murphy was telling Shrek.

Mattie screeched with laughter as if this were the first time he'd heard that line. Actually, this was probably his eighth viewing of *Shrek*.

Susan had tried to get him to take a nap after lunch, but he'd been too keyed up. So she'd compromised and let him lay on the sunroom sofa with a blanket over him and *Shrek* to keep him company.

With a leather-bound folder tucked under her arm, Susan glanced out the sliding glass door at the backyard. Then she went to the window above the kitchen sink and peered out at the woods. Finally, she took a long look out the living room window at the driveway. Since lunch, she'd been going through this routine every few minutes. There was still no sign of Allen. But she wasn't just keeping a lookout for her fiancé. She also needed to make sure that hunter hadn't come back.

The folder belonged to Allen, and he'd brought it along for the trip. It was full of information he'd gathered for this weekend getaway. He was always very organized when they traveled. Susan had seen him refer to the papers inside his folder a few times this week, but she'd never really looked at it herself. She'd just retrieved it from the nightstand on Allen's side of the bed upstairs.

Sitting down at the dining room table, she opened the folder and glanced at a printout of the MapQuest directions to the Cullen house—just like the one he'd given her.

In the sunroom, Mattie was giggling at the movie. This weekend vacation was supposed to be spent sailing, hiking, and appreciating the great outdoors. So far, her son had spent most of his time inside watching DVDs he'd already seen.

And so far, this *getaway* had been nothing but trouble. Allen had never really answered her question last night: "I don't understand why you felt you needed to bring a gun along this weekend. I mean, were you expecting trouble?"

There was something about his planning this trip that had seemed very rushed and forced. Early in the week, he'd suddenly decided they needed to go to Cullen. Susan wondered if he'd had some ulterior motive for this sojourn. Was there someone else he planned to see here, someone he expected trouble from?

Susan hoped to find something about his personal travel plans in Allen's folder, some clue that would help her figure out what had happened to him. He'd been gone for two and a half hours for an errand that should have taken fifteen minutes.

He had a printout with photos of the rental house here at Twenty-two Birch—along with a listing of all the dimensions and amenities. He had an e-mail confirmation, too. There was a similar printout of the boat he'd rented, *The Seaworthy,* and confirmation for that, too. Susan remembered the e-mail she'd read on the computer in the boat's cabin earlier: *We apologize again for the confusion with the other boat, and we're happy we could meet your specific request.* From the table, Susan glanced toward the dining room window at *The Seaworthy* moored at the rickety, old dock. She wondered, *Why that particular boat?*

She found a printout for a restaurant, The Willow Tree Inn, along with a coupon for a free dessert. Both the coupon and the printout had *Reservations Strongly Recommended for Weekend Dinners and Brunches* posted on it. Allen had talked about going there for dinner tonight, but they hadn't discussed a particular time yet.

She came across another page—from an Internet weather site, showing the five-day forecast for Cullen, Washington. It was supposed to go down to the mid fifties and rain tomorrow.

Finally, Susan uncovered some notes Allen had scribbled on a sheet of yellow legal paper:

CULLEN – Deprt by 8:30 Fri
–Bayside Rentals – ck everything works on boat &
  arrange delivery.
–Ck w/house rental, make sure place is cleaned.
  Pick up keys.
–Gas/coal for BBQ?

–Buy groceries.
–Sue & M arrive by 1 PM.
–SAT – sail w/Sue & M by noon for @ least 4 hrs.

Susan glanced at the back of the yellow piece of paper. It was blank. There was nothing about returning the boat or turning in the keys to the house on Sunday. Allen's notes to himself ended once he'd taken her and Mattie sailing this afternoon.

Another thing that struck her as odd: he hadn't jotted down any time for dinner at this restaurant, which *strongly recommended* reservations, and yet he'd allotted a specific time for sailing. Why did they have to sail for at least four hours?

That hunter had shown up in their yard around noon. Was that just a coincidence? It had been the same time they were supposed to be out on the boat.

There were no notes or printed e-mails indicating Allen was supposed to meet someone. But she couldn't get over the feeling it was part of a private agenda for this trip.

Susan closed the folder. If only she could, she'd pack up their stuff, load Mattie in the car, and just head straight for home right now. She really hated this place. The last straw had been the sheriff—of all people—stealing her panties.

Mattie let out a shriek of laughter in the next room.

Rubbing her head, Susan got up from the table and conducted another window check. She tried to figure it out. Allen had last been seen at Rosie's Roadside Sundries. Somewhere between there and this house, he'd disappeared. That teenager, Jordan Prewitt, he'd been at the store the same time as Allen. And he'd mentioned yesterday that he was one of their closest neighbors, a little over a mile away.

Susan went back to the dining room table and pulled a pen from her purse. She wrote on the back of Allen's MapQuest directions:

Dear A,

Where the H are you? We're worried! I even asked the local police to keep an eye out for you. I'm going nuts just sitting here waiting. Mattie and I are taking a quick drive around in hopes of finding you out and about. We'll be back within 45 min. If you get this message, just STAY PUT! Hope to see you soon!

XXXXXXX – Moi @ 2:25 pm

She'd hidden the flare gun and extra flares in the kitchen cabinet above the sink—just in case she needed it again. She retrieved the gun and some flares, then stuck them in her purse.

It was tough tearing Mattie away from *Shrek*, and then he insisted he write *HELLO!* with a smiling face in the *O* at the bottom of her note to Allen. After about ten minutes, they finally got on the road.

Rosie had mentioned where the Prewitt family cabin was, but Susan had forgotten the street name. Driving up Carroll Creek Road, she slowed down at every little avenue and private lane along the way. There was no one behind her, so she could take her time. None of the road signs jogged her memory, and she didn't notice a black BMW parked along any of those little arteries.

All the while, Mattie was in his safety seat in back with Woody, reciting his favorite lines from *Shrek* and trying to imitate the voices.

Susan decided to go to the grocery store and ask Rosie for directions to Jordy Prewitt's cabin.

"Their place is on Cedar Crest Way," Rosie told her, five minutes later. "It's really just a long private driveway. The Prewitts' cabin is the only house there. They're smack-dab halfway between here and where you're staying on Birch." She put on her glasses, and on the back of a flier, she sketched out a crude map.

Susan held on to Mattie's hand. She'd bought him a box of animal crackers.

"I'm awfully sorry your fiancé is still M.I.A.," Rosie said, leaning on the counter to draw her map. "You're smart to check with Jordan though—just to make sure he didn't see anything on his way home. Like I told you, he got sick all of a sudden and hurried out of the store while your fiancé was still—"

Rosie didn't finish. She glanced up and squinted at Susan. "Did I tell you earlier that Jordan left before your fiancé?"

Susan nodded.

Rosie sighed. "Oh, hon, I feel like the village idiot. Now that I think about it, Jordy left *after* your fiancé. He was still in the parking lot when your mister drove away." She took off her glasses. "You know, it's quite possible Jordy got a look at which direction your man was headed. At the very least, he could tell you that much."

Susan nodded again. At last, she finally had some

kind of lead. Peering over the counter, she studied the map Rosie had drawn. "So—Cedar Crest Way," she said. "Exactly how do I get there?"

In the basement of the brown-shingle cabin at the end of Cedar Crest Way, Leo was trying his best to comprehend what his friend had done. Jordan still stood between him and the helpless, gagged man face-down across the worktable. The knife ready in his hand, Jordan hadn't yet dropped that threatening stance. Leo knew his friend wouldn't ever use that knife on him. But he was almost certain that if he'd tried to pass him by and help the man, Jordan would punch his lights out.

He remained at the bottom of the basement stairs. He couldn't believe Jordan was capable of this. It didn't make any sense.

"I thought your mom died in a car accident," Leo murmured.

"I lied. I was ashamed, okay?"

"Ashamed?" Leo repeated.

Tears welled in Jordan's eyes. "I was there when he knocked my mother down and dragged her away. I was there, and I couldn't help her. I was eight years old at the time."

Baffled, Leo shook his head. The man moaned and whimpered past the gag in his mouth. His eyes kept pleading with him for some kind of intervention.

"Where's Moira?" Jordan asked. "You can't let her see this."

"She's still in the woods. She wanted to be alone. Listen, Jordan—"

"You need to do something for me," Jordan interrupted. He was still breathing hard, and his voice had a tremor in it. "Go upstairs, pack all your shit and her shit, and then wait for her outside. She can't see any of this; she can't know. I want you guys to go, just drive away. Go home. And you can't tell her about this, Leo. The biggest favor you can do for me is to forget all about it. . . ."

"C'mon, Jordan, you know I can't do that." Leo started to move toward him.

"Goddamn it!" he growled. "Do I have to tie you up, too? Because I will if it looks like you're going to screw this up for me. I swear to God . . ."

Leo took a deep breath. He wished his friend would put that stupid knife down. He pointed to the helpless man. "If this guy is a murderer—like you say—then let's call the police."

The muted whining from Jordan's prisoner suddenly escalated. Leo glanced at him, and the man nodded emphatically. Leo realized the poor guy wanted him to call the police.

"I don't trust the cops around here," Jordan said. "The sheriff's a scumbag. He let this son of a bitch get away at least twice—"

"What do you mean?" Leo asked.

"My mother was killed here in Cullen," Jordan explained. "Her family used to have a vacation house about a mile down the road—by the bay. She and my dad divorced, and I was staying with her for the weekend. The first day I got here," he turned toward his captive, "this piece of shit was stalking us. . . ."

The man started whimpering louder again, and he shook his head.

"My mom called the cops," Jordan said, almost yelling to be heard over him. "The sheriff came out and didn't do a damn thing. He treated my mother like she was crazy. And the next day, *he*"—Jordan nodded at his prisoner—"he showed up in the backyard. My mom was on the dock, and I was in a boat on the water. I watched him come down to the dock and attack my mother. He kept hitting her. I couldn't get to her in time. As much as I tried, I couldn't save her. I watched him knock her unconscious and carry her off."

The man was shaking his head adamantly. He tugged at the rope restraining his taped-up wrists; then he finally gave up and dropped his forehead against the worktable. He started crying.

Leo just stared at him—and then at his friend. It was all coming at him too fast. He still couldn't believe Jordan had been lying to him about his mother's death for so many years. Now, suddenly, he claimed to have found her killer. Leo couldn't help thinking his friend had snapped and lost his mind. Jordan didn't mess around with drugs. So what other explanation was there? Leo had never before been afraid of Jordan, but he was scared of him now.

"The sheriff didn't take it too seriously," Jordan continued, a bitterness creeping into his tone. He turned to glare at the man. "You left me a little sailor doll, your Mama's Boy calling card. The stupid sheriff thought it was mine. He didn't think to ask. He didn't think Mama's Boy would be working so far north of Seattle." Jordan rubbed his forehead. "The first few hours—the most important hours when we might have gotten to her on time—the damn sheriff hardly did anything. He just recruited a few flunky cops from neighboring communities to form a search party for her. Like I say, he just didn't take it seriously enough. What he really should have done was call the state police and the FBI. . . ."

"I don't understand," Leo murmured. "You said you saw her get abducted. You were an eyewitness. Why didn't he take it seriously?"

"Because," Jordan hesitated. "My mom had problems. He thought she'd wandered off with some guy, and I'd exaggerated about it."

"What do you mean your mom had *problems*?"

"What does it fucking matter?" Jordan screamed. He stabbed his finger in the direction of the man. "What matters is that he beat and strangled my mother to death. Then he came back. He got past the sheriff and all those other idiot cops and dumped her body in the forest by our house." Jordan swiveled around and grabbed his prisoner by the hair. Yanking his head back, he put the knife to his throat.

"No, Jordan!" Leo yelled, rushing to stop his friend. "Jesus, please, wait . . . don't . . ."

"You probably thought you were being so damn clever," he growled into the man's ear. His hand shook as he traced a thin line of blood on his prisoner's neck with the knifepoint. "Weren't you the smug bastard? Sneaking past all those police and throwing her in those woods so close to where you took her? I bet that gave you a big rush. Did it make you feel superior?"

"Please, Jordan, stop it!" Leo cried. "You don't do this kind of thing! The Jordan I know—the one who's my friend—he wouldn't do anything like this. . . ."

Jordan pulled the knife away from the man's throat, then let go of his scalp.

The man started coughing behind the gag in his mouth. His head slumped against the worktable, and his whole body shook.

Jordan stepped away from him. The knife slipped out of his hands and clanked on the cellar floor. Leo almost recoiled as his friend came toward him. But Jordan put his arms around him. "Oh, God, Leo," he cried, hugging him fiercely. "My mom was naked when they found her. He'd stripped off all her clothes. My mom . . . she always used to get so cold at night. . . ."

Leo felt his friend's tears against the side of his face. He patted his back and looked over at the man. He was crying, too—and choking. Leo wondered how he could breathe with a nose full of snot and that gag in his mouth.

"C'mon, buddy, sit down," Leo whispered, leading Jordan to the stairs. With a sigh, Jordan sank down on the third step from the bottom. He wiped his eyes.

Leo patted him on the shoulder. "I'm going to take the gag out of his mouth so he doesn't choke to death, okay?"

Jordan numbly stared down at the cement floor.

Leo went back to the man and carefully pulled at the wadded-up handkerchief in his mouth. "My God," he murmured. "This is really crammed in here. . . ."

Once Leo had pried out the handkerchief, the man gasped and went into a coughing fit. His scratched face was beet-red, and Leo stared at the veins protruding on the side of his forehead. "Thanks," he finally whispered in a raspy voice. "Thank you." Then he lapsed into another coughing fit.

Leo hurried over to the laundry sink. He grabbed a

plastic measuring cup off the top of the washer and filled it with water. But it foamed over with suds. He kept rinsing out the cup, and then filled it up and tasted it. There was still a faint under-taste of soap, but he figured the guy didn't care. He took the cup to him, and the man slurped it down. "Thank you," he said again. "My face is burning up. Please, if you could . . ."

Grabbing the handkerchief, Leo went to the sink again and ran the handkerchief under the faucet. He glanced over his shoulder at Jordan.

His friend stared back at him. "I'm not letting him go," he said quietly.

Leo returned to the man and patted his face with the cool, wet handkerchief. The guy hadn't been kidding. His face was hot, like something was cooking under the skin. Leo did his best to clean the dirt and dried blood off the gash on his cheek. This close, he could see a horrible bruise forming on his forehead—and a second bump on his skull, the bloody clot partially obscured by his thick, silver-black hair. Leo couldn't believe Jordan had done this to the man.

"Please," the man whispered. "Please, you need to call the police. . . ." He coughed again. "Your friend is making a terrible mistake. If I was really a murderer, would I be begging you to get the police?"

Leo looked back at Jordan.

"I wouldn't be surprised if he and the sheriff had some kind of deal," Jordan said. "I've read everything there is about Mama's Boy. I've become an expert on the subject. One of the theories was that Mama's Boy must have had a police connection of some sort, and that's why he was always able to keep one step ahead of the investigators. For a while there, they even thought Mama's Boy was a cop." He glared at the man and then shook his head at Leo. "No police."

"If you don't trust the sheriff here, then call the state police," the man argued. He glanced at Leo. "I don't care who you call. Just get me some help, please. He hit me in the head and knocked me out *twice*. I feel nauseous. For all I know, I could have a concussion. I belong in a hospital. . . ."

"You belong in the fucking electric chair," Jordan grumbled.

Leo turned to Jordan. "His forehead's awfully hot. He could be really sick."

"My fiancée and her son are waiting for me," the man explained. "We came up here for the weekend—from Seattle. They're probably climbing the walls wondering what's happened. . . ."

"That's bullshit," Jordan said, standing up. He clutched the banister. "You told me the kid was four years old. I saw your car, asshole. There wasn't a child seat in the back. There was nothing in that car to indicate a kid had ever been in it. You're lying."

"We came up in separate cars!" the man cried. "I wanted to open the rental house and rent a boat before she got up here—so it would be all ready for her. They drove up in an old-model red Toyota yesterday afternoon. Damn it, go to Twenty-two Birch and ask. Her name is Susan Blanchette, and her son's name is Matthew. We've known each other a year. Check it out, I'm telling the truth."

His mouth open, Jordan stared at him and blinked.

Leo remembered the woman with the little boy at the store yesterday. Jordan had shown some interest in her. Leo turned toward the man. "Is your fiancée thin and kind of tall—really pretty with dark brown hair?"

The man nodded. Then he looked at Jordan. "She got a flat tire yesterday in practically the same spot I did. Were you responsible for that, too?"

Jordan said nothing.

"Did you sabotage her car the way you did mine?" the man pressed.

Jordan shook his head. "No. And you're here to *answer* questions—not ask them." He stepped down to the bottom of the stairs, then reached behind his back. From the waist of his jeans, he pulled out a gun that had been hidden by his shirttail.

"My God," Leo murmured. His first inclination was to back away, but he held his ground between Jordan and the man. He'd never seen his friend with a gun before.

"Do you always take a Smith & Wesson along on family vacations?" Jordan asked.

The man seemed stumped for a moment. "It's registered," he said. "I bought it because I was carjacked once. I wasn't sure about the area here, so I brought it along—just to be safe."

Jordan cracked a tiny smile. "Didn't quite work out for you, did it?"

"Owning a gun doesn't make me a killer," the man argued. "I've never used it."

"You're right, *Mama's Boy*," Jordan replied. "You strangled all your victims—after stripping them and beating the hell out of them. But I'll bet you used a gun plenty of times—when you abducted those women. Not with my mom, you beat her unconscious with a blackjack before you took her away. But there were others. You must have had a gun on Anita Breckinridge at that Safeway in Lynnwood. How else would you have persuaded her to leave her kid sitting in the shopping cart and quietly walk out of the store with you? You must remember Anita, Allen. That was just a few days after Christmas, 1997. Poor Anita never got to see the New Year. You left her body by a jogging trail off Lake Union in Seattle."

Stepping closer to the worktable, Jordan showed him the Smith & Wesson revolver. "Was this the gun you used so she'd cooperate? Did you stick this pistol in Melanie Edgars' back? Is that why she went with you? All the newspapers wondered why a mother would suddenly leave her three-year-old son unattended in the kiddy pool. That was at the Burien Park and Recreation Center in the summer of 2000. You left a little plastic pail and shovel by Melanie's beach blanket. You held on to Melanie longer than the others—three days. Then you killed her and dumped her body on the beach in West Seattle. . . ."

"Oh, God, please," the man whispered to Leo. "You have to do something. This is insane. . . ."

Leo stared at his best friend. Jordan was practically a stranger to him. His buddy had never even hinted he knew about these murders. Yet obviously, he had all the names, places, and approximate dates committed to memory.

He wondered how Jordan could be so certain this man was his mother's killer. It had happened ten years ago. And from Jordan's own telling, he'd been in a boat on the bay, some distance from his mother and the man who had abducted her.

"Listen, I'm sorry your mother was murdered," the

man said. Stretched over the worktable, his whole body trembled. "That's horrible, and I—I—don't blame you for wanting to get even with somebody—*anybody*—for what happened to her. But you have the wrong guy, Jordan. You've made a terrible mistake. I'm begging you to call the police. I won't press charges. I'm just asking you to do the right thing, the sensible thing. If I'm really a murderer, the police won't let me go. And if you're wrong, you've just made a dumb, forgivable mistake. The only thing I'd ask is that you get some counseling."

"Nice try," Jordan said.

But Leo moved toward him and took hold of his arm. He pulled his friend away from their captive, toward the dust-covered washer and dryer. "What he's saying makes sense, Jordan," he whispered. "Let me drive over to that grocery store and call the state police. If this guy's really a killer, then they've got him. And they have you as a witness. . . ." He trailed off because Jordan was shaking his head. "What? What is it?"

"I need to talk to him first," he insisted. "I need to get a confession out of him."

"Well, how are you going to do that?" Leo asked. "Do you plan to *torture* him? Y'know, even innocent people will plead guilty when they're being tortured. Is that what you're going to do next? My God, Jordan, he's already been hit over the head and knocked unconscious twice. He's scared. You heard him, his fiancée and her kid are waiting for him, worried about him. How can you be so sure he's the one?"

Jordan put his hand on Leo's shoulder and leaned in close to him. "After he killed my mother," Jordan whispered, "the police and this special Mama's Boy task force had me look at all these books full of mug shots. They were hoping I might identify the guy who took her. Like I told you, I was eight years old, Leo. My mom was just murdered, and I was sitting there in this crummy police station, poring through hundreds of photos of criminals—rapists, sex offenders, and murderers. But I didn't find him in those books. I never saw that man again, not until today."

"Goddamn it!" the man bellowed. "Get me out of here. . . . Please!"

"Shut the hell up!" Jordan snapped at him.

"I still don't understand how you can be so sure he's the one," Leo whispered.

Jordan took a deep breath and then leaned in closer to him. "I heard him talking to my mother—very friendly at first. But then he hit her, and he called her a bitch. Even though I was pretty far away, I could hear him. I pissed in my pants, Leo. I was so horrified—and helpless. Earlier today, while I was in the store," he nodded toward the man, "*he* came in. I just heard his voice, and I almost pissed in my pants again."

"Then let me go call the state police," Leo said.

"No, what I need you to do is keep Moira away," Jordan insisted. "She could be back here any minute now, and she can't see this. She can't be a part of it. Drive her in to town, drive her home, I don't care what you do. Just keep your girlfriend out of here. I need some time with this scumbag."

Leo hesitated. He was afraid of what might happen if he left Jordan alone with the man.

Jordan rubbed his shoulder. "Like I told you before," he said under his breath. "I know everything there is to know about Mama's Boy. I'll catch him in a lie. I'll get a confession out of him."

Leo pulled away. His eyes wrestled with Jordan's. "And then what?" he asked. "What are you going to do with him then?"

Jordan stared at him and said nothing.

They both already knew the answer.

CHAPTER THIRTEEN

If any hikers had been roaming around that sloped section of woods, they might have noticed a pale grey object moving back and forth, hovering just above the ground. They might have heard a young woman crying for help.

But Moira had a feeling no one was around for miles.

She'd found part of a tree branch in the pit. Shedding her heather-grey sweater, she'd tied it to one end of the branch. She'd tried to stand up, but felt a sharp, grinding pain whenever she put her weight on her left foot.

So Moira leaned against the dirt wall of the pit. Even with her arm stretched above her head, it was still at least three feet from her fingertips to the top of the narrow trench. Her arm was tired from endlessly waving the makeshift flag over her head. Plus she had a cramp in her one good leg from standing on tiptoe for so long. All her screaming had left her throat sore and dry.

Moira had checked her wristwatch a few minutes ago: 2:30. She'd been stuck in this godforsaken pit for over an hour now. She'd tried several times to climb up the dirt walls, but her foot kept giving out on her. And there was nothing to hold on to—except fistfuls of loose soil and rocks.

The dark, dank hole smelled. In just her T-shirt and jeans, Moira shivered from the cold. She still had dirt in her mouth and in her nose, too. Mud, twigs, and God only knew what else had gotten tangled in her hair. She would have killed for a glass of water—and a couple of Tylenol. Every part of her body ached.

Every once in a while she heard a car in the distance driving along the road up ahead. Yet, obviously, they couldn't hear her screaming for help.

Moira also detected some noises in the woods—and not just birds chirping. She'd heard bushes rustling and an occasional scurrying sound. She figured it was wildlife in the forest, but she yelled out for help anyway—just in case.

Her arm was getting numb. She lowered the crude banner, then rubbed her shoulder and shook her arm to get the blood flowing again. She told herself that Leo and Jordan would start looking for her soon. They'd find her before sundown. She just had to hang in there.

She felt something crawling on the side of her neck. She let out a shriek and frantically swiped it off. Moira shuddered. She didn't see what kind of bug it was, but she figured there were more of the same down in the bottom of this smelly pit.

She heard high-pitched squealing in the distance, and she looked up at the patch of sky above her. At first Moira thought it was a flock of birds squawking. But then she recognized the sound as it got louder, more distinct. She listened to the same racket every day between classes in the hallways of Holy Names Academy. It was the sound of several girls—all talking, laughing, and screaming at once. Right now, it was a wonderful noise.

Moira quickly hoisted the makeshift flag and waved it above the edge of the crater. "HEY!" she screamed. "HELP ME! PLEASE, HELP ME, I'M TRAPPED!"

The din grew louder, and Moira guessed there were several girls—probably in an SUV or a small bus. Obviously, the windows were open. They had music booming. They were all talking over each other. It sounded like a party.

Moira kept screaming for help and waving the stick. She forgot about her ankle for a second and jumped up. When she came down on her foot again, the crushing pain shot through her leg, and she fell on her side amid all the mire and mud at the bottom of the pit.

The laughter and music faded, and Moira started crying. She picked up her sweater and saw that the branch she'd been using as a flagpole had snapped in two.

She had no idea how long she sat sobbing—and praying to God to get her out of there. But after a while, Moira wiped her tears with her sweater. Then she put it on. She was still shivering, but it was an improvement.

As she started to push herself up again, Moira felt something hard and bulky under her hand. Brushing away some dirt and dead leaves, she saw a blinking red light at the top of a device that looked like a clunky old answering machine. "What the hell?" she murmured. It felt heavy when she picked it up. Duct tape covered the back of it. She held the thing in the light and brushed some more dirt off it until she could read the printing across the side: SPY-TELL 300 MOTION SENSOR.

It confirmed what she'd thought when she'd first fallen into the pit. Someone was setting a trap here. Did the blinking red light mean somebody close by was picking up the signal on this device? They had to be in the vicinity. A small, portable thing like this couldn't have much of a range.

Moira wondered if a hunter had created this trap. But what kind of lame-ass sportsman would catch his game this way? Trap some creature in a pit rigged with a motion detector, and then come shoot it—if the poor animal hadn't already broken its neck in the fall? Yeah, that was really sporting. It didn't make sense.

She stared at the blinking red light on the device. If this was a lazy, dilettante hunter's trap for killing game, Moira shuddered to think that she might be sitting in dried animal blood. With reluctance, she felt around for shell casings or bullets. She imagined the creep who considered this way of hunting *sport*. Yet he might end up becoming her rescuer. Maybe he was on his way right now, with his gun loaded, eager to kill whatever defenseless creature lay in wait for him. Moira kept feeling around in the mud, twigs, and decaying leaves. She didn't find any shell casings or bullets.

But then her fingers brushed against something else. She grabbed it and then rubbed the dirt off it. She looked at it in the light from the opening up above.

"Oh, no," she gasped, tears filling her eyes. "Oh, my God, no . . ."

Moira suddenly realized what kind of game this cold-blooded hunter had caught down here in the past.

In her trembling hand, she held a woman's tortoise-shell barrette.

"I'll go pack Moira's stuff, wait outside for her, and send her away in your car," Leo said. He glanced over at Jordan's prisoner stretched across the worktable. Then he locked eyes with his best friend. "I won't say anything to her, I promise. But I'm not going with her, Jordan."

They stood in the corner of the cellar's big room—by an old blue plastic kiddy pool leaning against the wall and covered with dirt and dust. The man was out of earshot.

"You have to go," Jordan whispered. "You can't be part of this, Leo. You can't be involved."

"It's too late, I'm already up to my eyeballs in it," he argued. "Have you even thought this through, Jordan? I mean, the police are going to find his car soon. They'll be looking for him—"

"They won't find his car," Jordan replied, shaking his head.

"How can you be so sure?"

"Because I sunk it in a swamp about a mile away from here," Jordan said.

Leo stared at him and felt sick to his stomach. "You—you wouldn't have done that unless you were planning to kill this guy. You're going to make him disappear, aren't you?"

Jordan didn't answer.

There was a noise outside, gravel crunching under

tires. Leo glanced up toward the dirt-streaked basement window, but some bushes outside blocked his view.

"Jesus," Jordan murmured. He hurried toward his prisoner.

"HELP!" the man screamed. "HELP ME, PLEASE! DOWN HERE!"

Leo heard the car outside grinding to a halt in the driveway.

The man kept crying out for help. Jordan grabbed the handkerchief and wound it into a ball. He tried to stuff it into the man's mouth, but his prisoner kept turning his head away. "HELP ME! GOD, PLEASE HELP ME!" he yelled.

Leo heard a woman's muted murmuring as she talked to someone, and then the car door shut. Cell phones didn't work in these woods, so she wasn't talking on the phone. There had to be at least two people outside.

Jordan finally grabbed the man by the scalp and slammed his head against the worktable. The man gritted his teeth, but Jordan hit him in the ribs. His prisoner let out a yell, and Jordan forced the gag into his mouth.

Someone knocked on the front door. The sound carried down to the cellar as if it were just outside the room.

Jordan turned to Leo and hissed, "Whoever it is, get rid of them!"

Leo nodded and headed for the stairs. But Jordan rushed toward him and grabbed his arm. "Don't screw this up for me, Leo," he whispered. "I can hear you down here, you know. I'm counting on you."

Jordan's prisoner tried to cry out past the gag, but it was just muted whimpering.

Leo couldn't quite look Jordan in the eye. He nodded again. "I'll get rid of them," he muttered. Then he hurried up the stairs.

The person outside knocked again—longer and louder this time.

In the kitchen, Leo found a pen in a glass jar on the counter. He didn't see any paper, so he grabbed a napkin and scribbled on it. The thin paper tore in spots as he wrote:

SEND FOR THE POLICE. NO GUNS!!
MAN TRAPPED IN BASEMENT NEEDING
HELP . . . HURRY!

There was more knocking. Leo knew he was taking way too long to get to the door. Downstairs, Jordan had to suspect something was going on. "Coming!" Leo called, folding up the napkin. "Just a minute!"

He hurried to the front door and opened it.

He recognized the woman from the store yesterday, the pretty brunette. Standing on the front stoop, she wore a dark green windbreaker and jeans. Behind her was an old red Toyota, with the back window rolled down. Leo glimpsed her toddler in the child's safety seat in back. He had an animal cracker in his hand and was walking it along the edge of the open window.

"Sorry I kept you waiting," Leo said, a little out of breath. He stood in the doorway.

"Well, I'm sorry to bother you, so I guess we're even," the woman said with a timid smile. "My name's

Susan Blanchette. I understand Jordan Prewitt lives here."

Leo nodded a few more times than necessary. "Yes, but he—um, he's not in right now."

"Well, I was hoping he could help me with something. Do you know when he'll be back?"

One hand still on the doorknob, Leo shook his head and shrugged. "Sorry."

"I'm staying down the road at Twenty-two Birch Way," she explained. "My fiancé has disappeared. His name is Allen Meeker. He's a good-looking man in his late thirties—with silver-black hair. He drives a black BMW. . . ."

"Um, I wish I could help you," Leo said stiffly. Then he held out the folded napkin.

But she didn't see it. She was glancing just past his shoulder.

"Are you looking for me?"

Leo swiveled around to see his friend emerging from the kitchen and quickly stashed the napkin in his pocket.

Jordan looked a bit sweaty and frayed, but he put on his friendliest smile as he approached the fiancée of his hostage. Leo stepped aside. Jordan put a hand on his shoulder. "I was in the bathroom." He turned toward the man's fiancée. "Hi, again, how are you? Did I hear right? Did you lose somebody?"

She nodded. "Yes, my fiancé. I understand you were at Rosie's place when he was there—almost three hours ago. That's the last anyone has seen of him. I was hoping you could tell me something—anything. Did he by any chance talk to you?"

Jordan shook his head. "To tell you the truth, I didn't notice much. I wasn't feeling so well. In fact, I thought I was going to blow chow right there in Rosie's." He chuckled. "Huh, guess I had a bad ice cube last night. . . ."

She stared at him and blinked.

"I was hungover is what I'm saying," Jordan explained. "Hey!" He suddenly grinned and waved at the little boy in the car. "Hey, there, dude! How are you?"

Her son waved back excitedly. "Go Huskies!"

Jordan nodded and gave him a thumbs-up sign.

"You were very nice to us yesterday," the woman said to him. "Thank you."

Leo started to step back, thinking he might be able to signal to her somehow.

But then Jordan casually put his arm around him. He gave the man's fiancée a contrite smile. "Well, I'm sorry I can't be more helpful today."

But she wasn't giving up. "Rosie said you were in the parking lot when Allen drove away. Did you happen to see in which direction he drove off?"

Jordan thought about it for a moment. "It looked like he was heading toward town—that is, if I remember correctly. Like I said, I was kind of out of it."

Leo could hear a faint whimpering sound from downstairs. Jordan must have heard it, too, because he stepped outside and started leading Allen Meeker's fiancée toward her car. Leo trailed after them. He wondered if there was some way he could furtively slip the napkin into her hand.

"Not to alarm you or anything," Jordan said to her in a hushed voice. "But you don't suppose he got carjacked, do you?"

She shrugged. "I don't really know."

"Has anything like that ever happened to him before?" Jordan asked. "I mean, that looked like a pretty nice car he was driving. BMW's a classic. No one's ever tried to carjack him?"

She shook her head. "I don't think so."

"Well, maybe he got lost," Jordan said. "Does he know this area? Has he been to Cullen before?"

"No, this is our first trip here."

"Oh, right, you told me that yesterday." Jordan nodded. "Um, have you guys been together long?"

"About a year," Susan replied.

"You mentioned yesterday you live in Seattle. Is that where you guys met?"

"Yes. But listen, I—"

"Is your fiancé from Seattle originally?"

"No, he grew up near Chicago." She gave him a puzzled half smile. "I'm sorry. Why are you asking me all these questions about Allen?"

"Well, I wasn't being nosy," he said with a nervous laugh. "I—I just thought if I asked about him, it might help you figure out where he went off to. Y'know, trigger something in your memory? But I guess it didn't work, huh?"

Her gaze shifted from Jordan to Leo, then back again. "Didn't I see a young woman with you yesterday?"

Hands in his pockets, Leo nodded. "Yeah, that's Moira, but she went for a—a walk in the woods." He furtively took the napkin out of his pocket.

"You don't suppose she might have seen Allen, do you?"

"Who, Moira?" Jordan said. He shook his head. "I really doubt it."

"Well, could you check with Moira when she gets back from her walk? I'd be very grateful. . . ."

"Sure, no sweat," Jordan replied. "We're expecting her back soon."

"Maybe she noticed Allen or his car somewhere. Again, his name is Allen Meeker. He's about six feet tall, good looking—"

"Silver-black hair, little scar on his cheek, late thirties," Jordan finished for her. "And he drives a black BMW. I'll remember." He opened the driver's door for her.

Eyes narrowed, she stopped to stare at him. "I never mentioned Allen had a scar."

"Really?" Jordan let out a skittish laugh. "Huh, I thought I noticed a scar when I spotted him in the store."

She gave him a slightly wary sidelong glance. "Well, he does have one. You must have been more aware of things back at the store than you thought."

"Guess so," Jordan said. "Listen, if I think of anything else—or if Moira can tell us something—should we just swing by your place on Birch and let you know?"

"Yes, I'd appreciate that, thanks," she said. "If we're not there, just leave a note." She climbed into the car.

"I'm sorry we weren't more help," Leo piped up. He held out his hand for her to shake.

But Jordan stepped in front of him and closed the car door. "Take it easy, dude!" he called to the boy in the backseat.

Crestfallen, Leo backed up and watched her turn the

car around and head out of the driveway. He tucked the note back in his pocket.

Jordan put an arm around him. Leo started to wrestle away, but his friend held on tightly and pulled him inside the house. "Give it to me," he growled.

"What are you talking about?" Leo muttered.

"The note, goddamn it," Jordan said. "You were going to pass her a note. Twice you tried."

"Jordan, I—"

All of a sudden, his friend slapped him hard across the face. Leo reeled back, stunned. He bumped into the banister and almost knocked over a tall floor lamp by the stairs. The whole side of his head hurt. Stunned, he put a hand to the side of his face and numbly gazed at Jordan.

"Give me the note," his friend said.

Leo dug into his pocket. "The guy downstairs wasn't lying. He said she was his fiancée. Well, you heard her. She's his fiancée, and she's worried about him." He handed the napkin to his friend. "And I'm worried about you, Jordan," he added in a shaky voice. "Christ, in all the years we've known each other, and with all the fights we've had, you've never hit me before."

Jordan didn't seem to be listening. He frowned at the scribbling on the napkin and slowly shook his head. "I was counting on you," he muttered. "And you were ready to betray me—"

"That's because you're not acting rationally, damn it!" Leo cried. "I don't know who you are anymore! Good God, weren't you listening to her? It's just like he said. She's his fiancée. He wasn't lying—"

"What about the carjacking story?" Jordan shot

back. "He was lying to us about why he had a gun. She didn't know a damn thing about any carjacking. We've already caught him in a lie."

"Maybe he just didn't tell her," Leo argued.

"Something significant like a carjacking, you don't think he'd tell her?"

"Something significant like your mother being murdered, you don't think you'd tell your best friend?" Leo was still rubbing the side of his face. "You're acting crazy, Jordan. I'm sorry, but you are. He tried to make a deal with you downstairs. If we drop this in the lap of the law right now—and they find he's innocent—he won't press charges. God, take the deal, Jordan. Let me call the state police. . . ."

His friend turned and headed into the kitchen. Leo followed him in there and watched him open the refrigerator. "You can take some money out of your trust to buy him a new BMW," Leo suggested. "Let's get some damage control on this thing before it's too late. . . ."

Jordan leaned against the counter and drank a bottled water. He peeled at the label. "The first Mama's Boy murder in the Seattle area was Sarah Edgecombe in Auburn in November of 1997." His voice was void of all emotion. He may as well have been reading off that label he was peeling. "Mama's Boy broke into Sarah's house and dragged her away while she was giving her son a bath. He left a stuffed bear on the boy's pillow, and he left the mother's body in the woods at Discovery Park."

"Why are you telling me this?" Leo asked. He sank down in a kitchen chair.

"Two years before Sarah, there was a woman named Patricia Nagel," Jordan continued. "A few days before she was killed, Patricia told a friend that a man had followed her and her toddler son home from the El station. The investigators—"

"El station?" Leo repeated.

Jordan kept on talking: "The investigators figured he'd been following her and watching her for a while. Someone broke into Patricia's apartment on Diversey Street while she was waiting for her husband to get home from work. She was cooking dinner. Her little boy was there with her in the kitchen—in his high chair. Neighbors found one of those big, multicolored lollipops on the kitchen table. Three days later, a golfer at Skokie Country Club found Patricia Nagel's body in the rough near the seventh hole. She'd been strangled."

Leo's head still throbbed from Jordan's slap. He was amazed his friend knew all these facts and details. "I don't understand," he said, leaning forward in the kitchen chair. "What does all this have to do with the guy downstairs?"

Leaning against the counter, Jordan still seemed focused on the label on the bottled water. "A lot of the Mama's Boy investigators believe Patricia Nagel was his first victim, and that was two years before his first Seattle murder." He glanced over at Leo. "Patricia was killed in Chicago, buddy. And you heard the woman at our door. Allen Meeker is originally from Chicago."

With a sigh, Leo slumped back in the chair. "Oh, for God's sake, that's just a coincidence."

"Is it?" Jordan said. He put down the bottled water and moved toward the kitchen table. He sat down next to him and grabbed his arm. "I don't believe in coincidences, Leo. I don't think it's a coincidence that our guest downstairs rented the same house where my

mother and I were staying when she was abducted—
and about a quarter of a mile from where her corpse
was found. I don't think that's a coincidence at all.
There's a reason for it. Don't you see? He's returning
to the scene of his crime. And I can't help worrying
about that nice, pretty lady and her son who were just
here."

Leo stared at him. What Jordan said was starting to
make sense. And that scared the hell out of him.

"Don't you see?" Jordan whispered, squeezing his
arm. "He took them to my mom's old house for a reason."

CHAPTER
FOURTEEN

As she pulled onto Birch Way, Susan couldn't help hoping she'd find Allen's black BMW parked at the end of the driveway. She took one curve after another on the long, winding tree-lined drive. She couldn't see the house yet.

"Where's Allen gone?" Mattie asked, kicking at the back of the passenger seat.

"That's what your dear old mother would like to know," Susan muttered, eyes on the road.

She was thinking about her visit with Jordan Prewitt and his friend. At least she knew Allen had headed for town after leaving Rosie's. Maybe he'd gone to meet someone after all. She still couldn't dismiss the notion that he'd had some secret agenda for this trip.

Jordan and his friend had acted a bit strange. Why was he asking all those questions about Allen? And his pal had seemed so nervous and fidgety. Then again, they were teenagers. Acting weird came with the terri- tory. Besides, next to Sheriff Fischer—pilfering her panties—they'd come off as downright normal and nice.

Taking the last turn in the road, Susan saw the house ahead and the empty driveway. She figured there was always the chance Allen had come and gone. Maybe he'd left a note—alongside the one she'd written to him.

Susan had hoped not to come back to an empty house. But now as she took Mattie by the hand and headed for the front door, Susan prayed the place was indeed empty. She was terrified of running into that hunter again. She didn't care what the sheriff had said; that man had seemed far more interested in the house than he'd been in the woodlands surrounding it. Stepping inside, she didn't let go of Mattie's hand until she'd circled through the entire first floor. Then she parked him in the sunroom with his bin of toys so she could keep an eye on him.

Checking the dining room table, she found her note just where she'd left it. There was nothing from Allen. A weird thought suddenly occurred to her. What if Allen's hidden reason for this trip had been to meet up with another woman? What if he was with this woman right now?

Well, that would certainly let me off the hook, Susan thought, plopping down on a dining room chair. Then she immediately felt horrible for letting that notion creep into her head. Allen was so good to her and Mattie. And everybody liked him. Her parents were crazy for him.

Yet she remembered something that had happened on the last day of their visit down in Florida a few weeks back—before the engagement. While she'd been packing for the return flight, her mother had come into the guest room. "That Allen is a real charmer," she'd said with a smile and a hushed voice. "I think your father has just found a new best friend, and all the neighbors just adore him, dear. But I want you to know . . ." The smile had disappeared from her mother's still-pretty, lined face. "You shouldn't feel any pressure to make a commitment. Take your time, Suzy. It won't be the end of the world if he's not the one."

Susan had been rushing around to get packed and make their plane that afternoon. She hadn't had time to let her mother's words sink in. Besides, her mom had loved Walt so much; any man after him would fall short in comparison. So it had been easy to shrug off what her mother had said about Allen that last day in Vero Beach.

But maybe her mother had known then what Susan was just recently figuring out.

Perhaps that was why she felt so tempted to pack up their things right now, leave Allen another note, and drive home. But she felt duty-bound to stay—just as she'd felt duty-bound to accept his proposal of marriage.

Where the hell was he anyway?

Frowning, Susan stared out the sunroom's sliding glass door at *The Seaworthy*, tied to the dock. She wondered—once again—why he'd had to have that particular boat. And why had he allotted a specific time for sailing it this afternoon?

Susan opened up the leather-bound folder on the dining room table and glanced at the printout from Bayside Rentals. She folded it up and slipped it into her purse alongside the flare gun. Glancing at her wristwatch, she scratched out the time at the bottom of her note to Allen from forty minutes ago, and then wrote in: *3:05*.

"Sweetie?" she called to Mattie. "Better take a potty break. We're going right out again."

In the corner of the trench was a pile of broken plastic, metal, duct tape, and a battery. Moira had found a rock and smashed the SPY-TELL 300 Motion Sensor to pieces.

Until she'd destroyed the damn *Weatherproof-Waterproof* thing, its blinking red light had seemed like part of a time bomb. Each second that ticked away had her closer to meeting the creep who had set this trap.

Good luck picking up a signal now, asshole, Moira thought, with another glance at the mess of plastic and metal in the corner. One shard of plastic was particularly sharp, and she held on to it—just in case he showed up.

She'd been in this stinking pit for over two hours now. In the opposite corner from the broken sensor device, she'd finally succumbed to the call of nature and peed. So, basically, she was trapped in her own toilet now. Swell.

Weren't Leo and Jordan at all concerned? She'd thought by now she'd hear them calling for her. Was it possible that she'd been so awful to Leo that he didn't give a damn about her right now? Would he start to worry about her by sunset?

Moira didn't think she could stand it much longer. She was so cold, hungry, and scared.

She'd had only two more drive-bys, and had screamed and screamed—to no avail. She'd made another attempt to scale the wall, but hadn't even gotten a foot off the ground. There wasn't anything to hold on to— just loose dirt and mud. She felt so frustrated, only five feet away from freedom. It might as well have been fifty feet.

"SOMEBODY?" she yelled out—for the umpteenth time. She didn't need any car or forest noise to trigger her call for help, just frustration and panic. Somehow, screaming for help seemed more productive than sitting there crying. "SOMEBODY?" she repeated—a bit frail this time.

Then she heard something in the distance—a bass beat. Music again, someone in a car with their window rolled down.

"HELP ME! HELP!" she screamed, her head tilted back. She dropped the shard of plastic, then gazed up at the light above. "PLEASE, HELP ME, SOME-BODY!"

The music was louder and clearer now: *"Rock the boat. . . . Don't rock the boat, baby. . . . Rock the boat. . . . Don't tip the boat over. . . ."* A man was singing along with it. She could hear the car's motor purring, too.

"OH, GOD, HELP ME!" she screeched. "HELP ME!"

The music suddenly shut off.

"Oh, sweet Jesus, he heard me," Moira whispered. "Thank you, God." Her throat hurt from screaming, but she let out several more shrieks for help. She stopped for a moment and listened. She heard what sounded like a car door shutting.

"HELP ME! HELP!" She leaned against the dirt wall. "Help me, please!" she croaked. Her voice was giving out. Her throat felt raw, and her mouth was so dry.

"Somebody out there?" she heard the man call in the distance.

"YES!" she yelled. "I NEED HELP! I'VE FALLEN IN THIS HOLE. I'M TRAPPED DOWN HERE!"

"I hear you!" the man replied, his voice a little closer now. "Keep talking! I'm trying to find you. . . ."

Moira rubbed her neck. It hurt to swallow. "I'M HERE!" she managed to yell. "I SCREWED UP MY ANKLE WHEN I FELL! I'M STUCK IN THIS STU-PID HOLE!" She pulled her sweater over her head, and then tried to toss it up and out of the pit. It missed the edge and fell back in the trench. Moira caught it. She tried again, and it sailed over the top and disap-peared from her view. "LOOK FOR MY GREY SWEATER!" she yelled, wincing. She coughed to clear her sore throat. "CAN YOU SEE IT?"

"Keep talking!" the man called, but his voice sounded farther away now. "You're fading out. . . ."

Oh, no, she thought, slumping against the pit's dirt wall. "I'M HERE!" she screamed. "LOOK FOR A GREY SWEATER ON THE GROUND! IT'S RIGHT BY THE HOLE. . . ."

"Grey sweater?" he repeated. He seemed closer now.

"That's right," Moira said. She just couldn't scream any more. "I'm here. . . ." She glanced over at the smashed sensor device in the corner of the pit. She couldn't eliminate the possibility that the man now about to *rescue* her was the same person who had set this trap. Biting her lip, she searched around for that sharp piece of plastic.

"Keep talking! I—" he hesitated. Suddenly, his voice seemed closer. "Wait! I see the sweater now! Hold on!"

Moira found the shard of plastic and snatched it up. She couldn't take any chances. She took a deep breath and looked up at the edge of the pit. She half expected to see a rifle barrel pointed down at her—instead of a friendly face.

She heard bushes rustling, and the ground vibrated slightly as he zeroed in on her. A bit of soot shook loose from between the old, rotting boards at the top of the pit. Moira put her hand up to cover her eyes.

When she took her hand away, she could see a handsome man gazing down at her. "Oh, my God," he murmured. "Here I was thinking somebody was playing a prank on me. Are you hurt?"

Shivering, Moira smiled. He seemed nice. "I might have sprained my ankle when I fell in here," she said. "I didn't think anyone was ever going to come by. I've been stuck down here for two hours."

He cleared some branches away and then took off his navy corduroy jacket. Bending over the pit, he lowered the jacket down to her. "Grab on to the sleeve," he said. "I'll try to pull you up."

"Thank you, thank you so much," Moira said in a raspy voice. She dropped the plastic shard and then reached for the sleeve.

He let out a grunt as he tried to pull her up. More dirt came loose at the edge of the trench and fell onto her face. She kept her head turned away and held on. Her feet had just left the ground when she heard a tearing noise. "The sleeve!" she cried. "It's ripping!"

"Okay, okay," he said, gently lowering her back down.

Moira let go of the jacket, and he hoisted it back up. He examined the torn seam at the shoulder. "Goddamn cheap J. Crew!" he muttered. He glanced down at her again. "Hey, what's your name?"

"Moira," she said.

"I'm Jake. Listen, I'm going to get you out of there, Moira. I have some rope in the car. I'll be right back. Stay there, okay?"

"Stay here?" she repeated. "Yeah, I'll try not to wander off."

He laughed. "Hey, cut me a break. I've never rescued a damsel in distress before. Sorry if I suck at it." He lowered the jacket back down to her. "Here, you look cold. The sleeve's torn, but at least it's warm. I'm keeping your sweater out here for a marker." He let go of his end of the jacket, and it fell on top of her. "If you're hungry, there's a Twix bar in one of the pockets. I'll be right back, okay?"

Moira put on the oversized jacket. She glanced up— just as he started to move away. "Jake?" she called.

He peered down at her again. "Yeah?"

She smiled up at him. "I think you're a very good rescuer."

He smiled back at her and then ducked away. She could feel the ground shaking a bit as he ran off.

He was right. The corduroy jacket was warm—and it smelled of a musky, spicy men's cologne. And yes, there was a Twix bar in the pocket. She ate it slowly, savoring every bite. The smooth chocolate seemed to help coat her sore throat.

Moira glanced over at what was left of the SPY-TELL 300 Motion Sensor—the shattered plastic pieces and metal parts in the corner of the pit. She felt the lump in the pocket of her jeans, where she'd stashed the tortoiseshell barrette. If her theory was right about whoever had set up this trap, the son of a bitch wouldn't be hunting after today.

Once Jake got her to a hospital, she'd call the police. And while she was at it, she'd get word to Leo and Jordan that she was okay—if they even cared.

Moira glanced at her wristwatch. He'd been gone at least ten minutes. Every second dragged—now that she was so close to getting out of there. "Jake?" she called anxiously.

But there was no answer. Had he driven off? No, she would have heard his car. Maybe he'd run into the demented person who had set this trap. Or maybe there were other concealed pits around here, and he'd fallen in one and broken his neck.

"JAKE, ARE YOU THERE?" she cried out.

"Moira?" she heard him respond in the distance. "You didn't wander off, did you? Took me a while to—" He let out an abbreviated yell.

Moira heard a thud. She held a hand to her throat and listened to the silence.

"Jake, are you okay?" she nervously asked.

There was no answer, but she could hear a rustling noise, and the ground shook as someone approached the trench. Moira shrank against the dirt wall and gazed up.

"Jake, is that you?"

"I tripped over the stupid rope," she heard him say.

She let out a sigh and laughed.

He peeked down at her. "I figured you were thirsty— if you don't mind my germs. Here, catch. . . ." He tossed her a bottle of Evian.

She gratefully guzzled half of it while he lowered the rope down to her.

He told her to tie it around her waist and hold on. It was a struggle, but with her one good foot she got some leverage and pushed up while he tugged at the rope. Even with the cool breeze, she felt warmer as she got closer to the surface. The air was fresh. She could take a deep breath and not taste dirt.

Once he'd hoisted her up past the edge of the pit, they both collapsed on the ground. Moira lay there for a minute, half laughing, half crying. "Thank you," she gasped. "Thank you so much. . . ."

He helped her to her feet, but her ankle gave out. So she held on to her sweater and the rope while he carried her piggyback-style down the trail along the hill. Moira realized how horrible she must look—and smell. She was so embarrassed, yet she fiercely clung to him. "I'm not too heavy, am I?" she asked.

"I've gone hiking with backpacks that are a lot heavier than you—and not nearly as pretty," he replied.

He told her he was from Everett. He'd come up to Cullen to tour the winery and camp out for the night. He was supposed to meet some friends up here. "I think they're waiting for me," he said, out of breath, as they neared his car. His black Jetta was parked on the shoulder of a two-lane road. "My pals can wait a little longer. Let's get you to a hospital first—or at least the local country doctor."

He opened the back door and then gently set her down.

"I can ride up front with you," Moira said.

"With that bum ankle, you're better off stretching out in the back here," he advised. He took the rope from her and tossed it on the floor of the backseat. Then he put his arm around her.

Moira leaned on him as she hobbled the few steps to the backseat. It smelled like stale McDonald's French fries in his car.

"Let's take a look at that ankle," he said, crouching down beside her. He untied her tennis shoe and then carefully pulled it off. He rolled down her sock. "Does this hurt?" he asked.

"A little," she admitted.

"Sorry." He pulled off her sock and then handed it to her—along with the shoe.

Moira was more concerned—and embarrassed—about her foot odor. This guy really was getting her at her worst.

He put a hand on her shoulder. "Can you wiggle your foot a little?"

She tried, but it hurt. "Ouch," she said, forcing a laugh.

He rubbed her shoulder. "Feels like you're wearing a bra. Are you wearing a bra?"

Baffled, Moira gazed at him. "What?"

He glanced down at her foot again. "God, that looks really horrible. . . ."

Moira wondered what the hell her bra had to do with anything. Was he planning to make some kind of sling device for her leg or something? She let out a puzzled laugh.

He straightened up and pointed to her foot. "Take a look at it," he sighed. "That ankle is bad news."

Leaning forward, she gazed down at her ankle. It appeared slightly swollen, but not nearly as awful as he'd made out.

"I can't believe it," she heard him say. "You smashed up my motion detector, you bitch."

Moira looked up in time to see him raising a black-jack in the air.

"Wait!" she screamed.

He slammed it down on her skull.

Moira flopped across the backseat, unconscious.

On the floor in front of her was the rope he'd used to save her. He would use it again to tie her up.

But first, he pulled up the bottom of her T-shirt until it was bunched up over her breasts. He stared at her bra. It was pink.

"Pretty," he murmured.

CHAPTER
FIFTEEN

He didn't want to leave Jordan alone with Allen Meeker, not even for a few minutes. So Leo made a pact with his friend while they were in the kitchen. He would go upstairs, pack Moira's bag, and take it out to the car if—and only if—Jordan removed the gag from Allen's mouth.

"You don't trust me?" Jordan argued, frowning.

Leo slowly shook his head. "Not around him."

"Fair enough," Jordan muttered, patting him on the shoulder. Then they headed down the basement stairs.

Leo hated every minute of this. For the first time in their friendship, they both had good reasons not to trust one another. He just couldn't understand why Jordan wouldn't go to the state police with this. The only thing Leo could think of to do was keep this man alive while he tried to talk some sense into Jordan.

He stopped at the bottom of the cellar steps while Jordan went over to Meeker—just where he'd left him, strapped across the worktable with his arms stretched out in front of him. Their captive kept looking past Jordan—at him. Leo could see it in his eyes; the guy was counting on him for his survival.

Jordan pried the wet handkerchief out of his mouth. Meeker started coughing. "I—I heard Susan's voice," he said, once he caught his breath. "Is she okay?"

"As long as you're tied up here, I think she'll be okay," Jordan answered coolly.

"But don't you see now? I wasn't lying." Meeker glanced at Leo and then at Jordan. "I can't believe this. She was here, looking for me. Isn't that proof enough I'm on the level?"

"No." Jordan folded his arms. "Your fiancée said you've never been carjacked."

"It happened six years ago, before I even met her," Allen said. "I didn't see any reason to tell her about it. Y'know, she'll be calling the police soon."

"Six years ago?" Jordan repeated. "That's when you were living in the Washington, D.C., area wasn't it?"

Meeker frowned at him, then tried to tug at the rope around his bound wrists. "I don't know what you're talking about," he grumbled. "I've never lived in D.C."

"After the Seattle murders, Mama's Boy moved his business to the Beltway in 2003," Jordan said. "You abducted Natalie Boyer-Stiles one night in April while she and her little boy were walking to her car in the parking lot of Tysons Corner in Fairfax, Virginia. Her corpse was found in a ditch off Highway 236 in Annandale. You left an old toy fire engine in her shopping bag. And in June, you broke into the apartment of a single mother named Samantha Gilbert in Alexandria—"

"Not me," Meeker said, shaking his head. "I haven't been to D.C. since I was in college twenty years ago."

"A lot of people thought those two murders along the Beltway were the work of a copycat, but I always figured different. In a weird way, it made sense that you'd moved on to the *other* Washington." Jordan turned and gazed at Leo. "Don't you have some packing to do?"

Sighing, Leo gave him a guarded look and then retreated up the cellar stairs. In the kitchen, he could still hear their muted conversation. It was creepy the way Jordan talked to the guy—in a steady kind of monotone, until he got angry. Then he'd start screaming like a crazy man. Jordan didn't even sound like himself.

Leo stopped and glanced out the window in the kitchen door. No sign of Moira yet. He made sure the door was locked. Jordan didn't want her coming inside the house at all.

As Leo headed up to the second floor, the murmuring in the basement became more distant. He checked his wristwatch: 3:25. He'd left Moira in the woods over two hours ago. He knew she was ticked off at him. Still, she should have been back by now.

In Moira's bedroom, he peered out the picture window. He didn't see anyone out there. He stared down at Jordan's car. He could just barely make out the gift-wrapped package and bakery box in the backseat. He felt this horrible pang in his gut, a mixture of sadness and dread.

If only there were a working phone around here, he'd call the state police right now. He'd gladly endure Jordan's wrath in exchange for nipping this thing in the bud. His friend would thank him for it—maybe not for a while, but eventually.

It was only ten minutes by car to that store with the

pay phone. But Leo hated the idea of leaving Jordan totally alone with that man even for a few minutes. His friend had a gun with him—and he was like a loose cannon right now. He could so easily go nuts and shoot the guy—and then maybe himself.

One thing at a time, Leo thought. He'd get Moira's stuff packed and bring her bag out to the car. Moira couldn't get involved in this mess. She had to be kept away—and in the dark. It was one of the few things Jordan had insisted upon that made sense.

Leo set her overnight bag on the bed, then tossed in her robe and slippers. He found a fancy black dress under plastic on a laundry hanger in the closet. She'd planned to wear the dress to the restaurant tonight for his birthday dinner. He threw the clothes on her bed. Then he hurried down the hall to the bathroom. He stopped for a moment to listen to the murmuring in the basement. Jordan was doing most of the talking. The words were indistinguishable, but Leo recognized the weird monotone his friend had taken on with the man.

In the bathroom, he found Moira's paisley cosmetic bag on the shelf and snatched it up. Back in the bedroom, he tossed the paisley clutch in her overnight bag. Then he checked the top drawer of the dresser. The prescription bottle full of pills rattled as he tugged the drawer open farther.

Leo picked up the bottle and glanced at the label: MOIRA DANCEY—TAKE 1 CAPSULE BY MOUTH 30 MINUTES BEFORE BEDTIME AS NEEDED FOR SLEEP. DO NOT EXCEED DOSAGE.

Moira had told him a while back that she was taking something for insomnia. She was worried about getting too dependent on the pills.

Leo was still looking at the prescription label when he heard a scream from down in the basement. He threw the bottle back in the drawer and shut it. Then he raced downstairs. He could hear the yelling much more clearly now. It was Meeker—in an angry tirade: "Goddamn you! Are you crazy? HELP! JESUS, HELP ME!"

Leo ran through the kitchen and hurried down the wooden steps to the cellar. He balked when he saw Jordan hovering over his prisoner. Meeker was shirtless. He squirmed and shook against the worktable. It made a scraping sound against the cement floor. He cursed angrily while Jordan used garden shears to cut off his pants—in sections.

"Shut up and keep still!" Jordan growled. "Want me to cut you? I'm working on your inseam next. . . ." He maneuvered the shears up the side of Meeker's leg, toward the waist.

"My God, Jordan, what are you doing?" Leo shouted over the two of them.

Jordan tugged at the cut he'd made, completely tearing the trouser leg to one side—exposing Meeker's white briefs and his pale, hairy leg. "There wasn't a label along the back waistband," he said, eying something inside the pants lining on the back pocket. "Huh, *Polo, Ralph Lauren.* He could have gotten these khakis at any department store. . . ."

Leo still didn't understand what his friend was doing. "Jordan—"

"He's crazy, goddamn it!" Allen Meeker bellowed, writhing on the table and tugging at the rope around his taped-up wrists.

"Jordan, what the hell are you doing?"

Jordan grabbed Meeker's shirt from one side of the worktable and tossed it at him. "Take a look at that."

The pale blue oxford shirt hit Leo in the face before he had a chance to catch it. The shirt was soaked with perspiration and smelled of B.O. and Obsession cologne. Obviously, Jordan had cut it off Meeker's body. There were so many incisions it hardly looked like a shirt anymore.

"Check the label," Jordan said.

It took Leo a moment to find where the collar was. But then he saw the label: *Britches of Georgetown.*

"That was a chain of stores in the D.C. area," Jordan said. He set the garden shears down on top of the dryer. "I remember, because my stepmother took me shopping there during a trip to D.C. about seven years ago. I think it's closed now. Check out the material—and the buttons. Does that shirt look like it's twenty years old? More like five or six years old, wouldn't you say?"

Leo studied the shirt—or at least what was left of it. Jordan was right. It didn't look all that old.

"So—he hasn't been to the Beltway area in twenty years, huh?" Jordan said. "He's lying again. He bought that shirt in Washington, D.C., six or seven years ago, around the time he strangled those two women."

"For God's sake," Meeker moaned. "I got the shirt last year at a consignment shop in Seattle!"

Jordan let out a skeptical laugh and half smiled at Leo. "Does he look like the kind of guy who shops around secondhand stores? You think it's just another coincidence he's wearing a shirt from a store in the Washington, D.C., area—where they had two Mama's Boy–type killings six years ago?"

"Jesus Christ," Meeker grumbled, shaking his head. "I was going to take the high road and give you guys a break, not press charges. But I've had it! I'll see they throw the book at both of you!" His face was turning crimson. He glared over his shoulder at Jordan. "They ought to lock you up. You're a fucking lunatic. You belong in an institution. If you think for one minute there's any chance—"

Jordan didn't let him finish. He swiveled around and punched him in the kidney. Meeker let out an anguished cry. He might have crumpled to the floor if he hadn't been strapped to the worktable. "Screw you!" Jordan yelled, hitting him again—in the face this time.

"That's enough!" Leo shouted, grabbing Jordan and wrestling him away from the defenseless man.

His head drooped against the table, Meeker coughed and grimaced. His teeth were covered with blood.

Leo had to hold Jordan back to keep him from lunging at Meeker again. Jordan was shaking with rage. "You need to calm down," Leo whispered. "Just—just step back for a few minutes. Go upstairs and cool off, Jordan. Get a glass of water or something. . . ."

Rubbing his knuckles, Jordan nodded. "Watch him," he grunted, and then he lumbered up the stairs.

Leo still had the tattered shirt in his hand. He looked at Allen Meeker, slumped over the table, crying. Leo hurried over to the laundry sink and ran a section of the shirt under cold water. Then he went to the man and gently dabbed at the blood around his mouth.

"Could I have another glass of water, please?" Meeker asked in a quiet, shaky voice.

Leo quickly filled the measuring cup with cold water and brought it to him. Meeker drank from it and sighed.

"You—you seem like a nice guy," he whispered. "What's your name?"

"Leo," he said—a bit reluctantly. As much as he doubted Jordan's judgment right now, he didn't trust this guy either.

"Leo, can't you do anything to stop this?" he said under his breath. "All I'm asking is that you call the police. You know that's the best thing for you—and even for your friend. He—he's crazy. I'm not a murderer. If I was really this mass murderer, why would I be begging you to call the cops? Hell, I've never even been arrested. I sell hospital equipment, for Christ's sake. You met my fiancée. Does she look like someone who would hook up with a mass murderer?"

All Leo could do was shrug.

"She's worried. She'll probably call the police—if she hasn't already. And they'll come checking here. They'll think you were in on this whole thing." Meeker frowned at him. "Hell, Leo, for all I know, maybe this is some 'good cop, bad cop' routine you two dreamed up."

"It isn't like that at all," Leo sighed.

"Is his mother really dead? Was she really one of those Mama's Boy victims—or is this some kind of weird game you guys are playing with me?"

"Of course his mother's dead," Leo said. "And we're not playing any kind of game." He couldn't really answer the other part of the question for certain. It was all still too new to him. Until today, he'd never even heard Jordan mention Mama's Boy.

"Listen, I have reason to believe someone has been stalking my fiancée," Meeker said. "Ever since she and her son drove up here yesterday, someone's been following her and watching the house. I have a feeling it's your friend."

Leo shook his head. "That's impossible. I was with Jordan practically the whole day yesterday. He isn't stalking anybody."

"Well, someone's been following Susan around, and if it's not your friend, then the guy's still out there—and she's all alone, with her little boy." He tugged at the ropes. "Shit! God, I—I should be with her right now, watching out for her. Y'know, if something happens to Susan or her son while I'm stuck in this lousy stinking basement, it'll be your goddamn fault, Leo. I'm going to blame you."

Leo wondered if he was telling the truth about this stalker. He'd been on the level earlier when he'd said the woman was his fiancée. And while Jordan had claimed to have caught him in a lie twice, both times Meeker had a fairly rational explanation. Leo couldn't help putting himself in this guy's situation right now—if he was indeed innocent. What a nightmare this had to be for him.

Meeker lowered his forehead on the worktable and quietly cried. "Sorry," he murmured. "Here I'm trying to get you to help me. I'm hoping you'll look into your heart and do the right thing, and how am I handling it? I'm threatening you. I'm sorry, Leo. I'm just scared—and yeah, angry, too. Plus every part of me aches. My hands have fallen asleep. I can't feel them anymore." Tears in his eyes, Meeker gazed at him. He looked so pathetic and defeated. "Could you—could you help me blow my nose?"

Leo hesitated and then grabbed the cut-up shirt. "Is this okay?"

Meeker nodded.

Leo held the material up to Meeker's face, and the man blew his nose in it. There was a string of snot and blood attached to the makeshift hanky when Leo pulled it away. "Sorry," Meeker muttered. "Let me do it again." He blew his nose once more, and Leo was careful to wipe above his lip before he pulled the cloth away. "Thank you," Meeker whispered. "Leo, could you just loosen the rope a little? Please? He has it pulled so tight, it feels like I'm on a rack or something."

Leo stepped back from him. He shook his head. "I can't do that."

Meeker stared at him and winced. "Jesus, you're going to let him kill me, aren't you?" he whispered.

"No, I won't let that happen," Leo said resolutely. "I'm going to talk him into calling the state police. Until then, I'll try to make sure he doesn't hurt you again. But I'm not going to untie you or loosen the rope or do anything that might help you get away."

Meeker glared at him. "You stupid . . ." he said under his breath.

"If Jordan's acting crazy, it's because he saw you this afternoon, and it triggered something," Leo said. "He's been my best friend for six years. Maybe today I suddenly feel like I don't know him as well as I thought I did. But I don't know you at all, Mr. Meeker. And to be honest, I don't really trust you. I'm going along with Jordan on this."

"God help you," Meeker whispered.

The dark look in his eyes was so chilling Leo backed away even farther.

As he turned and hurried up the creaky cellar steps, Leo still had doubts. But he felt good about one thing. He was glad he hadn't loosened that rope.

CHAPTER
SIXTEEN

Susan was so relieved to see people and traffic and all the bustle—or, at least, what passed for bustle in downtown Cullen. It was a refreshing change from the quiet seclusion of the rental house, which was starting to feel like a prison. Sure, the house was lovely and in a beautiful spot, surrounded by trees and water. But for the last twenty-four hours—especially the last four— she'd felt so damn isolated.

Driving toward the town's harbor, Susan kept a lookout for Allen's black BMW. So far, she'd had two false alarms, but had yet to spot the real thing. She routinely glanced in the rearview mirror at Mattie, who seemed mesmerized by all the scenery. "Look it, look it, look it!" he said, pointing out the window at a twenty-foot weathered-bronze sea lion statue in a park, which also had benches, a garden, and a little playground. The town center was full of quaint shops and restaurants. At one intersection, Susan looked longingly at a rambling, white-trimmed, grey cedar-shake

building with a turret and a front porch. It was surrounded by a small garden of pansies, and the sign in
front, an old-fashioned shingle type, which read:

THE SMUGGLERS' COVE INN
The Captain's Table Restaurant
Pool – In-Room Movies – Jacuzzi Suites Available

Susan decided that if Allen didn't reappear by 4:30,
she'd pack their things, leave another note for him,
then come back and check into a room here at The
Smugglers' Cove Inn. She and Mattie could eat at The
Captain's Table and watch the in-room movies. She'd
wait for Allen there and do all her communicating with
Sheriff Fischer by phone.

Why couldn't Allen have booked them a suite at
The Smugglers' Cove? He'd never asked her where
she'd like to stay or given her any choice about this
weekend getaway. Ordinarily, they didn't even pick a
restaurant without discussing it first. She wondered
why he'd selected that particular house—in the middle
of nowhere.

Susan was questioning a lot of his decisions about
this trip. That was why she'd driven into town. She had
the Pier 12 address of Bayside Rentals on the printout
from Allen's folder. Maybe Chris was still on duty, and
he could give her some idea why that particular boat
was so important to Allen—that boat they were supposed to sail at noon for at least four hours.

She found parking by the waterfront and kept a tight
hold of Mattie's hand as they headed toward the pier. It
felt good to be walking amid other people, to see some

of them smiling and waving at Mattie and making a fuss over him. She also spotted a few passersby talking on their cell phones.

Susan realized they didn't have any cell reception problems in this part of town. She stopped, dug her cell out of her purse, and checked for messages: one from her sister, Judy, and that was it. She had to remind herself that Allen wouldn't have bothered calling and leaving a message if he thought she was still in the no-call zone.

She dialed his number. Jordan Prewitt had said Allen had headed for town after leaving Rosie's. If he was anywhere in the vicinity—anywhere outside those damn woods—she'd be able to get through to him. Susan anxiously counted the ringtones. A recording clicked on—and not Allen's voice. It was the automated response she always got when his phone was turned off or he was out of range. Even though he probably wouldn't get the voice mail any time soon, Susan left a message anyway. She turned her head away from Mattie and whispered into the cell after the beep: "Hi, it's me at four o'clock, going out of my mind worrying and wondering where in holy hell you are. Mattie and I are in beautiful downtown Cullen, by the waterfront. If you get this, call my cell. Bye."

Clicking off, she shoved the cell phone back into her purse and then pulled Mattie along. "C'mon, sweetie."

He was fascinated by all the boats and the screaming, swooping seagulls. He kept stopping to peek between the planks of the pier's wooden walkway at the water below them. The spicy aromas from Col. Mustard's Hot Dog Hut competed with the smell of fish and salt water. Just beyond the hot dog stand was a little brown shack with a blue and white metal sign above the door:

BAYSIDE RENTALS
CHARTER BOATS – TOURS – MOORAGES

The door was open, and Susan peeked inside. It was a dusty little room with a computer monitor and a keyboard on an old metal desk. In front of it was an empty chair on wheels with silver tape over part of the seat pad. Framed faded pictures of sailboats on the wall surrounded a large stuffed blue marlin that had seen better days. There was one window, and outside of it, Susan could see a tall, slim Asian man smoking a cigarette and talking on his cell phone. He was good looking with short, spiky black hair.

He glanced her way and then came around from the other side of the shack. Susan guessed he was in his mid twenties. He wore shorts, boat-sneakers, and an aqua blue sweatshirt that had *Bayside Rentals* over the left breast. By the shack's door, he tossed his cigarette in a coffee can full of sand and butts. He still had his cell phone in his other hand. "Hiya," he said. "Can I help you folks?"

"I'm looking for Chris," Susan said.

The man smiled. "Look no more. I'm Chris. How can I help you?"

"Well, you already have. I'm Susan Blanchette. You know, the woman with the emergency at Twenty-two Birch? Thanks so much for phoning the police for me earlier today."

He nodded. "I'm glad you're okay. You gave me a little scare there for a while. How's *The Seaworthy* working out for you folks?"

"We haven't had a chance to take it out yet," Susan said, pulling Mattie a little closer to her. "We were planning to go sailing at noon today. But my fiancé, Allen Meeker, who rented the boat from you, he went out on an errand and still hasn't come back yet."

Nodding, Chris glanced at something on his cell phone.

"Anyway," Susan continued. "I'm getting pretty worried about him."

"Well, he hasn't been by here," Chris said with a shrug, his eyes still on his phone.

Susan suddenly felt a little stupid for thinking this total stranger could tell her something about her fiancé's decision-making processes. Meanwhile Mattie tugged at her arm and rocked from side to side out of boredom.

Susan cleared her throat, hoping to tear Chris's attention away from his cell phone for a minute. "Ah, Chris, this is probably a silly question. But is there any reason someone would want to go sailing at a particular time today, specifically from noon until four? Is there anything going on this afternoon I might not be aware of—like a solar eclipse or something?"

He shoved his phone into his pocket. "Not that I know of."

She worked up a smile. "I read that e-mail you sent to Allen. It sounded like there was a mix-up with another boat. Apparently he was very much set on leasing *The Seaworthy.* I'm curious. Did he indicate why he had to have that particular boat?"

Chris ran a hand through his spiky black hair and frowned at her. "Our best vessel, *The Orcas Pearl*, a Catalina 309 cruiser, suddenly became available, and I thought Mr. Meeker would like that. It's usually more expensive, but I was going to charge him the same price we charge for *The Seaworthy*. I thought I was doing him a big favor securing him the better boat. But—um, well, he wasn't happy. In fact, he got really pissed off. . . ."

Wide-eyed, Susan stared at him. "I—I'm sorry," she murmured. "Did he say why it was so important that he have *The Seaworthy*?"

Chris shook his head. "No, but he sure got all over my case for making the switch. I tried to explain he was getting a better deal. But he didn't want to hear about it. He kept calling me a 'fuck-up' and threatening to get me fired."

Susan automatically pulled Mattie closer—until his head was against her leg. Then she covered his other ear.

"Sorry," Chris muttered. He pulled his cell phone out again, glanced at it, then wandered back into the small office.

With Mattie at her side, Susan stepped up to the doorway. "I apologize for my fiancé," she said. "Considering how Allen treated you, I'm extra grateful you helped me earlier today." Susan glanced around at the old, faded photos of sailboats on the wall, and she thought she recognized *The Seaworthy* among them. The name, written in the corner of the picture frame, confirmed it. "Is there any feature that's unique to *The Seaworthy*?" she asked him. "Maybe something this other boat doesn't have?"

Chris leaned back against the metal desk. "They both handle pretty much the same. The cabin space is bigger on *The Orcas Pearl*, and it's a newer boat. The only thing *The Seaworthy* has that the *Pearl* doesn't have is an old computer with Internet access. It was a novel feature when the boat was built twelve years ago. But with iPhones and notebooks, it's not really such a hot thing anymore." He shrugged. "Though I guess some people must still use it. We just had somebody call the day before yesterday to make sure the Internet connection still worked on *The Seaworthy*."

"Was it Allen—Mr. Meeker—calling?" Susan asked.

"I don't know who it was," Chris replied, shaking his head. "I didn't recognize his voice. He hung up as soon as I told him it was working fine."

"But if it wasn't Allen, who . . ." Susan didn't finish. He'd already said he didn't know who had called with that inquiry. Susan numbly stared at him as he started fiddling with his cell phone again. Then she glanced over his shoulder at the old, faded photo of *The Seaworthy* on the wall.

"Well, thank you," she murmured—though he clearly wasn't listening. She took Mattie by the hand and started back toward her car.

Moira woke up shivering from the cold.

Panic-stricken, she rubbed her bare arms and shoulders and realized someone had stripped her down to the waist. She still had her jeans on, but no shoes or socks.

Moira didn't have any idea where she was or how she'd gotten there. The room was so dark she could barely see her hand in front of her face. It smelled damp and moldy. She was curled up on a bare mattress or a futon—she wasn't sure which, but it felt low to the ground. She blindly patted around for her missing bra, T-shirt, and sweater.

When she finally sat up, it felt like something hit her between the eyes. Her head throbbed so badly she was nauseous. She would have thrown up if she'd had something in her stomach. Moira kept feeling around for her clothes until—at last—she found her sweater and T-shirt. But she still couldn't locate her brassiere.

Then she remembered the man who had helped her out of the pit. *"It feels like you're wearing a bra,"* he'd said. *"Are you wearing a bra?"*

Shuddering, Moira clutched the sweater in front of her breasts and kept searching in the dark for her bra—though she knew it was useless. Her handsome rescuer, the man calling himself Jake, had taken it. And he'd brought her to this black, cold place.

Moira heard a whistling noise and something flapping—like a boat's sail in the wind. She wondered if she was anywhere near a harbor.

Feeling around for the edge of the bed, she realized that she was right about the mattress. It was on an icy-cold cement floor. Something crawled over her hand. She recoiled and let out an abbreviated shriek. Moira wasn't sure if it was an incredibly large bug or a small rodent, but she scrambled to the opposite side of the mattress. She tried to get to her feet, but a bone-grinding pain shot up from her left ankle, and she fell back on the mattress again.

Catching her breath, she heard another sound: footsteps. Then there was a clank. The sound was in the room with her. When she turned in that direction, she saw a door opening—and a dim light pouring through it. For a fleeting moment, she could see the small, grimy, windowless room that was her prison. Beside the doorway was an empty metal bookcase—the only other piece of furniture besides the mattress.

The door opened wider. A shadowy figure appeared at the threshold.

Recoiling on the mattress, Moira clutched the sweater in front of her breasts. "Where am I? What—"

She didn't finish. A bright flash blinded her.

By the time Moira realized someone had taken her picture, she heard the door clank shut and then footsteps retreating. She quickly put on her T-shirt and sweater, but they weren't much protection against the unrelenting cold. She was still shivering.

She almost called out for the man to come back, but thought better of it. Moira started to cry. She tried to figure out where the door was. Even though she'd heard the lock clank, she still needed to know. It was the only possible way out. But all Moira could see now were ghost spots from the flash—and darkness.

And all she could feel was dread for the next time that door opened.

"I spy with my little eye something that begins with a *D,*" Susan said.

"Dog!" Mattie exclaimed, wiggling in his child seat in the back.

"No, there aren't any dogs around here," Susan said, glancing at him in the rearview mirror. "It's the same first letter as dog, the same, *deh . . . deh . . .*" She nodded toward a deer-crossing sign at the side of the road ahead. They were headed down Carroll Creek Road toward the house.

"It's a *deer*, sweetie," she finally said. "See the picture of the deer on that sign?"

"Mommy, are we gonna go home soon?" Mattie whined.

"Soon," Susan said. And she refused to get her hopes up that Allen was there, waiting for them.

She'd called the police while still in downtown Cullen and left a message with the woman who had answered the phone at the police station. She must have been Cullen's version of the 911 operator.

Fischer had said he'd check in with her in two hours. "My fiancé is still missing," Susan had explained to the woman on the line. "And it's been more than two hours, so I'm just following up with the sheriff. My little boy and I may relocate to one of the inns in town and wait it out there. I'll let you know."

"I'll make sure to pass along your message, Ms. Blanchette."

Susan figured it would take about twenty minutes to pack up everything and load it in the car. She also wanted to check the Internet connection on *The Seaworthy*.

She passed Rosie's Roadside Sundries and then continued along Carroll Creek Road. Just beyond the spot where she'd had the flat yesterday, Susan noticed a paved one-lane artery, Trotter Woods Trail. Susan quickly stepped on the brake. Through the trees, she'd glimpsed a black car parked down that road.

She backed up and then turned onto Trotter Woods Trail, which was so overshadowed by trees it was like driving at night. Susan switched on her headlights. The black car came into view. It was a Volvo, damn it. The car rocked slightly, and Susan noticed the startled shirtless young woman and man in the backseat. Mattie waved at them.

Susan sped up a bit and kept driving up the snake-like, narrow trail, figuring there was another way out— or maybe, just maybe, another black car along the roadside, a BMW next time. She slowed down as the paved road eventually became gravel—and a bit bumpy. Susan glanced in the rearview mirror. Smiling, Mattie seemed to enjoy the rough, jostling ride. Susan knew they were getting closer to the bay because she could smell salt water through her half-open window. She came to a turnaround area. Before the gravel road continued, there was a small, weathered wooden sign: PRIVATE PROPERTY.

Through a break in the trees, Susan spotted the top of a frame-style house. It sat on a hill, and the second floor had large picture windows and a deck encircling it. She realized this was their neighboring residence on the bay. She'd noticed the house from their dock— about a quarter of a mile down the shoreline.

It was a long shot anyone was home or had run into Allen earlier this afternoon. But Susan figured she was practically on their doorstep, so why not give it a try?

She continued along the bumpy, gravel drive. The forest thinned out, and she could see the bay—and the rest of the house. The gravel road merged with a paved driveway that looped around toward the back of the place. She followed it as far as the front door.

"I'll be right back, sweetie," she told Mattie, grabbing her purse. "Be a good boy and make sure Woody behaves himself. We'll go back to the house after this, I promise. You can watch a little more of *Shrek*."

"'Kay," he murmured.

Susan left the car windows open a crack and locked the doors. She walked up to the front door and knocked. There was no answer. Susan rapped on the door again, but to no avail. She glanced back at Mattie and then followed a walkway toward the other side of the house. There was a carport—and a red MINI Cooper parked in it.

"My God, it's him. . . ." she murmured.

She took another look at her car in the driveway to make sure Mattie was okay. She could just barely see his silhouette in the backseat.

Unless the guy was out for a sail or a hike in the woods, he had to be around. His car was there. She could hear a flapping noise coming from the backyard. It sounded like a boat sail.

She waved at Mattie and then stepped toward the back of the house. She didn't like leaving him alone in the car—even for a minute or two. But Mattie was better off sitting out this expedition. Without him tagging along, she stood a better chance of getting the hell out of there if she needed to leave in a hurry.

Susan remembered the flare gun in her purse.

The place was surrounded by trees and bushes. Staying close to the side of the house, she crept past a gas meter and some plastic trash cans behind the carport. As she approached the backyard, she saw the dock and a canoe tied to it. There was also a wooden picnic table in the backyard, and beside that a tall flagpole with a large American flag loudly flapping in the breeze.

She crept around the edge of the house. A sudden hissing noise made her turn her head, and she saw him. Susan froze. It was the man she'd met in Arby's yesterday, only his black hair looked wet and messy, his five o'clock shadow was even scruffier, and he didn't have a shirt on. She noticed his lean physique and hairy chest as he moved away from a stack of lumber piled against the house. The hissing noise came from the nozzle of a hose he carried. He twisted it to cut off the water flow, dropped the hose, and then reached for the front of his jeans. At that moment, he glanced up and saw her. "Whoa!" he said, quickly buttoning his jeans back up.

"I'm sorry," she muttered.

He scowled at her. "Oh, Jesus, Mary, and Joseph, it's you. What do you want?"

"Nothing!" she replied, taken aback by his blatant hostility. He'd been so friendly yesterday—*overly friendly*. In fact, that had been the problem. "Are you staying here?" she asked.

He looked at her as if she were crazy. "Um, yeah, I'm staying here. This is my place."

"Well, I'm sorry," she muttered. "I didn't know you lived around here. When I saw you at the grocery store yesterday, I thought you might have followed me from Mount Vernon."

"I wasn't following you at all." He grabbed a dirty grey sweatshirt from the stack of lumber and put it on. "In fact, after the Arby's incident, when I saw you again in the parking lot at Rosie's, I stayed in my car just to avoid you. What are you doing here?"

"Nothing, my mistake," she said. "God. . . ." She shook her head at him, then turned and started back toward the car.

He started after her. "Hey, excuse me if I seem rude, but y'know, I was just trying to be nice to you and your little boy at the restaurant yesterday, and you treated me like Jack the Ripper."

She passed the carport and glanced over her shoulder at him. "There's being nice, and there's being overly familiar. You have some major boundary issues, pal."

"I'm getting a lecture on boundary issues from a woman who just trespassed onto private property and snuck into my backyard? Listen—listen to me for just a second. . . ."

Susan stopped a few feet in front of her car. She could see Mattie in the backseat. She managed a reassuring smile for him and waved. He returned the wave. She didn't turn to look at the man.

"If I came across as overly friendly and pushy yesterday, I'm sorry," he said. His apologetic tone seemed genuine. "There was table full of guys in that Arby's, young, obnoxious, good old boys. I don't know if you noticed them, but they sure noticed you. . . ."

Susan remembered them staring at her. They hadn't seemed overtly obnoxious to her.

"I heard those guys talking," the man went on. "They were making bets on who could *nail* you in the parking lot at the back of the restaurant. I don't know how serious they were, but two of them started egging one guy on. It was pretty revolting. So I figured maybe they'd leave you alone if I joined you and it looked like we knew each other. If I came across as overly familiar, that's why. . . ."

Susan remembered how those three twenty-something guys had lumbered out of the restaurant shortly after he'd sat down with her and Mattie.

"So the road to hell is paved with good intentions, right?" he said. "Anyway, you're here now, and I'm sorry I was rude. What can I do for you?"

Standing in his driveway in front of his house, dwarfed by all the tall trees, Susan felt so stupid and lost. She turned to face him. She let out a little laugh, but tears came to her eyes. "I'm staying here with my fiancé," she explained, a tremor in her voice. "We were supposed to go sailing at noon, and he went to pick up something at Rosie's. And he never came back. This is totally unlike him. I've talked to Rosie, the police, and some neighbors. . . ."

She held back her tears, took a few deep breaths, and dug out a Kleenex from her purse.

"Would you like some lemonade or something?" he asked.

Nodding, Susan wiped her nose and eyes. "That would be nice."

"Good," he said. He tapped on Mattie's window. "Hello, Matthew Blanchette from Seattle. Do you like lemonade?"

"Yeah!" Mattie replied, nodding enthusiastically.

Susan opened the back door and took him out of his car seat.

"My name is Tom Collins, like the drink," the man said.

"Susan Blanchette," she said, "like your crazy neighbor down the bay for the weekend." She set Mattie on his feet and then closed the car door after him.

His smile vanished. "Are you staying in the house on Birch?"

She nodded. "Yes, why?"

He quickly shook his head. "Nothing. Listen, I hope you don't mind having your lemonade in the backyard. I'm remodeling, and the place is a construction zone in there—lots of exposed nails and stuff. It's not safe. C'mon, follow me to the back."

Taking Mattie by the hand, Susan trailed after Tom Collins. They moved along the side of the house, past the carport. He glanced over his shoulder. "So—you're engaged, huh?"

"Yes."

"Just my luck," he mumbled, with a crooked smile. "C'mon . . ."

Susan paused for a moment. *Yes, you're engaged*, she reminded herself. And her fiancé was missing right now. What the hell was she doing, stopping to sip lemonade in this man's backyard? Susan told herself that she should turn back, go to the house, and wait for Allen.

Then again, one glass of lemonade wouldn't hurt.

With Mattie at her side, she followed the man toward his backyard.

"Why that house on Birch? There are at least twenty other rental cabins around here, not to mention one of the inns or several B and B's in town." Standing in front of the worktable, Jordan folded his arms. "Why did you pick my mother's house this weekend? Why did you take that woman and her son there?"

Allen closed his eyes. "I already told you," he groaned impatiently. "I went shopping online for a rental, and it looked like the nicest place available. I didn't know anything about a murder there." He curled his lip at Jordan. "It wasn't one of the selling points they mentioned in the rental ad."

Leo sat on the cellar steps and watched them. But he was thinking about Moira. He hadn't finished packing her bag yet. They'd locked the front and back doors upstairs to make sure she couldn't let herself in. Once she knocked, he'd throw the rest of her stuff in the bag and meet her outside. He still hadn't thought of a good excuse to get rid of her. Maybe he'd just act like he was still mad at her, and he and Jordan wanted her to go. "We've voted you off the island," he imagined telling her.

At the moment, Leo wondered if she'd ever return. It was after four and would be getting dark soon. She'd been alone in those woods for three hours now.

Something had happened to her. Leo felt it in his gut.

They really needed to go back into those woods and search for her. But Jordan couldn't leave his prisoner. And Leo didn't trust his friend alone with that man.

Jordan and Meeker were glaring at each other right now. "Listen, kid," Meeker said. "If I murdered your mother in that house, I'd hardly go back there. It's not like some cheap detective novel. I wouldn't be returning to the scene of the crime—and I'd hardly bring my fiancée and her son along for the ride. It doesn't make sense."

"But you've already returned to the scene of the crime at least once before," Jordan maintained. Bending at the waist, he leaned forward so his face was close to Meeker's. "You came back to dump my mother's body in the woods right next to her house. And by the way, don't pretend to be ignorant of the facts with allusions to murdering my mother 'in that house.' You abducted her while she was standing on the dock off the backyard. You didn't strip, beat, and strangle her 'in that house.' You took her somewhere else and killed her there."

"I'm sorry for not getting all my facts straight," Allen shot back. "Since I wasn't even there, it's kind of difficult to keep track of what happened."

"Where did you take her, Allen?" Jordan pressed. "I'd really like to know where you killed my mother. Did you have a special place you took all your victims?"

"I haven't killed anyone," Meeker groaned. "I'll say it again, I'm really sorry your mother was murdered. You have my deepest sympathies. But c'mon, how can you be so sure it was me? I heard you telling your buddy about it. When was she killed? I mean, shit, how long has it been—seven or eight years?"

"You know how long it's been," Jordan growled. "Ten years last August."

"And you recognize me after all that time? Didn't you say you were in a kayak in the middle of the bay? You had to be pretty damn far away if you couldn't paddle to her in time to help her. You would have had to see the guy at a distance. How can you be so sure it was me?"

Jordan silently stared at him for a moment. "I never said I was in a kayak in the middle of the bay," he whispered. "I said I was in a *boat*. But let me tell you something. *It was a kayak*. And you knew—without me telling you. You knew, because you were there."

"Okay, so you said *boat*!" Allen yelled. He tugged at the rope around his wrists, and the worktable shook.

"I figured it was a kayak or a canoe. Goddamn it, I was just guessing!"

"You're pretending not to know, but you keep tripping yourself up," Jordan said.

"Oh, Jesus, please!" Allen cried. "I'm aching all over! I can't even feel my hands. I got to take a piss. I didn't kill anybody! I came here for a quiet weekend with my fiancée. I wanted to treat her to a break from the city. She's had a rough go of it. Her husband and her other kid died last year. I'm worried about her. God, please . . ." He glanced over at Leo. "I told you about this guy stalking her. She's all alone right now. . . ."

"If you're so worried about her, why didn't you just pack up your stuff and go back to Seattle?" Jordan asked.

"I wanted to take her sailing," Allen whispered. He started sobbing again. "I just wanted to do that for her. . . ."

Leo grabbed hold of the banister and stood up. "Jordan?" he said quietly.

His friend let out a long sigh. Scowling at his captive, Jordan walked around the worktable and approached Leo. "You can see I'm making headway here," he whispered edgily. "Still think he's innocent?"

Leo wasn't sure, so he didn't answer the question. "I'm worried about Moira," he said under his breath. "She should have been back here at least two hours ago. She could be lost or hurt or God knows what. We should be out there looking for her, Jordan." He glanced over at Meeker slouched across the worktable, weeping. "We can't keep doing this. It's not right. We need to call the state police and tell them we've captured a murder suspect. Then we can let them handle it.

And maybe they'll assign some cops to help us find Moira." Leo put his hand on Jordan's shoulder. "It's the smart thing—the right thing to do."

"Just give me another twenty minutes," Jordan whispered. He clutched Leo's hand on his shoulder and squeezed it. "Please, I need to hear him confess. Give me that much. I've waited ten years for this. Please, Leo."

He stared at his friend for a moment and then sank down on the step again. "Okay," he murmured. "Twenty minutes . . ."

From Tom Collins's dock, Susan gazed down the shoreline at the rental house on Birch. But it was too far away to discern if there was any activity in or around the house. The place looked very pretty from where she stood right now, but Susan wasn't eager to go back there—even just to pack up their things and leave.

Before stepping inside his house to make the lemonade, Tom had dug a twelve-inch plastic, multicolored beach ball and a plastic baseball bat out of a toolshed in the backyard. Mattie kept busy kicking and hitting the ball on the lawn.

Susan had offered to help make the lemonade, but Tom had insisted she and Mattie stay outside to avoid the construction mess in his kitchen and living room.

From the dock, she wandered over to the picnic table by the flagpole and sat down. The sun was just starting to set over the bay, and Susan felt a chill in the air. Above her, the Stars and Stripes flapped in the breeze. It was that magic time late in an autumn afternoon when the light made everything look beautiful and saturated with color.

Susan suddenly felt so lonely—and it didn't really have anything to do with Allen's unexplained absence. She couldn't quite put her finger on it. Maybe she was just feeling vulnerable.

Tom brought out a tray with a pitcher of lemonade, a bag of Chips Ahoy! and three tall, ice-filled glasses that had *Cheers! Tom & Viv Collins* written on them in gold script. He sat down with her at the picnic table. He'd combed his hair and changed into a sexy black V-neck sweater while he'd been inside.

"Mattie, come get some lemonade," Susan called to him. But he ignored her. He was having too much fun with the ball and bat. "Sweetie, did you hear me?"

Tom poured the lemonade. "Oh, let him play," he said. "Looks like he's having a blast."

"I suppose you're right. He'll sleep better tonight." She studied the inscription on her glass. "Did you get these in a divorce settlement or something?"

He shook his head. "No, I've never been married—engaged once, but never married. Tom and Vivian are my parents. They had a whole set of these cheesy glasses. I think the other ones said *Skoal* and *Salute*. My mom died in 2002. Dad moved to a retirement village in Arizona three years ago. He left me in charge of this place." He glanced toward the house. "It's been the family weekend and summer home ever since I was a kid. I used to hate coming here because all I ever did here was work on the yard and on the boat. Anyway, I teach high school in Everett. It gets a little crazy at times. I come here for a break—and once I set foot in the door, all I do is work. You go figure."

Susan smiled at him and raised her glass. "Well, *cheers*. This is very good lemonade."

"It's a mix, Country Time," he admitted, running the cool glass over his forehead. "So—be honest. Was I really that creepy at the restaurant yesterday? I mean, I was trying my best to be suave. On a scale from one to ten—with ten being I made your skin crawl—just how creepy was I?"

"You were about a twelve," Susan replied, cracking a smile.

He laughed. "I may go back to hating you."

Sipping her lemonade, she glanced over at Mattie while he chased the ball. "Can I ask you something?"

"Fire away," he said.

"Earlier, when I mentioned that I was staying at the house on Birch Way, you got this funny look on your face. Why is that?"

He frowned slightly and then let out a sigh.

"Is it haunted or something?" she pressed. "I ran into this nice young man at Rosie's yesterday, maybe you know him, Jordan Prewitt. His family has a cabin near here. When I asked him for directions to Birch Way, he got this strange, somber look in his eyes—sort of like you had when I mentioned I was staying there."

"You asked Jordan Prewitt for directions to the house on Birch Way?" Tom asked, as if she'd committed a major faux pas. He ran a hand through his dark hair. "Oh, God . . ."

"What? What is it?"

"So Jordan's staying at the family cabin this weekend? Is he here with his folks?"

"No, he's with some friends, another boy and a girl." Susan leaned forward, her eyes searching his.

"And you're changing the subject. What's wrong with asking Jordan Prewitt for directions to the house on Birch Way?"

Tom sighed. "Maybe I shouldn't say anything, since you're staying there. I don't want to give you nightmares, but—well, ten years ago, Jordan's mother was abducted from the dock behind that house. Jordan was out on a boat in the bay when it happened. He saw the whole thing, the poor kid." Frowning, Tom glanced down at the picnic table top. "Anyway, they found his mother's body in the woods nearby. I don't know if you're familiar with the Mama's Boy murders from about ten years ago, but Jordan's mother was one of the victims. Her name was Stella Syms. She dropped the *Prewitt* when Jordan's dad dropped her."

"My God," Susan murmured, shaking her head. "I knew one of the women was killed up here in Cullen, but I had no idea it happened at that house. . . ."

"The place belonged to Stella's family," Tom explained. "They wanted to unload it after that. But they had a hard time selling it, because of the murder. This local couple ended up buying it and turning it into a rental."

"Lord, no wonder Jordan reacted the way he did when I asked for directions. I feel like such an idiot. . . ."

Tom shrugged. "You couldn't know." He nodded toward his own house. "We used to have a landline phone here, but my dad had the service stopped a few years ago. When Mama's Boy came to the house on Birch, he cut their phone lines. Poor Jordan ran all the way here—through the woods. My folks weren't here that weekend. He broke that second window from the door there, climbed in, and called the police."

Susan just kept shaking her head. She felt so horrible for that sweet, handsome young man.

"He had a real rough go of it for a while after that," Tom said soberly. "I got a lot of this secondhand through my mom. But Stella—Jordan's mom—she had some psychological problems. I think she might have been bipolar. Apparently, that's one reason Jordan's parents split up. After she was killed, Jordan went a little crazy himself. Not that anyone could blame him, considering what he went through. . . ."

Susan felt a chill and rubbed her arms. "What do you mean when you say he went *a little crazy*?"

"Well, he tried to commit suicide. Eight years old, and he swallowed a bunch of pills. Can you believe it? His mother had some medications for her various conditions, and I guess he'd gotten ahold of them before they'd collected all her things. They put Jordan in the hospital for a while, but it really didn't take. After they let him out, on two different occasions, he attacked two different men on the street, both total strangers. He kind of hurt one of them, too. In both cases, Jordan was utterly certain the guy had killed his mother. I think he was about ten at the time. They put him in some private care facility after that, and I think he came out okay. But I hear his dad was really beside himself for a while. It wasn't just Jordan's breakdown after losing his mom that way. They were worried Jordan might have inherited some of Stella's disorders. Anyway, he got better, and the Prewitts moved from Bellingham to Seattle, where not so many people knew about them."

Tom sipped his lemonade. "Of course, my source for all this inside information was my mom and the local ladies she spoke with. But I think it's pretty reliable."

"Do you know Jordan at all?" Susan asked.

"Just enough to say hi," Tom replied. "He's a good guy. But I'm around teenagers all the time for my job, so I don't exactly seek them out when I come up here. All of us are kind of isolated in this section of Cullen."

"Tell me about it," Susan sighed. "I've been going stir-crazy from the isolation today—ever since my fiancé disappeared. I'm glad I didn't know earlier about the Mama's Boy connection to that house. My day there has been bizarre enough. Shortly after Allen— that's my fiancé—shortly after he left for Rosie's, I spotted this strange character in army fatigues lurking around the place. It scared the hell out of me. . . ."

"Well, not to downplay it, but that house is kind of a local landmark for the morbidly curious. When I see boats sailing around this section of the bay, about eight times out of ten, it's someone wanting a peek at the old dock—y'know, the scene of the crime and all that. They'll hover near the shore with their binoculars or their cameras for a good look or a good picture. I'm not surprised they're getting some foot traffic over there, too."

"Sheriff Fischer seemed to think it was a hunter," Susan said.

Tom ate a Chips Ahoy! and nodded. "Maybe. So— you had the police over there?"

"Yes, and the good sheriff decided to take a souvenir of his visit." Susan leaned across the table. "Do you know anything about him? Have you heard anything?"

"About the sheriff?" Tom shrugged. "Well, he's kind

of a good-old-boy chauvinist. He's been the sheriff here forever. What do you mean he took a 'souvenir'?"

"He stole a pair of panties from my laundry basket," she whispered.

"He did? Are you sure?" Tom began to laugh.

She slapped his arm. "It's not funny. I was really upset! It was incredibly creepy."

"I'm sorry. But on a scale of one to ten, with ten being it made your skin crawl—"

"It was a seventeen, okay?" Susan said, cutting him off. Then she found she was laughing, too—for the first time today. She slapped him on the arm again. "It's not funny!" she insisted, still grinning.

"I know it isn't," he said, a bit more serious now. "I've never heard anything like that about Sheriff Fischer. He's been married to the same woman for twenty-some odd years, and they have two children in college. But you never know about some people. One of the guys in my dorm quad at Western Washington University was this ladies' man jock named Ron, and he now lives in Portland and goes by the name Vanessa. You just never know." He shrugged. "Anyway, considering what you've been going through, it must have been the last straw to discover the person representing the law around here had stolen your underwear."

Susan nodded. "Yes, it was pretty disturbing." She rubbed her arms from the chill again and then glanced over at Mattie. He was still batting and kicking around the multicolored ball, but just starting to slow down. She could tell, soon he would be very sleepy or very cranky.

She thought about the house again, about waking up last night and going downstairs to find Allen on some kind of guard duty with a gun. Did he know the history of that house? In Seattle, Realtors were required to divulge if there had been a murder or suicide in a dwelling for sale or lease. Did that same rule apply to rental houses in Cullen? Maybe that explained why he'd seemed so on edge last night. But it didn't make sense that he'd stay someplace where he wasn't comfortable, where he felt on his guard all the time.

She wondered once again: Why that particular house? Why that particular boat with the Internet connection?

Mattie tossed aside the bat and wandered over to them. Susan was surprised that he sat down next to Tom and started talking to him as if they were old friends. Tom poured him some lemonade, and Susan said he could have only one cookie. She smiled across the picnic table at the two of them. It felt very comfortable here. Suddenly, she remembered Allen and felt very guilty.

So she announced they had to get going.

As Tom walked them to her car, he pointed out the main road to his house—by a blue mailbox at the end of his driveway. The paved road would take her all the way to Rosie's, but even with her having to backtrack a little, it was still quicker and less chancy than the winding gravel trail she'd taken earlier. He offered to follow her back to the house and keep her company until Allen returned.

"Can't he come?" Mattie asked, while she strapped him into the car seat. "Can Tom sleep over? There'll be lots of room in your bed if Allen doesn't come back."

Susan glanced over her shoulder at Tom, who was

shaking his head. "Out of the mouths of babes," he murmured. "I swear to God, I didn't tell him to say that."

She cracked a smile, then turned to Mattie and wiped some chocolate from the corner of his mouth. "No, sweetie, Tom can't spend the night. Now, watch your fingers and toes." She shut his door.

"My offer still stands," Tom said. "Sure you don't want me to follow you back—just to make certain you're all right?"

"Thanks," Susan said. "But if Allen isn't at the house, I'm packing up our stuff and relocating to one of the inns in town. And if Allen's there, I don't want to show up with this—this good-looking guy, and have to explain how I just had a lovely time sipping lemonade with him in his backyard."

"Well, thank you," Tom said. "You know, I just might go into town tonight, and if you're staying at one of the inns—well, they have better cell phone reception there in town. Would it be okay if I called you—just to check in?"

Susan shrugged uneasily. "I'm afraid not. I don't think Allen would like it. But thanks."

"I understand," he said, opening the car door for her. "So long."

Susan got behind the wheel and started up the car. He shut the door for her, and she smiled at him through the window. Shifting to drive, she headed toward the blue mailbox at the end of his driveway. But when she glanced at him in her rearview mirror, she moved her foot to the brake. She rolled down her window and then ducked her head outside. "Tom?"

He hurried toward the car.

"My cell phone number is 206-555-1954," she said. "Can you remember it?"

Stopping just shy of the car window, Tom nodded. "Yes, I'll remember that."

"Good," she said.

Then Susan rolled up the window and headed out of the driveway.

Sitting on the basement stairs, Leo rubbed his forehead and watched his friend question Allen Meeker. He still couldn't get over Jordan's expertise on the Mama's Boy murders and the way facts and dates just tripped off his tongue. It was a whole side of his friend he'd never known about—and he was learning a lot more about those serial killings, too.

After the murder in Chicago in 1995, Mama's Boy took his trade to the Seattle area in 1997, and that was where he did the most damage, strangling eleven women in three years. He killed two young mothers in Oakland in 2000. Then there were the two possible "copycat" murders in Virginia in 2003 and 2004 that Jordan attributed to him. The most recent case in 2007 had occurred south of Portland. No one had called it a Mama's Boy murder, not yet, but Jordan felt it had all the signs of one.

"I want to ask you about the scuff marks on the inside of your trunk lid," he said, pacing in front of the worktable—like a TV lawyer in front of the witness box.

But this witness was stretched across the table, bound, shirtless, and shivering. His torn trousers only partially covered one leg. Leo winced as he studied him. Considering how long Meeker had been tied to that table in that same torture-rack position, his back, shoulders, and arms must have ached horribly. The guy had to be in agony.

But Jordan was relentless. "I think those marks were made by Rebecca Lyden after you locked her in the trunk of your car," he said. "You remember her, don't you, Allen? She was the young single mother from Eugene. Rebecca disappeared in 2007. I looked at the dealer's slips in the glove compartment of your car. You bought that BMW in Seattle in 2006. Unless there's another victim I don't know about, Rebecca made those marks."

"If you say so, yeah, sure," Meeker grunted sarcastically. He didn't even raise his head from the table when he replied. "You're the expert; you know everything. . . ."

"Rebecca vanished from a rest stop along Interstate 5 near Wilsonville, Oregon," Jordan continued. "Her two-year-old son was found wandering around and crying outside the women's lavatory with a clown doll in his hand. Was that your gift to him?"

Meeker didn't reply. He just shook his head over and over.

"They never did find Rebecca's body," Jordan went on. "Maybe that's why the newspapers didn't call it a Mama's Boy murder. You never bothered to hide the others too well. Why were you so careful with Rebecca's corpse? Didn't you want anyone to know Mama's Boy was back?"

"Y'know, it's bad enough you're trying to pin the Mama's Boy murders on me, and now you're blaming me for all these other crimes. Jesus, pretty soon you'll have me in Dallas, assassinating JFK in 1963." Meeker let out a tired, labored sigh. "About the car, I load a lot of crap in that trunk. If there are scuff marks inside my trunk, I wouldn't be at all surprised. But it doesn't make me a murder suspect." He glared at Jordan. "Let me tell you something. I don't know nearly as much about the Mama's Boy killings as you do. But I remember they were already going on when I moved from Chicago to Seattle in August 2000. I wasn't even living in Seattle when the first several murders occurred. If you don't believe me, you can ask my fiancée, Susan, or call up any one of my Chicago friends."

"August 2000?" Jordan repeated. "Six months later, you must have been kind of sorry you'd made the move to Seattle."

"Why? Was there another Mama's Boy murder?"

"No, something else happened. Do you remember what happened in Seattle on Ash Wednesday, February twenty-eighth, 2001?"

Allen just shook his head.

"Around eleven in the morning?" Jordan pressed.

"I give up," Meeker grumbled.

Leo took hold of the banister and slowly got to his feet. He knew exactly what Jordan was getting at. Next to September 11, it was the other where-were-you-when event for Seattleites that year.

"February twenty-eighth, 2001, is when Seattle had the second worst earthquake in its history—a magnitude six point eight. Everybody in the area felt it. But you don't remember it, because you weren't there."

"Shit, that doesn't mean anything—"

"The last known Mama's Boy victim in the Seattle

area was Candice Schulman," Jordan spoke over him. "She was abducted in front of her four-year-old twin sons in their home on October sixteenth, 2000. You left the boys a couple of moldy hand puppets on the living room sofa. Some kids found Candice's body two days later in the woods by Shilshole Bay. By February 2001, you'd already left Washington state. The day before the Seattle earthquake, you were in Oakland, killing Leslie Anne Fuller. You tore her away from her toddler son in the parking lot of the Emeryville Food Court. You left a stuffed animal on the hood of her car. . . ."

"Not me," he shook his head. "I've never even been to Oakland, damn it! I didn't remember the exact date of the earthquake because I was out of town that week—in Spokane. I travel for my job—I already told you that! I heard about the quake, yes, of course. When I came back home that Friday, I was relieved because there wasn't any real damage to my place." His voice started to crack. "How do you expect me to know the exact date, for God's sakes?"

"I knew it," Leo piped up. "I remember it."

"Well, good for you," Meeker grumbled, tears brimming in his eyes. "Go to the head of the class, chum. You guys have already made up your minds I'm this—this heinous serial killer, and there isn't anything I can say to convince you otherwise, is there? What do you want me to say? What? Want me to confess?" Wincing, he looked at Jordan and then at Leo. "All right, okay, I did it! I killed them all! I murdered your mother in cold blood—and the rest of them, too! Is that what you want to hear? So are you going to get the police now?"

Jordan slowly shook his head. "It's not that easy."

"Oh, Jesus," Meeker cried. He glanced at Leo, his

eyes pleading. "He'll never let me go. There's nothing I can say or do to change his mind. I'm going to die down here. . . ."

Leo swallowed hard. He stared back at Meeker and knew the man was right.

Moira's eyes finally adjusted to the murky darkness inside the small, cold room, and dim images began to take shape. She was locked in some sort of storage room, probably a janitor's closet. From the icy cement floor, she figured it was in a basement or on a ground level. The empty metal bookcase was pushed against the wall—close to the door. The thin strip of light under the door was barely discernible. Up in the corner of the opposite wall was a fan box. Tiny slivers of daylight peeked through the built-in slats. There were some capped-off pipe ends along that wall, too. It looked like there might have been a sink in the room at one time.

She kept hearing that flapping noise. Sometimes it grew very loud as the breeze kicked up. She'd listen to the wind howling—and feel a slight draft through the fan slats.

Moira took the tortoiseshell barrette out of the pocket of her jeans, crawled across the mattress, and hobbled the rest of her way to the door. She still couldn't put much weight on her left foot without it hurting like a son of a bitch.

Catching her breath, she leaned against the door and slid the metal clip in the chink by the door handle until she felt the lock. She applied some pressure to it with the metal clip and rattled the knob, but it wasn't giving at all. "C'mon, c'mon," she muttered to herself, jiggling and jabbing the clip against the door lock.

She kept wondering about the woman who had owned this barrette. She must have been a hiker or big nature buff to be in those woods alone. Had the barrette fallen out of her hair when she'd plunged into that pit? Maybe he'd *rescued* her, too—if she hadn't already broken her neck from the fall. Had he locked her in this same janitor's closet and taken her photograph? Moira wondered if he'd stolen that other girl's bra, too.

Running her fingertips along the door frame by the knob, she could feel the wood was frayed there—as if someone had scratched and chipped away at it for a long time. Or maybe several people had, several women.

Moira imagined her photo and her brassiere as part of some maniacal murderer's private collection. As terrified as she was of dying, she also dreaded what he might do to her beforehand. She was still a virgin, and even the idea of *normal* sex was a bit scary to her. She shuddered to think what this man might want from her—before finishing her off.

Her hands shook horribly as she continued to wiggle the clip against the door catch. "C'mon, please," she whispered. She missed Leo and wished she'd never argued with him. She was thinking of her mom and dad, too, and how much she just wanted to be home right now. The barrette clip bent, and she shifted positions, forgetting for a moment about her sore ankle. As soon as she put weight on it, sharp pain shot through her leg.

Moira let out an anguished cry and slid down to the cold cement floor. She banged against the bottom of the door. "Let me out of here!" she cried. Her voice was still hoarse from all of her screaming earlier, and her throat felt raw. "Please! My parents, they'll pay you! If—if you just get me to a phone . . ."

But she knew, in all likelihood, this guy wasn't after money.

There was something else he wanted—something unthinkable.

CHAPTER
SEVENTEEN

Through the dirty corner of the windshield, where the wipers couldn't reach, Susan gazed over at the break in the trees along Carroll Creek Road. It was the turnoff for Cedar Crest Way, which eventually led to the Prewitts' cabin. Susan eased her foot off the accelerator. She was thinking about Jordan Prewitt and everything Tom had told her about him.

She couldn't help wondering if Jordan had anything to do with Allen's sudden disappearance. After all, as far as she knew, Jordan was the last person to see Allen before he went missing today.

The speedometer hovered around ten miles per hour as she approached the turnoff to the Prewitt cabin.

She'd left that place earlier feeling somewhat dissatisfied. Now that she knew Jordan was connected to the rental house, she wanted to go back and talk to him again. But talk about what—his murdered mother?

Shaking her head, Susan sped up and passed Cedar Crest Way.

In just a few minutes, she would be at the house on

Birch—"the scene of the crime," as Tom had referred to it. She told herself that she shouldn't expect to see Allen's BMW parked in the driveway or find him waiting for her.

Then she'd feel even worse for her dalliance with Tom Collins. For all she knew, Allen could have been in a car wreck. Right now, he could be dead—or in a hospital somewhere, hooked up to a respirator. And here she was giving her cell phone number to this charming, handsome man she barely knew. What was she thinking?

She glanced in the rearview mirror at Mattie. He was asleep in the child seat with that limp, absolutely-dead-but-still-breathing posture.

As she turned down Birch and approached the house, Susan didn't see Allen's car in the driveway. No surprise. She didn't see anyone lurking around the house either, thank God. Mattie barely stirred as she took him out of his car seat. She carried him into the house, up the stairs, and put him on the bed in his room. She covered him with a throw. She planned to start packing their things in just a few minutes.

Back downstairs, she checked her note to Allen, and it looked untouched, unread. She glanced out the sunroom's glass door at *The Seaworthy*—tied to that dock that had become a local landmark for the morbidly curious. The beautiful, orange-azure-streaked sunset reflected on the bay's rippling surface.

Susan unlocked the door and slid it open. She didn't want to leave Mattie alone in the house too long, even though he was sleeping. She trotted down to the dock and hurried across the same wooden planks where Jordan Prewitt's mother had been abducted ten years ago.

Susan was just about to climb aboard *The Seawor- thy* when she saw something that made her balk. There on the cockpit seat, someone had laid out Mattie's and her life vests, which she'd discarded on the dock ear- lier. She remembered stepping around those vests the last time she was on the dock. Now they were neatly folded up on the boat.

A chill raced through her. Who would do something like that? Susan convinced herself that the sheriff or deputy must have folded the vests and put them there when they'd checked around for that hunter character.

She boarded the boat, then took out the keys, un- locked the cabin door, and pulled it open. All the while, the boat gently teetered from side to side. Step- ping down into the darkened cabin, Susan turned on the power switch, and the interior lights went on. The computer started, but it took a while to warm up.

If someone had phoned Bayside Rentals asking if the Internet was working on *The Seaworthy*, perhaps that was how they'd planned to get a message to Allen. Had Allen seen something online when he'd been get- ting the boat ready? Maybe there was an e-mail or an instant message that might explain his sudden disap- pearance.

The Windows menu finally came up on the screen. Sitting on the edge of the captain's swivel chair, Susan pulled out the drawer with the keyboard and mouse and clicked on the Internet Explorer icon. It was an old computer and took a few more moments to make the connection.

Waiting impatiently, Susan stood and gazed out the thin, long horizontal window at the house. No one was prowling around the woods; at least, she didn't see anybody. Then she glanced around the interior cabin. She spotted something pink on the couch cushion. At first, she thought she'd left behind a toy from Mattie's bin. But then she stepped toward the settee and saw it was a brassiere.

Susan picked it up. One of the straps was torn. She automatically moved toward the V-berth—to make sure no one was in there. The place was empty.

"You've got mail!" the computer announced.

Susan set the brassiere on the table, moved over to the navigating station, and sat down again. Biting her lip, she clicked on the MAIL icon. There were three un-read e-mails within the last two hours, all of them from secretadmirer@ mbfan.com. The e-mail subjects were blank.

Susan clicked on the earliest e-mail, sent at 1:55 PM. The screen came up:

Where R U?

It didn't say anything else. Susan clicked on the next message at 2:40:

R U there yet? U can't avoid me.

If these messages were for Allen, obviously, the sender didn't know where he was either. The last e-mail was at 3:50:

U need 2 respond 2 me or I come 4 S & M in 1 hr.

"Oh, my God," Susan murmured. She glanced at her wristwatch. The hour was almost up. She peered out the

long window at the house again. She didn't see anyone.

Turning toward the monitor again, she clicked on
the REPLY icon and typed furiously. She tried to adapt
Secret Admirer's amateur shorthand:

> Sorry 2 B late. Unavoidably detained. R U close by? I'm
> here & awaiting instructions.

She clicked the SEND icon, and—true to her word—
waited. She glanced over at the brassiere on the table.
Someone had left that bra there for her or Allen to
find—no doubt the same person who had moved and
folded up the life vests. The police hadn't moved those
vests, she knew that now. The vests had still been out
on the dock after the sheriff and deputy had left.

Susan peered out the window again. She couldn't
linger, not if this person intended to come for Mattie
and her within the next few minutes. She had to grab
Mattie and get the hell out of there—no stopping to
pack or update the note to Allen. She'd drive to Rosie's
and call the police from there.

She heard a click from the computer—and saw the
MAIL icon blinking. It was another message from secre-
tadmirer@ mbfan.com. This one had a subject—*Pink
Souvenir*—and it had some kind of image attachment.

Susan clicked on READ MAIL, and an automatic warning came up advising that she shouldn't open e-mails
with download files unless she knew the sender. Susan
bypassed it. The text popped up on the screen:

> She's waiting 4 U. I'll send U another message soon. U
> know better than 2 involve police. Yes, I M very close. . . .

Below the text, a photo began to emerge—one section at a time from the top of the picture to the bottom. It was a blurry shot of a pale young woman with short-cropped dark hair. Susan recognized her. She'd been at the store yesterday with Jordan and his friend. They'd said her name was Moira. Naked from the waist up, she was sitting on a stained mattress in the dark. She had a dirt smudge on her forehead and looked startled and scared. She was covering her breasts with a bunched-up towel or sweater. Someone had obviously taken her top and her bra.

Susan turned and glanced at the brassiere on the galley table, the *pink souvenir*.

She heard a scream in the distance.

"Mattie!" she whispered. "My God . . ."

Rushing up the ladder to the deck, she leapt off the boat and stumbled onto the dock. She heard him scream again. "Go away!" he yelled. "Mommy . . . Mommy!"

Susan raced up the hill toward the house and the sound of his voice. The sunroom door was open, just as she'd left it. Inside the house, she stopped suddenly. She couldn't hear him anymore. The place was deathly quiet.

She rushed toward the front of the house, where the door was closed and locked. "Mattie?" she called, running up the stairs two steps at a time. "Mattie? Sweetie?"

Stopping in his doorway, she froze. His bed was empty.

"Mattie?" she screamed again, panic-stricken. She swiveled around and checked the bathroom—empty. Then she hurried down the hall to the master bedroom. He wasn't in there either. But she noticed the closet door was ajar. She heard a quiet whimpering.

"Mattie, honey?" she asked, trying to catch her breath. She moved toward the closet. "Sweetie, are you in there?"

"Mommy?"

"Oh, thank God," she whispered. She opened the door and found him sitting curled up amid Allen's and her shoes. Knees to his chest, he clutched Woody against the side of his face. She crouched down and reached out for him. "Sweetie, what happened?"

He threw his arms around her neck. "I woke up and you were gone!" he cried. "There's a monster in my room. I'm hiding from him. He—he—he's under the bed. . . ."

"It's okay, Mattie," she said, hugging him and patting his back. Finally, she lifted him up and carried him out of the bedroom. She headed for the stairs. "Everything's going to be all right," she cooed reassuringly. "We're leaving here now. Okay, sweetie? I'll make sure this monster doesn't get anywhere near you. . . ."

Susan meant every word she said.

It didn't work worth a damn.

Moira gave up trying to manipulate the lock with the flimsy, bent barrette clip. She moved away from the door and blindly felt around the shelves of the metal bookcase for something else she might use to trip the lock. The tall shelving unit had been put together with thin perforated metal pieces and screws. She found a discarded bracket lying in the back corner of the second-to-top shelf. The perforated piece was a bit longer than a nail file and only slightly thicker.

She slipped it in the door hinge by the lock, wiggling and maneuvering it while she twisted the knob. "C'mon, please, God," she whispered.

Suddenly she heard a click, and the knob turned.

With a grateful little cry, she pushed at the door with her shoulder. But it didn't budge. She couldn't understand it. She'd tripped the stupid lock. She kept twisting and turning the knob. What was going on?

Then Moira realized what was going on was the door must have another lock, probably a dead bolt.

"Goddamn it!" Moira cried, her voice raspy. Frustrated, she almost threw the metal piece across the tiny room. But she thought better of it. She might need the metal bracket as a weapon against that man when he came back for her, and he almost certainly would. Of course, she might as well defend herself with a butter knife. But it beat nothing.

Moira told herself that she wouldn't become one of his victims. That photo of her and her pink bra—they would be the last in his collection. She would survive this. She'd have to crawl or hobble, but she would get out of this cold, stinking little dungeon.

And stink it did. She was probably contributing to the foul smell herself after all her time in that dirty pit and then here in this little closet. Not much fresh air passed through the fan box near the ceiling.

Moira squinted up at it. She saw by the slivers of daylight seeping through those slats. There was no other light source. She wondered if she could fit through that opening. *Maybe*, she thought if she could pry or unscrew the slat covering.

A while ago, she hadn't been able to see her hand in front of her face. But Moira's eyes had adjusted to the darkness, because she could now see the thin metal bracket in her grasp. She probably had a snowball's chance in hell of clearing that opening and making it through to the outside. But she had to try.

And she had to work fast. Any time now, her abductor could come for a second visit. Another concern was that the light through those slats was starting to dim. It was getting dark out.

Pretty soon, she wouldn't be able to see anything—except blackness.

And then she might as well be dead.

Strapped in his car seat, Mattie kicked and wiggled in protest. His pinched-up face got red as he cried—a cranky, staccato whine that was, erratically, loud and then quieter.

Susan handed him Woody, and he immediately threw the doll on the car floor. The aborted nap definitely hadn't agreed with him. If Susan only could have put him back to bed, he might have calmed down and slept for another half hour and then been fine. Instead, she'd swept him up in her arms and carried him downstairs, where she grabbed her purse and his jacket. He'd started crying just as she'd headed out the door.

"That's no way to treat your pal, Woody," Susan said, having to talk loudly over his wailing. She picked up the doll and set it on the car seat—out of his reach. "I need you to be a good boy, Mattie. Okay?"

But he was cranky, scared, and disoriented. Susan knew exactly how he felt. Obviously, Allen was in some sort of secret communication with the person who had sent that e-mail. The photo of that teenage girl and the *pink souvenir* were meant for him. Susan wondered if Allen knew the girl. Whatever the case, the e-mails confirmed it: Allen definitely had an ulterior motive for this weekend getaway—but what exactly? And why did he have to drag her and Mattie up here for this trip?

She wondered about that poor girl. Jordan and his friend had said she'd gone for a walk in the woods. Were they lying? Were they the ones who sent that e-mail to Allen?

Susan hurried around the car to the driver's side and climbed behind the wheel. She was about to shut the door when she heard the sound of gravel under tires. She hesitated, unsure who it could be—maybe Allen, finally pulling into the driveway, or maybe the man who had sent him that horrible e-mail.

Susan shut her door and locked it. She started up the engine, but waited. That other car, when it arrived, would block the driveway. Susan reached into her purse for the flare gun and set it beside her. One hand, white-knuckled, on the steering wheel, she warily gazed in the rearview mirror, waiting for the other car to come into view. *Please be Tom*, she thought. It was crazy, but the most comforting sight right now for her would be that red MINI Cooper coming up the driveway.

Mattie's irritable cries competed with the sound of the approaching vehicle, but Susan could still hear it, coming up the driveway. "Mattie, sweetie, enough is enough," she growled. She nervously twisted the loose indicator handle. She kept fiddling with it until she'd completely unscrewed it from the steering column. "Shit," she muttered under her breath, screwing it back into place. Mattie didn't hear her swear. He was still crying.

In her rearview mirror, Susan watched a police car come around the tree-lined curve in the driveway. "Oh, great," she grumbled, switching off the ignition. It was the sheriff, *that panty-bandit*. But maybe he'd come with some news; maybe they'd located Allen.

Biting her lip, she glanced over her shoulder as the patrol car parked behind her Toyota.

"I don't wanna ride in the car!" Mattie was complaining.

"Sweetie, please," she said, shushing him. She watched and waited while the cop remained in the front seat of his prowler for a few moments. When he finally stepped out of the patrol car, Susan saw it was the deputy. A notebook in his hand, he started toward the house.

Susan opened her door. "Deputy?" she called.

The solidly built blond cop turned. "Oh, Ms. Blanchette, there you are. . . ."

"Did you find Allen?" she asked apprehensively.

"I'm afraid not," he said—talking a bit loudly to be heard over Mattie's cries. He waved at him, but it didn't do any good. Mattie kept screaming. "Somebody's not too happy. . . ."

"He got shortchanged in the nap department this afternoon," Susan explained, rubbing her forehead. From this part of the driveway, she had a view of the backyard—and the boat by their dock. *U know better than 2 involve police,* the e-mail had said. Then again, maybe the police were already involved. Maybe they were looking for that poor girl.

"Ah, if you didn't come about Allen, what—what can I do for you, deputy?" she asked.

"Oh, please, call me Corey," he replied with a cordial smile. "Nancy gave me your message. . . ."

"Nancy?"

"Yeah, Nancy Abbe, our operator at the police station," he explained. "She said you'd called and left a message for the sheriff. He's off duty now. So—I'm just following it up. If you'd like, I can put out a statewide APB to be on the lookout for your fiancé's vehicle." He glanced at his notepad. "Black 2005 BMW with Washington plates, KKC405. Is that correct?"

Susan nodded eagerly.

"While I'm at it, I'll notify my buddies in blue at Mount Vernon, Anacortes, Bellingham, and Everett. I'll get word to the ferry terminals, too."

"That would be terrific," Susan said with a dazed, grateful smile.

"Okay then," the deputy said. "I'm on it." He headed back to his patrol car.

Susan opened the back door of her Toyota, then unfastened Mattie from his car seat. He was still crying—but more softly now, as if he might fall asleep soon. Susan grabbed his Woody doll, then shut the car door with her hip. She carried Mattie to the police car, where Deputy Corey—she'd forgotten his last name—was sitting in the front, talking on the police radio to the woman she'd spoken with earlier. Susan recognized her voice—even through all the radio static and Mattie's whining. The deputy was instructing Nancy to phone and fax all the surrounding police stations and the ferry terminals to keep a lookout for Allen's car. In the middle of it, he stopped and looked up at Susan. "Hold on a sec, Nancy," he said into the radio mike. Then he nodded at Mattie. "Ms. Blanchette, if you'd like to take our buddy there inside the house, that's cool. Maybe you can give that nap a second try. I'll check in with you once I'm finished up here."

"Of course, I'm sorry," she said. Then she headed toward the house's front door. She could hear the deputy talking into his police radio.

"We're looking for Meeker, Allen, male, thirty-nine, black-grey hair. . . ."

She began to feel a little bit better, enough so she could talk calmly to Mattie once she'd laid him down on the sunroom sofa. She put his Woody doll in his hand, then took off her windbreaker and covered him with it. "You know, we're going back home tomorrow," she said. "Won't that be nice, sweetie? Just you and me, and we'll take it easy. Maybe we'll order a pizza and watch TV. What do you think? Just a boring night at home, doesn't that sound pretty wonderful right about now?"

"'Kay," he murmured, nodding tiredly. "Can we watch *Shrek* when we go home?"

"Of course," she said, smoothing back his light brown hair. "Anything you want, sweetie." She watched his long-lashed eyelids flutter and then close.

While he dozed off, Susan glanced over toward the sliding glass door—at *The Seaworthy* moored to the old dock outside. She thought about the e-mail warning her—or more specifically, warning Allen—not to involve the police. The person who had sent that e-mail had said he wasn't far away. Well, if he was watching the house, he knew police were here now. He probably figured she was telling the police everything anyway. She wasn't putting that girl in any more danger by letting this deputy know what was going on.

Just then, the deputy lumbered up the steps to the back porch. As Susan tiptoed over to the glass door, slid it open, and stepped outside, he took off his police cap.

"Well, we're getting the word out there," he said. "Someone's bound to spot his car soon."

"Thank you very much," Susan whispered. "Listen—ah, Corey, have you had any other missing persons cases today?"

Frowning, he shook his head.

"There's this teenager named Moira, and I think she's in trouble. . . ." Susan glanced back at Mattie on the sofa. She didn't want to be gone too long—and have him wake up to find himself alone again. "Could I—very quickly show you something on the boat?"

At a brisk clip, they started down the back lawn together. Susan told the deputy about the pink brassiere she'd found and the cryptic e-mails. Listening intently, he kept scratching his blond head. He stepped aboard the boat first and then reached out his hand to help her onto the deck. Susan had been in such a rush earlier she'd left the cabin open and the power on. She took one last look back at the house before she went below.

In the boat's cabin, she pointed out the bra with the torn strap on the galley table. The deputy advised her not to touch it again. "This is way out of my league, and Stuart's, too," he murmured, bent over the table with his hands behind him as he closely studied the bra. "We'll have to get the state police on this pronto. Let's leave this right where it is. . . ."

Susan sat down at the navigation station. The computer screen had turned black except for the floating Windows logo. She clicked the mouse, and a porn site came up on the screen: *BOOBS BONANZA—XXX-RATED!* flashed across sexually explicit photos of nude, large-busted women in various provocative positions.

"Now, that's some evidence I don't mind reviewing," the deputy remarked.

Susan tried to clear it, but the pornographic images remained on the screen. She couldn't even go back to the menu screen. "What is this?" she muttered, frustrated. "This wasn't here before. . . ."

Corey was looking over her shoulder. "You said you downloaded a picture of the girl? I bet you anything the guy sent you a virus. Mind if I get in there?"

Susan surrendered the chair, then anxiously glanced out the window at the house again. The deputy managed to clear the screen, but he was having difficulty bringing up anything else. "If you can bear with me for just a few minutes," he murmured, "let me try a few things, here. There's still a chance we can get something off the hard drive. . . ."

"I'm sorry, but I really don't want to leave my son alone in the house," Susan said. "I need to be close by in case he wakes up."

Eyes on the screen, the deputy nodded. "Go, go," he urged her. "I'll meet you on the back porch. I won't be more than two minutes here. If this is a dead end, I don't want to waste any more time on it—especially if this girl's in any kind of real danger."

Susan nodded and then headed up on deck. She jumped back onto the dock and scurried up the lawn toward the house. At the porch steps, she slowed down and crept up to the sliding glass door. Mattie was on the sofa, fast asleep. She caught her breath, then turned and glanced back at *The Seaworthy*. The boat's outside and interior lights glowed against the darkening sky.

After a few minutes, the boat's lights went out, and the deputy climbed up from the cabin. Susan watched his silhouette as he stepped onto the dock and hurried up the sloped lawn toward her. As his face emerged from the shadows, she could see he was frowning. "No luck," he grumbled, shaking his head. "But maybe if we got some computer geek to tinker with it, we'd recover those e-mails." He gave her the keys to the boat and then glanced toward the glass door. "Is he still sleeping?"

Susan nodded. "Thank God."

"Any clue at all who might have sent those e-mails?" he asked. "Anything more you could tell me about the girl would be a helluva lot of help."

"Her name's Moira, and she's here for the weekend with Jordan Prewitt and another friend. They're staying at this house on—ah—"

"Cedar Crest Way?" the deputy finished for her.

Susan nodded again. "I stopped by there about two hours ago, hoping they might know where Allen was. Jordan was the last one to see him." She sighed. "Anyway, Moira wasn't there when I dropped by. They didn't invite me in or anything. They were acting sort of peculiar. I can't put my finger on it exactly. They were just acting kind of funny. . . ."

"Well, Jordan Prewitt's a pretty strange kid," the deputy said. "Then again, I can't blame him. He's been through a lot."

"I know," Susan murmured. "I talked at length about him with our neighbor, Tom Collins, this afternoon. He told me about Jordan's mother—and what happened at this house with Mama's Boy ten years ago."

The deputy nodded glumly. "Huh, that Collins guy is a pretty weird character himself."

Susan didn't like hearing that. "What do you mean?" she asked warily.

He shrugged. "The guy's a real hermit, all holed up in that house every other weekend. No friends or visitors. I don't think anyone besides him has ever been inside that house since his father moved away. God knows what he's up to."

Susan stared at him and shook her head. She hated to consider it, but indeed there was something odd about Tom not even letting them inside the house for a moment.

"Anyway, you were telling me about your visit with Jordan Prewitt," the deputy said.

"Yes, well . . ." she shrugged. "I asked Jordan and his friend if I could talk with Moira in case she'd run into Allen or seen his car. They said she'd gone for a walk in the woods. They said they'd get back in touch with me once Moira returned from this nature hike. But that was over two hours ago. Anyway, I have a feeling something's going on over at that cabin."

The deputy nodded. "I'll go check it out." He

glanced toward Mattie in the sunroom. "I think you
and your son will be okay here for the next half hour.
But you better double-lock your doors just to be safe.
When I radio in about the girl, I'll have Nancy pull
some strings and get you a room at one of the inns in
town. They're usually booked solid on weekends. But
we've got some clout. I don't like you two staying out
here alone any longer than you have to. Do you have
anything for self-defense besides that flare gun?"

Susan shook her head. "Allen had a revolver, but it
was in the car with him."

The deputy's eyes narrowed at her for a moment,
but then he just nodded. "Well, you could start a fire
with that flare gun. Listen, there's a whole arsenal in
the trunk of my prowler. I'll loan you something. Be
right back. . . ."

Susan followed him as far as some bushes near the
side of the house. She watched the deputy duck into
the driver's seat of his patrol car. He left the door open,
so she could just make out what he was saying on the
radio: "We have a possible kidnapping or hostage situation involving a teenage girl, too soon to tell for sure
right now. But put Stuart on alert. I'm headed to the
Prewitt cabin on Cedar Crest Way for a follow-up.
Stay tuned, over and out."

He popped the trunk, then climbed out of the car
and lifted the hood. Susan watched him hover over the
trunk for a minute. Finally, he shut the hood, turned,
and then swaggered toward her with a pistol in his
hand.

From the corner of the house, Susan glanced toward
the open sunroom door. Not a peep out of Mattie so far.

The deputy came through a pathway in the bushes and plopped the pistol in her hand. "This is a semiautomatic pellet gun," he said. "It won't do as much damage as a regular handgun or your flare, but it's still very effective. It's used for riot control, and we don't get too many violent demonstrations here in Cullen. That's on loan for the next half hour. Don't tell Stuart I let you borrow it, or he'll have my ass in a sling. It's all loaded and ready. FYI—you can do a lot of damage if you aim for the head or groin. But you're probably not going to need it. . . ."

Susan looked at the gun in her hand and nodded nervously.

"Give me forty-five minutes," the deputy continued. "And if I'm not back by then, you and your boy hightail it to Rosie's, and then call Nancy at the police station. Until then, stay inside and keep the doors locked, okay?"

She nodded again. "Thank you."

"Be back soon," he said. Then he turned and hurried toward his patrol car.

The pistol felt awkward and heavy in her hand. A cool wind came off the bay, and Susan shuddered. She watched the police car back into the turnaround and then head out the driveway. It took a curve in the drive and disappeared behind some trees.

Susan retreated back inside the house and quietly slid shut the sunroom's glass door behind her. She locked it. Then she checked the front door to make sure it was locked and bolted. Returning to the sunroom, she checked on Mattie. He hadn't stirred.

She tucked her windbreaker around his neck. Then she sank down in the nearby easy chair. She glanced at her wristwatch: 5:20.

Susan held on to the gun. She didn't think she'd ever get used to the feel of it. All she could do for the next forty-five minutes was wait.

CHAPTER
EIGHTEEN

"**M**OIRA, ARE YOU OUT THERE?" he called.

Leo stood at the edge of the darkened woods behind Jordan's family cabin. He'd switched on the outside lights in back of the house, hoping that might help Moira find her way in the dark. It was officially nighttime, and he was officially scared for her now. Tears came to his eyes as he stared at the blackness past the first cluster of trees. Leo had quickly thrown together a cold ham and cheese sandwich to keep his blood sugar in balance. He had it in his hand, but couldn't eat or swallow just now. His throat was closing up from crying.

He was so worried about her—and worried about Jordan, who was acting like a crazy man—a dangerous, crazy man. His buddy had asked for just twenty more minutes to get a confession out of his captive. But that had been almost an hour ago. Meeker had tried to confess, but Jordan still wasn't satisfied. Leo had a feeling Jordan wouldn't be satisfied until the man was dead.

And all the while, Moira was missing. He should have driven to the store and phoned the police at least two hours ago—while it was still daylight and they still had a chance of finding her in these woods. Why the hell had he left her alone earlier? It was his fault she was lost.

And if anything happened to Susan Blanchette and her little boy, it would be his fault, too. Meeker had sworn up and down his fiancée and her son were in danger. He'd said if any harm came to them, he would blame him.

It was all Leo could do to keep Meeker alive, to keep his friend from killing him.

At the moment, he was pushing his luck by leaving them alone in the basement for just these few minutes. Any time now, he half expected to hear a muted gunshot from within the house, and then he'd know that Jordan had murdered the man.

He called out for Moira again. But there was no response from within the gloomy woods, just leaves rustling in the wind.

Turning toward the house again, Leo wiped the tears from his eyes and managed to take a few bites of his sandwich. He noticed Jordan's car parked in the driveway. It was only a five- or ten-minute drive to that store and the pay phone, where he could call the police—and finally put an end to this. Then they could start looking for Moira, too.

But he didn't dare leave Jordan alone with that man for even the short time it would take to drive to the store and back. Plus, Jordan was acting so crazy right now. What was to keep him from shooting at the police when they arrived? A lot of people—including Jordan—could end up dead.

At the kitchen door, Leo took a long last look at the darkened woods. He thought of how three hours ago, he'd been worried Moira would return to the cabin and discover the bizarre, horrible thing Jordan had done. He'd started packing her things to head her off when she returned. He remembered the prescription bottle in the dresser drawer of Moira's room: TAKE ONE CAPSULE BY MOUTH 30 MINUTES BEFORE BEDTIME AS NEEDED FOR SLEEP. DO NOT EXCEED DOSAGE.

He tossed aside what was left of his sandwich and then hurried into the house, through the kitchen, and up the stairs to the master bedroom. Taking the prescription bottle from the dresser, he shook out five capsules and shoved them in his pocket.

He swung by the bathroom, waited a few moments, and then flushed the toilet—just in case Jordan wanted to know why he'd gone up to the second floor.

Returning to the kitchen, Leo dug out a half-full bottle of citrus-flavored Vitaminwater from the refrigerator. Jordan had been drinking it earlier. Leo reopened it and set it on the counter.

The basement door was open, and he could hear Jordan talking. "Why the toys?" he was asking. "It always struck me as an empty gesture, since the cops took away those mangy, used toys as evidence. You had to know that. You knew us motherless boys would never get a chance to play with them—even if we wanted to. Was it all for show, just something for the newspapers?"

"I give up," Meeker replied in a weak, raspy voice. "I don't know what you want me to say. . . ."

"Some of the toys were eventually traced to a Value Village secondhand store in Seattle," Jordan continued. "But I always had a feeling that a few of those consolation prizes might have been yours when you were a little boy. . . ."

He heard Meeker mutter something but couldn't make out what he said.

Hovering over the counter, Leo nervously twisted open the sleeping capsules and dumped the powder into Jordan's Vitaminwater. He shoved the empty capsules in his pants pocket. Putting the cap back on the bottle, he gently shook it until he couldn't see the sediment anymore. Then he quickly shoved the bottle back in the refrigerator.

"For me, you left a little sailor doll," Jordan was saying. "Remember? It was very appropriate. How did you know I was going to be in a boat when you took my mother away?"

Leo crept down the stairs, and every step creaked. Both Jordan and Meeker glanced at him for a moment. Jordan was standing directly in front of his prone captive.

Jordan sighed and gazed down at the man. "Answer me."

Meeker closed his eyes and pressed his cheek to the tabletop. "I had a whole collection of old toys in the trunk of my car," he murmured. "Some of them were mine, and some were from secondhand stores, like you say. Leaving the toy was my trademark. When I saw you in the boat, I remembered I had the sailor doll, so I snuck back to the car and grabbed it from the box of stuff."

Leo froze at the bottom of the steps. He felt the hair

on the back of his neck stand on end. Meeker was admitting it now. He was even giving details.

"Were you following my mother and me around the day before you abducted her?" Jordan pressed.

"Yeah, I did that sometimes. If I could, I'd watch them for a few days before I made any kind of move."

Jordan started breathing heavily. "How did you decide on my mother? Why her?"

"I don't know. I guess because she was pretty."

"How long were you watching her?"

The man sighed. "I don't know, about a week."

Suddenly, Jordan slapped him across the skull with the back of his hand. "Fucking liar!"

Meeker grimaced in pain.

"Jesus, Jordan, what are you doing?" Leo started toward him.

"He's lying!" Jordan yelled. Some spit flew out of his mouth. "He's just been saying what he thinks I want to hear! But he's lying." He swiveled around and glared at Meeker, who started to weep again. "You couldn't have been following my mother around for only a week. It had to be a lot longer than that—or maybe she was just an impulse kill."

Leo shook his head. "Jordan, you're not making any sense—"

"The day my dad dropped me off at the house on Birch—the day before my mother was killed—I hadn't seen her for three weeks. Don't you understand? He wouldn't have been following her around for a week just because she was pretty. He only went after women with sons. In my mother's case, he couldn't have known she had a son until the day before he killed her. Like I say, I hadn't seen my mother in three weeks."

He turned and swatted him on the back of the head again. "You think you're being so clever. You're purposely making mistakes like that so you can point out later that you were making it all up."

"Oh, God, please, stop it!" the man cried.

"She was an impulse kill, wasn't she?" Jordan hissed, raising his hand again.

Leo grabbed his arm. "No! Jordan, that's enough. . . ."

Jordan pulled away from him, then retreated to the stairs and sank down on one of the lower steps. He put his face in his hands. "There were a few boats out on the bay the day I arrived, even with the choppy water," he murmured, his voice cracking. "I always figured Mama's Boy must have been on one of them. With a set of binoculars, he could have seen my mom and me in the backyard. Maybe he saw me trying out the kayak. I think he started following us around that first afternoon."

Standing over his friend, Leo said nothing. But he remembered Meeker mentioning that he was going to take his fiancée and her son sailing today. So Meeker was an experienced sailor. He remembered something else Meeker had said: *For all I know, maybe this is some "good cop, bad cop" routine you two dreamed up.*

He reached under the banister, between the posts, and patted Jordan's shoulder. "Why don't you take a break?" he whispered. "Go upstairs, get something cool to drink. Let me ask him some questions for a while."

Rubbing his eyes, Jordan nodded. "I'll go up in a minute," he murmured.

Leo glanced over at Meeker, half naked and shivering, stretched across the worktable. Leo moved over toward the washer and dryer, where he grabbed a plaid blanket from a laundry basket. He shook out the dust and brought it over to Meeker and laid it over his shoulders. Over the blanket, Leo rubbed Meeker's taut, tense back and arms. The man shuddered and moaned gratefully. Leo returned to the laundry sink and refilled the measuring cup with cold water. He brought the cup to Meeker and then set it to his lips. Meeker quickly drank the water down. Leo rubbed his shoulders again.

"Why don't you give him a goddamn manicure while you're at it?" Jordan mumbled.

Leo shot his friend a look; then he went back to rubbing their prisoner's aching shoulders and arms. With a sigh, Meeker seemed to melt against the table.

Leo didn't know very much about the Mama's Boy murders. He certainly didn't have Jordan's expertise. But Moira read like a fiend, and true crime was one her favorite subjects. She'd once told him that studies revealed serial killers and mass murderers were often the victims of violence and abuse in their own childhoods. A serial killer with the nickname Mama's Boy certainly had a good shot of being among those childhood victims.

Jordan, the bad cop, had tried to get their Mama's Boy suspect to talk about his crimes. But that hadn't worked out. Leo figured it was now his turn to be the good cop and get Meeker to talk about the crimes committed against him when he was a kid—if there were any.

The notion that he was rubbing the shoulders of a possible serial killer—even with an old blanket between them—sickened Leo, and he stepped back. He wiped his hands on his shirt and then nervously stuck them in his pants pockets. "Okay, I—I'd like to ask you some questions now—ah, Allen," he said, trying not to stammer. "Then we'll wrap this up, I promise. But I—I really need to warn you, we can check all this out with your fiancée to find out if you're telling the truth."

"Go ahead," Meeker murmured.

"Were you an only child?"

The man squinted at him. "What?"

"Were you an only child?" Leo repeated.

Meeker was scowling. "What the hell?"

"It isn't a tough question," Leo said. "Do you need time to think up an answer?"

"I—I—have a younger stepbrother. We were never very close." Meeker closed his eyes. "If I hesitated, that's why. I don't really count him as a sibling."

"So—you have a stepbrother. That means either your parents divorced or one of them died. What happened?" Meeker hesitated. "Why are you asking all this shit?"

"Why can't you just answer?"

"I just don't understand what this has to do with anything—"

"Answer the goddamn question!" Jordan bellowed, getting to his feet.

Leo furtively shook his head at him.

With a sigh, Jordan sank back down on the step. But his hand still gripped the banister, and he watched them intently.

"Was it a death or a divorce, Allen?" Leo asked him quietly.

Meeker turned his face away. "A death, my mother died. Okay?"

"How old were you when she died?"

"Eleven," he muttered.

"How did she die?"

He hesitated again. "It was a car accident."

Leo said nothing for a moment. He glanced at Jordan and then at Meeker. Finally, he sighed. "I'm sorry, but I don't believe you. It's too vague. 'Car accident' is how Jordan said his mother died. And I know now, he wasn't telling the truth. So—how did your mother *really* die, Allen?"

He didn't respond.

"Keep in mind," Leo said. "We can double-check with your fiancée. She's only five minutes away by car."

Meeker's shoulders started to shake beneath the blanket. Leo couldn't quite tell if he was laughing or crying. Then he realized it was a little bit of both. "Susan will tell you that my mother died in a car accident," he said. "But the truth is that one March afternoon, she locked herself in the family station wagon inside the garage, and she left the motor running. Guess who found her. Me, that's who. She didn't leave a note or anything—nothing at all."

"So you have a pretty good idea what it's like to lose a mother very suddenly," Leo said quietly.

"That doesn't make me a murderer," Meeker said. "In fact, I sympathize with those kids whose mothers were killed."

"Is that why you left each one of us a toy?" Jordan asked.

"I never killed anybody!" he cried. "You were right earlier, okay? I was making up everything, because I thought if I confessed, you'd turn me over to the police. Listen to me—for the last time, I'm not a murderer. I'm a nice guy, damn it! Ask anyone!" He glanced at Leo. "You said you were going to wrap this up. Well, when?"

Leo nodded. "Just a few more minutes, okay? We were talking about your mother. You said she didn't leave a note when she killed herself. You—um, after all these years, you must have come up with some idea about why she committed suicide."

Meeker pressed his forehead against the table again. He said nothing.

"Why do you think she killed herself, Allen?"

"I don't know," he muttered

"You must have been pretty angry at her for deserting you at such a young age," Leo said quietly.

"I don't know what you're talking about."

"Well, don't kids sometimes resent a parent who dies on them?" Leo pointed out. "My father was killed in Iraq when his jeep ended up in a ditch two years ago. And when I think about it, I still kind of get pissed off at him for dying on me. I know it sounds crazy. But I sometimes think he should have tried to get out of going overseas or he should have been more careful behind the wheel. This grief counselor the army fixed us up with—she said it was perfectly normal to have that kind of anger and resentment. She said that with some therapy, I'll get over it. But I think maybe I feel that way because I really miss him." He gazed at Meeker. "Weren't you ever angry at your mother for killing herself?"

The man slowly shook his head. "Nice try. I know where you're going with this. Because I'm mad at my dead mother, I go out and kill all these mothers, right? Where'd you get this shit, Psychology 101?"

"You're not answering his question!" Jordan piped up from the stairs.

Leo didn't want to admit it, but Meeker pretty much had his number. He did hope to make a connection between Mama's Boy and this man who felt some resentment for a mother who had abandoned him. He also wanted to find out if Meeker had been abused as a child—by either parent.

"Weren't you angry at your mother?" Leo pressed. "Didn't you miss her enough to be angry, Allen?"

Meeker said nothing.

"Maybe you were happy to see her die," Leo dared to say. "Was that it? Did she beat you or something?"

"My mother was a sweet, gentle woman," Meeker said steadily. "She never laid a hand on me."

"But did she ever raise a hand to defend you?" Leo asked, hoping he might hit on something. It was worth a shot. "I'm—I'm talking about when your dad came after you. Didn't she ever try to stop him?"

"Of course she tried to stop him!" Meeker blurted out. "He was much worse on her than he ever was on me. He beat the shit out of that frail, little woman. The son of a bitch once threw her across the kitchen, and she hit her head against the edge of the refrigerator. She got thirteen stitches that time. She always took the blows meant for me. She was like his goddamn punching bag. He—" Meeker seemed to choke on his words. He suddenly clammed up and glared at Leo.

"But then she killed herself and left you all alone with him. You didn't have your mother to run interference. It must have been a nightmare. And you can't admit you're mad at her for that?"

"Screw you!" Meeker yelled. He had tears in his eyes. "Think you're so goddamn clever. So what's your point? Just because I had it tough as a kid, I'm supposed to be some kind of serial killer? That's ridiculous. You have your head up your ass. . . ."

Leo turned to his friend. But Jordan was looking toward the basement window. "Oh, shit," he murmured, quickly getting to his feet. He rushed toward the work-table.

It took Leo a moment to realize what was happening. Then he heard tires squealing and a car engine purring outside.

Meeker must have heard it as well, because he started to yell out: "HELP! HELP ME! OH, GOD, PLEASE . . . !"

Jordan nearly plowed into Leo to get to their captive. He yanked the blanket off Meeker's shoulders and tried to stuff one corner of it into his mouth. Meeker kept turning his head. He frantically tugged at the rope, and the whole table shook. He wouldn't stop screaming.

Leo hurried to the window. Through the dirt-streaked glass, he could see the cop car in the driveway. "Oh God, it's the police. . . ."

This made Meeker shout even louder—until Jordan punched him in the face. Their prisoner let out an aborted cry and then slumped against the table.

Leo could only see part of the patrol car, but he heard the door open and shut. He turned to his friend, who hastily stuffed one corner of the blanket into Meeker's mouth. "Jordan, here's our chance," he said. "Let's hand him over to the cops now. We've gone as far as we can with this guy. We have enough on him to make the cops *suspicious* at the very, very least. And we have to let the police know about Moira. . . ."

But Jordan was shaking his head. He pulled at the rope around Meeker's wrists to make sure it was tight. "We can't quit now, Leo," he said, out of breath. "He's finally starting to crack and tell the truth. He—"

A knock on the front door upstairs interrupted him.

Jordan grabbed Leo's arm and pulled him close. "Please, Leo," he whispered, his mouth against his ear. "Don't screw this up for me. I'm counting on you. Please . . . just wait down here. . . ."

He turned and pulled the gun out from the back of his jeans. He checked it, then tucked it back under his shirttail and hurried up the cellar stairs.

The rapping on the front door only got louder and more intense.

At the bottom of the basement stairs, Leo listened to Jordan's footsteps above. Why had he checked the gun like that? In his crazy plan to keep this man his prisoner at any cost, did Jordan actually consider shooting a policeman an option?

Leo glanced over at Meeker—his eyes closed, lifelessly sprawled over the worktable. One corner of the old blanket was stuffed in his mouth. If he hadn't seen him breathing, Leo would have sworn the man was dead.

He heard the front door opening, and then Jordan's voice—with strained cheerfulness. "Well, hey, hi again. I hope I'm not in trouble or anything. . . ."

Then there was some muttering from the cop, but Leo couldn't make out what he was saying. He crept up the stairs and quietly opened the basement door to hear them better.

"Well, it's just like the lady told you," Jordan was saying. "We were in the store at the same time—around noon. He didn't say squat to me. I saw him get into his car and drive toward town. End of story. I don't know what else I can tell you."

"Where did you go after you left the store?" the cop asked.

"Here, I came here—but, um, my friends were gone, so I decided to go exploring. Then I ran into you. . . ."

"At the old Chemerica plant," the cop said. "You just went there to *explore*?"

"Yeah—I mean, yes sir."

"Sure you weren't up to something else?"

"Nope," Jordan said. "I was just hanging out, killing time."

"A lot of kids go there to get high. . . ."

"Well, not me. I don't do drugs."

"Oh, yeah, I guess you got your fill of drugs back when they put you in that institution—or *care facility* or whatever they called it. Sure must have taken all the fun out of pharmaceuticals for you. . . ."

Standing on the cellar stairs, Leo wondered what the hell the cop was talking about.

"It was the Patrick-Hannah Clinic," he heard Jordan grumble. "They called it a *clinic*. And yes, they had me on different medications for a while."

"If you don't mind me asking—I mean, as long as we're on the subject—did they ever give you shock therapy?"

"No. They didn't do that there. P.H. Clinic was a very advanced, swanky place, only the most affluent nut jobs were welcome."

"Hah, at least you got a sense of humor about it, that's good," the cop said with a chuckle.

Leo couldn't believe what he was hearing. Jordan spent time in some kind of mental health clinic? He glanced over the banister—down at the half-naked, half-dead Allen Meeker, strapped to that worktable. No sane person would have done this—and here he was practically going along with Jordan on the whole thing. Meanwhile, his friend was upstairs with a concealed gun, talking to a policeman.

"Is there anything else I can do for you?" Jordan said. "Sorry I can't be more help tracking down this Alex Meeker person."

"Allen," the cop corrected him. "Allen Meeker. Where did your friends disappear to?"

Leo hesitated for a moment, then hurried up the last two steps to the kitchen. "Jordan?" he called, moving toward the front of the house.

Turning, Jordan stepped aside to gape at him. Leo saw a good-looking, beefy blond-haired cop standing in the front doorway. He tried to smile at the policeman, and all the while, figured he must have a dazed, dopey look on his face.

"Hello," he said, a bit out of breath.

Directly below them, a very conscious Allen Meeker heard the cop talking to Jordan's buddy. He recognized the cop's voice. He was the same patrolman who had stopped Jordan hours ago, while Allen had been bound and gagged in that dark, tiny, cramped trunk.

He listened to them upstairs. For a moment, Allen

thought Jordan's friend would put an end to all this and tell the cop that they'd taken someone prisoner in the basement. But no, Leo was pretending he didn't know who or where "this Alex Meeker person" was.

Allen could hardly breathe with part of the foul-tasting, moldy blanket crammed in his mouth. His head ached horribly. That last punch Jordan had dealt should have knocked him out, but it hadn't. He'd merely faked unconsciousness, hoping Jordan would stop hitting him—and maybe, eventually they'd think it was safe to leave him down here alone. To his surprise, his ploy had worked.

What he needed to do now was make a lot of noise. But he couldn't scream past the makeshift gag in his mouth. He tried to throw his weight from one side to another—to get the worktable to move. The legs scraped and yawned against the dirty cement floor, but the noise wasn't very loud.

He'd lost all feeling in his arms. But the blood was still flowing in his legs. A small section of material from his pants remained on his right leg—down near the ankle, which was duct-taped to the worktable leg. Sweat and hours of wiggling that foot had loosened the tape, but Allen had made sure Jordan and his friend didn't realize that.

Upstairs, he heard Leo tell the cop that he was worried about their friend. "Her name is Moira Dancey," he said. "We went for a walk in the woods this morning. And close to one o'clock we had this stupid argument, and she said she wanted to be alone. So I left her there . . . and . . . and she's still not back yet."

"Well, if you're so worried about her, what are you

doing here?" the cop asked. "Why aren't you in the woods looking for her?"

"I don't know. I just kept hoping she'd come back before dark. . . ."

At least an hour ago, Allen had first spotted a flat-blade shovel leaning against a support beam. It was about two feet behind him on the right. If he could knock over that shovel, it would make a loud clatter. The cop was bound to hear it.

"Well, Ms. Blanchette was concerned about this Moira girl, too," the officer was saying. "Sounds like Allen Meeker and your girlfriend disappeared around the same time. I'm wondering if there's a connection."

"Why is Allen Meeker's fiancée worried about Moira?" Jordan's pal was asking. "She's never even met Moira. . . ."

Allen wiggled his foot, then pushed and turned his ankle against the loose duct tape. He heard the police-man answer, but couldn't make out what he was say-ing. His voice sounded a bit farther away. Allen wondered if the cop was starting back toward his pa-trol car. He tugged and tugged at the tape around his ankle—until his shoe fell off his foot.

"Well, I can tell you practically for sure that Moira has never met Allen Meeker either," Jordan's friend was saying. "I don't think there's a connection. But I'm really worried about her. Moira's not familiar with the area, and she's all alone in those woods. . . ."

"Wasn't exactly smart of you to ditch her there, was it?" the cop replied.

Allen heard him clearly that time. He still had a chance of being heard himself. With one last yank, he managed to squeeze his sweaty, swollen foot past the loose duct tape. His leg was cramped up, but he managed to wave it around behind him. He tried to tip over the shovel with his foot, but his toe kept missing the handle by an inch or two. He pulled down at the rope around his bound wrists and then stretched his leg out farther—until he thought his arms would pop out of their sockets. Every muscle in his body ached. Perspiration dripped down from his forehead and the back of his neck.

He kept swinging his leg back. His toe brushed against the shovel handle, but it just grazed it. Still the shovel moved slightly, and the flat blade made a dull scraping sound. Allen tried to kick it again—and again. At last, he connected. The shovel toppled over and landed on a rolled-up drop cloth on the other side of the support beam.

It barely made a sound.

Exasperated, Allen wanted to scream, but he couldn't.

"Well, if you and your girlfriend had a fight in the woods," the cop said, scratching the back of his neck, "there's a good chance she's just avoiding you. Maybe she hitched a ride to town. . . ."

"No, she wouldn't have done that," Leo interrupted, shaking his head. He heard a scraping noise in the basement, and he could tell Jordan had picked up on it, too. Standing on the front stoop, the policeman must have been just out of earshot. If the noise got just a little bit louder, the cop would certainly hear it.

"I'll tell you what," the blond deputy said with a sigh. "Maybe you guys can do a little of the legwork for me. Get yourselves some flashlights and go look in the woods for your girlfriend—like you should have done a couple of hours ago. . . ."

Suddenly a loud thump reverberated from down in the basement.

The deputy blinked. "What the hell was that?"

Leo watched Jordan reach back toward his shirttail. "It's just the furnace finally starting up," he said. "It was freezing in here last night."

Brushing past both of them, Leo stepped outside. "That's where we were," he said, pointing toward the forest in back of the house. "There's a stream about a half mile into those woods, and we walked at least another mile beyond that."

The cop stepped away from the door and gazed at the dark woodlands. "Well, like I say, why don't you guys get off your asses and go look for her?" he said impatiently. "That's step one. But do me a favor and stick together, so you don't get lost. I don't need any more missing persons on my plate tonight."

Leo noticed Jordan stepping out to the front stoop. He closed the door behind him.

The deputy swaggered back toward his patrol car. "I'll check in with you in an hour or so," he grunted. "If you haven't found your girlfriend by then, I'll start to get a search party organized. Meanwhile, I got to track down this Allen Meeker character before his fiancée has a conniption. The broad's going out of her mind with worry." He opened the door to his patrol car, but paused and glanced at Jordan, his eyes narrowed. "You sure you can't tell me anything else about this Meeker guy, anything at all?"

Jordan shrugged and shook his head. "Sorry."

"Okay, well, see you dudes in about an hour." He ducked inside his car, started up the engine, turned around in the driveway, and drove off.

"Whew," Jordan said, putting his hand on Leo's shoulder. "That was close. I thought for sure we were screwed. You totally saved the day, getting him away from the house. . . ."

Leo recoiled from him. He shook his head. "Jesus, Jordan I can't believe it. You were going to shoot him."

His friend frowned at him. "No, I wasn't—"

"Yes, you were," Leo argued. "I saw you start to reach for your gun."

"It was just a reflex. I wasn't going to shoot anybody." Jordan turned and hurried back into the house.

Leo trailed after him. "If that cop tried to go down to the basement, you would have stopped him. You were ready to pull that gun on him. Don't deny it."

He followed Jordan inside the cabin. He heard another loud crack from down in the basement.

"Listen to that!" Jordan barked, stomping toward the kitchen. "If you'd have stayed down there with him like I asked you—"

"What were you talking about with that cop about spending time in an institution?" Leo interrupted. He kept on Jordan's heels. "What's this Patrick-Hannah Clinic? Were you ever going to tell me about that?"

Jordan ignored the question and tromped down the cellar steps. "The cop's gone, asshole!" he yelled at Meeker. "You can cut that shit out now!"

Their captive had managed to free one of his legs. And he was using his foot as leverage to raise the front of the worktable and then drop it on the basement floor. Jordan almost tripped over the fallen shovel as he bolted toward the worktable. "Damn it!" he growled. He grabbed the shovel and swung it at Meeker, whacking the flat blade against the backs of his thighs.

Past the blanket-gag in his mouth, Meeker let out a muted howl of pain.

"Jordan, stop it!" Leo yelled. It looked like his friend was about to hit Meeker with the shovel again. Leo lunged toward him and wrestled the shovel from Jordan's grasp. Jordan tried to push him away. Before Leo knew what was happening, he threw the shovel aside and hit his friend in the face.

"Jesus!" Jordan cried, shrinking back. A hand over his mouth, he bumped into Meeker.

Leo backed away, too. He unclenched his fist. "This ends now," he whispered.

Jordan stared at him for a moment. He took his hand away from his mouth, and Leo could see his lower lip was bleeding.

Silent, Jordan turned toward a storage rack against the wall and took a roll of duct tape off the shelf. He tore off a long strip. The ripping sound seemed to echo in the cellar. He squatted down in back of Meeker and grabbed his ankle. Meeker didn't resist as Jordan taped his ankle to the table leg. Jordan pulled another long strip from the tape roll and wrapped several loops around his captive's ankle and the table leg.

Leo gazed at the bright red mark on the back of Meeker's thighs. Slumped over the table, the man sobbed. Only a muffled whimpering could be heard past the makeshift gag in his mouth.

Leo turned toward his friend. "Jordan?"

Without looking at him, Jordan straightened up and then returned the roll of duct tape to the shelf. Touching his lip, he glanced at the blood on his fingertips and then brushed past Leo as he headed up the stairs.

Leo moved to the worktable, where he pulled the corner of the old blanket out of Meeker's mouth. "Thank you," Meeker gasped. Then he started coughing.

Leo went to the laundry sink and filled the measuring cup with cold water. He brought it to Meeker and put the cup to his lips. Meeker drank greedily. He pulled away and caught his breath. "Thanks," he said again, with another gasp. "Listen, you need to stop him. He's crazy. He's not going to—"

"Shut up," Leo whispered. He put the cup to Meeker's lips once more. "Please, don't say another word. Don't say another goddamn thing."

He found Jordan in the bathroom off the kitchen. The door was open. His friend stood in front of the sink, staring at himself in the mirror. He dabbed at his bloody lip with a wadded-up Kleenex.

Leo leaned against the doorway. Jordan eyed his reflection in the mirror for a moment and then went back to nursing his lip.

"I'm sorry I hit you," Leo murmured.

"Well, I hit you earlier," Jordan said with a limp smile. "Guess we're even."

"It scared the crap out of me when I saw you check your gun before going upstairs to meet that policeman at the door," Leo admitted.

"It's not my gun; it's Meeker's."

"Whatever, you still started to reach for it when the cop asked about the noise. Conscious or un, you started to reach for it, Jordan. You came that close to drawing a gun on a police officer. Do you know how screwed up that is?"

Jordan eyed him in the mirror. "Pretty screwed up, I guess," he muttered. "Maybe you think I belong back in Patrick-Hannah. . . ."

"What's it going to take for you to be satisfied?" Leo asked quietly. "What does he have to say for you to end this and turn him over to the police?"

Jordan winced, and Leo thought it was because his lip hurt. But then he saw the tear sliding down his cheek. "I really don't know, Leo," he admitted in a shaky voice. "I just want him to confess—and know it's genuine. I want it to be over, too. I hate this." He lowered the toilet lid, then sat down and started sobbing. "I'm sorry, Leo," he cried, rubbing his eyes. "I didn't mean to do this to you. You shouldn't be involved in this mess. I'm so ashamed." He tore off some toilet paper and blew his nose. Then he took a deep breath. His face was red, and his eyes were bloodshot. "You asked about that—that clinic. He's the reason I had a breakdown and had to go to that place. He's the reason I'm so screwed up. He took my mom away right in front of me. I couldn't save her, Leo. I couldn't get to her in time."

Leo sighed. "You could have told me, you know— about your mom, about the clinic, all of it. I wish you hadn't kept it a secret. It wouldn't have made any difference to me, Jordan. I mean, you're still my best friend. Even after all this shit, you're still my best friend."

"Well, it ain't over yet," Jordan murmured.

Leo worked up a smile. "C'mon, let's take this into the kitchen," he said. "I feel like I'm talking to you while you're taking a dump in here."

Jordan let out a weak laugh; then he got to his feet.

Leo led the way into the kitchen. He stopped at the refrigerator. He took out Jordan's citrus-flavored Vita-minwater and a Coke for himself.

Jordan sat down at the breakfast table. "I'm sorry you got sucked into this, buddy. Some happy birthday, huh?"

Leo just shrugged, and then he reopened the Vitamin-water and set it in front of his friend.

"I got you the jacket," Jordan said, with a sad little smile. "You know the one from Nordstrom, the one you had your eye on? You look cool in that thing. Anyway, it's out in the car."

Leo felt a tightness creeping into his throat. He swallowed hard. "Thanks," he whispered. He mussed Jordan's hair. "Thank you. . . ."

Leo's heart ached as he sat down at the table with Jordan. He raised his Coke can and nodded at the Vita-minwater. "C'mon, Jordan, drink up."

CHAPTER NINETEEN

Her hand was bleeding, but she couldn't see it.

The little cell had become pitch black—except for faint traces of moonlight through the slats of the box fan. Moira had been working in the dark for an hour now.

She'd managed to move the moldy, fetid mattress aside. Then she'd felt her way back to the metal shelving unit and dragged it over to the wall that had a built-in fan up near the ceiling. The metal bookcase had made a loud scraping noise against the cement floor. Every few moments, Moira would stop, catch her breath, and listen for his footsteps. But she didn't hear him. She didn't hear anything except that constant flapping noise outside.

Moira wondered if the slime bucket was even around. Maybe he had another motion detector going off in another location, or perhaps another girl in another little room somewhere.

Her ankle hurt like hell every time she put weight on it. But Moira managed to climb up three shelves of the wobbly metal bookcase. There she precariously stood, praying the damn thing would hold her up without tipping over. With the bracket piece she'd found, she tried to unscrew the frame around the fan box. But the screws, once she'd located them, didn't move easily. In fact, at first, they didn't budge. Moira's fingers ached from putting so much pressure on the bracket piece until each screw began to turn. The apparatus's sharp edges kept cutting into her finger and thumb.

It seemed to take forever extracting the six screws from the rusty metal frame. And after all that work, the stupid fan still stuck to the wall. Moira tried to pry it out with the bracket, but the frame wouldn't budge. Finally, she shoved the bracket piece in her jeans pocket, grabbed the dusty fan blades, and started tugging. "Please, God . . . please . . ." she whispered. She was so tired and hungry and scared.

After a few more tugs, she started to get angry. "Damn it, you son of a bitch, move!" Moira frantically pulled at the fan blades until they started to bend. At last, she heard something snap, and she felt the fan piece shift. Her hands and arms were so sore—and her back ached from balancing herself on the rickety shelving unit. But she was suddenly filled with a renewed determination.

She grabbed another pair of blades and yanked at them until the fan box started to give. It sounded like pebbles rattling inside the wall, and Moira knew she was so close. She kept tugging at the fan until the contraption finally let out a loud creak and popped out of the wall.

But Moira lost her balance and fell. She landed on the mattress, but the impact knocked the wind out of her. It was too dark for her to see the metal bookcase teetering, and with an earsplitting clatter, it came crashing down—just missing her. The sound seemed to echo in the cold, tiny room.

Moira caught her breath and listened for his footsteps. He certainly would have heard that noise if he was anywhere in the vicinity.

She waited, her heart racing against her chest. She didn't hear anything—just the wind and that constant flapping noise outside.

A dim light seeped through the slats on the other side of where the fan had been. From plaster-caked cords and wires, the fan contraption loosely dangled against the wall. It swayed back and forth like a pendulum.

Moira kept waiting for the footsteps—or that dreaded clanking sound on the other side of the door. But there was nothing.

She was alone.

He was gone—probably hunting down his next victim.

Susan heard a car coming up the driveway.

She got up from the easy chair and glanced over at Mattie. Curled up on the sofa, he didn't stir. Her windbreaker still covered him, and he had Woody tucked under his chin.

The pellet gun in her hand, she tiptoed past the locked sliding glass door and peeked outside. Moths and bugs fluttered around the porch lights. The sailboat gently rocked on the silver-rippled inky water.

Susan continued on toward the front of the house. She noticed the glare of headlights through the sheer curtains of the living room windows. She glanced out and saw the red MINI Cooper pulling up beside her car in the driveway. "Thank God," she murmured.

Susan hurried to the door and unlocked it. But then she remembered what the deputy had said about Tom living like a hermit, and how no one had seen the inside of Tom's house in years.

She'd been taken in by his good looks and his charm this afternoon. But perhaps her first impression of him at the Arby's in Mount Vernon had been more accurate. She'd specifically told him not to come here. Yet, here he was, being overly solicitous again.

With one hand on the doorknob and the other holding the pellet gun, she wasn't sure what to do. At this point, even if Allen pulled into the driveway, she wasn't sure she could welcome him without some qualms. With all his secrets, she didn't think she could ever trust him again. Right now, the only person she really wanted to see was the deputy—and maybe another cop who could escort Mattie and her to the Smugglers' Cove Inn.

Better yet, she wanted someone to come here and tell her Allen was fine and she could take Mattie home. She would have gladly endured the two-hour drive at night if it meant going home right now. It was strange, that ideal scenario didn't include Allen. How could her feelings for him change so much during just part of one weekend?

She listened to the car door open and shut.

Susan took a deep breath and then opened the front door.

Tom looked very handsome. He'd changed into a sports jacket, a white shirt, and khakis. He came up toward her, but stopped just a few feet short of the front stoop. "Hey," he said with an uncertain smile. He seemed to read the apprehension on her face. Then his gaze shifted to the gun in her hand. He let out an awkward chuckle. "Wow, you're packing heat. . . ."

Susan kept the barrel pointed down—not at him. She nodded. "Yes, it's on loan from the local police force," she explained. She decided not to tell him that it only discharged pellets. "There have been some new, strange developments since I saw you last."

"What happened?" he asked. "Are you okay? Is Mattie okay?"

She gave him a tight smile. "We're all right, just shook up a little."

"Well, what happened?" he pressed. "You don't seem all right to me. You—you're acting like it's Arby's all over again, like you're not happy to see me."

She just shrugged uneasily.

He let out a long sigh. "Listen, Susan, I know you told me not to come here. But I called your cell number and kept getting this automated recording. So I started to worry."

"Well, that's very nice of you," she said. "I appreciate it, Tom, I really do. The deputy should be here soon. They're getting Mattie and me a room at one of the inns in town. So we're okay, thank you."

He glanced down at his feet for a moment and then at her. He cocked his head to one side. "Is that your polite way of saying 'get lost'?"

She gave him a halfhearted nod. "For now, yes. I'm sorry, Tom."

"I'm sorry, too," he murmured. "Did I do anything wrong?"

She wanted to say, *Yes, you should have invited me inside your house this afternoon.* Maybe then she wouldn't be so wary of him right now, and he wouldn't seem like such a stranger.

"No, Tom, you didn't do anything," she said finally.

"So—be honest, on the creepy scale, where am I right now?"

"I just wish I knew you better," she admitted. "That's all."

"I'd like to know you better, too," he said with a guileless smile. "Can I at least call you later?"

"Of course." She wasn't sure if she'd answer the phone. She wasn't sure of anything right now. Even though she was asking him to leave, Susan didn't really want him to go.

"All right, I'm out of here," he said. "Can't I do anything for you, Susan?"

"We're fine," she replied, stepping back from the doorway. "Thanks for stopping by, Tom."

He nodded, then turned and lumbered back toward his car.

Susan stood there by the threshold. She watched the red MINI Cooper back into the turnaround and then head out the driveway. She hated not being able to trust him.

She'd thought once he was gone, she'd feel relief.

Instead, she only felt more scared and alone. And she wondered if maybe her last chance of being rescued had just driven away.

Deputy Corey Shaffer didn't quite believe everything Jordan had told him.

The last known person to see Allen Meeker today was this once-troubled teenager, and he seemed to be covering something up. Jordan had said he'd gone to the old Chemerica plant this afternoon—less than an hour after running into Allen Meeker at Rosie's Roadside Sundries—just to "explore," "hang out," and "kill time." Corey wasn't buying it. That squirrelly kid wasn't telling him the whole story.

That was why the deputy now sat at the wheel of his patrol car, headed down the cracked, potholed access road to the Chemerica plant.

It had been nearly an hour since he'd issued that APB on Allen Meeker's black BMW, and so far no response. He had a feeling Meeker hadn't left Cullen on his own steam. Perhaps he'd never left at all.

The squad car's headlights cut through the darkness and illuminated the little shack that was once a guard station in front of the sprawling two-story plant. His car window was halfway down. He could hear the old window shades flapping and the wind howling through the dark, deserted building ahead.

Earlier this afternoon, Jordan's Honda Civic had driven out from behind that lonely, decrepit edifice. Corey headed back there now. He switched on the driver's side searchlight and studied the woods next to the driveway and loading area.

He noticed some tire marks in the mud at the edge of the cracked pavement. He remembered the mud on Jordan Prewitt's shoes earlier. It was even on the cuffs of his jeans.

Corey switched on the strobe and grabbed his flashlight before stepping out of the patrol car. He made sure he had his nightstick and then checked his gun. He didn't think he'd be running into anyone, but he wasn't a nature lover, and there were bears and coyotes in some of the woods around here. Directing the flashlight on the ground, he followed the tire tracks along a mud trail though the darkened forest. There was only one set of tire tracks. It looked as if the car had made a one-way trip—toward a marsh that was dead ahead.

Corey kept looking for a second set of tire tracks. But all he saw were footprints, one set—probably belonging to Jordan Prewitt.

He picked up a few stones along the way and started to toss them in front of him—one after another—until he heard one hit water with a hollow *thwunk* sound. The swamp was in front of him, and those tire tracks went directly into the mire. He threw out another stone and heard another hollow *thwunk*. He tossed still another stone in the muddy water, just a little farther out. He saw it splash, but the sound it made was totally different—a hard, tinlike *ding*—as if he'd hit something metal just under the murky surface.

Corey had a feeling he'd just found a black BMW.

One more kick would do it.

Moira had been telling herself that for the last few minutes. The outside piece to the exhaust fan was a metal frame with slats. She'd tried pushing and pulling at it, but the damn thing wouldn't budge from the wall. In the darkness, she'd discovered several pipes overhead. She'd found if she grabbed the pipe and hoisted her butt up on the fourth shelf of the metal unit, she had the leverage to give that slatted frame a forceful kick.

But it was more like twenty forceful kicks.

Her one good foot started to hurt like hell. Still, Moira kept kicking. The frame bent and shifted a bit more each time. But the shelving unit teetered with every blow, and her arms ached from hanging onto the pipe. *One more kick* became her mantra.

This close to the hole in the wall, she was pretty certain she could squeeze through to the outside. But once she was out there, she'd have to make her escape crawling or hopping. She prayed to God her abductor wasn't anywhere out there. *One thing at a time*, she told herself, *one more kick.*

Gritting her teeth, she shoved her foot into the porthole with all her might. The battered metal frame finally flew off the outside wall. From the clanking it made, Moira guessed the thing landed on some rocks directly below the opening.

At last, she could see outside. A dried-up dead bush blocked her view of anything else—except a little patch of night sky. She breathed in the fresh air and allowed one hand to let go of the pipe above her. She shook it out to get the blood flowing again. She did the same thing for her other arm. Then Moira hoisted herself up—headfirst—through the porthole.

The opening was rough and jagged. Little sharp bits of concrete scratched her hands and arms as she squeezed through to the outside. She was halfway out when the tall shelving unit toppled over again and went crashing to the floor. Her legs flailed and kicked in the air for a few moments as she struggled through the hole.

Moira kept thinking that if her abductor was around, he certainly would have heard that last loud crash. Panic-stricken, she clawed at the rocky ground and finally pulled herself outside. She rolled onto the dirt.

She'd been right earlier. Her dark little cell was in a basement. Moira found herself at the side of a run-down, deserted, beige-brick building. The flapping sound she heard came from some torn shades in the broken windows of the second floor. They looked like blinking eyes. The windows on the first floor were boarded up. Along the side of the building, among the dead shrubs, she noticed old beer cans, pop bottles, and other debris.

Moira tried to get to her feet. But she couldn't put any weight on her left ankle, so she braced herself against the side of the building. She caught her breath and glanced around. The place was surrounded by woods, but up ahead, she saw a row of streetlights that were out. She guessed it must have been a parking lot at one time. And where there was a parking lot, there was a road out of here.

Leaning against the side of the building, she hobbled toward the old parking area. Every muscle in her ached, and she started to feel faint. But Moira pressed on. She glanced down at her sore hand and now saw all the little bloody cuts on her thumb and fingers from working that bracket to unscrew the fan box. She checked her jeans pocket to make sure she still had the bracket piece. But then she realized it wouldn't be very effective warding off her abductor. So she bent down and retrieved an empty beer bottle.

Up ahead, she thought she saw a light sweeping through in the parking lot.

Moira staggered forward and watched the beams of

light. Past the flapping window shades and the howling wind, she heard the purr of a car engine.

She was about to scream out for help, but hesitated. What if the car she heard was that black Jetta—the one driven by that man calling himself *Jake*?

Moira peered around the corner, and for a moment, the headlights blinded her. She ducked back and fell to the ground. When she peeked around the corner again, she saw the vehicle veer around a little guard house toward a driveway. It was a police car.

"WAIT!" she cried. She tossed aside the empty beer bottle. On all fours, she scurried onto the cracked, potholed pavement. She frantically waved at the patrol car. "Help me! Please, help me. . . ." But her throat was so dry and sore. As much as she tried to scream, all that came out was this pathetic, squeaky little voice.

Helplessly, she watched the squad car turn down the driveway.

Moira got up and hopped on one foot to chase after it. She kept waving her arms above her head and trying to shout. "Please . . . please . . . stop. . . ."

The patrol car's taillights got smaller in the darkness as it drove farther and farther away down the narrow road. But Moira kept pursuing it, always on the brink of tripping and falling on her face. She couldn't give up. It looked as if the squad car was about to disappear in the night. But then Moira saw the brake lights go on.

"Yes!" she cried, staggering down the road toward it. "Yes . . . please . . . dear God . . ."

Moira watched the prowler make a U-turn. Exhausted, she stopped and collapsed to her knees. She began to laugh and cry at the same time. She kept waving her arms.

The cop car slowly approached her, and its high beams went on. Squinting at the patrol car, Moira dragged herself up from the cracked pavement. The squad car came to a stop about twenty feet in front of her. Past the headlights' glare, she saw the cop step out of the car and hurry toward her.

Moira smiled gratefully at him.

Then she saw him reach for his nightstick. And she saw his face.

"Oh, God, no!" she screamed, recoiling.

"How the fuck did you get out?" he asked.

Deputy Corey Shaffer didn't wait for an answer. He cracked her over the skull with his nightstick.

CHAPTER TWENTY

Susan never packed so quickly in all her life.

With Mattie at her side and the pellet gun in the pocket of her russet cardigan sweater, she quickly gathered up all her clothes and toiletries, then shoved them in her overnight bag. At this point, she didn't give a damn about wrinkles. She just wanted to get the hell out of this house.

Deputy Shaffer had told her to stay inside and keep the doors locked. He'd also said he would be back in forty-five minutes.

That had been nearly an hour and a half ago.

Susan glanced at her wristwatch: 6:45.

She'd waited all this time downstairs in the sun-room, sitting in the same chair where Allen had pulled guard duty with his revolver last night. She'd done the same thing, only with a different kind of gun. While Mattie had slept, she'd sat there, afraid she'd suddenly see that man in the army fatigues on the other side of the sliding door—his face against the glass.

Ten years ago, she and Walt had been so concerned because one of the Mama's Boy victims had been abducted in a park five blocks away from their home.

And here she was now, in a house occupied by another Mama's Boy victim.

As Susan zipped up her suitcase on the bed, she thought about Jordan Prewitt's mother, spending the last night of her life in this very room.

"Okay, sweetie, we're out of here," she said, grabbing the overnight bag. She'd already packed Mattie's suitcase—in less than three minutes. It was now by the front door, along with the bin full of his toys. She hadn't packed Allen's things. When he came back, he could do his own packing.

As she started down the stairs after Mattie, Susan half expected to hear a sudden pounding on the door— or perhaps a window shattering. She couldn't get past the weird notion that Mattie and she were reliving Jordan Prewitt and his mother's last night in this house— and they might not make it out alive.

Her purse was hanging on the newel post at the bottom of the banister. Susan realized she still had the flare gun in there. She took out the gun and the extra flares and set them on the half table in the front hallway. She thought about stashing the pellet gun in her bag, but decided to keep it in the deep pocket of her cardigan. That way, it was easier to reach—in case of an emergency.

"You don't have to go potty, do you?" she asked Mattie, pausing by the door.

"Nope," he said, tapping Woody's head against the doorway frame.

"I want you to stay right here like a good boy while

I load up the car." She mussed his hair, then opened the door and took her suitcase outside.

The car was parked just a few feet from the burnt rain barrel—by the trees where that hunter had been lurking. Susan made three trips back and forth, loading up the car, and for each brief trek she glanced at those woods with trepidation. She kept waiting for someone to leap out of those bushes.

Finally, she strapped Mattie into his child's seat, then hurried around and ducked behind the wheel. She quickly locked her door and then started up the car.

As she pulled out of the driveway, Susan glanced in the rearview mirror. She took one last look at the house—and hoped to never see it again.

"You only have a few more sips left," Leo said, nodding at the near-empty bottle of citrus-flavored Vitaminwater. "Why don't you polish it off?"

They sat at the kitchen table. Leo had half a peanut butter and jelly sandwich on a paper plate in front of him. He felt horrible as he watched his trusting best friend swill down the rest of the Vitaminwater he'd laced with sleeping pills.

If that wasn't bad enough, a few minutes earlier when Jordan had mentioned he wanted to go back down to the basement again, Leo had lied, saying he felt another diabetic episode coming on. So Jordan had gotten all concerned and made him the PB and J.

"This isn't exactly the birthday dinner I'd planned for you," he'd said, setting the sandwich in front of him.

Leo had noticed Jordan slurring his words a bit. And

the way he'd moved around, he'd seemed slightly drunk. That had been about ten minutes ago.

"We gotta go back down there, Leo," he announced with a sigh. He rubbed his mouth as if it weren't working right. "I know you hate it, and I hate it, too. But we're so close to making this son of a bitch crack. We're so close. . . ."

Jordan got up from the kitchen table, but started to lose his balance. "Whoa, head rush," he muttered. He went to grab his chair and tipped it over. It clattered against the tiled floor.

"Are you okay?" Leo asked, springing to his feet. He grabbed Jordan's arm. He felt like such a weasel, pretending he didn't know what the problem was. He wondered if he'd put too many pills in that drink.

Weaving slightly, Jordan numbly gazed down at the fallen dinette chair.

"Y'know, maybe you ought to lie down for a few minutes," Leo suggested. He picked up the chair and set it by the breakfast table. "You're tired. You've been through a hell of a lot today. It's catching up with you. . . ."

But Jordan was shaking his head. "No, no, we gotta go down there and get a confession out of him. We— we can't give up now."

Leo tried to take hold of his arm again, but Jordan pulled away and staggered toward the basement door. "That deputy is coming back in less than an hour," he said sluggishly. "We don't have much time. As soon as we get a real confession from this son of a bitch, we can—we can go look for Moira. Poor Moira, lost all alone in those woods . . ."

Leo hovered behind his friend as he teetered down

the basement stairway. Halfway down, Jordan stumbled, but he grabbed for the banister and landed on his butt. He sat in a stupor on one of the lower steps. "Geez, what's going on?" he murmured.

"Like I said, you're tired," Leo whispered. "Really, you ought to go upstairs and lie down—for just a few minutes. This can wait."

As he helped Jordan get to his feet, Leo glanced down at Meeker, sprawled across the worktable. With a cold look in his eyes, he seemed to study their every move.

Leo ignored him. "C'mon, Jordan, let's get you upstairs. You can catch a few Z's. A fifteen-minute break, and you'll be good as new." He led Jordan up the cellar steps. All the while, he felt Meeker's eyes on him.

He almost had to hold Jordan up as they staggered through the kitchen to the next set of stairs. They made their way up to the second floor, but at the landing, Jordan stumbled once again—almost falling down the staircase. Leo caught him and steered him toward Moira's room.

"Jesus, what's wrong with me?" Jordan mumbled. "All of the sudden . . . did you . . ." he shook his head. "No, no, you wouldn't have. . . . You wouldn't have done anything like that to me. . . ."

Leo knew what he was talking about. But he pretended not to hear. He pulled back the quilt and sat Jordan down on the bed. Reaching back under his friend's shirttail, he took away the gun and set it on the nightstand.

Jordan flopped to one side, then rolled over and laid his head on the pillow. "We got him, Leo," he murmured sleepily. "We got Mama's Boy."

"Yeah, we got him," Leo said. "Justice will be served, I promise." His heart ached as he pulled off his friend's shoes. He kept telling himself this was for the best—even if it meant betraying his best friend. Eventually, Jordan would forgive him.

He reached into the pocket of Jordan's jeans and took out his car keys.

His friend squirmed. "I'm going to let all the others know," he said, closing his eyes. "I'm going to look them up, all the Mama's Boy orphans like me. Maybe they—maybe they'll finally be able to live with themselves and move on, y'know?"

Leo covered him with a blanket.

"Wake me in fifteen, okay?" Jordan asked.

Leo patted his shoulder. "I'll make it twenty," he said.

He figured that was how long it would take to drive to the store and back. Just one phone call and the state police would be on their way to resolve this whole mess—and no one had to die. He watched Jordan start to doze off. "I'm sorry," he whispered, his hand lingering on his friend's shoulder for a moment.

Then he took the revolver from the nightstand and headed downstairs. He hid the gun in the kitchen cabinet—behind the Cap'n Crunch. At the top of the basement stairs, he hesitated. He hadn't been down there alone with that man—not without Jordan alert and close by.

Leo started down the creaky cellar steps.

Meeker was watching him. "You drugged him, didn't you?" he asked, his voice raspy. "What, did you slip something in a drink of his?"

Leo said nothing. He wondered how the man could have figured it out. Perhaps he'd had several opportunities to observe someone who had been drugged. Maybe Mama's Boy hadn't always taken his victims by gunpoint. Maybe he'd drugged a few of them.

Leo warily moved toward the worktable.

Meeker laughed and shook his head. "I don't care what you did," he sighed, "as long as that crazy-shit friend of yours is out of commission. Thank you. Thank you, Leo."

Biting his lip, Leo avoided Meeker's eyes. He tugged at the rope around his wrists.

"That sucker's so tight, you'll need a knife to cut it loose," the man said.

But Leo made certain the rope was secure. He bent down and checked the tape around Meeker's ankles.

"What the hell are you doing?" Meeker asked. "What's going on? Aren't you going to untie me?"

"I'm driving to the general store, so I can call the state police," Leo said, backing away from him. He thought of Jordan upstairs, asleep and vulnerable. "I'm taking Jordan with me," he lied. In truth, it would slow him down terribly if he attempted to move his unconscious friend into the car. But Meeker didn't need to know that. "When we come back—"

"NO!" Meeker shouted. "You gotta untie me! At least, loosen the rope, for Christ's sake. I'm dying! You can't do this to me. . . ."

"We'll come back here and wait for the police together," Leo said, edging toward the stairs. "All of this will be over in about a half hour."

"Goddamn it, don't leave me here like this!" Meeker

bellowed. He squirmed on the table and tugged at the rope around his bound wrists. "Don't leave me alone! You gotta untie me!"

Leo headed up the stairs.

"You son of a bitch!" he heard Meeker scream. "Get back here!"

Leo shut the basement door, but it didn't block out Meeker's tirade. The man downstairs kept screaming and cursing at him. Leo locked the basement door. Then he dragged one of the dinette chairs across the kitchen floor and wedged it under the doorknob.

Fishing the car keys from his pocket, he hurried out the front door and climbed into Jordan's Honda Civic. It smelled like a bakery cake inside the car. Leo turned the key in the ignition. But then he hesitated, turned, and pulled at the string around the bakery box. He opened the top flap.

Inside was the cake with Speed Racer's likeness in the frosting and a tiny green plastic race car by the words *Happy Birthday, Leo!*

He let out a little laugh, but then tears stung his eyes and he began to cry.

Leo closed the top flap of the cake box. He wiped his eyes, took a deep breath, and started out of the driveway.

"Hi, um, Nancy, this is Susan Blanchette calling again," she said into the telephone. Rosie had let her use the corded slim-line phone by the register. Susan leaned over the counter to glance past the lottery machine at the play area, where Rosie was keeping Mattie entertained. He was in Fisher-Price heaven.

"Yes, Ms. Blanchette," the police operator said on the other end of the line. "Can I help you?"

"I'm wondering if you've heard from Deputy Shaffer. He stopped by where I'm staying this weekend—at Twenty-two Birch. He said he'd be back in forty-five minutes. And that was nearly two hours ago. Do you know where he is? Has he radioed you?"

"No, Ms. Blanchette," the operator said. "I haven't heard from him since we put out that APB on Mr. Meeker's car. And that was just about two hours ago—like you say."

Susan anxiously tugged on the phone cord. "Have you had any response to that bulletin yet? Any leads as to Mr. Meeker's whereabouts?"

"I'm afraid not. I'm awfully sorry."

"What about the girl? Do they have any updates on the girl?"

There was a pause on the other end of the line. "What girl?"

"The teenager, Moira," Susan explained. "The deputy radioed you about her just a few minutes after he spoke to you about Allen—Mr. Meeker."

"I'm sorry, Ms. Blanchette. Corey didn't report anything to me about a teenage girl—at least, not today."

Susan didn't understand. "But I heard him on the radio with you. He said it was a possible kidnapping and that you ought to notify the sheriff."

"Well, Sheriff Fischer has the night off. Corey knows that. Stuart and his wife left for Whidbey Island late this afternoon. He's had it on the schedule for weeks now."

"But that doesn't make sense," Susan murmured.

"Well, maybe you heard him talking to the state

police," the operator said. "Or maybe you misunderstood. I'll try to get ahold of him and straighten this out. His radio was off when I tried him about twenty minutes ago. The caller ID shows you're phoning from Rosie's store. Is that a good number to call you back?"

"Yes, thank you," Susan said numbly.

"Okay, stay put, and I'll give you a call there," the operator said. Then Susan heard a click and the line went dead.

Susan hung up the phone. Leaning over the counter, she glanced toward the play area. Rosie caught her eye and shuffled toward her. "Any luck?" she asked.

Susan sighed and shook her head. "They're supposed to call me back here. I hope you don't mind."

"Oh, please," Rosie said, with a wave of her hand. "Are you kidding me? I could use the company. It's deader than Hector here. *Mi casa, su casa!*" Donning her glasses from the chain around her neck, Rosie got busy at the cash register. She pressed a button on her credit card machine, and it began to spit out a long roll of paper with tabulations on it.

Susan wandered over to the play area and watched Mattie crawling in and around the mini jungle gym.

She kept thinking that it didn't make sense, what the police operator had told her. Susan had heard the deputy on his car radio earlier. She remembered him describing a "possible kidnapping or hostage situation," and he'd said, "put Stuart on alert." Then he mentioned that he was headed to "the Prewitt cabin on Cedar Crest Way." He wouldn't have talked like that to the state police. He had to have been talking to someone local.

On the way here to Rosie's, she'd slowed down near the turnoff to Cedar Crest Way. But she hadn't been able to see if a patrol car was in the driveway to the Prewitts' cabin. She wondered if the deputy was still there—or if he'd gotten a hot lead from Jordan Prewitt and was now following it up someplace else.

The Prewitts' place was only five or ten minutes away.

She watched Mattie, entertaining himself in the play area. He was looking the happiest she'd seen him all day—except for when he'd been frolicking in Tom Collins's backyard.

"Rosie?" she said, starting back to the register. "Could I ask you for a big favor? I need to check on something down the road. It shouldn't take more than fifteen minutes. Would you mind—"

"Looking after the little one?" Rosie finished for her. She put down her credit card printout and took off her cat's-eye glasses. "Honey, I'd be delighted. Mattie and I are like old friends already. He's a peach."

"Well, the police operator is supposed to call back here."

"No sweat, I'll take a message for you," Rosie said.

"Rosie, thank you. You're a lifesaver." Susan moved back toward the play area and crouched down on the recreation mat. Mattie was playing with a big plastic dump truck. "Sweetie, I'm going out for a few minutes. I want you to be a good boy for Rosie while I'm gone. Okay?"

Nodding, he barely looked up from the toy truck. "'Kay."

"Kiss me good-bye?" she asked. She needed to

make sure he understood she was leaving. Often when she left him with a babysitter, he didn't comprehend what was happening until she stepped out the door—and then he'd scream bloody murder.

But not now. Mattie looked up from his truck, put an arm around her neck, and kissed her on the cheek. "Bye, Mommy."

She kissed him and hugged him back. On her way down the aisle toward the front of the store, she thanked Rosie again. Heading toward her car, Susan listened for the sound of Mattie's cries. But it was quiet in the store. Susan told herself that he would be all right without her—for a while.

She remembered in the heyday of the Mama's Boy murders, she used to wonder if Michael would be all right without her.

Susan wondered why she'd thought of that now.

She jumped in her car and headed toward Cedar Crest Way.

A loud banging echoed from the basement of the Prewitt cabin.

Allen Meeker kept pushing out with his foot, trying to break the leg off the worktable—or at the very least, tear the duct tape securing his ankle to that table leg. Like a crazy man, he repeatedly threw his weight to slam the table against the cellar wall.

With every crashing blow, saws, wrenches, and other work tools that had been hanging from hooks on the wall dropped to the floor—some two or three at a time. The pile of fallen tools lay on the cement floor, just out of his reach. Allen had thought he'd lost all feeling in his hands, arms, and shoulders, but now, every time he banged the worktable against the wall, he felt a painful reverberation in his limbs.

But Allen was relentless. He figured if he could break the table, he'd be as good as free. He wasn't sure which one of them would give out first—him or the table.

After every violent blow, Allen caught his breath. Then he'd push and pull at the table leg until the joints in his own leg ached.

He was doing that now—putting as much pressure as he could against the wooden strut. His face turned crimson, and the veins protruded in his neck and forehead. "C'mon, you son of a bitch," he growled.

Then he heard the crack.

It was a lovely sound.

Leo wondered what that noise was. It sounded like he'd hit a tin can along the snaky road to Rosie's Roadside Sundries. He'd been driving for nearly five minutes and hadn't seen another car yet. He hadn't seen any lights either. If there were any other homes or cabins along this route, they were tucked away behind the trees—like Jordan's place.

The car didn't seem to be handling right. He'd only gotten behind the wheel of the Honda Civic on the rare occasions when Jordan needed a designated driver. But he could tell something was wrong. He felt as if he were driving over a path of potholes, and yet the road ahead looked smooth. The steering wheel resisted as he tried to maneuver the many curves. "This isn't good," he said to himself. "Please, God, don't let it be a flat. . . ."

Hunched close to the wheel, he eased off the accelerator and felt the car tilt and buckle. "Shit, shit, shit," he muttered—with a pang of dread in his stomach.

Leo switched on the emergency flashers and veered toward the shoulder of the road. The car limped to a stop on the gravel. He left the motor running, climbed out of the Civic, and checked the back tire. It was flat.

He took a few deep breaths. "Okay, okay, don't panic," he whispered to himself. "Don't wuss out. . . ." He'd changed only one flat tire in his day—and even then, Jordan had done most of the work. It had taken them about ten minutes.

Leo figured he was about halfway between the cabin and the store—about three miles in either direction. On foot, it would take him at least twenty minutes. He'd need the car to drive back to the cabin after calling the state police. He couldn't leave Jordan alone—fast asleep and defenseless—with that guy in the house.

Ducking back inside the car, he switched off the ignition and took out the keys. With the key ring, Leo tried to pop the hood, but nothing happened. Frowning, he tried to unlock it manually. That was when he found a metal piece—it looked like part of another key—jammed in the trunk lock.

"What the hell?" he murmured.

The lock had worked fine yesterday when he'd unloaded their suitcases.

Frustrated, Leo tried to wiggle the piece of metal

out of there, but the damn thing was stuck. It looked like someone had jammed the lock on purpose.

Then he realized the flat tire might be on purpose, too.

Leo anxiously looked around and felt swallowed up by the darkness. Jordan's crippled car—with its emergency blinkers going—seemed to provide the only pool of light for miles.

He couldn't just stand here. He'd have to run to Rosie's and call the police.

Leo shut the car door, but left the flashers on. He was just about to start running. But then, in the distance, he saw something on the dark, winding road.

Through the trees, the light seemed to wink at him.

It was coming his way.

Susan couldn't see anything beyond the twin beams of her car's headlights—just a small patch of road; the rest of the landscape was black. She'd left Rosie's just a few minutes ago, and yet she felt as if she were the only person around for miles, the only person in all this darkness. She couldn't believe it was only 7:20. It seemed more like three in the morning.

She was still trying to make some sense out of Deputy Shaffer's reporting procedure. Why would he radio the police operator to set up the APB for Allen, but then radio someone else about the girl, Moira? If anything, that helpless teenager's situation was far more urgent and life-threatening than Allen's disappearance. Why didn't the police operator know about it?

Susan took another curve along the dark highway

when suddenly a figure darted out from the roadside. The thin man looked ghostly in the harsh glare of her headlights. He ran right in front of her car, waving his arms.

Panic-stricken, Susan slammed on her brakes and jerked the wheel to one side to avoid hitting him. Tires screeched as the car swerved off the road and careened toward a tree.

All the while, Susan had this powerless, doomed sensation. She pumped the brake, but the car kept moving. Automatically, she reached for the backseat with one hand. Her fingers grazed Mattie's empty child seat, and she realized he wasn't there. He was all right.

But she wasn't—and neither was the car.

It slammed into the tree. Susan reeled forward, but the seat belt kept her from hurtling through the windshield.

She hadn't even had a moment to recover from the shock when the man rushed up to her car window. For a second, Susan thought he was going to attack her. But then she recognized Jordan Prewitt's friend—and he looked utterly terrified.

"Are you okay?" he called through the closed window.

Rattled, Susan caught her breath. She gazed at him and nodded.

He ran around to the front of the car. "Can you back it up?"

The motor was still running, and it looked as if both headlights were still on. Susan felt her heart racing. Her hands shook as she shifted to reverse and backed up the car a few feet.

"The bumper's a little dented, but it doesn't look too

bad," he announced. "I'm really sorry! I didn't mean to make you drive off the road. . . ."

Susan's first instinct was to step on the gas and get the hell out of there. But something made her hesitate. As he approached her window, she checked to make sure her door was locked. She rolled down her window an inch.

"Listen, I—I know where your fiancé is," he admitted, hovering by her window. "I need to call the state police. If you'll give me a ride to the store, I'll explain everything to you on the way."

"Where is he?" Susan asked. "Is he all right?"

"He's okay," the teenager told her. "I'll tell you all about it—if you'll just give me a lift."

Susan didn't trust him. She shook her head. "Tell me now. Where's Allen?"

Jordan's friend winced and then gave the ground a kick. "Please! My car got a flat, and I'm stuck out here. I really need to call the police—"

"Why?" Susan asked, shouting at him. "Tell me what the hell is going on!"

The young man let out an exasperated sigh. "My friend, Jordan, he's pretty sure your fiancé is the guy who killed his mother."

Susan stared at him. She wondered if she'd heard him right. Hadn't Jordan's mother been one of Mama's Boy's victims?

"I know it sounds crazy, but I think Jordan might be right. Jordan has him tied up in the basement at the cabin. We've been talking to him, asking him questions, trying to get a confession out of him. . . ."

Stunned, Susan kept shaking her head.

"Jordan has a gun, and I was worried he'd—he'd *do*

something. He's been acting kind of crazy. I put some sleeping pills in a drink and gave it to him. He's sleeping right now—and—well, your fiancé is all right. I promise. But I need to call the state police and let them handle this before somebody gets killed."

"Your friend believes Allen murdered his mother?" Susan asked, incredulous.

He nodded glumly. "I'm sorry, but I think he might be right."

"Do you know that, when he was younger, your friend attacked two total strangers on the street because he thought *they* murdered his mother?"

The teenager frowned. "Where—where did you hear that?"

"One of his neighbors here in Cullen told me today," she said. "Allen's been in your basement all this time?"

He nodded. "Since early this afternoon. I wanted to tell you when you stopped by, but I couldn't. Please, I can explain everything in the car if you just—"

"Have you two been communicating with Allen before this?" she interrupted. "Did you coerce him into taking this trip?"

"No, Jordan didn't even know who he was until today. He spotted him at the store this afternoon, and suddenly recognized him. . . ."

"What happened to that girl you came here with?" Susan pressed. "Do you have her tied up in the basement, too?"

"God, no—"

"Then you didn't e-mail that picture of her to Allen?"

"What picture? What are you talking about?" His hand came up to the glass.

"Did a police deputy come by your cabin earlier tonight?" Susan asked.

"Yes," he nodded quickly. "But you started to say— did something happen to Moira?"

He seemed genuinely concerned—panicked even. But Susan still wasn't sure she trusted him. Maybe this was a case of three bored teenagers preying on a tourist couple as part of some twisted, deadly game. She'd seen plotlines like that in the movies. They picked some couple and terrorized them.

"Please, tell me," he pressed. "Did something happen to Moira?"

"The deputy didn't say anything to you?" Susan asked.

"Not much," he answered. "He seemed a lot more concerned about finding your fiancé. He asked if we knew where Moira was, but that's about it."

"Well, do you? Do you know where she is?"

He shook his head. "She and I went for a walk in the woods earlier. We had a fight, and she told me to get lost. So I left her there." He heaved a sigh. "That was five hours ago, and I haven't seen her since. I told all this to the deputy, and he said Jordan and I should get some flashlights and go look for her in the woods."

Susan stared at him and blinked. It didn't make any sense. Earlier, she'd made it clear to the deputy that the poor girl was being held prisoner someplace. Why would Shaffer tell the two boys to go look for her in the woods?

Nothing this young man was telling her made any sense—especially the part about Allen being a murderer.

"Listen, please," he said. "We're wasting time here.

If you could just drive me to the store . . ." He hurried around the front of her car and then reached for the passenger door.

Susan swallowed hard and then stepped on the gas.

He pounded on the car window. "No, please, wait!" he screamed.

But Susan pulled onto the pavement.

"God, please, no, don't leave me here!" he cried, chasing after her.

Susan pressed harder on the accelerator. She just couldn't believe anything he was saying—except maybe the part about them holding Allen prisoner in the basement of that cabin.

She was headed there now.

Picking up speed, she watched Jordan's friend in the rearview mirror as he ran after the car. For just a few seconds, she thought about turning back. What if he was telling the truth?

But Susan pressed on. She looked at him in the mirror again. He'd stopped running. And he became smaller in the distance until darkness swallowed him up.

CHAPTER
TWENTY-ONE

He glanced out the kitchen window toward the bay. He watched his kayak rocking and banging against the side of the dock—though the blue-grey water didn't look all that choppy. There were only a few whitecapped ripples on its surface. And it was strange how the little, hollow boat made such a loud clamor against the dock pilings.

But Jordan didn't really question it. Nor did he question that he was sitting at the dinette table in the *Spice Rack*–wallpapered kitchen in the cabin—and yet his view of the bay was from the sunroom in the old house on Birch Way.

"Drink up, kiddo," his mother said, setting a tumbler of orange juice in front of him. She wore a cardigan sweater over her nightgown. She didn't seem to notice the loud banging outside.

Jordan started to drink the orange juice, but then something clicked against his teeth, and to his horror, he saw shards of glass floating in the juice. He set the tumbler down and pushed it away—toward a wire cage on one corner of the dinette table. Inside the cage was a grey rabbit with pink eyes. It was trembling.

"You're going to have to kill him," he heard his mother say—over the constant banging.

Jordan leaned closer to the cage. The nervous little rabbit turned toward him, and its face morphed until it resembled some kind of mutant rat. The thing hissed and bared a mouthful of sharp, pointed teeth. It leapt toward him, crashing into the cage's thin bars.

Jordan suddenly bolted up in bed, gasping.

He heard another loud crash. It seemed to come from downstairs or outside. In a stupor, Jordan glanced around and realized he was in the master bedroom at the cabin. The digital clock on the nightstand read 7:39 PM. He'd been asleep for nearly an hour.

Jordan tried to move, but his limbs felt so heavy. He patted his pockets, but his car keys weren't there. He vaguely remembered Leo taking them. His friend had walked off with the gun, too.

"Damn it, Leo," Jordan muttered.

He was pretty sure Leo must have slipped something into his Vitaminwater. He'd gotten awfully punchy and sluggish immediately after drinking it. Jordan had spent enough time medicated in his younger days to know when he had some kind of drug in his system. Back at the Patrick-Hannah Clinic, the sleep aids they gave him usually knocked him out, but he'd always be wide awake an hour or two later.

The stuff Leo had slipped into his drink must have been pretty potent, because Jordan felt a bit woozy as he sat up.

He guessed his friend had gone to Rosie's to phone the police.

There was another loud crack. Jordan could tell the sound came from the basement.

He sat in a stupor for a few moments. He had to do something—go downstairs and maybe even hit Meeker over the head to knock him out again. It sounded like Meeker was breaking up the worktable. There were plenty of tools down in the cellar the scumbag could use as a weapon once he freed himself. Overpowering him wouldn't be easy—especially since Leo had taken the gun, damn it. Jordan contemplated making himself throw up—so he'd get the rest of the sedative out of his system.

His limbs still ached, and his head felt like a big wad of chewing gum. He wasn't sure he could even make it to the bathroom without collapsing. But he had to try. He couldn't just sit here and allow Mama's Boy to escape.

He couldn't let that thing get out of its cage.

His lungs were burning, and cold sweat flew off his forehead. Leo was exhausted and scared, but he kept running along the shoulder of the snaky road. Every time he came around another curve, he prayed he'd see the lights from the store up ahead. But all he saw was darkness and the shadows of trees looming over both sides of the winding highway.

He couldn't believe that stupid woman had left him stranded on the roadside. Then again, he couldn't really blame her. After all, he'd made her crash her

car, and he probably sounded like a total nutcase—
explaining how he and Jordan were holding her fiancé
prisoner. Hell, he was lucky she didn't back up and
mow him down.

What she'd said about Moira baffled and worried
him. Why had she asked if they'd tied up Moira in the
basement, too? And what was that about an e-mail
with Moira's photo? He had a feeling Moira was no
longer lost in those woods and that something far more
terrible had happened to her.

The more he wondered about it, the faster Leo
sprinted along the roadside. It seemed he'd been running forever. He thought for certain he would have
reached that store by now.

It had been almost an hour since he'd left Jordan
asleep in the house—with that man who could be a
murderer. Even if the guy was tied up and locked in the
basement, Leo couldn't help worrying. He also wondered if he'd given his buddy too many pills. Would
the police have to pump Jordan's stomach when they
got to the cabin—or would they be too late by then?

Up ahead, Leo saw a pinpoint of light on the bleak,
dark horizon. He thought it might be the store in the
distance. But then the light disappeared. He pushed on,
though his throat was dry and his chest hurt.

Then he saw the light again, peeking through the
trees, closer now. Leo realized it was a pair of headlights. The vehicle came around a curve in the road,
and the twin lights became brighter.

Leo slowed down and waved his arms over his
head. He told himself not to run in front of the car like
an idiot. *Please, please, stop,* he prayed.

Directly above those approaching headlights, a red strobe went on. It was a cop car. Its siren briefly wailed as the vehicle veered onto the shoulder. Leo heard gravel crunching under the tires as he staggered forward a few more paces. The squad car stopped directly in front of him.

Leo let his arms drop to his sides, and he managed to smile and nod at the patrolman. He couldn't quite get his breath yet. His vision was a little blurred, but he could see the cop stepping out of the driver's side. "Thank you!" he managed to gasp. "Thank you for stopping!"

"So what's going on here, hotshot?" the cop asked, swaggering toward him.

Leo recognized the deputy. "I was—I was trying to get to the store to call you guys," he explained. It hurt to talk because his throat was so dry. He still couldn't get his breath. He leaned forward and put his hands on his knees. "My car got a flat a few miles back. Listen, I wanted to—I wanted to tell you earlier when you came by the house, but I couldn't. . . ."

"Tell me what?" the deputy asked.

At last, Leo got a few good breaths. "My friend Jordan and I—we have that guy you were looking for. He's tied up in the basement of the cabin." Hands still on his knees, he glanced up at the cop to see his reaction.

Stone-faced, the deputy stared back at him and said nothing.

"Jordan thinks he's the one who killed his mother," Leo said, straightening up. "And I have to tell you, I think he's right." Leo took a few more breaths. He explained to the cop everything he'd just told Susan Blanchette a few minutes ago. He said how he didn't want anyone to get hurt, so he'd drugged his friend. "Jordan conked out pretty quickly," he said. "I was just so worried he'd use that gun. Anyway, I put him to bed upstairs. In fact, I'm wondering if maybe I gave him too many pills. . . ."

"What about the gun?" the deputy asked.

"I hid it," Leo said. "That was almost an hour ago. I—"

"So let me get this straight," the cop interrupted. "You have Allen Meeker bound and gagged in the basement of the cabin, and your friend's upstairs—unconscious and unarmed."

Leo nodded. "I wanted to make sure when the police arrive there, nobody gets hurt."

The deputy cracked a tiny smile. "Well, you did a good job, kid. You've made it really easy for me."

Leo smiled back at him, then leaned forward and set his hands on his knees once again. He drew a few more breaths—and started to feel normal.

"What did you say your name was?" the cop asked.

"Leo," he said, still bent over.

"Well, thanks a bunch, Leo," he heard the cop say.

Leo looked up in time to see the cop reaching for his nightstick.

"What are you doing?" Leo asked. "Wait—"

But he didn't get another word out.

After that, everything turned dark again.

She saw the turnoff for Cedar Crest Way up ahead. Susan squirmed restlessly behind the wheel. Something in the car had been rattling ever since she'd plowed into that tree. But all her dashboard indicator lights—fuel, battery, and temperature—looked okay, and she didn't see any smoke wafting from under the hood, so she tried to ignore the rattling noise. Similarly, she'd been trying to ignore the notion that Jordan's friend had been on the level with her a few miles back.

She'd passed his abandoned car—with its emergency flashers going—on the shoulder of the road a few minutes ago.

Part of her still felt horrible for leaving him stranded. But it would have been incredibly foolish to give him a ride. How could she trust him? He'd admitted he and his friend had abducted Allen. What was to keep him from attacking her?

He'd said Allen was tied up in the basement, and Jordan was asleep. She might have turned around and gone back to Rosie's and phoned the police once more. But why—so she could talk to the operator again? And she was no longer sure how reliable the deputy was. She had to see for herself if Allen was really at that cabin.

Susan switched off her headlights as she turned into the driveway. Then she slowed down to a crawl. White-knuckled, she clutched the steering wheel and kept looking for a little break in the trees and bushes on either side of the drive. Up ahead, she could see the cabin. There weren't any other cars in the driveway.

Susan noticed a clearing on her right. She veered off the drive and wound around some bushes and trees until she figured the car couldn't be seen from the driveway. The motor made a weird wheezing sound as she switched off the ignition. She hoped it wasn't an indication that the car might not restart.

Fishing the pellet gun from her sweater pocket, Susan climbed out of the car and quietly closed the door behind her. She glanced at the front of her Toyota—and the dented bumper. The license plate was mangled and precariously hanging to one side. Otherwise, the car really didn't look too bad. Jordan's friend had been telling the truth about that.

She shivered in the cold night air. Clutching together the front of her cardigan, she crept to the edge of the wooded area lining the driveway. She studied the quaint, two-story brown-shingle cabin. A light shone in the second floor window—and it looked like some outside lights were on in the backyard, too. One side of the house stood in the shadow of a towering elm tree. Some tall, wild bushes nestled against the other side. Their branches swayed in the breeze. Susan noticed a light in the basement window behind those shrubs.

She wondered if it was true. Was Allen really tied up in that cellar? Could it be that all this time he'd been their prisoner? Meanwhile, she'd convinced herself that he'd had a secret, sordid agenda for this trip, that he was devious and untrustworthy. She'd even let herself get interested in another man—a stranger, practically. What the hell was wrong with her?

Susan imagined how awful the last few hours had been for him, held captive by two teenagers—maybe three, if the girl was in on it. And one of those teens suffered under the insane delusion that Allen had killed his mother. Susan remembered what Tom had said—

how Jordan had actually hurt one of those innocent men he'd attacked, and he'd only been a little boy at the time. Jordan's friend had mentioned they'd tried to get a confession from Allen. He hadn't explained exactly how they'd gone about that.

All at once, a loud crash came from inside the Prewitt cabin. It gave her a start.

Susan looked for some movement inside the house, but saw nothing.

Weaving around trees and shrubs, she silently made her way toward the side yard. She raced across the driveway, hoping no one spotted her for those few fleeting moments she was out in the open. But she stumbled across something on the gravel. It rolled across the driveway and clattered against a rock. Susan quickly regained her footing and ducked amid the bushes alongside the house. Catching her breath, she reached for the metal object she'd kicked. It looked like the head of a rake—with thick pointed prongs.

Jordan's friend had said he'd gotten a flat. Had he run over this thing with his car?

Another loud crack reverberated from inside the house.

Susan dropped the hunk of metal and crawled toward the basement window.

"My God," she murmured. Past the dirt-streaked pane, she spotted Allen in the cellar. He was shirtless, and his trousers were all torn. Sweaty and panting, he looked like a wild man. He held a hammer in his hands. A rope hung from his wrists, which were bound with duct tape. The same tape had been wound around his ankles. One ankle had a splintered piece of wood still taped to it. It looked like he'd smashed up a table. The wood pieces were scattered around him. Allen kicked aside the tabletop and reached for something on the floor.

Susan was about to knock on the window, but she heard a car approaching. She turned and saw the headlight beams sweep across the trees bordering the driveway. She retreated from the window and hid behind a shrub. Then the headlights suddenly went out. But she could still hear the motor running. It sounded like the car had stopped halfway down the driveway. Had someone discovered where she'd hidden her car?

Susan scurried out from the shadowy bushes and darted behind one tree, and then another. Finally, she dashed into the wooded area by the drive. Catching her breath, she tried to get a glimpse of the car that had stopped just short of the Prewitts' driveway. She couldn't see it through the bushes and trees. But she heard a voice on a static-laced radio. Susan couldn't make out what the woman was saying, though it sounded like the police operator.

Then she heard Deputy Shaffer talking in a whisper: "Well, hell, Nancy, I don't know anything about that. Ms. Blanchette never said anything to me about a missing teenage girl. She must be confused. If you ask me, that woman is N-U-T-Z, nuts. She's got me running around in circles looking for her missing fiancé. I tell ya, these damn tourists are going to be the death of me. . . ."

Susan hid behind a tree and tried to fathom what she was hearing.

Now she understood why the police operator didn't know anything about the girl. It all started to make sense in a weird, frightening way. Earlier, when she'd heard Shaffer on his police radio reporting a possible kidnapping or hostage situation, he must have faked the call. Susan hadn't heard any response when he'd made that second radio report.

She listened to the static-marred reply from the operator now. The woman said something about Rosie's store. Susan couldn't make out the rest of it.

"Well, I'm way out here by the winery," the deputy lied. "I was chasing down a potential DUI, but the guy got away. So call Rosie's and tell Ms. Blanchette I can meet her at the house at Birch Way in about forty-five minutes. That's the soonest I can get out there, okay? Let's keep her happy, and tell her I'm looking into this thing with the teenage girl. We'll figure out what she's talking about later. Okay?"

There was a garbled response on the other end. But Shaffer must have understood it, because he chuckled a bit and then said, "No kidding, over and out."

From the wooded area, Susan watched the patrol car—with its lights still off—slowly round a curve in the driveway. She threaded through the trees and bushes and followed the vehicle toward the front of the cabin.

Shaffer shut off his motor and then climbed out from behind the wheel. The car's interior light went on, and from what Susan could tell, nobody was in the backseat. He must not have run into Jordan's friend on Carroll Creek Road; otherwise, he would have picked him up.

Shaffer wasn't wearing his police hat, and the front of his uniform shirt hung over his pants. He looked as if he'd recently been in a tussle or something. Pausing outside his patrol car, he tucked in his shirt and smoothed back his short blond hair. He took out his gun and crept toward the front door.

A hammering noise erupted from the basement.

Stopping in his tracks, Shaffer glanced over toward the side of the house. He seemed to notice the light in the basement window. He skulked along the side of the house, then bent down and peered into the window.

The pounding from inside the house continued. Shaffer gazed into the basement for another minute. When he finally turned away from the window, Susan saw he was grinning.

He moved over to the front door and tried the knob. He put an ear to the door and then shoved the gun back in his holster. From a side pocket of his trousers, he took out something that looked like a ruler. He slid it in the door hinge a few times and then quietly opened the door. Putting the rulerlike device away, Shaffer took out his gun and stepped inside the cabin.

Susan sprinted across the driveway to the bushes at the side of the house. She crawled back to the basement window.

The pounding noise had been replaced by a creaking, splintering sound. She couldn't see Allen in the basement anymore. She had to put her face close to the ground before she finally saw him near the top of the rickety-looking cellar stairway. He had a crowbar in his hands. He must have found a knife or some shears to cut the duct tape because his hands were free now. She guessed he'd also found some clothes in the basement, as he now wore a too-tight white T-shirt and white painter pants. With the crowbar, Allen alternated between hammering at the door and trying to pry it open. She couldn't see his face, but she heard him cursing.

Susan gently tapped on the window, trying to get his attention. But he obviously couldn't hear her past all of the racket he was making. She wasn't sure about Shaffer's intentions. Whatever they were, the guy couldn't be trusted, and she had to warn Allen. She knocked on the glass again.

Then directly above her, a light went on in the living room window. Susan ducked and rolled against the side of the house. Sweeping across the bushes was the shadow of someone in the living room. He was at the window, looking out.

Lying on the cold, damp ground, Susan pressed against the side of the house. She held her breath—until finally, that figure moved away.

From the basement she could hear wood splintering. Susan scooted over and peeked down into the cellar again. But she didn't see Allen anywhere.

Getting to her feet, she glanced over the ledge of the living room window. The deputy stood in the front hallway with his gun drawn. Then Allen staggered out of what looked like the kitchen area. He saw the deputy and stopped dead.

The deputy smiled at him. "Hello, Mama's Boy," he said. "We meet at last."

Gasping for air, Allen looked exhausted and stunned. "So—the kid called you, huh?" Slump-shouldered, he leaned against the newel post at the bottom of the stairs. "Well, they're both crazy. I'm no serial killer. I came here with my fiancée and her son for the weekend. These two teenagers, they've had me tied up in the basement here for—"

"Shut up," Shaffer said firmly. He shook his head. "No one called me."

Allen stopped talking. Susan could see he was still breathing heavily.

"You have to take my word for it, Allen," the cop said. "When I made you come here, I didn't think this was going to happen."

Allen stared at him. "You? My God," he whispered. "You're the one who's been sending me all those e-mails and letters. . . ."

The deputy nodded. "That's right, Mama's Boy. I'm your number-one fan."

Clutching a fireplace poker in his fist, Jordan stood in the bedroom doorway and listened to the two men. He still had an awful taste in his mouth from forcing himself to throw up ten minutes before. His throat felt raw, too. He'd swallowed down some cold water and gargled with Listerine, but it just hadn't done the trick. He'd been in the bathroom when he'd heard the car pull up outside.

He'd figured Meeker must not have heard. The son of a bitch had been too busy wrecking the basement or whatever the hell he'd been doing. Jordan had grabbed a poker from the fireplace set and been about to go downstairs when he'd heard the car. He'd gone to the window and seen the cop doing something odd. The guy had snuck up to the house with his gun drawn, and then he'd let himself in. Jordan held on to the poker and waited in the bedroom. He'd been tired and punchy before, but he was wide awake now.

"You know, I thought you were dead," the deputy was saying. "Earlier today, I ran into Jordan Prewitt at the abandoned chemical plant off Coupland Ridge Trail. I went back an hour ago and figured he must have sunk that sweet little BMW of yours into a swamp. I thought maybe you were in the trunk."

"Was that your plan?" Meeker asked edgily. "Is that why you wanted me to come here to Cullen? Did you set something up with that lunatic and his friend?"

Jordan tightened his grip on the poker. He was starting to shake.

"Hey, I already told you, Allen. I didn't expect anything like this to happen. See, I've always wanted to get you to come back here. And well, I've been banging a woman at Orcas Property Realtors, which gives me a chance to check out who's leasing the different properties and where there are rental openings. I'm always on the lookout for a woman vacationing here by herself. Anyway, I knew Jordan Prewitt would be staying here this weekend, and I knew his old house on the bay was available. I thought it might liven things up if you were here the same time as him—and in the same house where you abducted his mother. Honest to Pete, I had no idea you'd actually run into him, and he'd remember you. . . ."

"Listen, we don't have much time," Meeker interrupted. "The skinny one, Leo, he drugged his pal. I think he might have dumped him in the car. They're headed off to the store to call the state police. They left about an hour ago. We can't stay here."

"Relax, we have plenty of time," the cop said.

Jordan strained to hear as Meeker's voice dropped to a whisper: "What the hell do you want from me?"

"Haven't you figured it out by now?" the deputy said. "I want to work with you, Allen. I saw you kill her. I was living here when you helped put Cullen on the map. I was seventeen years old, perpetually horny, bored, and tired of just killing dogs and torturing cats for a cheap thrill." He chuckled. "You know what I mean. You know what that's like. I had a little crush on Stella. I used to sneak up to the house on Birch and watch her undress at night. Then one evening in August, while she was here with her kid, I realized I wasn't alone outside. I was already a big fan of your work, Allen. But I had no idea I was in the company of the maestro. I still didn't know the next day—when I watched you from the woods by the house. It was like I had a front-row seat to your performance. You showed up in the backyard, knocked her out, and carried her away. I can still hear little Jordan screaming and crying. It was beautiful. That's when I knew who you were. . . ."

His back against the bedroom wall, Jordan couldn't stop shaking. A tear slid down his cheek.

"I thought for sure you might have noticed my old, beat-up Ford following you and Stella," the deputy continued. "I followed you all the way to your dumpy little shack in North Seattle. It served you well for a while—isolated as it was. There was no one around to hear the women screaming. I saw you take Stella in there. And the next day, I saw you deposit her naked body in the woods by her house on Birch Way. I could have turned you in, but I didn't. That's when I became your number-one fan, Allen."

"And that's when the letters and e-mails started," Meeker muttered.

Jordan could barely hear him. But it was the confirmation he needed. Meeker was admitting it. He was Mama's Boy.

"Didn't slow you down any, and I'm glad," Shaffer said. "I'd like to think it kind of excited you to know someone else was in on it. I used to take weekend trips down to Seattle and sleep in my car. I'd check out your house at night. I missed a couple of murders. But seven months after Stella, I saw you take Rhoda Mundy out of the trunk of your car and then carry her into that house, Allen. She was a real step down from Stella, though. In fact, from her photo in the newspapers, I'd say she was kind of a skank. You must have thought so, too, because just six hours later, you were carrying her in a Hefty back to the trunk of your car. Something about her must have gotten under your skin, because one of the newspapers reported that you'd beaten her so badly, it looked like she'd been trampled by a horse. I don't know how they figured it out, but they said it appeared as if she'd been strangled up to a point and revived several times—until you finished her off. I wish I'd seen that. But you were always so careful about closing the shades. Was that repeated-strangulation thing something you did with any of the others? I imagine it was like watching them die several times. . . ."

Jordan heard Meeker mutter something, but he couldn't make out the words. It tore him up inside to imagine that might have happened to his mother.

"Were my letters the reason you moved in 2000—after you killed that woman with the twins?" Shaffer asked. There was a hint of melancholy in the deputy's tone.

"Partly," Meeker replied.

"That wasn't what I wanted," Shaffer said. "I just wanted to be in on it, Allen, be a part of it. I didn't mean for you to move away. Hell, you're the reason I became a cop. I realized it gave me access to all sorts of things that helped me keep track of you. When those women were killed down in Oakland, I knew it was you. I knew exactly where you were living at the time. Then there were the murders in Fairfax and Alexandria in 2003. I've visited all the spots where you've abducted woman—and the places where you deposited their bodies when you were finished with them. I know you and your work better than anyone else. You may have tried to go straight and set up house with Susan and her kid. But I wasn't buying that cover. Maybe you figured you'd lose me if you laid low for a while. But I never lost track of where you were, Allen . . . never."

Jordan didn't move for fear they'd hear the floorboards creaking. He kept his back to the bedroom wall. But he could see the clock on the nightstand: 8:09 PM. Leo had been gone for over an hour. It only took ten minutes to drive to Rosie's from here. Why had Deputy Shaffer been so confident that they had plenty of time? Had he spotted Leo on his way to Rosie's and pulled him over?

Jordan imagined his Honda Civic parked along a dirt trail off Carroll Creek Road, a birthday cake in the backseat, and behind the wheel, Leo with a bullet in his head. Jordan prayed it wasn't true. He felt sick to his stomach again.

For the last several hours, he'd desperately wanted some kind of confirmation that Allen Meeker was indeed Mama's Boy. Now he had it—thanks to Deputy Shaffer. But the person downstairs confronting Meeker wasn't an accuser.

He was an admirer.

And it sounded like he planned on helping this mother-killer get away.

CHAPTER
TWENTY-TWO

Hovering outside the living room window, Susan was in shock.

She couldn't believe what they were saying. She kept waiting for Allen to tell the deputy that he was mistaken, that he had the wrong guy.

Allen wasn't a murderer.

But he just stood there in that ill-fitting white T-shirt and those painter pants, leaning against the newel post—sometimes even nodding as Deputy Shaffer attributed these horrendous murders to him.

Susan thought of Allen abducting that poor little boy's mother right in front of him, and the others he'd abducted and murdered. She thought of the motherless boys left behind. Allen was responsible for all of it.

She remembered when that woman had vanished in Volunteer Park ten years ago and how terrified she'd been. A police artist had made a sketch of Mama's Boy, and she'd had nightmares that one night the man in that sketch would invade her home. She'd locked her doors and carried around a canister of pepper spray to protect her family and herself from that monster.

But he'd gotten in, despite all her precautions.

She'd let him into her life—and her son's life. She was engaged to him. He'd been inside her.

Susan felt sick. Her legs were shaky, and she couldn't get her breath. She leaned against the side of the house and clung to the window ledge.

"I'm sorry things got screwed up, Allen," the deputy was saying. "I was going to get in touch with you while you were out on the boat today—between noon and four, like I told you. I thought you might agree to a little plan I had. I won't go into the details just now, but it would have looked like a sailing accident. They'd have found the little brat washed up on the shore, but no sign of Susan. I was hoping you'd hand her over to me. . . ."

Susan watched Allen shake his head over and over.

"Why not?" the deputy asked. He still held the gun in his hand, but it wasn't pointed at Allen anymore. Instead, he casually caressed it. "I'm very good at making women disappear, Allen. They're still looking for two ladies I had a little fun with. *Missing, presumed dead.* It could have been the same scenario with Susan. . . ."

"What the hell makes you think I'd have given her up to you?" Allen asked, frowning.

"Maybe the notion that if you didn't cooperate, you'd find the state police waiting for you when you returned from your afternoon sailing excursion," Shaffer replied. "I started to e-mail you on the boat. I thought you were avoiding me for a while. That's when you must have run into Jordan. What those boys put you through, was it rough?"

"I've been through worse," Allen muttered. He turned and walked into the living room.

Susan saw him approaching the window, and she dropped to the ground. She could see his silhouette directly above her. "What makes you so certain those two haven't gotten hold of the state police by now?" she heard him ask. He was so close to the glass, it sounded as if he were talking to her.

"Relax," the deputy said, with a cryptic smile. "They won't give you any more trouble."

Susan watched the shadow move away from the window. She remained crouched down below the ledge.

"I've come up with a plan for them that I think you'll like," Deputy Shaffer went on. "By tomorrow morning, there will be three dead teenagers in this house. The two boys—and the third, I don't think you've met. She's Jordan's girlfriend, a very pretty girl. You'll like her. In fact, your lovely Susan pulled a fast one on me and e-mailed me from the boat, pretending to be you. I thought you'd finally come around, so I sent you a photo of this pretty, young thing. I have her tucked away in a closet at the old Chemerica plant. I was going to kill her myself, but I'd really like to do her with you, Allen. You know, like Bianchi and Bruno—the Hillside Strangler? Wouldn't that be fantastic—if we killed together, and they ended up giving us one name like that? We'd be a team, Allen. Maybe the Cullen Killer? This sweet teenager is just waiting to be our first joint effort. . . ."

Susan finally dared to peek over the window ledge.

She saw Allen sitting in a chair at the far corner of the living room—near the stairs. He was hunched over, rubbing his back while Shaffer stood in front of him. The cop still had the gun in his hand, but the barrel was aimed at the floor.

"Here's the part you'll really like," Shaffer continued. "We'll leave her body in the woods back here. Everyone will think those two asshole teenagers did her in and then shot each other—until we team up for another kill and then another. They'll start to see a pattern and realize we're a force to be reckoned with. There are plenty of women out there for us, Allen. It doesn't matter how cautious they are either, we can still get to them. One of the nice things about being a cop is that I make a pretty girl pull over on a lonely highway whenever I want. What do you think, *partner*? Are you interested?"

"What if I were to say no?" Allen asked warily.

The deputy let out a long sigh. "Well, you're going to want these two teenage avengers dead, am I right?"

Allen just nodded.

"This girl is going to disappear anyway. She's already ID'd me. Unfortunately for you, her bra can be found somewhere at Twenty-two Birch—among your things. Plus I've been inside your place in Seattle—and Susan's place, too. I've cleaned your hairbrush for you, Allen. Wouldn't it be bad luck for you if they found this girl with some silver and black hairs clutched in her fist?"

Allen said nothing. He slumped forward in the chair and buried his face in his hands.

"By the way, speaking of unfinished business," the

deputy said, digging into his pocket. "Susan will have to disappear."

"What?" Allen looked up at him.

The deputy lobbed something at him—and it hit Allen in the face. Susan realized the white item now landing in Allen's lap were her missing panties.

"She knows too much, Allen. Besides that, she'll be a detriment to our work together. I know you're fond of her. But she has to go. We'll have to put our heads together on how to handle this. . . ."

Out of the corner of her eye, Susan saw a shadow creeping behind her.

She ducked below the ledge and swiveled around. She saw the shadow was within a patch of light that spilled across the bushes and part of the lawn. It came from the second-floor window, where someone was standing.

Susan raised her head and peered into the living room again. The two of them had stopped talking. The deputy had his gun ready. He put his finger to his lips and shook his head at Allen. Then he pointed up toward the ceiling. Susan realized they must have heard the footsteps above. The deputy didn't seem at all surprised. In fact, he was smiling.

She crouched down again and scrambled toward the lawn and that little patch of light. She saw Jordan Prewitt upstairs, trying to open the window—possibly to escape. He tugged at it, but the window squeaked. He hesitated.

Susan straightened up and started to wave at him. She had to warn Jordan that they were on to him. Stepping back, she accidentally kicked the metal rake head she had stumbled over earlier. She heard it clatter against the same rock it had struck before.

Susan glanced over and saw Allen approaching the living room window. She quickly darted behind some bushes.

"I think someone's outside," she heard him say, his voice muffled in the distance.

Crouching close to the ground, she glanced over at that patch of light—and Jordan's silhouette as he struggled with the window. It squeaked again, and as far as she could tell, he didn't even have it halfway open yet. From his shadow, it looked as if he was shaking his head. Then he turned away, and the silhouette disappeared.

Holding her breath, Susan peeked around the shrub. Allen wasn't at the living room window anymore. She crept back to the ledge and gazed into the house again.

His gun ready, Deputy Shaffer skulked up a few steps toward the second floor. Behind him, Allen waited at the bottom of the stairs.

Susan remembered the pellet gun and took it out of the pocket of her cardigan. She didn't expect to do much harm with it—except perhaps create a diversion by blowing a hole through the window. Maybe Jordan could get away if she distracted them. Trembling, she stepped back, aimed the gun at the glass, and squeezed the trigger.

Nothing happened.

Of course, nothing happened. Shaffer had given her the damn gun.

Susan was about to hurl the gun through the window, when she heard Allen yell: *"Shoot him! Shoot the son of a bitch!"*

Two loud shots rang out.

Through the window, Susan watched in horror as Jordan Prewitt tumbled down the stairs. Near the bottom of the steps, Shaffer stepped aside and brutally shoved him. Jordan went crashing through the banister. There was a loud crack as the wooden railing broke and the pieces snapped off. A poker flew out of Jordan's hand. He fell to the floor amid the scraps of wood.

Allen marched over to his prone body and kicked him in the ribs.

Covering her mouth, Susan turned to run, but she tripped and hit the ground with a thud. The useless pellet gun fell out of her hand. She was almost certain they had heard her. As she pulled herself up, she noticed the rake-head contraption. She swiped it up and scraped her hand on the sharp prongs. But she barely noticed. She was already heading for the police car. She wedged the device—prongs up—under the rear tire.

Then she raced for the wooded area at the side of the driveway. She ran as fast as she could toward her Toyota. Bushes scratched at her hands and face as she sprinted through the thicket to her car. By the time she climbed into the front seat, Susan was shaking violently. She could hardly get the key in the ignition, and once she did, the car wouldn't start. She tried it again, and the car responded with a loud wheezing sound. No doubt they heard it in the cabin. Finally, the engine turned over with a roar. The Toyota started to make that rattling noise again.

Susan backed up to the driveway, plowing over a few shrubs in the process. Turning the car around, she peeled out of the driveway.

Tears streaming down her face, Susan sped down the dark, winding road. Her tires screeched at each bend, and the rattling seemed to grow louder. She kept checking the rearview mirror. The road was dark in back of her. Maybe that pronged device had crippled the patrol car.

Up ahead, she saw the disabled Honda Civic. But the emergency flashers were off. Shaffer must have switched off the lights. It didn't look like anyone was in the car. Was it too much to hope that Jordan's friend had made it to the store and called the state police by now?

Wiping the tears from her eyes, Susan glanced in the rearview mirror again. "Oh, no," she whispered.

A pair of headlights appeared in the distance behind her. They began to loom closer and closer—disappearing behind the tree-lined curves every few moments and then reappearing again. Susan wondered if there was a chance it might *not* be the deputy. Wouldn't he use his police flashers and the siren? Could it be Tom? The back road to his place was somewhere around here.

She didn't want to risk slowing down to find out who it was. At the same time, she didn't want to lead them to Rosie's—and Mattie.

The headlights in her rearview mirror seemed larger and brighter now. Susan bit her lip and then switched off her own headlights. For a few moments, it felt like she was driving blindfolded. Her hands taut on the steering wheel, she tried to find a trail off Carroll Creek Road. She felt the tires go over some gravel on the side of the highway, and she heard a spray of pebbles hitting the underside of the car. She quickly steered back onto the pavement.

At last, amid the shadows, she spotted a dirt road to her left. The car swerved and skidded as she made the last-minute turn. For a few seconds, Susan thought the Toyota might flip over. She couldn't help slowing down once she hit the unpaved path. But she couldn't step on the brake, for fear they'd see the red brake light in the woods. So she just steered and kept her foot off both pedals. The car reverberated with every rock and bump it encountered along the crude trail. Sans headlights, Susan couldn't see all the obstacles in front of her. She navigated by the contour of the trees and the tops of bushes—and even then, she could barely make out their shapes in all this darkness.

She hit something that finally made the car stop. Maybe it was a tree stump or a boulder, she couldn't be sure. But the Toyota's engine kept purring and rattling while the car remained stuck.

She glanced over her shoulder in the direction of Carroll Creek Road. Beams from the approaching car's headlights swept across the trees. Susan prayed the car would just stay on the main road. For a moment, the headlights illuminated her car—and the surrounding woodlands. Then she was in the darkness again, and the other vehicle sped on down the highway. It was the cop car.

Susan felt so relieved—for about five seconds. Then she realized if they continued down the road, they'd hit Rosie's store and find Mattie. Allen could easily talk Rosie into letting him take Mattie off her hands. And Mattie would go with him, too.

Susan couldn't let that happen. She had to catch up

with them. She'd do whatever she had to, even if it meant running them off the road or getting herself killed. They weren't getting her son.

She switched on the headlights and saw a clearing up ahead—a bald spot in the forest, where she could turn the car around. Susan stepped on the accelerator, but the car just wheezed and bucked. Her hands shaking, she shifted to reverse and tried to back up. But she hit a divot, and the whole left side of the car dropped suddenly. "Damn it!" she cried.

She shifted to drive again, and the Toyota lurched forward a foot before it slammed against something again. The rattling noise became louder every second.

Frantic, Susan jumped out and checked the front of the car. The trunk of a tilted tree had created a barrier at least a foot high. "Oh, dear God, please," she murmured.

She jumped back into the driver's seat and started working the gear shift. She inched forward and inched back—at least ten times. All the while, she kept thinking that Allen and that horrible policeman were getting closer to Rosie's store—and Mattie.

Finally, Susan drove over the tip of the tree trunk, and she felt the underside of the car scrape against it. She headed into the clearing and started to turn the car around. Past the rattling noise, she thought she heard another car's engine. Switching off her headlights, Susan glanced around for another vehicle along the dark, hidden trail. All around her, shrubs and tree branches swayed in the breeze. A leaf danced across her windshield.

She could still hear another car nearby. It seemed to be coming up behind her. Susan glanced over her shoulder but didn't see any headlights. She heard footsteps, someone—or something—running. Maybe the forest was playing tricks with sound. Maybe it was the echo of her own engine she heard.

Susan switched on her lights again. Looking up, she saw something that made her heart stop. She let out a startled, little cry.

Bathed in the headlights, Allen stood in front of her car. He glared at her. Wearing the tight white T-shirt and painter pants—and with that haggard, cold expression—he looked like a total stranger. He put a hand on the hood of her Toyota.

She heard the other car. All at once, a bright light went on in back of her. Glancing over her shoulder, Susan was blinded for a moment by the patrol car's high beams. The squad car crawled to a stop a few feet behind her. Susan realized the deputy must have seen her turn. Obviously he knew about another artery to this hidden dirt road.

The cop's high beams illuminated the interior of her car. No doubt, Allen saw how terrified she was. He probably noticed her trembling, too. He approached her window.

Susan took a deep breath and opened her door. "Oh, Allen, thank God!" she cried, jumping out of the car. "Are you okay? I've been worried sick!"

She figured if she played dumb, they were less likely to restrain her. It would buy her time, and maybe she'd live a little longer. Though it sickened her, she forced herself to hug him and even kissed his cheek.

He seemed slightly taken aback.

"I kept thinking those teenagers down the road from us had abducted you as part of some kind of—twisted game or something." She pressed her head against his shoulder. "I was going out of my mind with worry. I thought they might have killed you." Susan pulled back for a moment to glance at him.

He was looking toward the patrol car—a furtive, slightly dubious look on his face.

"I drove over to their cabin," Susan explained breathlessly. "I got halfway down the driveway and heard gunshots. Then I got out of there. I could see a car behind me. I thought it was those awful kids. I had no idea it was you. Thank God you're okay. . . ."

She waved at the deputy in the front seat. "I can't believe you found him! Thank you!"

Allen kissed her cheek. "Wait in the car, okay?" he said. "I want to talk with this guy and find out how soon we can go home."

She nodded obediently.

He started toward the police car, but hesitated and turned toward her. "Where's Mattie?"

"He's okay," Susan said, forcing a smile. Then she climbed back behind the wheel. She grabbed her purse and frantically searched for something she could use to defend herself. The closest thing to a weapon she had was a Bic pen.

She glanced in the rearview mirror. Past the patrol car's high beams, she could just make out Allen, hovering by the driver's window. He and the deputy were talking.

She thought about stepping on the gas and making a run for it. But the deputy knew these roads too well, and her dinged-up, old Toyota was no match for his patrol car. He'd catch up with her in a matter of minutes.

Susan sat frozen behind the wheel. Staring at her side mirror, she watched Allen in conference with his cohort, his fellow murderer. She knew what they were talking about back there.

They were discussing how they should kill her.

CHAPTER
TWENTY-THREE

His head was splitting, and he felt nauseous. His arm—pinned against the floor of the backseat—was dead asleep. But Leo didn't dare move a muscle.

He didn't want them to know he'd regained consciousness.

He remembered the deputy clubbing him with the nightstick. The next thing he knew, he'd found himself lying on the filthy floor in the backseat of a car. His head was behind the driver. Allen Meeker's voice had come from outside the vehicle. "Hold it, hold it!" he'd called. "There's something back here by your tire. . . ."

Leo had heard the clatter of a metal object hitting the driveway. The two men had muttered to each other, and then the car doors had opened. "Is he dead back there?" Allen had asked.

"Might as well be," the deputy had replied.

"Why didn't you stash him in the trunk?"

"I got a shitload of stuff in the trunk. He's fine back there. He can't get out. The door and window controls are up here. C'mon, move your ass. She's getting away. . . ."

Leo hadn't any idea where he was. He'd opened his eyes briefly and noticed a crisscrossed thin steel grid separating the front seat from the back. The car smelled like sour milk and stale coffee. He'd heard the doors shut, and the engine starting up. He'd felt every little bump and divot on the driveway, but he'd remained still.

Up front, they'd started talking about how Allen would take Susan Blanchette and her son out on a boat in the morning. Leo hadn't really been able to follow the conversation. In fact, he'd blacked out for a spell.

The next thing he knew, he'd been jostled awake by the rough, stomach-churning ride. The windows had been totally black on either side of the car, and Leo hadn't been able to see a thing outside. After a few grueling minutes, they'd finally stopped and Meeker had gotten out of the car. The cop switched on his high beams, and Leo glanced up again. It looked like they were in the middle of the woods someplace. He felt a cool breeze wafting through the driver's open window.

He heard someone approaching that same window. "I don't think she knows anything," Meeker whispered.

"Bullshit," the deputy grumbled. "She knows about Prewitt's mother. She knows someone lured you here to Cullen. And then the kid abducted you. She's a gnat's eyelash away from figuring out you're Mama's Boy. She's got to go, Allen."

Leo kept his eyes closed and remained perfectly still. The cop had just confirmed what Jordan had been saying for most of the day. Allen Meeker was Mama's Boy.

"We can kill her together," the deputy said eagerly. "There are plenty of closets over at the old Chemerica plant. We can stick her down the hall from that sweet little bitch I've saved for you. We'll do them both tonight—and take our sweet-ass time about it. But first, a few chores. I'll need your help changing the tire on Jordan's Civic, and then you can drive it back to the Prewitts' cabin. I have a stash of cocaine on me. Wouldn't it be a nice touch if I planted some blow in Jordan's glove compartment? When we finish with the girl, we'll dump her body in the woods behind the house. I'll torch the place in the early morning and then call the fire department. They'll find what's left of the two dead guys inside the burnt-out cabin. They'll think they were freebasing when things got out of hand. And whatever you and I do to that tasty teenage morsel, they'll blame on the dead boys."

"You think of everything, don't you?" Meeker grumbled.

"Well, I had time to ponder it after I dumped Sleeping Beauty in the back there," the cop said. "Now, you can take Susan to the Chemerica plant and lock her up until later tonight, or we'll finish her off right now and dump her body at the plant for safekeeping. Either way, we have less than an hour to get to Rosie's and pick up the kid. Tell Rosie that Susan's at home, and I'll back you up on it. First thing in the morning— while I'm calling the fire department—you go sailing with the little brat. You'll have a little accident out there on the bay. We'll go over the details later. But the result is this: Susan's lost at sea, the dead kid washes up on shore, and you survive. Then you and I can become a team. . . ."

"There's no reason why Mattie has to be killed," Meeker whispered. "He's a toddler, for Christ's sake. He doesn't know anything. . . ."

"Okay, okay, fine, we'll let the kid live," the cop grumbled. "That's your thing, isn't it?"

"What do you mean?"

"You spare the boy. With every job you pulled, you always left behind a motherless son."

There was a pause—and neither one of them spoke. Leo held his breath. For a second, he thought Meeker might have been staring at him and somehow noticed that he was awake. Leo's eyes fluttered open just a sliver, and he could make out Meeker's silhouette as he leaned close to the driver's window.

The man heaved a weary sigh. "Okay, let me take care of Susan—alone. I'll drive with her out to the old plant and kill her there. We'll come back for the body later tonight."

"All right then," the deputy said. "But I get first crack at the girl. Like I told you, I have some cocaine—and condoms, too. We'll have ourselves a regular party."

Leo realized the girl he'd referred to—that "tasty morsel," the "sweet little bitch"—was Moira. He tried to remain perfectly still.

"You know how to get to the plant?" the cop asked.

"Yeah," Meeker answered. "I remember from when I was here in ninety-eight. Afterward, I'll swing by Rosie's and pick up the boy. Then I'll meet you at the cabin."

"It's going to be a long night working and partying," the deputy said. "How exactly do you plan to keep the kid out of our hair?"

"I'm sure Jordan's pal didn't use up all the sleeping pills." Meeker answered. "We'll find them."

The deputy chuckled. "You're getting into this now, I can tell."

"See you in an hour," Meeker said.

Leo opened his eyes. Meeker had walked away from the window.

"Sorry to take so long, honey. . . ." he heard him say in the distance. Then a car door opened and shut. Something was rattling on the other vehicle as it took off down the road.

Leo listened as the rattling noise grew fainter. He carefully reached behind his head and felt for the door handle. He gave it a gentle tug. Nothing. The cop had said he controlled the locks, but Leo had figured it was still worth a try.

"You awake back there, asshole?"

Leo didn't answer him. He didn't move.

"Hmmm," the cop grunted.

After a moment, Leo felt the car moving again—over the bumpy road.

As Susan steered down the crude, narrow trail, she glanced in her rearview mirror at the idling patrol car. She kept waiting for the deputy to start following them. Or had they decided that Allen would kill her by himself?

He said he'd taken so long with the deputy because they'd gotten into an argument. "This cop insists you and I go to the Skagit County Police precinct in Anacortes to answer questions while he files a report," he explained. "Christ, all I want to do is go home with you and Mattie. Where is he, by the way?"

"He's all right," Susan said, watching for rocks and other obstacles in the road ahead. "We were in town earlier today. One of the hotels has a babysitting service. I left him there while I went looking for you."

She'd be damned if she'd make it easy for him to find Mattie. But then, it really wouldn't be too difficult. Rosie at the store was probably wondering why she hadn't returned yet. Susan prayed the nice lady would hold off calling the local police about it.

"Well, you were right," Allen said, tipping his head back. "It was like you said. What a goddamn nightmare! These two teenagers ambushed me on the road. They were holding me prisoner in the basement of that cabin. I don't know why—maybe for some kind of sick, cheap thrill. Jesus, it was horrible. . . ."

"You poor man," Susan murmured.

She wondered if he saw through her lies as clearly as she saw through his. She probably should have asked for some details, but she didn't want to hear any more fabrications. She didn't have it in her to feign gullibility and concern.

"The deputy shot one of the kids in self-defense, and the other got away," Allen said. "Those were the gunshots you heard."

Susan just nodded. She came to a stop as the dirt trail merged into Carroll Creek Road. She nervously fiddled with the loose indicator handle. "So I take a left here?" she asked.

"Yeah," Allen answered, cracking his window a little. "The deputy told me about a shortcut. We have to look for Coupland Ridge Trail. It's another one of these pain-in-the-ass, little dirt trails, but it'll cut our travel time in half—which is okay with me. I just want to get this over with."

Susan turned onto Carroll Creek Road. She figured this remote route he talked about was where he planned to kill her.

"Jesus, I need a shower," he said, sniffing himself. "I also need about four aspirin and a very tall drink. Would you look at the clothes I scraped up? Sons of bitches stripped me. I was gagged and tied up, practically naked. . . ."

All Susan could do was click her tongue against her teeth and shake her head. She figured whatever he'd suffered at Jordan Prewitt's hands hadn't been nearly enough to make up for what he'd done to that boy. It was all she could do to keep from spitting in Allen's face.

She checked the rearview mirror and noticed the cop car emerging from the darkened forest. But the deputy turned in the other direction—toward the Prewitts' cabin, or perhaps to wherever he'd hidden that poor girl.

"There it is," Allen said, pointing to a dirt path coming up on their right. "The cop said to ignore the sign. . . ."

The small wooden placard read: COUPLAND RIDGE TRAIL – NO MOTORIZED VEHICLES.

Nodding, Susan veered onto the narrow pathway. She felt as if she were driving to her own execution. She thought of those people who were forced at gunpoint to dig their own graves. She felt like one of them, compliant, doing whatever she could to buy a little more time.

As she maneuvered the Toyota over the rugged,

winding trail, Susan knew she didn't have much time left. From the way the deputy had talked, he'd already killed Jordan's friend or had him locked up someplace so they could do away with him later. That girl shared the same fate. Susan wondered if they planned to stop there. Would they spare Mattie?

"You aren't saying much," Allen observed. "I guess you've had a pretty rough day, too, huh?" He put a hand on the back of her neck.

Susan cringed inside. She stared at the dirt road ahead and pushed harder on the accelerator. "Yes, I was very worried," she said tonelessly. She thought about picking up speed, switching to cruise control and jumping out of the car. But she could break her neck in the jump, and Allen might walk away with just a scratch. She considered bracing herself and smashing into a tree—aiming on the passenger side. No, with the car wrecked, she'd be stranded, unable to help Mattie or any of the others.

"Susan, slow down," Allen whispered. He braced his hand on the dashboard. "Goddamn it, I said, *slow down.*"

She glanced at Allen and found him glaring back at her. She realized so many women had taken their last breath staring into those same cold green eyes.

Susan eased off the accelerator. Up ahead, she noticed a high chain-link fence with a large gap in it. "Is this our shortcut?" she asked.

"Past the break in the fence you'll see a driveway," he said. "Take a right."

She followed his instructions—and the wheezing, rattling Toyota made it over a big bump just before the gap in the fence. Merging onto the pavement, she turned right and started down what must have been a private driveway at one time. Rocks, tree branches, and trash littered the long strip of cracked, potholed pavement. In the distance, she noticed a little shack that looked like a guard house. Beyond that stood a squat, decaying, two-story beige brick building. It must have been the old Chemerica plant, where the deputy had that girl "tucked away" in one of the closets.

Susan started to slow down. "Is this our shortcut, Allen?" she repeated.

"No, I lied about that," he murmured. "There's a girl who's in trouble here. . . ."

Susan stopped the car just past the decrepit little guard house. She glanced at Allen again. Those eyes that had been so cold moments ago were now brimming with tears. He looked so tortured. He kept shaking his head. "Oh, God, Susan . . ."

She wondered if he was actually going against the deputy's plan to murder this helpless teenage girl. Was it possible Allen had a decent streak and he wanted to rescue her? He put his hands over his face, and he let out an agonized cry. She'd never seen him cry before.

"You mean you really want to save her?" Susan heard herself ask. She switched off the car's ignition. She started to fidget with the indicator handle again. "You're not going to kill her—or me?"

He wiped his tears away and then gazed at her. "Then you know. . . ."

She nodded. "I was outside the Prewitts' cabin while you were talking with Deputy Shaffer. I heard everything. It made me sick. . . ."

"I never wanted to hurt you, Susan," he said. "I thought for you and Mattie, I could change."

Susan slowly shook her head at him. "Then it's true. You killed all those women. You snatched them away—right in front of their little boys. Then you beat them and strangled them." She shuddered. "The night I first met you, I was with Mattie outside that restaurant. I had car trouble. You did something to my car, didn't you?"

He glanced down at the floor of the car and then nodded.

"You were going to kill me—like the others," she said. "Why did you change your mind?"

"You were different. . . ."

Susan shook her head. "That's not why," she whispered. "I remember now. The lawyer's paperwork was on the front seat of my car—where you're sitting now. You asked me, and I told you about the lawsuit—one and a half million dollars. Then you invited me to join you for Thai food. Up until that point, no one had seen us. You were going to take me away from Mattie and kill me. . . ."

She glared at him, but he wouldn't look at her. Slouching in the passenger seat, he rubbed his forehead.

"You faked that call to Triple A in the restaurant's parking lot, didn't you?"

He nodded. "I called them for real when you and Mattie were cleaning up in the restroom of the Thai place."

"The idea of that one and a half million changed your mind, didn't it?" Susan asked. "You figured on holding off for a few months, so you could play the dutiful husband and stepfather. What did you have in mind for later—an accident for Mattie and me? Why kill me in that parking lot, when you could do the same thing later and end up with a million and a half? Was that the plan, Allen?"

"Maybe at first," he admitted. "But you've changed me, Susan. I'm different from the guy who killed all those women. . . ."

Susan just shook her head in disbelief.

"Haven't I been a good fiancé?" he continued. "Haven't I been good to Mattie? That cop, he wants me to kill you—and Mattie. I took you out here so we could get away from him." Allen nodded at the old, abandoned chemical plant in front of them. "I figured maybe we could find this girl he's got trapped in there. Then I'd let you take the car, and the two of you could go to the state police. As for me, well, maybe you'll just let me disappear. . . ."

Susan stared at him. He had to know she wouldn't let that happen—not after what he'd done. He seemed so tormented and tired. He still wouldn't look at her.

"Now that we're here," he whispered. "The more I think of that helpless, scared teenage girl, trapped in there, probably crying for her parents—" He shook his head. He had tears in his eyes. "The more—God help me—I want to kill her. . . ."

Horrified, Susan edged back from him. She tightened her grip on the indicator handle—now, almost completely unscrewed from the steering column.

"I don't expect you to understand, Susan," he said, a coldness creeping into his voice. "I can't help it. She's so close. Knowing she's practically within my reach, I've got to do her. That cop, he knows me. He has my number. He knew I couldn't pass up an opportunity like this. He wants you dead. And I'm sorry, but he's calling all the shots here." He gazed at her and half smiled. "I want you to know, I got him to agree that Mattie won't be harmed. He'll be okay." He gently patted her knee. "I—I'll give him a nice toy."

Susan held the thin steel rod in her grasp—one more twist and she'd have it freed from the steering column.

"I meant it when I said you're not like the others, Susan," he said. "Prove me right and make it easier for both of us. Don't struggle. It'll be quicker. . . ."

Suddenly, he lunged toward her.

Susan tried to recoil, but he grabbed her around the throat. He shoved her against the car door, and she let go of the indicator handle. He started choking her. Susan kicked and struggled. All the while she tried to grab the rod on the steering column. But it was just out of her reach. Her hand fanned at the air.

She couldn't breathe. The more fiercely she fought, his grip only got tighter. He was practically on top of her now. He had this cold, calm look on his face. His eyes seemed dead. He brushed his lips against hers.

With every ounce of strength she could muster, Susan pushed him back. But one of his hands was still on her throat.

Grabbing the indicator handle, Susan wrenched it away from the steering column and slashed the metal rod across his face—just missing his right eye. Allen shrunk back and howled in pain. She'd made a deep, bloody laceration down his left cheek.

Susan pulled the keys out of the ignition—just as he started to lunge at her again. Recoiling, she flung open her door and staggered out of the car. She ran toward the old, neglected building. It was all boarded up—except for the broken windows on the second floor.

She glanced back at Allen as he crawled out of the car. He held a hand over the wound on the side of his face. Blood seeped through his fingers. He could hardly stand up straight.

"Goddamn it!" he bellowed. "You're going to die in there, Susan! You and that bitch are going to die in there!"

Susan turned toward the darkened warehouse and ran.

Leo felt the car take a turn. Then the road changed. For the last five or ten minutes, the ride had been relatively smooth. But they were driving over gravel now.

He had a feeling they were back at Jordan's cabin. He also had a feeling—a terrible notion—that they'd killed Jordan. But he couldn't think about that now or he'd start bawling. Besides, he wasn't positive his friend was dead. Meeker and the cop hadn't actually mentioned killing Jordan. All he knew for sure was that he and Jordan were supposed to be found dead in the burnt-out cabin tomorrow morning—and it would appear as if they'd killed Moira while on some cocaine binge. Meeker's fiancée had a death sentence hanging over her head, too.

And here he was, lying in the back of this smelly cop car, unable to do a thing about it. The car doors were locked, and the mesh screen separated him from the deputy in the front seat. All he could do was play 'possum and wait until the creepy cop stopped the car and opened the back door. Then he could either attack the cop or make a run for it—or both. But Leo didn't have anything he could use as a weapon. Meanwhile, the deputy had a gun and a nightstick and God only knew what else.

Leo felt a few more bumps in the gravel road, and then the patrol car came to a halt. He heard some static from the police radio. "Hey, Nancy, you there?" the cop asked.

It didn't exactly sound like the way they talked on TV police shows.

"Corey, we have a noise complaint at 2113 Louise Court," the woman said through a hiss of static. "Some teenagers are having a wingding. I also got a call from Rosie at Roadside Sundries. She's closing up the store in ten minutes. Seems she's been babysitting for that Ms. Blanchette's little boy. Ms. Blanchette was supposed to be gone for only fifteen minutes, she said—and that was over an hour ago. . . ."

"Tell Rosie not to get her panties in a twist," the deputy said. "I've found Ms. Blanchette's missing fiancé, and I found Ms. Blanchette, too. They're both at the house on Twenty-two Birch, and everything's copacetic. Either the fiancé or I will be over in about twenty minutes to pick up the kid. Tell Rosie to sit tight. As for the noise complaint, I'll check out Louise Court when I get around to it. Okay?"

"I'll pass the word on to Rosie," the police operator said.

"Over and out," Shaffer said. Then the static died. "You awake back there?" The deputy banged on the mesh screen. "Hey, kid . . ."

Leo let out a drowsy groan. He heard the ignition shut off, and then the front door opened and shut. After a moment, the back door opened by his feet. "C'mon, hotshot, it's the end of the line for you. . . ."

His eyes half closed, Leo watched the deputy lean into the car and reach for his leg. Leo kicked his foot at Deputy Shaffer's face, but missed and hit his shoulder. Still, he stunned the cop, who reeled back and fell to the ground.

Leo crawled out from the back of the patrol car.

"You little shit!" Shaffer growled, scrambling to his feet.

Out of the corner of his eye, Leo saw the cop pull out his nightstick. Leo tried to run but suddenly felt the club come crashing down on the side of his head.

His legs went out from under him, and he slid down on the gravel. Dazed, he tried to get up, but couldn't.

The deputy grabbed his foot and dragged him across the gravel toward the cabin. Through his jeans, Leo felt stones and pebbles digging against his backside. He tried to yank his foot free, but he was too weak and stunned. He felt utterly helpless. His vision was blurred. He tried to focus on the cop, but he could only hear his voice.

"C'mon in here and join your buddy," the deputy said.

CHAPTER
TWENTY-FOUR

Allen kept screaming that she was going to die.

Susan ran away from that taunting, angry voice—and toward the abandoned building. She ran until the sound of the old, heavy shades flapping in the wind began to drown him out. The plant's front door and first-floor windows were boarded up with graffiti-marred plywood. Racing around to the side of the building, she weaved through dead shrubs and litter. The ground floor windows on the side of the building were barricaded, too, but she found one plywood board that was askew. She managed to boost herself up to the broken window and climb inside.

Once inside the dusty, dank building, she took a moment to adjust to the darkness. Susan found herself in a tiny office—with two broken chairs and a pile of trash on the floor. Starting for the office door, she accidentally kicked some old beer bottles and cans. She winced at the thought that Allen might have heard the clattering.

Susan hesitated and listened for a moment. She didn't hear him. She couldn't hear anything except the wind howling through the second floor—and those shades banging.

In the narrow corridor, she poked her head into several dark offices—all full of cobwebs and discarded broken furniture. On the floor of one room, she saw two rats crawling around by some trash, and she quickly ducked out to the hallway again.

"Hello?" Susan called softly. "Moira? Can you hear me? I've come to get you out of here!"

No response. Then again, Susan was afraid to yell too loudly. She didn't want to make it any easier for Allen to find her. She wondered if the girl was really here—or if she was dead already. For all she knew, the deputy might have lied to Allen.

Her heart racing, she searched through the maze of offices, going from one gloomy room to another, unsure of what was around each corner. Susan's voice cracked as she kept calling out to the girl—each time a little louder. She poked her head into an old laboratory. The built-in counters and some archaic equipment were covered with dust. Moths fluttered around the big, unlit room. Against the wall were two large, refrigeration units. One was missing a door; the other still had its door attached, and it was shut. She pulled on the handle, but it didn't budge.

"Moira?" she called again. "Yell out if you can hear me! Moira—"

Susan fell silent at the sound of a distant, muffled scream. She realized it wasn't coming from inside the refrigerator unit. "Moira, keep yelling!" she shouted, heading out of the laboratory—then down the dim hallway. "Keep yelling! I'm trying to find you!"

She listened to the girl's stifled cries and realized

she was getting closer to her. The garbled whimpering became louder—and more frantic. It sounded like she was trying to scream past a gag in her mouth.

Susan kept wondering about Allen. Why hadn't she heard his footsteps? Had he already found a way inside the building? For all she knew, the deputy might have told Allen exactly where to find the girl, and Allen was with Moira now—waiting for his unwitting fiancée to come to him.

Susan noticed a leg from a broken table on the floor, and swiped it up. It was about the size of a baseball bat.

She could still hear the girl's muted screaming. She followed the sound—to a larger office at the end of the hall. With the table leg ready, she poked her head into the room. She didn't see anyone and almost moved on. But then she noticed an old chair wedged against the door to a closet or a connecting room. She moved toward the door and heard Moira's stifled cries on the other side of it.

Pushing the chair away, Susan opened the door. She found Moira curled up on the closet floor in just a torn shirt and panties. The teenager was shaking violently. It looked like her arms had been tied behind her, and she was pushed up against a pipe that ran from the floor to the ceiling. Moira tried to talk past a rolled-up rag stuffed in her mouth.

"It's okay, I'm going to get you out of here," Susan said, reaching for the gag.

As she pulled it out of Moira's mouth, the girl gasped. "Oh, God . . . thank you . . . thank you . . ." Then she started coughing. Susan tried to help her to her feet, but Moira shook her head. She turned away from Susan to show that her hands were handcuffed around the pipe.

"Oh, Jesus," Susan murmured. She tugged at the handcuffs. "Okay, listen, I'm going to look for something to free you up from these damn things. Just hold on."

Moira let out a weak laugh. "I ain't going anywhere. . . ."

The table leg clutched tightly in her fist, Susan headed down the shadowy corridor until she spotted an old fire box with a broken alarm, a coiled hose—and peeking out behind it, an ax. The glass on the firebox door was cracked. Susan struggled to open it up. She finally dropped the table leg and pulled at the door with both hands. When it finally gave, a shard of glass fell off and shattered on the floor.

"Are you still there?" Moira called weakly.

"Yes, that was me!" Susan replied. She pushed the coiled hose aside and reached for the ax stashed behind it.

The thing was heavy and awkward to carry, but the blade still looked sharp. Susan ran back down the corridor with it. Ducking into the office, she hurried to the closet where Moira had managed to stand up. She was leaning to one side, putting all her weight on one foot. When she saw Susan with the ax, a look of horror swept over her face. "My God," she gasped. "I thought you were going to get a bobby pin or something to trip the lock." She started coughing again and shook her head at Susan.

"Listen, I don't know a thing about picking a lock," Susan admitted. "But my aim's pretty good. Okay?"

Moira winced at her. "I don't know—"

Susan hesitated. But then she heard the rattle of bottles and cans in another part of the building. She realized Allen had found his way into the plant.

Moira must have heard it, too, because suddenly she nodded several times and turned her body away from the pipe. Susan adjusted the girl's hands so the inch-long chain between the cuffs was vertical and taut against the pipe.

All the while, she listened to the footsteps of someone running in the hallway.

"You—you were at the general store yesterday, weren't you?" Moira asked nervously.

"Yes, my name's Susan. Now, I need you to keep very still."

"Don't you have a little boy?"

"Yes. The woman at the store is looking after him right now—I hope." Susan took a deep breath, then lifted the ax.

"You were talking to my friend, Jordan. I think he's got a crush on you. . . ."

Susan didn't want to tell her that her friend was dead. "Moira, I need you to be quiet," she whispered.

"I'm sorry. I talk a lot when I get nervous. I'll shut up."

In the silence between them, Susan could hear the footsteps in the corridor getting louder—and closer. She swallowed hard and swung the ax. Moira let out a startled yelp as it hit the chain. The pipe made a loud, hollow, bang. But the handcuffs' steel links were intact. "Do it again," Moira said under her breath. Her hands were shaking.

In the dark little closet, Susan felt lucky she hadn't chopped off one of the poor girl's arms on that first try. But she hauled back and swung the ax again. There was another clatter that echoed from the pipe. Susan barely waited a beat before giving the ax a third swing. At last, the handcuffs' chain snapped. Moira let out a grateful cry and leaned against the wall. She rubbed her arms.

Susan figured the sound of that ax hitting the pipe had reverberated through the whole building. She paused, but couldn't hear the footsteps anymore. She wondered if he was just outside the office door, waiting for them.

"Thank you," Moira whispered. "Thank you, Susan."

Draping her cardigan over Moira's shoulders, she grabbed the ax and started to lead her out of the closet. The girl could hardly walk. "I—I think I sprained something," Moira explained. "I'm sorry I can't move very fast."

Susan glanced down at the girl's swollen, discolored ankle. "Looks like a bad sprain," she whispered. "Just lean on me, okay?" Susan held her up with one hand and clung onto the ax with the other. Before they stepped out to the hallway, she paused, put her finger to her lips, and then left Moira leaning against the wall. With the ax ready, Susan peeked into the corridor. She didn't see anyone, just the shadowy hallway and the office doorways.

She ducked back into the office and nodded at Moira. The girl grabbed hold of her shoulder, and together they started down the gloomy corridor. They moved past the open doors to several dark offices. Susan was terrified that Allen could be lurking in any one of them.

"This guy, he's a cop—he's the one who did this to me," Moira started to explain.

Susan shushed her, then nodded. "I know, I know," she whispered. She'd lost track of which office window she'd used to enter the building. She couldn't stop trembling—and neither could the girl. They passed the old laboratory and turned down another corridor.

She spotted a very faint light coming through one doorway near the far end of the hall. Susan bypassed the other offices and hurried toward it. Moira hobbled alongside her. Stepping into the room, Moira accidentally kicked some old bottles. They both hesitated for a moment. Susan wondered if Allen was close by, listening to them. There was a reason those footsteps had stopped. He was hiding.

She saw a shaft of moonlight pouring through an opening in the broken window where the plywood board was askew. She peeked out the window to make certain he wasn't waiting for them there. Holding the plywood board back, she helped Moira through the opening to the ground below. She lowered the ax down to the girl and then climbed out after her.

They crept alongside the building, toward the old parking lot. Susan kept thinking that any minute now, Allen would come up and grab one of them from behind. She saw the Toyota ahead and reached for the car keys in her pocket. All the while, Moira clung to her, and Susan clung to the ax.

She noticed the drops of blood around the passenger door as she opened it for Moira. Then she checked the backseat to make sure Allen wasn't hiding in there. "Lock it!" she said, once Moira shut the car door.

Susan glanced at the tires. There was nothing wedged beneath any of them to give her a flat. The back tires looked a bit low, but seemed okay. Opening the driver's door, she quickly stashed the ax in the backseat. As she climbed behind the wheel, she saw blood on the dashboard.

"What is that?" Moira asked, staring at it, too.

Susan shut her door, locked it, and then put the key in the ignition. Giving it a turn, she prayed the car would start. The engine let out a roar—and that rattling noise started, too. Starting up the driveway, she glanced in the rearview mirror at the dark, abandoned building. She didn't see anyone. There was no sign of Allen.

"What is this?" Moira asked again, nodding at the blood on the dash.

Susan's heart was still racing. But she started to catch her breath. She glanced at the dark red spots and smears on the dashboard. "I had a disagreement with my fiancé," she said.

Susan hadn't noticed that the same kind of markings were on the hood of the trunk. It didn't dawn on her why the rear tires were riding low. Nor did she realize the trunk was propped open—only a sliver.

It was just enough for him to breathe a little easier.

Rosie heard the bell tinkle over the door. On a dead night like tonight, it usually gave her the willies when someone wandered into the store three minutes before closing. That was what had happened one evening six years ago, and the guy had held her up at gunpoint.

But tonight she was expecting Susan Blanchette's fiancé or Deputy Shaffer to come pick up Mattie. With a groan, she pulled herself off the play-area floor mat, where she'd been supervising Susan's son on the mini jungle gym. "Howdy!" Rosie called, not sure yet to

whom she was talking. She waddled around from behind the counter and saw Tom Collins coming up the
soup and canned foods aisle.

"Hey, Rosie," he said. "How's it going?"

Mattie jumped off the pint-sized jungle gym and
scurried in front of her, almost tripping her. "Hi, Tom!"
he said, looking up at him.

Tom stopped and smiled at Susan's son. "Well, hi,
Matthew Blanchette," he said. "Where's your mom?"

"She's running Aaron," Mattie replied. "I'm going
to ride in a police car!"

"Well, how about that?" Tom gave Rosie a puzzled
look.

She mussed Mattie's hair. "Sweetheart, why don't
you put the toys away, and maybe old Rosie will give
you a treat for being such a good boy." She waited
until Mattie hurried to the play area.

"What going on?" Tom whispered. "Is Susan okay?"

"She swung by a little while ago and said she had to
run an errand," Rosie explained in a hushed tone. "She
was only supposed to be a few minutes. Well, after an
hour, I started to panic, and I called the police. But it
turns out everything's all right. See, her fiancé's been
missing since noon—"

"I know," Tom nodded. "She came by my place this
afternoon, looking for him. We had lemonade."

"Lemonade, huh?" Rosie gave him a knowing smile.
"Well, honey, from the smitten look on your face, I hate
to tell you this, but that pretty lady found her man.
They're staying at the old Syms house on Birch. She's
there right now with him. I'm expecting him or Deputy
Shaffer to come pick up Mattie. One of them is sup-

posed to be here any minute. I think Mattie's hoping for the deputy. He wants to ride in the police car."

Tom frowned at her.

"Is anything wrong?" she asked.

He sighed. "Well, for starters, I just came from the house on Birch, and nobody's home."

"You sure?"

"Yes, I was worried about her. I was there nearly two hours ago. She told me she was checking into one of the hotels in town tonight. But I just tried both hotels, and she's not registered at either of them. So I swung by the house on Birch again, and nobody's home." His eyes narrowed at her. "Who told you she was there?"

"Nancy at the police station told me," Rosie said, shrugging. "At least, that's the skinny she got from Corey Shaffer."

Tom wandered toward the counter and leaned against it. "Let me ask you something. Does Susan strike you as the kind of mother who would unload her child on you way longer than she said she would—and then not come by to apologize or explain? Instead, she sits on her ass in her rental house and sends a cop to come pick him up?"

Rosie slowly shook her head. "No, sir, she doesn't strike me as that kind of mom at all. And you say the house is empty?"

Tom nodded.

"Well, why the heck would the deputy sell me that bill of goods?"

"I'm not sure," Tom muttered. "I know he represents the law around here, but I've always had a bad feeling about Corey—ever since when he was a kid and my mother told me he killed a cat in his backyard with a lawnmower."

"I've heard that story, too," Rosie said grimly.

"I don't trust the guy. Where's Sheriff Fischer tonight?"

"With his Missuz on Whidbey Island," she answered.

"Something screwy is going on here," Tom said, rubbing his chin. "Maybe this is jumping the gun, but do you mind if I use your phone to call the county sheriff in Anacortes?"

Rosie stared at him for a moment, and then she nodded. "Honey, I'll even dial the number for you."

"Oh, God, no," Susan groaned.

The headlights of her Toyota illuminated two big cement barriers at the end of the abandoned plant's driveway. They totally blocked any motor vehicle access to the road.

For the last five minutes, Moira had been describing what had happened to her—from getting lost in the woods to falling into a pit to being locked in a janitor's closet. She'd mentioned twice that her friends were probably worried about her. Susan didn't have the heart to tell her that both her friends were probably dead. She didn't need the poor girl to get hysterical on her, not now.

"What is this?" Moira said. Staring at the barricades, she clutched Susan's sweater around her. The dashboard light exposed her panicked look. "What is this?" she repeated.

"I'm afraid this is us having to turn around," Susan muttered.

As she pulled a U-turn, Susan dreaded the notion of heading back toward the deserted plant. They'd just narrowly escaped from there. Allen was probably sprinting up this same neglected, old driveway. Any minute now, she expected to catch him in her headlights.

"Listen, Moira, there's a gap in the fence on your side," she explained. The car's rattling became louder as she picked up speed. "It's the way we came in here. If I was smart I would have gone out that way, too. It should be coming up soon. Keep your eyes peeled."

Moira nervously peered out her window. Meanwhile, Susan watched out for potholes, rocks, and the little shrubs that had grown through holes and cracks in the road. She kept a lookout for Allen, too.

"I see it!" Moira announced, pointing to an opening in the chain-link fence on their right.

Slowing the car down to a crawl, Susan veered off the driveway and headed toward the gap in the fence. The ride over the rugged trail jostled them. As they hit a big bump at the fence line, the car suddenly buckled and tilted to one side.

"Oh, God, no," Susan said for the second time in five minutes. She tried to accelerate, but the Toyota didn't move. Past the constant rattle, Susan heard one of the tires spinning.

"Christ, this is a goddamn nightmare," Moira muttered.

"Can you work the accelerator pedal with your sore foot?" Susan asked her.

Moira nodded. "I can try."

"I'll get out and push." Susan stepped out of the car.

Its headlights illuminated the trail winding through the darkened forest. Staring toward the back of the car, Susan glanced at the driveway on the other side of the fence—bathed in the red glow of her taillights. There was no sign of Allen.

Biting her lip, she studied the rear tire on the driver's side. It was stuck in a small, mud-filled crater. "Okay, give me a minute. I think we can get out of here," she announced.

Moira was hobbling around the front of the car. She ducked behind the wheel.

Susan quickly gathered up some fallen branches and wedged them in front of the tire. As she moved to the back of the car, she noticed some blood smeared by the trunk lock. Then she could see the trunk was open—just an inch.

All at once, the lid sprung up.

Recoiling, Susan let out a shriek. Allen scrambled out of the trunk and charged toward her. The car lurched forward. He looked like a madman. The side of his face was covered with blood. It ran down his neck and stained the shoulder of his tight white T-shirt. He drew back his fist and punched her in the face.

Susan flew back and slammed into a tree. Dazed, she crumpled to the ground.

She heard Moira screaming. She blinked and helplessly watched as Allen swiveled around and dragged the girl out of the driver's seat. The car rolled forward again. He noticed the ax in the backseat and grabbed it. Moira was crying and shrieking in pain at every step he forced her to take on her swollen ankle. With one hand, Allen grabbed her by her short, pixie-style hair. His other hand held the ax blade to Moira's throat.

Susan managed to get to her feet, but she clung to the tree to keep from falling again. The whole side of her face was throbbing. A high-pitched ringing assaulted her left ear. She numbly gazed at Allen.

Tears were streaming down Moira's face. "Oh, God, please," she cried. "No, don't. . . ."

"Shut up!" he growled. Still holding her by the hair, he gave Moira's head a shake.

Moira took one last gasp, then stood there, wincing and trembling.

Allen glowered at Susan. "Get in the car," he hissed. "You're driving us to the cabin on Cedar Crest Way. The two of us will sit in back." He pressed the ax handle to Moira's throat and cracked a tiny smile. "Oh, and, Susan, mind the bumps."

As the deputy dragged him into the cabin's front hallway, Leo noticed the stairway's broken banister. Amid the splintered and broken pieces of wood, he saw a trail of blood on the beige carpet. The crimson path started at the bottom of the stairs and led into the kitchen.

Leo realized Jordan must have been shot on the stairs and that his body was moved into the kitchen or the basement. His heart sunk, and tears welled in his eyes. He tried to struggle as the deputy hauled him farther into the cabin, but he was still too dazed and weak.

"What the hell?" the deputy murmured. He dropped Leo in a heap on the hallway floor and then followed the blood trail toward the kitchen. "Shit, I should have put a bullet in his brain. Little bastard, where the fuck are you?"

Leo felt a surge of hope. Maybe his friend had been wounded and somehow escaped.

Pulling out his gun, Shaffer stepped into the kitchen. He called for Jordan in a soft, mocking voice. "C'mon, kid, show your face. . . . Give me your best shot. . . ."

Unable to stand, Leo crawled toward the front door. His head was spinning. He kept thinking, if only he could get outside and hide someplace in the woods. Maybe that was where Jordan was now. He heard the deputy's footsteps on the basement stairs.

The front door squeaked as Leo tugged it open. On all fours, he crept out to the front stoop. He managed to get to his feet and stagger a few steps before he fell to the ground. He didn't have any equilibrium. He started crawling again.

"Jordan?" he called in a hushed voice. No answer. Leo blinked a few times and tried to focus on the patrol car.

A shot rang out from within the house. "Little shit!" Shaffer bellowed.

Leo wasn't sure if the deputy had been shot—or if he'd just gunned down Jordan. Maybe he'd merely been spooked and, in a panic, fired his weapon.

Struggling to his feet again, Leo managed to lurch to the patrol car. He opened the front door and flopped across the seat. He tried to figure out how to use the radio. Fiddling with the switches and buttons, he heard a muffled voice through the static. Leo wasn't sure if he'd reached someone, but he pressed the button on the mike and whispered into it: "Is anybody there? Can anyone hear me? I've been assaulted by this deputy. . . ." Leo paused and released the button. All he heard was static. He pressed the button on the mike again. "This deputy—his name's Shaffer. He—he's a murderer. He's got a gun. I think he killed my friend, Jordan Prewitt. I'm at the Prewitt cabin in . . . in . . . in Cullen. Can you hear me? Please, send help. . . ."

He released the button on the microphone and heard someone responding through the static, but the words were indistinguishable. Leo glanced back at the cabin and saw the deputy standing in the front doorway.

Panic-stricken, Leo looked around the patrol car for something he could use to defend himself. But there was nothing. He scurried out of the vehicle and left the car door open as he made a run for the woods bordering the driveway. He only made it a short way from the car before his legs stopped working and he stumbled again. He hit the gravel hard and got the wind knocked out of him.

Leo blinked and saw the deputy stomping toward him, his gun drawn.

Leo desperately crawled toward the forest, grabbing at thin tree branches, or stones—anything he could use to throw at the cop. He hurled whatever he could find at him, but kept missing.

The deputy descended on him. His swaggering stride only seemed more determined as he got closer.

Crawling toward the edge of the woods, Leo felt something stab his hand. He glanced at his bleeding palm—and then at a strange metal contraption that looked like the head of a rake.

"Where do you think you're going, asshole?" he heard Shaffer ask.

Leo twisted around and gazed up at the cop. He shook his head. "No, please, wait. . . ."

The deputy aimed his gun at Leo's face. But then

something in the woods caught Shaffer's attention, and he glanced away for a moment.

Leo quickly grabbed the pronged metal contraption, pushed himself off the ground, and swung it at the deputy's head. He knocked off his police cap.

He heard the gun go off, a resounding *bang*. Then Leo felt a sharp, burning pain in the side of his stomach.

Stunned, Deputy Shaffer stared down at him with his mouth open. The spiked metal piece stuck to his left temple. Blood leaked from the side of his blond head and down his neck. His eyes started to roll back.

Leo watched the deputy hit the ground with a thud.

After a moment, Leo's vision started to blur again. He felt a horrible, searing pain in his side. The rest of his body felt so cold. He turned toward the woods—where the cop must have seen something earlier. Through the trees, he thought he saw someone.

Then everything went black.

She kept glancing at them in her rearview mirror.

Crammed in the back with Mattie's child seat, Allen practically held Moira in his lap. One arm slung around her shoulder, he pulled her in close while pressing the ax blade to her throat. Tears glistened on Moira's face, and every few moments, she let out a terrified whimper. She was shaking uncontrollably.

At one point, Susan had heard him say under his breath to the girl. "I heard you were pretty, Moira. But I didn't know just how pretty until now."

Moira said nothing. She just closed her eyes and grimaced.

Navigating the dirt road ahead, Susan remained quiet, too. The Toyota's constant rattle did nothing to alleviate the tense silence inside the car.

As she merged onto Carroll Creek Road, Susan reached for her turn indicator, but then she realized it was on the car floor some place. The thin metal rod was hardly a match for the ax Allen wielded. But at least it was something. With a tight grip on the steering wheel, Susan glanced around the car floor for it. She started to feel gravel under the tires and looked up in time to see she was veering off the road.

Allen jabbed her shoulder. "Eyes on the road, god-damn it."

She steered back into her lane, but still felt him hovering behind her. She glanced in the rearview mirror, and their eyes met.

"I look pretty beat up, don't I?" he asked. "Do I look like I've been in a boating accident?"

Susan said nothing.

"Because that's how it's going to look for you, too, bitch," he whispered. "And to think, I used to like you." Then he sat back again and pulled Moira closer to him.

As they passed Jordan's abandoned Honda Civic on the roadside, Susan glanced in the rearview mirror to see if Moira had noticed it, too. She saw the girl's eyes widen. "That—that was Jordan's car," she murmured, baffled. "What—what's happened?" She started to squirm—until Allen grabbed her by the hair again and snapped her head back.

"You'll see him soon enough," he growled.

Trembling, Moira didn't say another word for the rest of the ride—not even when he pressed the side of his face against hers. His blood smeared her cheek. She didn't try to move away. She just winced and sat very still.

Susan turned down Cedar Crest Way. Taking a curve in the tree-lined road, she spotted the police car in the drive-way ahead. The driver's door was open, and the interior light was on.

"Stop the car," Allen said.

Susan stepped on the brake. Glancing at the floor again, she searched for the metal rod but couldn't see it anywhere.

"Shut off the motor, and hand me the keys," he commanded.

Wordlessly, she obeyed him.

"You get out first," he said. "We'll be right behind you."

Susan took one last glance toward the front passenger side, but still didn't spot the indicator handle. Reluctantly opening the door, she stepped outside. She couldn't see the front of the house from where she stood. But as she took a few steps up the drive, Susan saw something else—and it made her stop dead.

Not far from the squad car's open door, on the edge of the driveway, Deputy Shaffer was lying on his side. His police cap had been knocked off. The pronged contraption Susan had noticed earlier was now wedged between the side of Shaffer's head and the gravel.

A hand over her heart, Susan took another step closer.

The police car's interior light illuminated the pool of blood around Deputy Shaffer's head—and the startled look in his open eyes. A fly landed on his cheek, grazed around for a moment, then flew away. Shaffer didn't move.

She heard Allen and Moira behind her, climbing out of the car. Susan jumped at the sound of the car door slamming. She glanced over toward the cabin. The lights were off, but she could see the two young men on the front stoop. One of them was half sitting, slumped against the door. He had his arm around his friend's prone body. With their faces in the shadows, Susan couldn't tell which boy was sitting and which was lying there, but neither one of them was moving. It appeared as if the one boy had tried to pull his friend's body into the house before he'd given up and died. Or was he breathing? Susan couldn't tell. It looked like he had a gun in his hand. She stood there frozen.

"What the fuck happened here?" she heard Allen mutter.

She knew he'd just spotted the deputy's body. Susan swiveled around to face him.

Dumbfounded, Allen gazed down at Shaffer's corpse. He still had Moira by the hair and the ax blade against her throat.

Susan shook her head at him. "You don't have to do this now, Allen, not anymore. He's dead. He has no power over you. You no longer have to do what he says. You can just turn around and drive away. . . ."

Moira started to struggle, but it was in vain. His grip on her didn't slacken.

"I can't have any witnesses," he muttered. "And there's a matter of payback for what those two pricks did to me this afternoon. One of them is still alive."

"No—no, they're both dead." Susan pointed to the

two bodies by the front door. She started backing up toward the cabin. "They're both dead. No one holds anything over you now. You can just drive away, Allen. Please, let her be. . . ."

At the news that her friends were dead, Moira let out an anguished cry. "Oh, God, no . . ." She tried to wrench free from Allen. The ax blade nicked the side of her neck, but she didn't seem to notice. She sobbed hysterically.

Allen took in the scene by the front door. Then he smiled a little and turned to Susan. "I can't have *any* witnesses," he said loudly—over Moira's weeping. "None at all . . ."

Susan kept shaking her head over and over. Out of the corner of her eye, she glimpsed the boys by the front stoop again.

The one with the gun in his hand was moving.

Cradling his friend in his arms, he leaned against the front door and watched Meeker's fiancée. Her back to him, Susan Blanchette kept stepping into his line of vision, blocking his view of Meeker and Moira. But he could hear Meeker's voice, so close.

Jordan had the deputy's gun in his hand.

He glanced at his leg—and at all the blood around the tear in his jeans, where the bone stuck out below his knee.

It had happened after the deputy shot at him—twice. One bullet had grazed his shoulder; the second had hit him in the gut. He fell down the stairs and broke through the banister. Jordan remained on the living room floor, keeping perfectly still—despite the horrible pain. He didn't even move when Meeker kicked him in his side. The bastard probably fractured a couple of his ribs. He knew he'd wrecked the hell out of his leg during that fall, too. Jordan had no idea just how bad it was. He couldn't look at it, not while they were standing right next to him.

He didn't move a muscle. Fortunately, they didn't stay there long. The deputy heard someone outside. "I have a feeling that's your intended, Allen," Shaffer said.

Jordan had waited until after they left and he had heard the cop car peeling out of the driveway. Then he crawled into the kitchen, grabbed a dish towel, and clutched it to his stomach. With a *Kiss the Cook* apron, he made a tourniquet for his leg. He stared at that bone jutting out and cringed. He tried to tell himself he'd seen worse in one of his lacrosse games, but he really couldn't remember anything quite this gory.

He hobbled out the back door, around the cabin, and past the driveway, bracing himself against the side of the house or trees, anything he could grab to keep from keeling over. If he could reach the road, he might flag down a passing car—on the off-off chance someone drove by. He staggered through the woods on the other side of the driveway.

Jordan had just reached Carroll Creek Road when he spotted the deputy's patrol car approaching. He ducked back into the bushes and watched the prowler pull into his driveway. It disappeared behind the trees.

Jordan thought he might pass out from the pain and exhaustion, but he hobbled through the woodlands—all the way back toward the cabin again. He heard a car door slam, then Shaffer's voice in the distance. But he couldn't make out what the deputy was saying. He heard the cabin door open and shut—and then nothing for at least two or three minutes. Jordan kept hobbling through the shadowy woods until he started to see the cabin through the trees again.

Then he heard Leo softly calling out to him.

Jordan was so stunned and elated, he forgot about his leg for a second. He moved toward the sound of his friend's voice and immediately felt a horrible pain shooting up from his knee. Falling down on the forest floor, he let out a groan. He was about to call back to Leo when he heard a gunshot from within the cabin.

Jordan dragged himself through the woods toward the driveway. Helplessly he watched Leo, by the patrol car, trying to fend off the deputy. Panic-stricken, Jordan struggled to his feet. Twigs snapped beneath him. He saw the cop standing over Leo with the gun.

For a split second, the deputy glanced his way. Their eyes met.

That was when Leo hit the cop in the head with the pronged device. The gun went off with a startling bang. The blond deputy teetered there for a moment, looking baffled. Then he collapsed onto the gravel driveway.

Hopping on one foot, Jordan made his way to his friend. At first, he thought Leo was dead. But then he saw his buddy was breathing. It looked like Leo had been shot in the abdomen, almost the same place where the deputy had put a bullet in him—only with Leo's wound there was a lot more blood. A crimson stain bloomed on his shirt, and it alarmed Jordan to feel how cold Leo was.

Taking the dish towel away from his own stomach

wound, Jordan pressed a part not soaked with blood against the bullet hole in Leo's shirt. His bloodstained hands were shaking, and he started to cry. He kissed Leo on the forehead. "Hang in there, buddy, okay?" he murmured.

Dragging himself over to the deputy, he took the dead cop's gun and his car keys. He stashed the gun in the back of his jeans, under his shirttail. Then he managed to crawl back to the patrol car and tried to radio for an ambulance. "Two people have been shot at number one Cedar Crest Way in Cullen," Jordan gasped into the mike. "It's right off Carroll Creek. Another person's dead. But two of us are badly wounded. We need an ambulance right away." His voice started to crack. "Please, hurry, for God's sake, my friend's looking really bad. . . ."

All he got for an answer was a distant voice through the static. Jordan couldn't make out what they were saying. He knew Cullen pretty well, and the nearest hospital was in Mount Vernon, about twenty-five minutes away. He wondered if he might be able to drive that far. *No, not a chance.* He couldn't operate the pedals with his broken leg. The bullet in his gut wasn't helping either.

Frustrated, Jordan wiped the tears from his eyes and tried the police radio one more time. He glanced down at his pal. Leo's breathing seemed to be getting shallow. All Jordan could think to do was get him inside the house, give him some water, and try to stop the bleeding.

He left the door open as he climbed out of the cop car. Grabbing Leo underneath the arms, he began dragging him across the lawn toward the front door. He couldn't get to his feet or bend his bum leg. So he crawled most of the way, with Leo's limp body on top of his. Jordan felt the gun barrel digging into his tailbone. Cold sweat poured off him. He was so depleted, but he pressed on toward the cabin. He listened to his friend's breathing. It was like a death rattle.

On the front stoop, Jordan felt himself starting to black out.

He'd paused there and caught his breath. Just then, he heard another car approaching. He knew it wasn't a cop or an ambulance because there would have been a siren. Instead, he heard gravel under tires, a rattling noise, and then quiet. Two car doors opened and shut.

He saw Allen Meeker's fiancée approaching the dead cop. Then he heard Meeker's voice: *"What the fuck happened here?"*

That was when Jordan reached back for the gun.

He heard Susan Blanchette begging the son of a bitch to spare Moira and drive away. She pointed to Leo and him. "They're both dead," she said. "No one holds anything over you now. You can just drive away, Allen. Please, let her be. . . ."

He only glimpsed Meeker for a few seconds. His face was bleeding. He had Moira by the hair and held an ax blade to her throat. He kept saying he didn't want any witnesses. Moira was screaming and crying.

Jordan was about to raise the gun and fire. But he was too far away and didn't want to risk shooting Moira. Just when he thought he had Allen Meeker in his sights, Susan would move between them, blocking the way. It was almost as if she were doing it on purpose.

* * *

Stepping back toward the cabin's front door, Susan glanced over her shoulder again. Now she could see the boy with the gun was Jordan, and he was alive. But she couldn't let Allen see that. So she kept obstructing his line of vision by placing herself between Allen and the boys.

The more she pulled back, the closer she drew Allen toward the young man whose mother he'd murdered. And that young man had a gun. Susan just hoped his aim was good.

Allen still had Moira in his grasp.

"You can't kill her, Allen," Susan said, taking another step back. "Not yet. If you do, then you'll never get a description of Deputy Shaffer's partner. He'll always be hounding you. . . ."

"What are you talking about?" Allen grumbled.

"Moira told me—after I found her in that old warehouse," Susan continued. "She said that *two* men abducted her."

"Shaffer never mentioned a partner in any of his e-mails or letters," Allen said, eyes narrowed at her. "He didn't say anything today about it either. You're lying. . . ."

"No, she's not!" Moira insisted, her voice shrill. "There were two of them—a good-looking cop, and th-th-the other one's an older guy with red hair. He breathes funny. I think he's got asthma or something. . . ."

That a girl, Susan thought. Moira was going along with the whole fabrication—and it was buying them time.

"Lying bitches, the both of you," Allen grumbled.

Susan furtively glanced over her shoulder. She was close enough to see the gun in Jordan's trembling hand.

She turned to look at Allen. "We're telling the truth," she said, clutching her fist against her chest. "On our way to the car, Moira asked me, 'Who is Allen Meeker?' She said the two kidnappers were talking about you. This other man knows who you are. . . ."

Allen yanked Moira's head back. "Did you get the other guy's name?"

"I think—I think the cop called him Jake," she answered, trembling. "They kept talking about you. . . ."

Susan took one more step back and then snuck another glance at Jordan. She saw him raising the gun and the determined look in his eyes.

Then she moved aside.

Jordan suddenly had him in his sights. He was so close.

But Meeker still held Moira in front of him. "Jake *who*?" he asked, screaming in Moira's ear. "Did you get his last name? What did they say about me? Tell me, goddamn it. . . ."

Beyond the yelling, Jordan heard something else—the distant wail of a police siren. Meeker must have heard it, too, because he suddenly shut up and glanced toward the driveway.

All at once, Moira let out a shriek. She elbowed him in the face and broke away. She faltered as she tried to run. But Susan rushed forward and pulled her up.

Meeker was only momentarily stunned. He hadn't

even dropped the ax. He gave his head a little shake and then started after them.

Holding up the crippled Moira, Susan tried to retreat toward the house. But they were too slow. Moira couldn't run. Meeker was just a few paces behind them—with the ax raised.

"Do it!" Susan shouted.

Jordan realized she was talking to him. He squirmed out from beneath his friend's dead weight. The gun wavered in his trembling hand.

Meeker suddenly seemed to realize who Susan was talking to as well. He stopped in his tracks, turned toward Jordan, and blinked.

Their eyes met.

Jordan aimed the gun at his mother's killer and squeezed the trigger. A loud shot rang out, and Jordan felt an electriclike jolt surge up his arm.

But Allen Meeker was still standing, still gaping at him.

Jordan dragged himself across the ground. He tried to keep the gun pointed at Meeker. He had to get closer. For a moment, he was in that kayak again, an eight-year-old boy rowing frantically, desperate to reach his mother and ward off her attacker.

He gazed at that same man now. Jordan felt as if he were about to pass out from the exhaustion and pain, but he kept crawling toward him.

Meeker lunged forward and grabbed Susan's arm. He wrenched her away from Moira, who cried out and helplessly collapsed on the ground. Meeker twisted Susan's arm behind her back. She shrieked in pain, but didn't acquiesce. She kept struggling. *"Jordan, help!"*

It was his mother's voice he heard.

And it was his mother's murderer now turning to look at him as he was about to kill again.

Jordan fired the gun once more.

He hit the son of a bitch in the neck. Allen Meeker gasped, and the ax dropped out of his hand. Susan broke free from him and rushed toward Moira.

Clutching his throat, Meeker grimaced as blood oozed between his fingers. He seemed to be choking. A look of astonishment passed across his face—as if he'd never imagined he could have been stopped by one of his victim's sons.

Jordan watched Meeker fall to his knees. He flopped forward, and he hit the ground, face-first. A spasm convulsed his body for a moment; then he was utterly, perfectly still.

Mama's Boy was dead.

Jordan had waited ten years to see that.

Past the sound of a siren in the distance, he heard something else. It was his mother reassuring him. *It's okay, kiddo,* she was saying. *It's all over. You can finally rest now. . . .*

Then everything went out of focus. He squinted up at Moira and Susan as they hobbled toward him. He looked back at Leo, still slumped over the front stoop. His friend was just a blur. Jordan dragged himself over to him and took him in his arms. Leo was still breathing, he could tell that much. Then Jordan felt himself slipping away.

It wasn't just one siren. There were several.

The state police cars and ambulances pulled up the

driveway on Cedar Crest Way, behind the deputy's car and Susan's old Toyota. The front of the Prewitt cabin was suddenly bathed in a swirling red light. But Susan and Moira weren't looking at all the emergency vehicles descending on the remote cottage. They were more concerned about the two wounded young men sprawled across the cabin's front stoop. Susan held Moira up, and the girl hobbled alongside her as they approached the door.

Jordan held Leo in his arms. He started to list toward one side, and his head tipped back against the door. The gun he'd used to shoot Mama's Boy fell out of his hand.

Susan couldn't tell whether or not he was alive.

But she could see he was smiling.

EPILOGUE

After the death of Corey Shaffer, the people of Cullen started telling stories about him—stories they'd suppressed while he'd been their deputy. It was a small wonder Corey had never been arrested, considering all the trouble he'd gotten into. At least a quarter of the townspeople had heard about his, at age twelve, running over a cat with a lawnmower. And now folks began to wonder what had really happened to the two dogs young Corey had owned that he claimed had "just run away." Former classmates recalled he'd been an obnoxious bully, a not-so-practical joker, and an anything-for-kicks daredevil.

Far more disturbing were recent stories now emerging about the town's deputy. Several women came forward to say that while driving alone, they had been pulled over by him for no apparent reason. Often he did this at night. According to twenty-seven-year-old Cullen resident Rachel Porter, he'd acted rather peculiar after stopping her one night along Carroll Creek

Drive for a broken taillight. And after she returned home to her husband, she discovered nothing wrong with the light. Rachel was convinced that if a motorcyclist hadn't passed by and waved at her and the deputy during their brief exchange, she would have ended up like Wendy Matusik.

Investigators combed through Corey's ranch house, located in a residential area near the center of town. The place was a mess, with plates of moldy, half-eaten food everywhere. The Ikea furnishings were tattered and dirty, and dust covered the two mounted deer heads on his wall. But he had a state-of-the-art computer and sound system.

In his basement was an entertainment room with a big-screen TV. In front of the black leather sofa, an old locked trunk doubled as a coffee table. They found more than 200 pornographic DVDs in the trunk, most of them advertising S & M and bondage on the cases. The detectives also discovered sexual paraphernalia such as handcuffs, leather masks, and mouth gags.

Next door, in Corey's exercise room, they uncovered what they were looking for in another locked trunk: a scrapbook full of clippings about the Mama's Boy murders. Beside the grisly headlines, Corey had pasted gold and blue stars.

In the same trunk were Corey's journals—with photos of Wendy Matusik, of Bellingham, and Monica Fitch, of Vancouver. In some shots, they were still alive—half-dressed, looking scared and disoriented in a darkened little cell. They were curled up on that same moldy, stained mattress on which Moira Dancey would later find herself. The other pictures were taken after he'd finished with them. His journals described in detail abducting both women. Wendy with her flat tire, and Monica, trapped in a narrow pit, had been so happy to be rescued at first. For Wendy, he'd even been in uniform, driving in his squad car. Corey buried both of them within ten feet of each other, very close to the spot where the police had found the eighth known Mama's Boy victim, Stella Syms.

For the families and friends of Corey's victims, the waiting, wondering, and dreading were over. The bodies were excavated, autopsied, and transferred to their loved ones. Monica and Wendy, who had planned on merely passing through Cullen months and months before, finally returned home.

Allen Meeker's various residences were tracked through his tax records. He had indeed been living in Chicago when the first-known Mama's Boy victim, Patricia Nagel, was abducted in front of her toddler son in their apartment—not far from the El station where Allen had first spotted them. He'd been in Oakland, California, and in Annandale, Virginia, when the Mama's Boy murders occurred in those areas as well. But it was at his residence on Camden Mills Road in North Seattle where he'd done most of his killing. The remote, two-bedroom, dark red cedar-shingle rambler was slightly run-down. It had a small, hidden room he'd created in the basement—behind a built-in bookcase in the storage closet. The current owner of the house, a sixty-seven-year-old retired art teacher, Eileen Miller-Johnson, had no idea the room existed. In the seemingly empty little cell, investigators found blood and hair samples matching nine of the eleven murdered women from the Seattle area.

The vacated house on Camden Mills Road was still a boarded-up crime scene when Eileen Miller-Johnson contacted a real estate agent about eventually selling the property. The house remained unoccupied for weeks and weeks after that. Several times a day, people drove by to gawk at Allen Meeker's former home. Many of the license plates were from out of state. Some of those people took photos with their cell phones, or they got out and walked up to the windows of the empty house. A few of them even broke off pieces from the cedar shingles for souvenirs.

Apparently, Corey Shaffer wasn't the only fan of Mama's Boy.

There was a three-year gap, from the 2004 murder of Samantha Gilbert in Alexandria, Virginia, to the disappearance of Rebecca Lyden from a rest stop near Wilsonville, Oregon, in 2007. Meeker's tax records showed he lived in Jacksonville, Florida, in the interim.

Two months after Meeker's death, FBI and local police were still trying to connect him with the disappearances of three Florida women, all young mothers, between 2004 and 2007.

The morbid tourists who made pilgrimages to the house on Camden Mills Road weren't very interested in Allen Meeker's residence for the last two years—a one-bedroom unit in a modern condominium in Seattle's First Hill neighborhood. From what investigators could discern, Meeker hadn't committed any murders while living there—and while he knew Susan.

That didn't keep Susan from feeling hurt—and violated and incredibly stupid for letting herself be taken in by him.

She and Mattie became reluctant celebrities. The tabloids, TV, newspapers, and Internet always identified her as *the fiancée of Mama's Boy*. Despite the fact that she'd saved the life of a teenage girl and helped bring Allen Meeker down, Susan seemed suspect to a lot of people who didn't know her. After all, she'd been engaged to a serial killer. If she hadn't shared his secrets, she'd certainly shared his bed—and that made her guilty by association.

Though Allen was dead, Susan still couldn't completely expunge him from her and Mattie's lives. She went through her photo collection and tossed all the pictures that had Allen in them; even if just his hand or half his face was in the shot, out it went. She donated to the Salvation Army every gift he'd given her and Mattie. Though she'd been living in the same duplex on Prospect Avenue since her first son, Michael, was born, Allen had spent so much time there, Susan felt compelled to move.

In December, the two-year lawsuit over the deck collapse was finally settled out of court, and Susan put some of that money down on a small two-bedroom house in West Seattle. News about the lawsuit settlement made Internet headlines on AOL: SERIAL KILLER'S FIANCEE AWARDED $1.5 MILLION. Even though the article pointed out that Susan had won the money in a lawsuit in a negligence case involving the deaths of her husband and older son, the "user comments" below the story showed that 90 percent of the readers hated her:

KayeM2 says at 2:52 PM 12/4/09: I can't believe this woman would take money after sleeping and having sex with a serial killer. They should take her kid away from her. She's trash.

MarcusvXXX says at 2:58 PM 12/4/09: I agree with the last person! Ive seen her on TV, & she's a HAG & stupid sounding. My wife & I call her Susan Bullshit. She acts like she was never engage to Mamas Boy & had no idea he was a killeer but I don't believe her for one minute. She's a BIG phoney. I feel sorry for her son. Now their giving her money! She should give it to all the people Mamas Boy killed.

MelissaS says at 3:04 PM 12/4/09: I think people are forgetting that Susan Blanchette was given that money after she was injured in an accident that also resulted in the deaths of her husband and child. It has nothing to do with the Mama's Boy murders. From what I've read, Allen Meeker had intended on killing her, but changed his mind in hopes of eventually getting her lawsuit money. I don't understand how people can't have more compassion for this woman who was duped by a charming psychopath. In the end, she's one of the people who stopped him. I'd say she's a hero.

MarcusvXXX says at 3:09 12/4/09: That last comment was SO STUPID!!!! If you consider that EVIL bitch a hero, you don't know WHAT THE F—K your talking about!!!! She should give that money to the family of people her boyfriend killed. Its too bad he didn't strangel her like he did the others . . .

"I can't believe you actually read that crap, Susan," Tom Collins told her on the telephone. He'd called her on a Saturday night in early December, two days after that story with all the comments had been featured on-line. He'd caught her cleaning out kitchen drawers in preparation for the move.

Two months before, it had been Tom's call to the Skagit County police—followed minutes later by two radio transmissions from Deputy Shaffer's squad car about a shooting—that prompted the police and medical response to Cedar Crest Way. Tom's red MINI

Cooper had arrived on the scene right after the police and ambulances. He'd parked on Carroll Creek Road, just far enough away from all the chaos and carnage so that one of his passengers couldn't see what was going on. Rosie had ridden shotgun with Mattie in her lap. One of the cops on the scene had written him a $124 ticket for violating the state's child-restraint laws. But Tom still claimed that it had been well worth it to see the ecstatic look on Susan's face when she'd spotted Rosie at the end of the driveway with Mattie in her arms.

She and Tom hadn't seen each other since. But that hadn't been Tom's fault. He'd called several times, asking to get together, but Susan kept putting him off. It just wasn't the right time to start seeing him—or any man for that matter. Still, she looked forward to his calls.

"Listen, you have to scroll down to read those user comments, right?" he said on the other end of the line. "Do yourself a favor and don't scroll down. I feel sorry for the intelligent people who get on there and try to talk some sense into the idiots making those comments. I mean, that one guy who really hated your guts, he was borderline illiterate. Do you really give a crap what he thinks of you?"

"I give a crap when people are saying on the Internet that I'm a terrible mother," she admitted, standing in a kitchen full of boxes.

"You're a good mother and a good person," he replied. "Just ask anyone who actually *knows* you, Susan. Hell, that's how Rosie and I figured out Shaffer was lying that night. He sent word that everything was okay and you were at the rental house—and he or Allen would pick up Mattie at the store. I saw the house was empty, yeah. But that could have been a mistake. I knew he was lying, because that story didn't sound like you at all, Susan. You're way too kind and considerate to have left your son with Rosie that long and not come back to explain or apologize in person. And you're too good a mother to have sent some cop or your boyfriend to pick up your child. In the short time I spent with you that day, I figured out that much about you. It's why I want to see you again. I think you're pretty wonderful."

"Well, that's sweet of you, Tom, but—"

"I'm not being sweet, I'm being honest," he interrupted. "Listen, do you need any help moving next week?"

"No, I'm fine," she said, leaning against the kitchen counter. "I've hired some movers."

"Well, I'd like to check out your new digs in West Seattle," he said. "Let me pick you up and take you and Mattie out to dinner, maybe Jak's Grill or Buddha Ruska for Thai. You said the new place is on Forty-sixth and Alaska, right? They're both pretty close by."

"Now just isn't the right time, Tom," she said with a sigh. "I'm sorry. I—I hear Mattie crying. He must be up from his nap. I really should go—"

"You like me, don't you?" he interrupted.

"Yes, of course I like you, but—"

"Well, if you keep shooting me down, I'm going to give up. And that would be a real shame—for all parties involved. What's going on, Susan? I mean, do you really believe those idiots on the Internet? Do you really think you don't deserve to be happy? Is that it?"

"Tom, I don't have time for this right now, I really don't. Mattie's crying—"

"All right, fine. Take care, Susan." Then he hung up.

Frowning, Susan clicked off the line and then wandered down the corridor. Stacked boxes, a big mirror, and some framed pictures were on the floor against the wall. She caught her reflection in the mirror. Dressed in old jeans and a frayed black sweater, and her brown hair in a ponytail, she didn't look very much like a millionaire. She just looked tired and sad.

She continued down the hallway and poked her head into Mattie's room. Nestled under a throw, he slept soundly on his bed, holding his Woody doll under his chin.

She'd explained everything the best she could to him the day after Allen was killed. Mattie seemed to understand, but still asked about Allen from time to time. Just yesterday, he'd asked while she'd been emptying out his closet: "If Allen wasn't a nice person, why did you want to marry him?"

Sometimes, he sounded so much older than his age. And this had been one of those times. Susan had put some toys in a packing box, and then she'd sat down on his bed with him. "Well, sweetie," she'd said. "There are bad people out there, and sometimes they can fool you into believing in them. That's what happened with Allen. He fooled me into thinking he was a nice man. But I know better now. I've learned to be more careful. Sometimes, it's hard to admit when you've made a mistake. But that's the only way you can move on and make sure you don't repeat the same mistake. Do you understand?"

Mattie had nodded pensively, and then he'd squinted up at her. "Do you think my dad could beat up Allen?"

Sometimes, too, he sounded just like a four-and-a-half-year-old.

Now, Susan watched Mattie sleep for a few moments. She heard the dryer bell go off. Weaving around stacks of boxes, she shuffled into the laundry room off the kitchen. She started to unload the dryer and fold clothes. Susan came across a sage-and-black striped pullover she'd bought about a year ago. She remembered how Allen really liked the way it looked on her.

She knew it would take a while before she felt completely rid of him.

Susan stopped folding the pullover, took it into the kitchen, and threw it into the garbage.

"So—Leo, how are you, son? How long were you in that hospital again?"

"Six days, Mr. Elliott," Leo told the paunchy, squinty-eyed, sixty-something man. Mr. Elliott sat at the four-top with his wife and another couple, who were their guests at the country club. Dressed in his busboy's mustard-colored jacket, white shirt, black tie, and black pants, Leo refilled their after-dinner coffees. "But I'm feeling okay now," Leo said. "Thank you for asking, sir."

Mr. Elliott reached inside his suit jacket and pulled out his billfold. "Well, I know hospitals cost money—even if you're covered by some G.I. plan from your dad. Are you going to college next year?"

"Yes, sir, Western Washington up in Bellingham," he replied.

Slipping his fat hands under the table, Mr. Elliott took some bills out of his wallet. "Well, here's a little something to put toward school—and those hospital bills," he said in sort of a stage whisper. Then he held out his hand for Leo to shake it. The folded-up bills were in his palm.

Leo set the coffeepot down on a nearby empty table and then shook the man's hand. "Thank you very much, sir."

Elliott patted his arm. "Merry Christmas, son."

"Merry Christmas, Mr. Elliott," Leo said. He smiled at Mrs. Elliott—and nodded to the guest couple, whom he realized were totally ignoring him. "Um, Happy Holidays."

An hour later, he changed out of his uniform in the club's employee locker room. As he zipped up the leather aviator jacket Jordan had given him, Leo felt a little pang of regret. He missed his friend.

Stepping out of the employee entrance, he saw the car waiting for him in the driveway turnaround behind the tennis courts.

Leo hurried up the driveway, jumped into the passenger seat, and kissed Moira. They'd been a couple ever since he'd gotten out of the hospital seven weeks ago. Hobbling in on her crutches, she'd visited him there every day. The two of them had achieved a kind of celebrity status because of what had happened. Some publishers and movie agents were even trying to get Moira to sign over the rights to her story, but she wasn't interested. "I don't want one of those *Gossip*

Girl stars to play me. I'm holding out until they get Ellen Page to star in it," she claimed, only half joking. Leo wasn't getting any serious offers, which was too bad because he could have used the money.

They were a popular couple, especially at her high school. And now that Moira was off her crutches, they were constantly going out. Leo found himself spending what little free time he had with Moira and her friends from Holy Names—and their boyfriends. They had a regular routine of going out for late-night pizza at Pizza Ragazzi in the University District after he finished his shift at the country club on Saturday evenings. It was kind of heady to have a bunch of people catering to his schedule like that. At the same time, he wasn't crazy about hanging around with a pack. Tonight it was just the two of them, thank God.

Leo told her about Mr. Elliott's making a fuss over him and slipping him the money to put toward school—and the hospital bills. Then at a stoplight, Leo showed Moira the money: a five and two singles.

"Oh, my God!" she laughed. "What a cheapskate loser!"

Shrugging, Leo stuffed the money back in his jeans pocket. "Oh, he's kind of a doofus, but he means well." In fact, since his return to the country club, Leo had been getting lots of gratuities from club members who hadn't paid any attention to him before. Now they knew his name, asked how he was doing and what his plans were for school. He wasn't sure if it was a club member or not, but someone had even paid his first full year's tuition and board at Western Washington University. That was over fifteen thousand bucks. It was arranged by some anonymous party through a Seattle law firm, which also sent him a cashier's check for four thousand dollars. On the bottom left-hand corner of the check, it said, *For Schoolbooks & Supplies.*

Moira would be attending Marquette University in Milwaukee. They hadn't yet discussed the relationship challenges of attending schools half a continent away from each other. Though he didn't say anything, Leo had a feeling she would end up breaking his heart before they even graduated. She'd say, "Let's be friends," and, damn it, they probably would be.

But until then, he'd enjoy being her boyfriend. Moira made him feel important. With her he was *somebody.* And under his class photo in the yearbook, it wouldn't say *Pathetic Virgin.*

"I missed you today," Moira said, watching the road ahead.

Leo smiled and studied her pretty profile in the dashboard's light. She had one hand on the wheel, and the other on the console between them.

Leo put his hand over hers, and she didn't pull away.

Not anymore.

Garfield's varsity football team had lost by two points. So the overall mood of the crowd that cold December afternoon was pretty somber. The light, cold drizzle didn't help either. Once the final whistle blew, the fans quickly cleared the bleachers.

During the game, he'd felt like he was onstage, sitting in the first row, half a bench length away from the cheerleaders. But with his crutches, he couldn't make it up the bleacher steps. Last time he'd tried at one of these games, everyone had gawked at him and whispered to each other. So he sat there at ground level, very conspicuous with his leg in a fiberglass cast and his titanium crutches at his side.

Jordan stared out at the vacant, muddy football field. He could see his breath and felt the rain on his face. He could also see people staring at him as they passed by, so he put the hood of his navy blue slicker over his head.

He figured this sitting-on-the-sidelines business was a dress rehearsal for spring—and lacrosse season. The leg injury had benched him, permanently.

He'd spent three weeks in the hospital—unfortunately, not the same hospital as Leo. Jordan's dad wouldn't hear of him staying in a public hospital. It was only the best for his son. So Jordan had a private room, around-the-clock nurses, a TV, and a telephone so he could phone his friend.

After everything they'd been through, they should have been together. Apparently, Leo had thought he might be ticked off about the sleeping pills thing. But Jordan wasn't angry, not really. In fact, one of the interns had told him the sedatives in his system might have saved his life. The pills Leo had given him had possibly slowed the bleeding and reduced some of the pain. Whether it was true or not, he passed the story on to Leo. It made his friend feel better.

They'd sprung Leo from Harborview Medical Center after six days. Jordan figured he could have gone home around the same time, but they transferred him to another wing at Swedish Hospital and kept him there for observation—in other words, to make sure he wasn't crazy. During that time, he wasn't allowed to use the phone or have visitors. He found out later that a ton of reporters had wanted to talk to him—along with some guys from the lacrosse team; Leo, of course; Moira; and even Susan Blanchette. She'd sent flowers with a card that simply said: *Thanks for saving my life. Get well soon. Susan Blanchette.*

One of the stipulations to his release from the hospital was that he had to see a therapist twice a week. At least that was the consensus from the higher-ups, "the people who decide these things," as his mom used to say. By the time he got out, Jordan learned that Leo and Moira were dating. Things were suddenly different. He didn't see so much of his friend anymore.

He used to pick up Leo for school in the morning, but he couldn't drive with his leg in a cast. So Jordan's dad hired some limo service to chauffeur him to and from Garfield. As if he already didn't feel like a freak, now he had a limo dropping him off at school.

Meanwhile, Moira drove Leo to school now. She took up nearly all of his time. Jordan actually had to plan ahead if he wanted to hang out with his best friend—and Moira almost always wanted to join them. It just wasn't the same. He missed his friend.

Things felt different with his lacrosse teammates, too—or maybe he just felt isolated from them because he couldn't play anymore. He'd never really gotten into being a big jock hero, but now that he'd been sidelined, Jordan kind of missed it. He felt so isolated. And of course, everyone knew his mother had been murdered by Mama's Boy, and they all knew about him abducting Meeker, sinking his car in a swamp, and tying him up in his basement. One of his lacrosse buddies even asked him in a hushed voice: "Is it true you had that guy bare-assed down in your basement and you were torturing him?" They all knew about his early breakdowns, and the two extra weeks he'd just spent in the hospital under *psychiatric observation*. So a lot of the kids at school were treating him like a dangerous character.

It wasn't just people at school either. Total strangers would stop and stare at him on the sidewalk or in the mall. Some of them would even walk up and ask, "Aren't you Jordan Prewitt?" And then they'd ask about Mama's Boy.

He talked about all this with his therapist, who said he was "in a better place" than he'd been last month. Jordan figured that meant he wasn't so damn crazy— maybe just a little lonely. He and Leo had made a date to get together this coming Friday night. Moira had a girls' sleepover and would be out of the picture, thank Christ.

It would be nice to see his pal again.

The rain seemed to come down a bit harder, and except for a few stragglers, the bleachers had emptied out. Jordan reached for his crutches, and saw a kid coming down the steps. The red-haired boy was about twelve years old. He was kind of a goofy-looking kid, wearing a yellow rain-slicker poncho. He walked toward him, but hesitated for the last few steps. The boy looked a bit apprehensive. Of course, he did. After all, he was approaching a guy everyone knew was a dangerous character. He used to be kind of a hero. But now, he was just kind of crazy. Jordan wondered if he suddenly said "Boo!" how quickly this curious kid would turn around and run.

He glanced over his shoulder and saw a forty-something guy who had to be the kid's father. Standing under his umbrella a few tiers up, he had glasses and receding reddish-grey hair.

"Excuse me," the kid said. "Are you Jordan Prewitt?"

Frowning, Jordan turned toward him and nodded. "Yeah, that's me."

The boy in the yellow slicker nervously held out his hand. "I wanted to say hello—and—and—and thank you," he said. "My name's Andy Milford...." He glanced back at his father, and then at Jordan. "Eleven years ago, that guy killed my mother. My—my dad, he wanted me to thank you and shake your hand."

Jordan knew the name. Pamela Milford had been abducted while pushing her ten-month-old baby in his stroller in Volunteer Park. He looked over his shoulder at the boy's father. The man nodded respectfully and mouthed the words, *Thank you.*

Jordan worked up a smile and nodded back. Then he looked the sweet, funny-faced boy in the eye and shook his hand. "It's really great to meet you, Andy," he said.

The father came down the bleacher steps. "Okay, Andy, let's get a move on," he called gently.

The boy turned and ran back to his dad. He hovered under the umbrella with him.

Jordan reached for his crutches again and caught the

boy's father looking at him. "Are you okay, Jordan?" the man asked, a little tremor in his voice. "Do you need any help?"

"No, thank you, Mr. Milford," he said. "You and Andy have helped me enough already today. I'll be okay."

The father nodded at him once more, then turned and walked away with his arm around his son.

Jordan sat and watched them for a moment. "Yeah," he whispered to himself, still smiling. "Yeah, I'll be okay."

She heard the movers' truck churning as it pulled away from the curb in front of her new house. Susan stood in the living room. She wearily stared at the maze of stacked boxes amid her furniture—which, somehow, didn't seem to belong in here. She was tired and hungry, and she missed the old duplex. She didn't think this new place was ever going to be home.

Of course, when she'd taken one last look at the empty duplex this morning, she'd been flooded with memories of Walt and Michael and Mattie when he was a baby. Funny, she hadn't thought at all about Allen Meeker, and the nights he'd spent there. Yet that had been her main reason for moving. Now it all seemed so pointless.

Allen had been the reason she'd pushed Tom away, too. Tom hadn't called back since last week. He'd warned her that if she kept shooting him down, he would give up. And, apparently, he had. In her campaign to expunge Allen Meeker from her life and never make the same mistake again, there had been some heavy, unnecessary casualties.

Tom had been right. She didn't feel she deserved to be happy. For a while, she'd even considered what some of those people on the Internet had said about giving the lawsuit money to the families of Allen's victims. Instead, she'd paid off her hospital debt, put some away for Mattie's college, and anonymously gave $20,000 to pay for Leo Forester's first year of college. She figured it was the least she could do for not giving him a ride that night.

Another big chunk of the money went as a down payment for this stupid house.

Susan stared at the mess of a living room, and tears welled in her eyes.

"Mommy, are you crying?" Mattie asked. He'd been having a blast, running around the new house. She'd unpacked the linen, and with two sheets and the stacks of boxes, Mattie had already built a fort-tent in his bedroom. Now he stood at her side, gazing up at her. He seemed mystified, probably wondering how she could think all this wasn't fun.

Susan managed to smile at him and then wiped her eyes. "No, sweetie, I just have something in my eye, that's all."

Taking a deep breath, she looked at all the boxes again and spotted a dolly one of the movers must have accidentally left behind. She also noticed two big boxes with *Christmas Stuff* and *X-Mas Tree* scribbled on the sides.

"You know, honey," she said. "We only have a little more than two weeks until Christmas. I think we should put up the tree, don't you? As the song says, 'We need a little Christmas, right this very minute. . . .'"

So while Mattie marveled at the ornaments and decorations, Susan unpacked the fake, pre-lit tree and started assembling it. She found an old mixed tape Walt had made of Christmas favorites—everyone from Ella Fitzgerald to the Kingston Trio to Bruce Springsteen. She put it in the CD/ tape player. Walt used to go out to one of those farms and cut down a tree every Christmas. But after he died, she'd gotten this fake one and settled for that. Right now, she was very glad to have it.

The first two of the three tree sections were up and lit, and Mattie had only broken one ornament, when the doorbell rang. Susan figured it was probably one of the movers, coming back for his dolly cart. She hurried to the door and opened it.

Tom stood on the front stoop. He looked handsome in his brown leather jacket and with his black hair tousled by the wind. He held up a big Arby's bag.

Susan numbly stared at him. "Um, hi," she said.

He peeked into the living room. "Looks like Christmas in here," he said. "I—um, well, I saw the moving van leave about forty-five minutes ago and took a chance this was the right house." He shrugged. "I guess that means I was stalking you."

A hand still on the doorknob, she half smiled and nodded. "I guess."

"So—on a scale of one to ten, with ten being incredibly creepy . . ." He trailed off as Mattie came to Susan's side. "Hi, Matthew Blanchette, do you remember me? I'm Tom."

Hugging her leg, Mattie squinted at him for a moment. "Did you bring fries?"

Tom laughed and then nodded. "I brought fries, and Arby's regular, Arby-Q, potato cakes, and salad. And the Cokes are in my car." He looked at Susan. "Is this okay? I know you told me you weren't ready to see anyone, and now I'm pulling this surprise visit on you. But I like you, Susan. And I think you like me. If I'm wrong, well, then I can just drop this off. . . ."

Susan sighed. "You know, while you're standing there talking, our potato cakes are getting cold."

Tom grinned at her.

She smiled back, opened the door a little wider, and let him inside.

Please turn the page for an exciting sneak peek of
Kevin O'Brien's newest thriller

THE BETRAYED WIFE

now on sale wherever print and e-books are sold!

CHAPTER ONE

"**I** have only a few sunny days left."

That's what Antonia recently announced in a Facebook post several days ago. Like we're all supposed to give a shit.

Antonia and her tan. Okay, I admit: at forty-four, she looks pretty good—what with all her exercising and all that sun. But the way she talks about her tanning sessions and how important they are, you'd think she was doing work for the United Nations: "Oh, no, I can't be there for that . . . I'll be tanning!" Every damn summer, it's the same thing. As soon as she gets off work at the Hilton, Antonia hurries home, makes herself a Cosmopolitan (still thinking she's Carrie Bradshaw in Sex and the City), changes into her bikini and heads up to the roof of her apartment building with her Coppertone, her blanket, and the Cosmopolitan in a thermos. All her friends and former boyfriends know about her sacred routine.

The roof has no protective railing, and it's seven stories high. No one's supposed to be up there. If Antonia stumbled and plunged to her death from that roof, would anyone be all that surprised?

Would anyone really care?

She's a terrible mother. I'll certainly vouch for that. I guess a couple of her work friends at the hotel might miss her, but hell, they don't really know her—not like I do. She's currently single (it's been an off-month for her), so she won't leave behind a devastated boyfriend to shed any tears for her. And I sincerely doubt her two loser ex-husbands or any of her loser ex-boyfriends will show up at the memorial service.

I can imagine the preacher giving the eulogy, struggling to come up with something nice to say about her: "Okay, so she was a self-centered, uncaring bitch, but Antonia had a killer body and a terrific tan. And by all accounts, she was great in the sack. She lived fast and died young . . ."

Too bad she won't leave a good-looking corpse, not the way she's going to die.

And she isn't exactly young . . .

I admit, I'm being hard on Antonia here. I read a while ago—I don't remember where—that some people, when they know they're going to die, they push their loved ones away. It's supposed to make the separation easier for the survivor. Maybe I've been doing something like that in reverse—to make it easier for me to pull this off. But I really don't think I'll miss her when she's gone.

I know she has her good side. She can be a hell of a lot of fun at times, and she has a great laugh.

But really, right now, she's just in the way.

If everything is going to happen as I want it to, Antonia can't be around. I've known that for weeks now. And I've prepared myself for it.

According to the weather report, Portland is supposed to be warm and sunny tomorrow, so it's a sure bet that Antonia will be soaking up some rays on the roof.

But she won't be completely alone.

Antonia was right. She's used up the last of her sunny days.

Thursday, September 6—4:12 P.M., Portland, Oregon

Antonia Newcomb—"Toni" to most of her friends—had a conflict of major proportions. It was a perfect afternoon for a rooftop tanning session. But she'd come home from work five minutes ago to find a second notice stuck to her mailbox in the lobby of her apartment building: The post office was holding a package for her. She'd ordered an item online from Barney's a couple of weeks ago. It was supposed to be like Botox in a bottle, and cost a small fortune: $180. The trouble was that her neighbors in the building had recently complained that someone was stealing their packages. So for the time being, no parcels were left in the lobby.

Antonia had to work late tomorrow. If she didn't pick up the package now, she'd have to wait until Monday afternoon—and hope it was still there at the post office.

Meanwhile, it was gorgeous out, and the Weather Channel predicted rain for next week. It was probably the last decent afternoon before autumn rolled in. The days were already getting shorter.

For a few minutes, Antonia stood, staring through the window of her messy sixth-floor apartment. The appeal of "Botox in a bottle" was strong, but the appeal of her rooftop tanning time was even stronger. She'd been looking forward to it all day. And with every minute of indecision, she was losing precious sun time.

"Screw it," she said, heading into the kitchen to make her usual rooftop cocktail. So she'd have to take her chances at the post office on Monday.

Ten minutes later, Antonia stepped out of her apartment and locked her door. She wore sandals and had a Chris Isaak T-shirt over her bikini. In her backpack, she carried a beach towel, her smartphone, sunglasses, Coppertone and the thermos with her chilled Cosmopolitan.

In the dim hallway, she turned toward the back stairwell and spotted old Mrs. Pollakoff stepping off the elevator with two bulging grocery bags. Mrs. Pollakoff lived next door and was a nice old biddy. But she liked to talk, slowly, and usually about something excruciatingly boring. All it took was one "Hey, Mrs. Pollakoff" to get her started, and then Antonia would have to stop everything and listen to the old woman drone on and on: "Well . . . I . . . heard . . . from . . . my . . . niece . . . today. And . . . her . . . son . . . has . . . this . . . particularly . . . terrible . . . ear . . . infection . . ."

A coworker at the Hilton once told Antonia that you can always tell if someone is engaged with you and really listening by looking at their toes. If their toes were pointed toward you, they were engaged. If their toes pointed in another direction, they wanted you to shut up so they could move on. That was how it was with old Mrs. Pollakoff. Antonia's toes were always pointed in another direction whenever Mrs. Pollakoff stopped to talk to her.

Antonia thought about ducking back inside her apartment, but it was too late. The old woman had already spotted her. "Well . . . where . . . are . . . you . . . off . . . to?" she asked, between gasps for air as she lugged her grocery bags toward her unit.

"A friend's pool," Antonia lied. Her toes were already pointed away from Mrs. Pollakoff, who looked like she was about to have a heart attack from the load she carried. The roof access was one flight up the back stairwell, and the last thing Antonia wanted to do right now was stop and help Mrs. Pollakoff with her groceries.

"Would . . . you . . . mind . . . giving . . . me . . . a . . . hand . . . here?"

Antonia tried not to wince. She quickly nodded and grabbed one of the bags. "I'm just going to take this to your door, Mrs. P," she said, walking ahead. "Hope you don't mind, but I'm running kind of late . . ."

"Have . . . you . . . noticed . . . lately . . . at . . . the . . . Safeway . . . that . . . more . . . and . . . more . . . people . . . are . . . bringing . . . their . . . dogs . . . into . . . the . . . supermarket . . . even . . . though . . . it's . . . supposed . . . to . . . be . . . against . . . the . . . law?"

Antonia ended up carrying the bag into Mrs. Pollakoff's kitchen, which was about ninety-five degrees and smelled like sour milk. She also listened to the old woman go on and on about how no one paid attention to the "No Pets Allowed" signs anymore.

The good-deed side trip took only three or four extra minutes, but it felt like an eternity before Antonia was out of there. She hurried down the hallway to the back stairwell. Up on the top floor, there was a metal spiral staircase blocked by a chain. A faded sign hung from the sagging chain: DO NOT ENTER.

Antonia swung her leg over the chain and started up the slightly wobbly stairway to a little room, no bigger than a closet. The caretaker kept a broom, a dustpan, and a bucket in there for the rare occasions when he swept the roof. The beige paint on the walls was peeling, and cobwebs swathed all four corners of the high ceiling. A door—with a fogged, mesh, safety-window—led outside to the roof. It had one of those push bars that activates the fire alarm when the door was opened. But the janitor had a key to a lock just below the bar, and that bypassed the alarm trigger.

Antonia had "borrowed" the key from the previous janitor years ago. She kept it on a rubber bracelet specifically for these sessions. No one else in the building had access to the roof. She wasn't supposed to be up there, either, but so far, she'd never been caught. She slipped her key into the door.

It wasn't locked.

"Oh, crap," she muttered.

Was someone out there now? She hoped not. It would ruin her whole afternoon.

With a bit of trepidation, Antonia opened the door

and stepped outside. She didn't see anybody, and nothing looked different. A couple of puddles had formed from the rain two nights before, but that was all.

Antonia figured maybe she'd forgotten to lock up when she'd been up here on Monday afternoon.

Ducking back inside, she grabbed the broom, stepped out again, and wedged the broomstick in the doorway. She was always slightly paranoid about the door slamming shut and getting stuck, leaving her stranded up there.

Outside at last, Antonia felt the sun's delicious warmth. Heat seemed to waft up from the faded black tar covering the rooftop. She took her sunglasses out of her backpack, put them on, and ambled over toward her usual spot.

Ten chimney-like air ducts were staggered across the flat roof. The ledge around it was only about two feet high. Beyond the ledge, she had a beautiful view of Portland's Northwest neighborhood. There weren't any other tall buildings within two or three blocks, so Antonia had some privacy.

That was why, once she laid out her blanket, she usually sunned topless. This afternoon would be no different. Antonia sat down on her beach towel, pulled the T-shirt over her head and removed her top. As she rubbed Coppertone on herself, she breathed in the lotion's scent. It always reminded her of orange blossoms, trips to the beach, and sex. She often imaged some slick, handsome executive vice president in a high-rise office building a few blocks away, looking at her through high-powered binoculars. Maybe he knew about her tanning sessions and looked forward to them as much as she did. Maybe he got off on seeing her sunbathing semi-nude. It was a nice fantasy. In reality, no one had ever bothered her while she was up there on the roof—except two summers ago, when a low-flying helicopter revisited her on few occasions. She'd figured it carried a rush-hour traffic reporter for one of the radio stations. The first time the chopper hovered over her, Antonia had automatically covered herself up. But during the return visits on other afternoons, she'd decided to give them a peek—more than a peek, a good long look. She was proud of her body, and liked showing it off.

She set her thermos and the backpack on top of her T-shirt and top so they wouldn't blow away. Then she poured some of her Cosmopolitan into the thermos cup and sipped it. Popping in her earbuds, she listened to Sheryl Crow on Pandora, blocking out the noise from the street seven stories below. Antonia sipped her drink once more.

She reclined on the blanket and felt the warming rays on her smooth, lubricated skin.

Antonia was about to close her eyes when she heard something slam. Was it the door to the little shed? She sat up and squinteded at her only entry back into the building. The broomstick was still lodged in the door.

She figured the noise had probably been from a dumpster lid shutting in the alley below. All Antonia had to do to check was walk a few feet and peer over the ledge. But she didn't want to put her top back on. The apartment building's garbage and recycling bins were in the alley directly below the roof's ledge—just a few feet away from her.

She glanced once more at the rooftop shed. Was

someone hiding behind there—or maybe crouched behind one of the air ducts?

Despite her bravado about being nearly nude outdoors, Antonia couldn't help feeling a bit skittish this afternoon. Off and on, for a couple of weeks now, she'd had the feeling someone was following her, watching her.

On several occasions, she had spotted her daughter Eden's creepy new boyfriend hanging around the apartment building—even when her daughter wasn't there. Was he the one stalking her? Antonia thought she saw him in the Hilton lobby earlier this week, too. His name was Brodie, and at nineteen, he was three years older than Eden. Antonia wouldn't have been a bit surprised if he was into drugs or some other kind of criminal activity. In fact, when her neighbors in the building started to complain about their missing parcels, Antonia immediately figured Brodie was stealing them. She didn't understand what Eden saw in him. He was all skin and bones—with a mop of dirty, blond hair. She often wanted to remind the scrawny SOB that every time he touched her underage daughter, he was setting himself up for a statutory rape charge. But Antonia decided any efforts to interfere in her daughter's love life would only push Eden closer to the worthless creep.

But why the hell would Brodie be hiding on the roof right now? Had Eden told him that her mother liked to sunbathe topless up here?

Well, if he'd come up for a peek, and she caught him spying on her, then maybe she could convince Eden to dump his sorry, skinny ass. Of course, knowing her daughter, if anything like that actually happened, Eden would merely blame her.

Antonia finished off what remained in her thermos cup and refilled it. Removing her sunglasses, she lay back on her blanket and listened to her music. After a few minutes, her mind started to drift. She might have even fallen asleep for a spell. But then, past the music, she thought she heard footsteps.

With a start, Antonia sat up again. She automatically crossed her arm over her bare breasts. She plucked out her earbuds. "Who's there?" she called. "Is anyone there?"

She glanced toward the janitor's shack. She didn't see anyone. The shack's door was still propped open with the broomstick.

Yet Antonia called out once more: "Is anyone there?"

No one answered. She could hear cars down on the street below—and someone tinkering on a piano in a neighboring building.

A cloud passed over the sun. Shuddering, Antonia grabbed her T-shirt and clutched it to her chest. She didn't know why she was so spooked. But she no longer felt safe muting the outside noise with her music, so she switched off her phone and stashed it in her back-pack—along with the earbuds. "Shit," she muttered. She liked listening to her tunes while she tanned. Maybe this rooftop sun session was a bust after all. Maybe she'd be better off going back to her apartment and finishing what was left in her thermos down there.

Frowning, she glanced up at the sky. There was just the one little cloud. Was she going to let it ruin her afternoon?

She wouldn't let her silly paranoia spoil things, either. This could be her last tanning session of the year, the last of her sunny days.

Antonia took another gulp of her Cosmopolitan.

The sun came out from behind the cloud, and she basked in its reassuring warmth once more. She reclined on the towel. Antonia was just starting to relax again when she heard something squeak, followed by a little tap. *It's not the shed door, stupid,* she told herself, keeping her eyes closed. *You're all alone up here, and that sun feels delicious.* She wasn't going to sit up again. There was a creaking sound, which might have been footsteps—or just about anything else. *Ignore it,* she told herself. It was probably just a neighbor moving around directly below in one of the top-floor apartments—or maybe someone down in the alley, taking out their garbage.

She felt the kiss of a slight breeze against her naked skin. It gave her goose bumps.

A part of her wanted so much to sit up and check one more time to make sure no one was creeping toward her, but she didn't move. It was like a contest now. How long could she lay here with her eyes closed? Besides, even if someone else was up there, why would she care? What did she think would happen? So they'd see her boobs. Big deal. And if it was the janitor, ready to chew her out for sneaking up here, she'd simply tell him this was her first time on the roof, and the door was unlocked. Wasn't it his responsibility—to keep the roof door locked? And how long had he been staring at her practically naked before he'd made his presence known?

Antonia giggled at the thought of turning the tables

on Sid, the building janitor, who had never seemed to like her much.

Something blocked out the sun once again. Probably another cloud.

Without opening her eyes, Antonia blindly felt around for her thermos cup. Her fingers brushed against something: a foot. She felt the laces of a sneaker.

Antonia opened her eyes and gasped. She couldn't see who was standing over her—just the shadowy silhouette between the sun and her. Sitting up, she quickly grabbed her T-shirt to cover herself.

Past all the sounds she'd been ignoring, Antonia could hear her visitor's voice, though it was merely a whisper.

"Why did you have to be in my way?"

The custodian, sixty-two-year-old Sid Parsons, lived in the basement of Antonia's apartment building. He was proud of the job he did keeping the building clean, safe and secure. That was why it irked him to find that some jerk had left a near-empty, sixteen-ounce cup from McDonald's on the newel post at the first-floor stairway landing. The same jerk must have tossed the used McDonald's bag onto the lobby floor. Now the entryway smelled like old cheeseburgers. Outside, crows were fighting over scraps of greasy paper and French fries on the small front lawn. The birds scattered the fast food trash over the walkway and trimmed grass.

Sid had a pretty good idea who the guilty party was.

It was probably that seedy creep who hung around with the daughter of Newcomb in 6-B. The scumbag and the daughter seemed high half the time. Talk about a couple of lowlifes. Since the guy had first started coming around a few weeks ago, several residents' packages had been stolen. Also, someone had broken into the storage room and made off with all sorts of things, leaving behind a hell of a mess. And Sid kept finding trash in and around the building. He often noticed the guy's cigarette butts out by the front door, too.

Sid had already said something about it to Newcomb the Nympho. That was what he called her, though he kept the nickname to himself. She was always buzzing in some new guy. She didn't seem to have any problem getting boyfriends, but she sure couldn't keep them. Each one would move in and make himself very much at home there. But by the time Sid learned the guy's name he'd be gone, and there would be another to take his place. The woman's taste in guys wasn't all that much better than her daughter's.

As he gathered up the sorry son of a bitch's trash, Sid figured he'd send an email to the condo board about it. Maybe one of them would give Newcomb the Nympho a talking-to.

Opening the dumpster lid, Sid tossed the garbage inside.

Suddenly, he heard a scream directly above. He thought it was a seagull. But when he looked up, he saw a nude woman plummeting down from the roof. Arms and legs flailing, she hurled right toward him—and the open dumpster.

Horrified, Sid reeled back.

Her body hit the edge of the bin with a loud, terrible, ripping thump.

But Sid didn't see what happened to her.

He couldn't see, because of the blood that had splattered into his eyes.